A STONE FOR MADDIE GREEN

EBEN BEUKES

A Stone for Maddie Green

Copyright © 2020 by Eben Beukes.

Paperback ISBN: 978-1-952982-43-9
Ebook ISBN: 978-1-952982-44-6

Published by Golden Ink Media Services   10/27/2020

Golden Ink Media Services
(302) 703-7235
support@goldeninkmediaservices@gmail.com

1
CHAPTER

She liked staring through her window. The green lawn seemed to go on forever, down to where she knew the sea was. Sometimes Martha took her for a stroll around the gardens but always avoiding the long driveway that would lead down to the gates at the bottom of the hill.

There were bad people at the other side of those gates Martha would say and they had promised mommy that she would be safe until she could come for her.

Sometimes she would watch Ken mow the lawns, riding on his big orange tractor with Artos lying in the shade of a large tree watching him. He was a huge black dog and she had been instinctively wary of approaching him.

At night she could hear him roaming the grounds. She had never heard him bark.

The shadows were long now over the lawn and the birds were returning to the trees for the night. There were huge flocks of them, white and making a lot of noise as they swarmed. They were corellas, Ken had said, parrots, and he hated them. They would come here from down south in winter and destroy his vegetable patch and every now and then he would take his big shotgun and kill some but they would always come back.

Like the 'flu, Ken said. Every bloody year you get it.

Martha would scowl at him and say if you stopped smoking you wouldn't get so sick. Ken would grunt and say nothing and reach for the bottle of the brown drink he liked so much and which seemed to make him angry and sad at the same time.

Once he slapped Martha so hard that she fell off her chair.

Even then, Martha did not leave her alone with Ken, not until they had finished their evening lesson.

It was almost time for the lesson now and she wondered which dress Martha would have her wear to-night. She quite liked the pink fairy queen dress, the one with the gossamer wings and the lace up ballet slippers. Also the little tiara with its glimmering white stones. The tiara reminded her of the one mommy had given her one Christmas when they had that big party on daddy's boat.

She had called her a little angel and promised they would always be together.

Laid out on the bed was a black dress with a lace edged white apron and next to it, a fluffed out linen cap. Also a black pantyhose with a pattern much like the net daddy had used that time they went fishing on the river in England. A French Maid costume Martha called it and she knew there would be a feather duster somewhere to go with it. Also those nice frilly white knickers that would peek out from under the frock when she bent over to dust, like they showed her during the lesson.

Lying against the pillows on the bed was the sleeping doll the uncle had brought her when he visited yesterday in the afternoon. Her name was Mabel and she was heavy and at the same time soft, just like a real baby. The hair was real too with a pretty little headband that had a flower in it. Like the fashion was now with baby photos.

She liked Mabel, there was something in her blue eyes that made her look alive, like she was there with her in the room and would not leave her. Like mommy.

She did not like this uncle, he smelled like old men do and the skin on his neck and hands were wrinkly with spots on it and red showed under his bottom eyelids, the eyes watery while he dribbled even when he wasn't sniffing her arms and legs and licking.

She was glad that Martha changed the bedsheets and pillow cases every time an uncle visited, they would smell, especially the old ones and sometimes the sheets would be dirty.

But he did not hurt her, not like the other uncle who used to visit, the one with the hoarse voice and stained fingers who smelled of cigarettes and whose hands would shake when he touched her. He would make her do bad things and then that last time he bit her and Ken rushed into the room and slapped him hard and bundled him out of the room, tossing his clothes after him.

She never saw him again.

There were other toys and gifts some of the uncles had given her and they were arranged on a shelf at the other end of the room, next to the dresser with the large mirror. You could see through the mirror from the other side and that was where the video camera was and from where Ken would be watching. She knew that because one day she left the room to go to the toilet and the door to the next room was ajar and peeking inside she could see Ken busy with the camera and she could see through the mirror into her own bedroom.

She had wondered about that because this was not where they filmed her dancing and posing like they taught her. That was in the big lounge room where there was an elevated area reached by two stairs and leading to the dining room and beyond that the kitchen.

Sometimes Ken liked to film her from the lower level, saying to Martha that it made for more seductive angles. They would always tell her that these films would be sent off to mommy who was sick at present but was so happy to see her little girl in those pretty dresses and learning to dance and all.

At last night's lesson there was an upright pole in the middle of the floor and they had shown her how to slide and twirl around it, all to some new music and remembering to smile at the camera. It was a good thing they had not rubbed the shiny oil on her again because that would have made the pole too slippery to climb! They had a good laugh about that!

She was still thinking about that when Martha came into the room. 'Time to come and have your tea, poppet. Then we'll do your makeup and get ready for some fun!'

Martha always called her poppet and when she brushed her hair and sometimes plaited it while she watched in the mirror there was a sad look in her eyes. Not like the nannies she had in London who were much younger and always chatting away about boyfriends and how cold it was back in Sweden where they lived.

She liked Martha.

The woman known to the world of fashion as the supermodel Sarah Green recrossed her long legs and declined a soft drink from an off camera assistant with a slight wave of a beautifully manicured hand. Exquisitely made up sapphire blue eyes smiled wanly at the reporter from Vogue who paused, pen hovering over notebook, as she anxiously wondered whether the last question had possibly been too sudden, too intrusive.

'My husband, Mr Abdul-Karim, has offered a reward of five hundred thousand US dollars to any information leading to the safe return of my – our—daughter, Maddie. As you have correctly pointed out no ransom note has been received, nor any word of Maddie.'

An unseen signal from the hovering fashion photographer had her tilt her head slightly, changing the angle of her famous profile while the makeup artist stood by should repairs be required to counter the effect of the lighting. Prancing about like a jitterbug the photographer oohed and sighed as he angled his camera every which way, all the time marvelling at how the camera just loved her. Every picture a masterpiece!

'It has now been—' checking her data sheet the interviewer frowned, '—one hundred and twenty one days since the disappearance of Maddie from your house in Melbourne. A month ago you left Melbourne to be with your husband here in Kuwait City. I take it you are in regular contact with the police in Australia?'

'Of course. My husband is an international businessman who travels a lot and as his wife it is expected of me to be by his side whenever possible. We can leave for Australia at a moment's notice should there be any news at all. It was just—just too depressing to stay there in the house all alone, sitting by the phone, waiting, wondering—'

The assistant stepped up to hand Sarah Green a tissue which she used to carefully dab at an eye before checking herself in the small hand mirror and handing it back and putting on a brave smile once more. The interviewer, a veteran of the celebrity media world, was not born yesterday and thought the performance wasn't bad but her advice would be to stick to the day job.

She thought the tremor of the hand that held the offered glass of water was a trifle overdone.

'So, no progress by the Australian Police?'

Eyes downcast and replying in a whisper Sarah Green shook her head, 'No—'

'And, no proof of life?' The interviewer hated herself for asking that question but it was the elephant in the room.

'Wh...What do you mean?!' Sarah asked in a shocked voice, widened blue eyes glittering with fresh tears.

'I—well—it's just that recent history tells us that, opposed to teenagers who run away from home, when children that young disappear – are kidnapped – the outcome is usually not – ' At a loss for words she fumbled with her notepad before adding somewhat plaintively, 'positive?'

The sudden silence was tangible, the only sound in the room the soft hum of a distant air conditioner. Searching the face of her subject the interviewer, a veteran of a thousand such discussions, wondered what was reflected there. Fear, horror, a deep sadness? Or was it something else, something less tangible yet there alright. For a fleeting moment she thought it was almost a hint of triumph but that was ridiculous, impossible.

'Maddie is alive,' came the soft answer. 'She is alive and I will find her.'

'There have been reports over the years that your daughter has had some ongoing health issues? That there had been hospital admissions of undisclosed nature. Are you worried that Maddie is receiving the necessary medical attention she may require?'

Sarah Green visibly stiffened, leaning forward in the lounge chair and waving the photographer away.

'I have always endeavoured to keep my family life strictly private while realising that, as a public figure, a celebrity if you will, I have a certain obligation to the public. Maddie has always been kept out of the public eye and any health issues are of no concern to your readers, I'm sure.'

Which, the interviewer concluded, put paid to her next question on how her husband, who was reputed to dote on Maddie, was holding up. Instead she changed tack 'You have been the face of the Dolce Vita fashion empire for some years now and we believe there is a launch for a new range coming up, are you planning to be there? I mean involved in the modelling and active promotion as before?'

'Life goes on,' Sarah Green said, an unseen motion ushering over her hovering assistant who informed the woman from Vogue that Ms Green had another engagement scheduled, thanking her and the photographer while reminding the latter that prior approval of any photographs would be needed before publication.

Rising to shake hands and gathering up her bag and notepad the interviewer thought how odd the whole exercise had been. Here they had flown all the way to Kuwait City, hardly a fashion hotspot, to interview the famous clothes hanger – at her suggestion – for nothing new, really. No profound announcement, no heart rending baring of the soul, the stuff of tabloid fodder, just a few new outfits being modelled, a show around just another millionaire's home and that was that. All the way from New York to this shithole city and for what?

More pertinently, just what did Sarah Green get out of this?

There was no other pressing engagement for Sarah Green, at least not with the media but as eleven o' clock approached on the diamond studded Cartier on her wrist there was a keenly awaited phone call pending. As the visitors were ushered out she strode quickly to her study, firmly closing the door behind. Hasan, her husband, was at his downtown office as usual and the servants knew better than to disturb her when she was behind closed doors.

Reaching for the mobile nestling in a desk drawer with a shaking hand, she sank into an armchair and waited as the excitement mounted inside her bosom.

The phone buzzed at one minute past eleven, punctual as promised. She answered immediately, her voice strangled and breathless, 'Hello, this is Sarah?'

There was a few moment's silence punctuated by heavy breathing, then a husky voice spoke a single word. A term of endearment and at the same time foreign, a language from a distant past that, although she did not speak it, at once filled her with a strange mix of dread and nostalgia.

2
CHAPTER

The boy ran his fingers lightly over the oiled stock while gazing down at the sensuous lines and curves of the object. It was heavy, heavier than the previous models he had been practising on, more realistic all the time as the levels of the game went forever deeper, more intense, more challenging.

This one even had the smell of gun oil, the way he had always imagined it would smell. Haptics, the Master had called it; first the feel and the sound effects and now even the smell of the controls.

And had the Master not said that this time there would even be the shudder and shake, just like the real thing, when he pulled the trigger. All the more reason to take careful aim, he had said, then squeeze gently and use short bursts, always remembering to keep the barrel from lifting.

With a barely suppressed shudder of excitement that raised the fine hairs on his forearms he stepped up to the parapet of the balcony to stare down at the small gathering of men seated three floors below and diagonally across the street. Eight, nine, ten, he counted them. Seated on two cushion strewn wooden benches at right angles to one another as a manservant moved amongst them serving mint tea in small glass cups while a television, sound turned down, flickered and yellow light spilled from the open doorway of the house and onto the pavement.

How incredibly realistic it all was now, the boy mused. Right down to the people, out for their evening stroll, going by, having to step into the street to pass the seated men of the *diwaniya* blocking the pavement, even the small kids still out and kicking a ball. The hum of traffic on the distant Gulf Road.

The graphics will astound you, the Master had warned, adding that much work had gone into creating the life like effects of blood and gore, the sound effects of people screaming. He had to be ready for this.

Sweating now as the adrenalin sent his heart racing, the heavy metal slippery in his grip as he lifted it slowly from behind the parapet and settled the stock into his shoulder before carefully taking aim. This was his moment, the incredible honour that he had been picked to be the first gamer to try out Lone Striker – The Devil's Workshop.

But then he *was* the best of his group, had not the Master said so himself? And that was the reason he had been chosen.

Remembering to brace himself, he squeezed the trigger.

The staccato death roll of the AK 47 shattered the steady buzz of a summer's eve with all the sharpness and inherent violence of a car crashing through a plate glass shop window. For a surreal microsecond all sound was supplanted by an impossible silence, then the screaming started.

Stunned the boy looked down at the now smoking object in his hands before letting it slip from his grasp to fall with a dull clang on the stone chip tiles of the rooftop balcony. By Allah that was more real than he had ever expected, disturbingly so. It was everything the Master had said it would be but still... How had the designers managed to get those sound effects? And the feel of the thing in his hands, even the acrid tang of the smoke from the barrel!

Suddenly uneasy he stepped back from the parapet and glanced around. Where was he? It bothered him that he could not remember how he had got there, found himself inside this incredibly realistic new studio. Instinctively reaching to remove his headgear he stared dumbly down at his hands before dropping it on the hard cement where it rocked for a moment before coming to a stop, the single baleful eye of the camera staring back at him. Then suddenly, without warning it exploded, a muffled sound accompanied by a small puff of smoke.

Shocked he staggered back as his numbed mind tried to make sense of this new development. Maybe it was all a dream was his bewildered thought as he stumbled down the stairs of the building only vaguely aware of startled faces staring back at him from half opened hallway doors. The Master, must find the Master! Did he not say he would be waiting outside the games room for him to come out?

The man sitting behind the wheel of the parked Mercedes tossed his cigarette out of the window and cursed softly as the Master's voice came over his earpiece, the boy had pulled off the mask which was supposed to kill him, he had to be terminated immediately, do it! Revving the engine he nudged the big car into drive as he scanned the front entrance to the building through slitted eyes. Any moment now! Then he saw the boy bursting out onto the pavement and pausing for a moment to scan his surroundings, not seeming to notice the surrounding chaos as people milled about with the sounds all around now at a demonic level.

A single sharp tap of the car's horn and the boy saw him, a look of relief instantly replacing that of sheer terror as he recognised the man behind the wheel and came running towards the car now coming his way. Timing it so the boy was less than twenty feet away the driver stomped down hard on the accelerator and aimed the big car straight for where the target now loomed large, the boy's eyes widening as he saw. Then he was struck, the driver swerving sharply to crash into a SUV parked half on the pavement and crushing the boy with sickening force, the dying look on the face of fourteen year old Ali El Mashri one of total bewilderment.

CHAPTER 3

The early evening traffic was building when Waleed turned onto Highway 30 heading for Fahaheel, most of the stream heading into the city and the shopping malls that would be open by now that the good citizens of Kuwait had risen from their afternoon siesta. In the passenger seat Riad stirred and turned to toss the folder he had been studying onto the back seat of the unmarked police cruiser.

'You think he'll be home?' Waleed asked as he tail lighted a slower vehicle until the driver cut off another car to let the road hog through with a shouted curse and a waving fist. Ignoring the angry bleat of horns in their wake Riad grunted a reply as he let his thoughts drift back on what had brought them there at a time when he should be home with his daughter and enjoying a home brew as he watched Bill O'Reilly on TV.

Almost two weeks ago now when the golfer at BP's Ahmadi golf course had discovered the body and called it in. During a game on the sand and oil course he had sliced a ball way over the raised sand wall marking the border between the par five third hole and the open desert beyond. Still cursing the stone strewn rough that dinged his clubs and vowing to use the small Astroturf mat in future, even when not on the so-called fairway, he breasted the rise to peer over the featureless hard wasteland where the sprawling city was just visible on the distant horizon.

At noon the heat was dancing off the stones in shimmering waves, distorting images and hurting his eyes even with the sunshades. The man, a British expat engineer, cursed as he searched in vain for his golf ball, once again wondering why on earth even a yellow ball could be so hard to find. Next time he would just leave the bloody thing, play an old ball instead and then he saw it.

Fifty, maybe sixty yards away and half hidden where the uneven terrain dipped into a shallow gully something stirred. Just for a second and then it was gone. For a moment he hesitated, running a hand over his sweat soaked neck. An illusion perhaps – a mirage even? Twice in the past he had suffered sunstroke and vividly recalled the flashing images that went with the blinding headaches.

But no, this was real. There was something there where there should just be nothing.

'Tom! For God's sake, your five minutes is over! Leave the goddam ball and let's get on with it. A man can die of thirst out here!' It was his playing partner calling out but still, he had to have a look. Shouting back that he would just be a moment he strode quickly over to the gully, slipping and sliding over the loose pebbles as he went down its side to reach the object the dog had been dragging from the sand.

The animal, a starving saluki mongrel, had released the bundle of rags to retreat to a safe distance where it hunched down on all fours as it watched the intruder through hooded yellow eyes.

Even from six paces away Tommy Smith could see it was a human body, a woman to be precise. Still half buried in soft sand the animal had dug up most of the body and he could see it was a young Asian girl and that judging by the bloated body and the buzz of blowflies she had been dead for a while.

Reaching for his cell phone he suddenly felt faint and had to sit down as he hoarsely called out to his friend before vomiting up the breakfast of hours earlier.

Riad had been over in nearby Fahaheel investigating a cold case that had recently come alive again when he got the call. It took him twenty minutes to get there and at that stage a small crowd of mostly golfers and employees of the golf course had gathered. Two police officers from the nearby Ahmadi police station had been first on the scene, managing to secure it and keep the crowd a fair distance away.

Saluting the sergeant led Riad over to the body where he was relieved to see that the scene appeared largely undisturbed. 'This one's a young Filipina, Lieutenant, probably not been here too long. Looks like she was killed elsewhere and buried here.' He waved in the direction of the group of golfers now watching them with interest, 'A golf player found a stray dog digging the body up and called us. He is over there and I have already taken his statement.'

Kneeling next to the body Riad nodded and drawing a disposable glove from a pocket carefully swept the long black hair away from the face to find himself staring at a woman of no more than twenty, perhaps younger, red veined open eyes bulging and a further examination revealing a bluish tinge around the neck which was the other tell tale sign of a strangling.

Keeping his thoughts to himself he straightened up and turned to scan the surrounding flat landscape seeing nothing but hard desert with the occasional dust caked shrub, lizard burrow and hardscrabble bush. 'Any vehicle tracks?' he asked returning the silent stare of a large blue tongue lizard sunning itself twenty yards away.

The sergeant shrugged, 'Quite a few but mostly motorbikes, the area is popular amongst kids riding their scramblers. SOCO is on their way and we'll take some prints. The few fresh footprints belong to the people who found the body.'

Taking a photograph from an inside pocket Riad studied it. It was her alright, taken from her *iqama* ID photo. The Kuwaiti family she worked for had stated that the girl had been unhappy, the prevailing thought being that she had run off with persons unknown and had possibly returned home to the Philippines.

Kuwait police deal with dozens such reports on an annual basis, most being found fairly quickly and deported but with the occasional murder, usually a prostitution transaction gone wrong. This one had however been different. The girl, eighteen year old Dinah Reyes, had visited the Philippines consulate a week before her disappearance enquiring about changing her employers, the reason being personal. After some probing she had reluctantly hinted at being "bothered" by certain members of the family she worked for.

All expatriates in Kuwait must by law have sponsor who is responsible for that employee's accommodation, health care and general behaviour. Switching between employers is not allowed under any circumstances. This had been explained to the young woman who seemed quite upset but declined to elaborate, something the interviewer had put down to homesickness, a not too unfamiliar phenomenon amongst these young women who suddenly find themselves far away from family and friends and often working under abusive circumstances.

From poor background and with little or no education their lives were often even worse in their own countries.

Feeling sorry for the girl the consulate had arranged for her to attend a group meeting of young expat girls a week later, the idea to help her establish a circle of friends and hopefully feel less alienated.

So Dinah Reyes had gone back to her short unhappy life and her disappearance only came to the notice of homicide when two things happened. Firstly the Philippines consulate, when notified of her disappearance as required by the police, reported the earlier interview with the deceased and her failure to turn up for the arranged meeting. Secondly the anonymous letter delivered to the Shuwaikh Precinct and posted in Fahaheel, stating that the girl had been petrified of being pregnant, claiming to have been raped by the men in the family.

It was not the first time Riad had been confronted by this all too familiar scenario. These young women, girls really, were at the mercy of their employers and little more than slaves. The wives often aware of the abuse only to place the blame on the girls and punishing them in turn.

In the world Riad found himself in there was the culture that a thing was only a sin if found out. No discovery no sin. And no crime. The penalty for any low life expatriate who dared complain to anyone, especially the authorities, would more often than not lead to the termination and deportation of the complainant without compensation and without the sought after "letter of no objection" that would enable them to find employment at some other hellhole in the Middle East.

Hence the anonymous letter in a child's handwriting on a crumpled piece of paper and littered with spelling mistakes and pidgin English.

He could track down the author, of course, it would be easy enough from the dead girl's small circle of friends but what was the point? He knew it was true, what was written there. Knew why the girl had died, knew who the killer was.

The problem was proving it.

So, once the identity of the deceased had been established they had interviewed the family. As expected the father was the spokesman, the mother, a morbidly obese woman of indeterminate years with the faint hint of a moustache, a silent presence in the background.

The girl had been with them for six months and there had never been the hint of trouble. She had her own room and her duties were mainly cleaning and cooking as well as going grocery shopping.

She went alone on these occasions? Riad had asked as he sipped his mint tea while taking in the surroundings of the living room. Spacious with a high ceiling the walls were hung with tapestries including a silk prayer carpet. Heavy drapes at the windows, the furniture ersatz Louis XIV, the centrepiece a giant flat screen TV that was switched to a breakfast show with the sound turned down.

Glass tipped doilies covering the coffee tables. Assorted multicoloured junk displayed all around.

'Mostly,' the husband had replied, adding that occasionally he would drive her to the Sultan Shopping Centre when a big list had to be filled. It turned out his wife did not like leaving the house so he was tasked with driving the maid. 'I would wait in the car while the maid did the shopping. I would not look right for me to...'

'I know,' Riad had said, holding up a hand and then switching direction to take another biscuit from the offered plate. Oreos, they were rather nice and he made a mental note of buying some.

'But you also sometimes drove her on other errands, did you not?' Riad had asked casually while watching the flickering images on the television. This was information already gleaned from the neighbours when Waleed had gone knocking earlier.

'Er...yes, sometimes, when she had to go to get her *iquama* renewed or when my son had to be picked up from school and there would be no parking at the...'

'Ah, yes, your son,' Riad had said replacing his glass cup on the table and waving away the offer of a refill. 'That would be the boy we saw just now, when we came in?'

The father, who went by the name of Jassim, nodded silently, glancing uncertainly at the wife who was a hovering spectre somewhere out of Riad's line of vision.

'How old is your son?'

'Hossam is eighteen,' the mother said, a distinct note of defiance in her voice.

'He and the young girl got along well?' Keeping it casual, making a show of studying something on his mobile while feigning a frown.

'She was a *maid*,' the mother said with some emphasis, this statement being deemed self explanatory. A mere servant, not someone whose presence was acknowledged other than when her service was required.

An *untouchable.*

But what exactly did that service entail?

Riad thought he knew.

Next they inspected the girl's room, on the upper floor of the dwelling. Larger than anticipated one half of the floorspace was taken up by stacked cardboard boxes and several items of random furniture indicating a storage function. In a far corner were two large plastic drums and peering into the half open lid of one box Riad could make out the green hue of spring topped glass bottles.

A slight stickiness underfoot completed the picture, in addition to this being the maid' sleeping quarters it was also the beer and wine brewing room, now quickly and discreetly disguised as just another storage space.

The walls of the room were as bare as the family lounge was stuffed with enough cheap bric-a-brac to fill a second rate tourist shop. A single bed took up centre space against the far wall next to small side table on which sat a gilt framed photograph of what was likely a family gathering. Smiling faces of the young with the adults clustered behind and the faces mostly hidden in shadow as the shot was amateurish, the sun at the wrong angle. Next to it a small well thumbed Tagalog bible.

The stand alone clothes cupboard contained half a dozen cheap print dresses and two pairs of denim jeans. Some underwear, a pair of sneakers and two pairs of black lace up shoes.

A full length black *abeya* and then a host of personal articles, mainly tiny pieces of costume jewellery and a stack of letters postmarked in Manila which would turn out to be from a concerned mother.

A few personal hygiene items.

And a slightly battered red canvas suitcase shoved under the bed.

From experience the detectives knew these items represented all of the girl's earthly belongings. Not the picture of someone who had left the country, especially not when her passport would be kept in the possession of her employers as had been confirmed earlier.

That was when Riad knew why she had to die.

4
CHAPTER

It came like it always did, without warning. The dream. Not every night but most nights. At one stage she thought of escaping the demons, banishing them from the dark recesses of her mind by sleeping in the light of day, with the windows open, just enough so the sounds of the big city could float inside and wrap her in their comforting embrace.

That had not worked, it only served to make the slow moving images of the dream even more real as they drifted past and mixed with the blurred half seen background of the room, the piercing scream somehow accentuated by the screech of brakes and the blaring of car horns outside.

She was in the dream now, knowing it was a dream yet unable to escape the horrible sight of the man in the water as the boat sailed slowly away, his eyes staring straight back at her in silent accusation as a hand, an arm, was raised in a last hopeless cry for help. Or was it a wave of farewell?

And as always she realised the scream of terror was not from the drowning man but tearing over her own lips.

Nooooooo!!!

'Sarah... *Sarah!*'

She was awake now, suddenly and completely and lying quite still as her eyes followed Hasan about the room, her husband rummaging through the drawers of his dresser as he searched for his cufflinks. 'You've been having the dream again,' he said without looking at her, a glance at his watch showing he was going to be late for the office.

18

She did not say anything, just lay there as the tension and the perspiration slowly drained away from her shivering body. Except she wasn't cold, the opposite in fact and with trembling hands she pulled the bedsheets off and lay there for a while just staring at the ceiling where she could still see that terrible face, those accusing eyes, as they flashed across her subconscious in a series of aftershocks.

'Are you alright, my love?' he asked, a frown creasing his handsome face.

'Yes,' she managed running a hand through hair that was plastered to her forehead, 'Yes, I'm alright –'

'Sure you don't want me to call someone, perhaps a sleeping tablet or – ?'

Stifling a yawn she shook her head, 'I'm alright, darling. I'm seeing a psychologist now, as you know, and she is helping me work through this until –' Unable to complete the last bit she stared up at him helplessly.

'Maddie will be back soon,' her husband said as he leaned over to gently kiss her on the forehead. 'Soon, you'll see. Then those demons will go away forever.'

'Yes darling,' she said softly as she raised herself on the pillows, 'the monsters will go away...'

'I'll send the maid up with your breakfast,' Hasan Abdul-Karim said as he reached for his slim briefcase and paused in the doorway to smile back at her. 'I'm finalising things here in Kuwait and we should be back in Melbourne in less than two weeks, this time staying as long as it takes. I promise.'

Then he was gone leaving her lying there and thinking of Maddie. *Oh my baby, dear beautiful trusting little Maddie, what have I done?! I had to Maddie, I had to!*

But the dream had been different this time, for there had been a man, a stranger in the shadows who stared back at her with the penetrating gaze of he who knew and, above all, understood. Then it came to her with such clarity that she sat upright in bed, aware of her heart beating in her chest. The man was the key out of this madness! Find that man who had been through what she had but also a man of the world who was experienced in finding the lost but above all, would understand her pain.

But here, in Kuwait? What were the chances of finding a man who would slay the monster?

And deep inside she knew that for so long now, long before Maddie was there, the monsters were. And they would never leave her.

For she was the monster.

⸻ ◆ ⸻

They sat in the same living room on the same chairs drinking the same mint tea as on their first visit fourteen days earlier.

The third visit now and this time the son was present, as requested by Riad during an earlier phone call. A tall gangly youth he wore a white dishdasha, cut short at the hem with black slip on loafers tucked into white basketball socks and with the obligatory Cubs baseball cap worn low over the ears and at an angle, the peak off to one side.

Wispy strands of a beard just visible in the sunlight filtering through a curtain and green aviator sunshades that, when removed at Riad's request, revealed large eyes with long girlish lashes that vaguely reminded him of a camel.

Jassim al Mashri was seated diagonally opposite his son whom he was studying with more than a hint of anxiety while trying not to appear anxious. Twitching fingers nervously rotating a string of prayer beads as well as the frequent nervous licking of his lips gave him away.

As on previous occasions the mother was a looming but unseen presence in the shadows somewhere behind the couch Riad and Waleed were seated on. (Didn't the woman ever sit down?)

'We were not expecting to see you again so soon, Lieutenant,' the father began hesitantly furiously rotating the beads while silently mouthing the ninety nine names of Allah. 'Is there news...?'

'There is,' Riad said slowly, seeing from the corner of an eye Waleed's wolfish smile as he sat on the edge of his chair to stare at a now clearly uncomfortable youth. 'Not good, I'm afraid,' he added after a pause to heighten the dramatic effect.

Silence in the room now, the only sound the asthmatic wheeze of the mother somewhere in the shadows. 'B...bad?' the father managed all but choking on the word.

Riad nodded, 'The DNA results have come back, Jassim,' he said, the other man's head jerking at the contemptuous familiarity incipient in the use of his first name. The prayer beads had dropped onto the carpet but the man appeared not to notice.

'DNA...' he mouthed silently, his eyes flickering between wife and son.

'Yes. We tested some nail scrapings from the girl's fingers as well as body fluids and found a match.' Lifting his gaze Riad stared directly at the boy who met his gaze with dark eyes that harboured no expression at all. *Looking at me like a horse over a fence, Riad thought. Wasn't that how Raymond Chandler's Philip Marlowe once described it?*

'You do recall that we took a swab from the mouth of each of you, as well as several others who knew the girl? Well, there's been a match.' Nodding at Waleed who had risen Riad said, 'Hossam al Mashri. I have reason to believe you were having sex with the deceased who has been found to be pregnant. I arrest you and must warn you that...'

'It was I,' Jassim al Mashri said in a voice gone weary and soft. After a pause he went on, his expression now one of hopelessness. 'I found out that my son had been sleeping with the girl and was afraid of a pregnancy. I... we, could not have that. Not with this maid! It, it would destroy us.'

'I understand,' Riad said softly, reflecting that he sadly understood only too well. 'So you drove her to the bus stop on her off weekend like you told us earlier but you never dropped her there, did you? Instead you killed her and took the body into the desert and buried it?'

Jassim nodded mutely then just sat there, shoulders slumped. An old man reviewing the ruins of his life.

'Cuff them both,' Riad instructed Waleed. 'We'll take their statements down at the station.'

As he watched father and son being handcuffed, the younger unceremoniously jerked to his feet by a grinning sergeant, Riad reflected on how often in their business it came down to a confession more than burden of proof to get a conviction. Truth was he had been bluffing all along. They had no solid evidence against these two, just a pile of circumstantial items that would not be enough for even a

Kuwaiti judge. The girl had not been pregnant after all. As usual it was simple logic that had them conclude early on it had to be one or both of the family males, the girl simply had no other life outside of this prison, knew no-one else. Would never have gotten into a vehicle with a stranger.

There was no DNA worth a damn, at least nothing even a half baked defence lawyer would not have discredited and then there was the question of the status of the deceased. How hard was the Kuwait police force going to pursue the death of a nobody? How long would it have been before Colonel Omar, that bastion of the city's finest, called him off?

Not long.

No, it had to be a confession. Staring at the two men, the old man crying softly, Riad thought how all Jassim al Mashri should have done was to say nothing. Nothing! And it would all have blown over like just another desert sandstorm. In their world little more than a storm in a teacup really.

Much ado about nothing as Shakespeare would have put it.

Why did this not make him feel any better? Wasn't justice about to be served? This pathetic man in front of him, this killer of innocence, would hang all too soon, probably the son as well. And for what? What would it change in the grand scope of things?

Shaking off the looming cloud of depression Riad motioned Waleed, who had finished reading them their rights, to take them outside when there was an ear-splitting scream from somewhere behind his back, an ululation from hell and then there was a terrible pain. A sharpness so intense that it took the breath clean from his lungs as his legs buckled and he twisted in a desperate attempt to get away from the sharpness.

His last vision as the blackness descended the sight of the mother, still screaming, standing over him with the kitchen knife in her hand red with blood. His last thought not again! NOT AGAIN!! That and two loud bangs in quick succession and the smell of cordite and darkness.

5
CHAPTER

'**D**o you have anger management issues, Riad?'

Leaning back against the soft enveloping leather of the easy chair he mulled this over for a minute. He did not have to close his eyes to relive the time he had stood on the deck of a yacht watching a murderer of babies drown while numb with rage. Or that time, long ago now, in the desert dunes outside Jeddah when he had dealt, if not exactly within the confines of the law, the debilitating physical blow that would have a rapist think twice in future...

'No.'

While the psychologist scribbled something on her pad Riad swivelled in the chair to take in his surroundings. So this is what a shrink's office looked like he decided. Spacious and airy with a large picture window looking out on the Marine Parade with the sea beyond and the Kuwait Towers just visible in a corner.

Tastefully decorated in the minimalist style with a few smallish artworks on the light green walls and fresh cut flowers in a corner hand painted vase.

Ikea furniture, a small open fronted wooden desk and office chair facing two plush backed chairs, all in light stained wood, one in which he sat. The only piece out of place a leather chesterfield at an angle next to the desk with two small scatter cushions in bright colours.

It was a shrink's office after all, there *had* to be a couch.

Ameera al Quarashi – her full name according to the Toronto University Diploma of Psychology on the wall behind her – was wearing a navy blue pants suit with a high collar white blouse, a silk scarf completing the picture while black stilettos adorned her slender feet.

The suit was Armani, the scarf he thought Chanel, the shoes either Jimmy Choo or possibly Manolo Blahnik. Riad knew these things courtesy of a woman that he never thought of more than about once every three or four hours. Fareeda, his wife and the love torn from his life.

The perfume was definitely Chanel. Number 5, he thought. Fareeda had worn that.

'Riad?' She looked at him quizzically, a pen poised above a pad she was writing on.

'Wha?... Oh, sorry, lost in thought there for a moment.'

He affected a smile, shifted in his chair and tried to focus. Important to make the right impression, get the nod from the lady so she would sign him off as fit to return to duty.

Ameera smiled in turn, carefully so the skilfully applied makeup would not spoil and went on, 'If your wound is hurting we can continue another time?'

Riad shook his head, 'No, I'm fine. Let's do this.' Truth was the scar on his back where his left kidney had been until recently was hurting but it was a good hurt. The kind of hurt a man could learn something from. *Deadlier than the male, Riad! Twice now you have been caught like that.*

'Let us go back to your earlier life, just to give me a better understanding of where you came from and what your true goals in life are. So I can help you,' she added somewhat unnecessarily.

Supressing a sigh Riad straightened in his chair wondering whether there was a reason the chair was that uncomfortable. 'Where to begin,' he said while thinking of Alice in Wonderland. *Start at the beginning, go through to the end. Then stop.* 'My father was a Saudi military attachè in Paris where he met my mother, a French Lebanese student. They were married with me the only child. The family travelled frequently as my father was posted to different countries and hence I was sent to a boarding school in England.'

'Harrow it says here on your official dossier.'

'Yes.' Wondering whether it also stated that he was almost expelled for playing tiddly winks with the dean's eighteen year old daughter.

'Your mother, Yvette Ayoub, is quite famous in the world of Arabian music and Lebanese Television, is she not?'

'Yes. She took back her maiden name when they divorced.'

'Why did they divorce? Do you want to talk about it?'

Riad shrugged, stole a look at one of the modern paintings on the wall, wondering what poor tortured soul had created that, someone who had sat in this chair perhaps? 'My father took a second wife. As a man of his status he felt it his duty. My mother decided to leave.' She also shattered a potted plant against the side of his head leaving a broad scar visible to this day but no need to mention that.

'So you have siblings? I mean half brothers or sisters?'

'Two brothers, one has died and three sisters. My father has more than one wife.' Three he thought but who was counting? For all the contact he had with the family in Al Hada there could be more little half siblings by now.

'The brother that died, it was when you were there, in Saudi?'

'It was from a drug overdose,' Riad said flatly. Might as well get it out in the open.

'Hmm.' He watched as she scribbled something. 'Let's go back to when you finished school. It says here you went to military college?'

'My father's idea, he wanted me to follow in his footsteps. Sandhurst wasn't my thing and I left and went to university instead.' A slight nod of understanding from the psychologist had him carry on, 'I came down from Cambridge with a bachelor's degree in English Literature.'

She smiled and leaned back in her chair, touching the tips of her teeth with the pen, 'And then you went back to Saudi Arabia and entered the police force, not so?' Before he could answer she went on with what he thought just a touch of the wry in her voice. 'It is our lot, here in the Arab world, not so? The government sends us overseas to study as much as we wish but always with the understanding that they own us, that one day we must return and work amongst our people.'

Riad said nothing. Just another beautiful little songbird in its gilded cage, he thought. Living a life of security and luxury but never

ever free like her western sisters. Where did this young woman go when she needed therapy?

'What made you leave the Saudi police force and come to Kuwait?' A frown indicated it was something inexplicably missing from his file.

'There was an incident, a criminal case. It involved a person of great *wasta*. (Wasta – influence. How he could never say that word without a touch of bitterness. Might as well call it by its real name, corruption.) I was persuaded not to bring a charge against this person –'

'A sheikh,' she prompted, 'a prince?'

'It was also explained to me that my usefulness in Jeddah had come to an end, that it would be wise for me to leave the country. So I came to Kuwait who was happy to have me. I was already a senior investigator then.'

He could have added that in the course of the resisted arrest the prince had sustained one or two embarrassing injuries but that might have brought up the anger management issue again.

'Tell me about your wife and child.'

'Fareeda and I knew each other from childhood days in Al Hada where our families lived. I spent school holidays there and we played together until it was time for her to wear the hijab, you know.'

Ameera al Quarashi nodded as she scribbled something. She knew all too well the Saudi custom, not the norm in Kuwait, where girls were segregated from males the moment they had that first period.

'She was sent to Boston in the USA where she became a gynaecologist. We met again when I returned from the UK and a marriage was arranged.' He regretted it the moment it rolled off his lips. "Arranged." Why had he said that? Because it was true, because she was pregnant to another man, an American womaniser on the Al Hada Hospital compound, her fate sure to be terrible? Had he really been that knight in shining armour who had married her to protect her honour, to raise little Rania as his own daughter?

No, that wasn't it. He had loved his wife with all his heart, loved his daughter for she was *his* daughter.

If the psychologist had noticed the slight catch in his narrative she did not let on, simply prompted him to continue.

'She stayed behind in Saudi when I left for Kuwait, we had some problems at the time that we were trying to work through. During my visit in 2001, it was the month of Ramadan, Fareeda was killed, murdered by her brother, a terrorist who is still being hunted by the Americans.'

There was a long pause during which Riad could hear the noise of a typewriter in an adjoining room. 'How do you feel about that?' Ameera asked at length.

Riad shrugged, 'It took me a long time to get over that. I felt I should have been able to protect her.'

'Do you feel that you may have failed your mother as well Riad?'

He said nothing as he returned her stare for deep inside nothing was what he felt right then.

He watched as she closed the pad, folding her hands to lean forward on the desktop. 'You show signs of suffering from the post traumatic stress disorder, Riad. During earlier sessions we had gone over your disturbed sleep, vivid nightmares and episodes of anxiety. None of this is surprising seeing as to what had happened to you in the line of your work as well as certain events in your personal life. I would like to introduce you to a few group therapy sessions I feel will be of benefit.'

'Group therapy?'

'Just a small circle of patients of mine who share similar traumatic incidents in their lives. Quite often it helps to share our experiences with others.'

'Do I have to?'

This time there was no warmth in her smile, 'If you want to return to your work, yes. The first session is to-morrow morning at ten, next door in our meeting room.'

And with that the consultation was over leaving Riad feeling stripped bare and utterly alone.

6
CHAPTER

etective Inspector Josh Reed looked down at the contents of the
paper cup which had once been an extra shot latte' but had after
being neglected for half an hour turned into a cold, unattractive
brown sludge. His fault and something he put down to becoming
engrossed once more in the file open in front of him. It had been a
nice coffee too, the little pattern the coffee shop barista created on the
top always tickled him, how did they do it? A colleague had suggested
they use a sieve but Reed preferred to think it was an artistic creation
requiring hours of patient practice and perseverance.

Much like his job, come to think of it. How did the old cliché go,
five percent inspiration, ninety five percent perspiration? Not at all
like on NCIS his wife liked to watch and which he suspected had more
to do with the good looks of the actors rather than any semblance of
reality.

Swivelling his office chair he gazed out through a window
streaming with rain, his gaze settling on a miserable looking pigeon
skulking under the little protection offered by an overhanging eave.
It was preening ruffled feathers with quick movements while a beady
eye appeared to be watching him. For some inexplicable reason
he felt a sudden twinge of deep sadness, melancholy even. For all
its misery – how could you not be miserable on a wet and windy
Melbourne winter's day – it was free. No possessions, no mortgage,
no increasingly aloof wife, no teenage son that called you a doofus
and not always behind your back.

No gut wrenching concerns about a case involving a missing little girl that was fast going as cold as his coffee.

With a sigh he picked up the Maddie Green file to stare at the A4 size photograph on page 1. The face that stared back at him was that of a four year old girl with large blue eyes under impossibly long natural eyelashes shining from a peaches and cream complexion, tiny freckles highlighting her cheeks. Rosy lips were slightly parted in a half smile and revealing tiny white teeth as she glanced up at the camera with, could it be, just a hint of apprehension? Wispy blonde curls framed the heart shaped little face with a tousled look peering out from under a red and yellow knitted woollen cap.

She was beautiful and she had been taken going on four months now. Four months with no clues, not even a hint of what could have happened. Was she still alive? The mere thought had him shudder for wasn't that so often the case with these paedophiles, use them and lose them?

Something about this case that just did not make sense. Technically it was still a missing persons issue until proven otherwise but everything pointed to Maddie being snatched. An opportunistic paedophile ring? Possible but on the other hand Maddie was the only child of a fabulously rich family, both parents millionaires in their own right. Wouldn't it make far more sense for the issue to be one of ransom? Even a million or two?

But no, in that case the kidnappers would have been in contact long before now. Rubbing his temples to ward off a dull ache which his chiropractor had suggested was due to tension induced muscle sprain in his neck, he thought back on a story he had come across years earlier when he still had the free time to read fiction. A young heiress is kidnapped by a two bit gang for ransom. Before they have time to issue the ransom demand, the gang is wiped out by another, larger outfit who decide to play it differently, mainly because the perverted psycho scion of the crime family falls for the girl in a big way and wants to keep her for himself. The rest too scared to intervene.

So the searchers go down a dead end trail looking for the original kidnappers and finding nothing.

Shit! Absently going through a dry spitting motion in a cupped hand, a normally well suppressed affliction of his Tourette's, he tried to remember how that story had played out. Wasn't it something like the Patti Hearst kidnap case some years later? The Stockholm Syndrome heiress who was turned by the gang to become a soldier for their cause?

Was that what was happening to Maddie Green while in the hands of whoever these perverts were? Would they turn this vulnerable clean slate young mind into another human being altogether if he didn't find her soon?

It did not bear thinking.

Paging through the casebook while scanning all recorded there, the work of a team assigned to the case, he saw evidence of solid hard slogging detective work. Every angle had been covered over and over again. From repeated interviews with both parents plus the couple they had dined with on the fateful evening to even tracing the cab driver who was unable to add anything. There had even been a phone interview with a Chrissie May, Sarah Reed's personal secretary who normally accompanies the family on overseas trips had been on holiday in Spain at the time of Maddie's disappearance.

Another interview with a London based young woman, a Scandinavian au pair, who had been the girl's most recent nanny. This one conducted by London's Metropolitan Police at his request, the Brits being very co-operative as Maddie was after all a British citizen. They had even offered to send down a detective to help in the case but Reed declined as they had enough manpower. Something that bothered him about that last interview though, the lingering impression that the woman was holding back, especially when it came to Maddie's frequent visits to paediatricians at the time or, more specifically, her visits to a child psychologists.

It was something that had bothered his London counterpart as well. What was she not saying? No matter how many angles the policeman tried she would always clam up when that issue was raised. He even went as far as stating, not in the report but in a subsequent phone conversation, that he suspected a cover up, to the point of wondering if hush money had changed hands.

Attempts at gleaning information from the psychologists had met with stonewalling under the mantle of patient confidentiality.

Later pages detailed all subsequent local investigations where the team had utilised fully the integrated resources available to the various branches of Australia's criminal investigation branches as well as Interpol and now the Child Protection unit of the Australian Federal Police.

All for nothing.

But Reed had been a cop for a long time now, over the years developing that sixth sense that all good detectives come to rely on. That and informants. Without those you were dead in the water but so often it started with a well thought out hunch, an instinct.

And all this instincts told him Sarah Green and husband Abdul-Karim, held the key to the disappearance of Maddie Green.

The question was how to get behind that beautifully presented mask that was the cold face of a supermodel.

———◆———

The picture of Maddie Green open in front of DI Josh Reed bore almost no resemblance to how the girl looked now as she studied herself in the full length mirror, turning from side to side while shyly looking up from under lowered eyelids just as Martha had taught her. The wig that hid her golden curls was black and cut in the pageboy style and the white face cream highlighted the sapphire blue eyes as did the cherry red lipstick.

Martha had called it the Japanese look saying that some of the uncles liked that as well as the black school jumper worn over a plain white shirt complete with a school necktie. The jumper ended well above the knees while long white bobby socks came all the way up to the knees.

Black patent leather shoes fastened with a single strap completed the outfit.

Ken had protested that Japanese girls don't have blue eyes but Martha had said that would be the titillating catch, the stand out feature that would fascinate the visitors.

———

Martha had told her that to-day was a big day for Maddie's training was now over and the next step was her dancing classes. Maddie was happy for Mommy had taken her to early ballet lessons and she had liked it and made many friends. But Martha had explained this was different dancing with added some tricks where she would swing around a pole while all the time smiling.

Also, for the first time, they would start taking pictures as she danced, with a movie camera. Many people would see this and she would have many friends. Would Mommy come to see me dance she asked, adding that Sarah always came to her dance classes, even when it was the nanny that took her.

Not to-day, Martha had replied while glancing at Ken, for Mommy was away on a modelling trip and very busy right now, that was why Martha and Ken were looking after her. But soon, she promised, she would see Mommy again.

Maddie was happy to hear this. She was four years old, she believed in the promises of adults.

7
CHAPTER

After leaving the office of the psychologist Riad decided to leave his parked car and take a walk down the Marine Parade heading for the Ras Kuwait where there was a little coffee shop that baked their own delicious baklava pastries. After the increasingly stifling atmosphere of the woman's consulting rooms he needed the fresh air and a cup of strong Americano.

Not that the air was all that fresh that morning, some construction was taking place at a new marina complex next to the city's amusement park and his nose told him the sewage works had been breached. In the wind still morning there was no escaping the mix of sewage and exhaust fumes and Riad decided he wasn't hungry after all.

Waiting at the counter for his takeaway coffee he glanced at the front page of a Kuwait Gazette a customer had left on a table. The mass shooting in Salwa still claimed the headlines. Nine people dead, a tenth clinging to life in hospital. The police still interviewing witnesses while the family of the boy identified as the shooter declared themselves as shocked as everybody else and completely at a loss to explain the behaviour of their only son.

The father, an employee at the Ministry of Health and by all accounts a good Allah fearing citizen, had disclosed that the boy had been doing well at school and that the family had plans for him to be an engineer. It was true that he did not appear to have any friends, at least not that the family was aware of and had no extramural activities such as sport.

Instead he was an avid video gamer who would shut himself in his room for hours on end playing an interactive game   and seemingly becoming so involved with it that at times it was difficult to persuade him to come to the dinner table.

The father's own computer skills were limited to logging on patients to the department's medical records system and chatting to friends on Facebook. He admitted to being fascinated by his son's dazzling computer skills while increasingly being unable to comprehend the games flickering across the laptop screen as well as, in the last few months, being excluded from being present when the boy was online.

A search of the boy's laptop had come up against a very sophisticated firewall that so far the experts had not been able to crack, help being sought from the FBI with the police confident that it was only a matter of time.

A greater puzzle was where the boy had gotten hold of the assault rifle and ammunition. Civilian ownership of small arms was not allowed in Kuwait and the armed forces were issued with American weapons which meant the rifle in question could only have been smuggled in, possibly from nearby Iraq. But by whom and why?

Was it a terrorist attack? Could the boy somehow have been radicalized online? There was no evidence that he had been unduly religious or attending meetings of disaffected others. Not that any such groups were known to be present in their city where any signs of dissent would quickly be rooted out by the ever watchful security police.

And why that particular target? That, Riad decided as he turned the page to read the rest of the article, was the real question. Answer that and the case would open up. An ordinary *diwaniya* of ordinary citizens like dozens of others that night in the city. No VIPs and no foreigners. Just a group of neighbours who gathered on that sidewalk every Wednesday evening to discuss the week's everyday events and relax in each other's company while enjoying the coolness of the evening air.

A list of the deceased had finally been released, there had been a delay as some family members had been travelling abroad and had to be informed first. Scanning the names, occupations listed next to each, Riad saw a random group of middle class Kuwaitis with occupations ranging from government workers to artisans to retirees. It was the seventh name on the list that had him pause while absently taking a sip from the piping hot coffee. Abdullah Farsi. 46 yrs. Police Captain in the Vice Division.

Breathing through his mouth in a vain attempt to cool his scalded palate Riad thought this over. He did not personally know the late captain but had come across the name somewhere before. Dismissing it from his mind for the moment he bade the shopkeeper good day and resumed his walk down the boulevard heading in the direction of the Imax.

Crossing the busy street he strolled past the main gates to the funfair, pausing for a moment to glance around at the carnival rides and stalls that adorned the place.

All but deserted during the day with only a handful of maintenance workers about the place would become a hive of activity at night. As the gaudy neon lights came on and the music started up the carousels and dive bombers and jumping castles would start gyrating and revolving to the screams of hundreds of small children as they slurped their ice creams and tugged parents every which way as the next thrill caught the eye.

A smile creased his lips as he thought back on how many times he had brought Rania there as a little girl, watching her as she screamed her way from ride to ride all the while wondering what he should do with the fast melting ice cream running over his hand or the sticky candy floss in the other.

Memories of happy times. Times when they managed to forget, even if just for a moment, the events of that Ramadan in the mountains of Saudi Arabia when death had stalked them all taking a wife and a mother away from them forever.

Now his little girl was little no more and no longer interested in funfairs and silly children's games. Now she was a teenager with posters of young men on her bedroom walls and strange tuneless music wafting from under her closed door. Of mood swings and unexplained tears and anxieties that somehow she found difficult to share with him.

Shaking off the thoughts he glanced at his watch. Not yet noon, too early to pick Rania up from school and his appointment with his surgeon was only later that afternoon. After a moment's hesitation he decided to catch a cab down to the Salmiyah Police Station, see if there was any paperwork waiting for him and hopefully catch up with Waleed.

He would get one of his colleagues to drop him back at his car later.

It was when he walked into the cool lobby of the police station and passing by the wall mounted board with photos of missing and wanted people that he remembered where he had come across the name of Captain Abdullah Farsi.

The late vice captain had been in charge of the investigation into the disappearance of four year old Maddie Green. The months old case that still gripped the imagination and nightmares of Kuwait's citizens.

'Lieutenant! *Sabah al Kheer!*' Waleed's shout had Riad pause halfway up the steps to the detectives room, ignoring a sharp stab of his wound as he whirled to locate the owner of the voice. The sergeant was at the charge desk with a handcuffed suspect which he summarily handed over to the desk sergeant while calling out to Riad to wait, he was coming up. Moments later, still shouting instructions at the desk sergeant, he joined Riad on the stairs, a sudden look of concern crossing his features as he enquired about Riad's wound. 'You shouldn't be back at work, boss. Get better first, better still, take a bloody holiday!'

Slightly out of breath after the climb and inwardly cursing the elevator that was still out of commission Riad paused at the entrance to the large shared office space taking in the familiar smells of the place, a heady mix of cigarette smoke, swirling dust and body odour.

A man's environment he decided, gender equality and indeed political correctness not yet having found its way to this little corner. Familiar sounds too, the hum of ageing desktop computers competing with the tired wheeze of window mounted air conditioners and the rustle of shuffled paperwork. All providing the background to a hubbub of voices, some rising above the others such as the all too familiar bellow emanating from the open door of Colonel Omar's office where some poor unfortunate bastard was being the stool pigeon of the day.

God he missed it! Only two weeks away, most of it in a hospital bed and already he missed the cosy familiarity of this dump of a place.

You have no life, Riad...

Behind him Waleed chuckled, nodding towards the room they were now entering, 'Already you miss, no?'

Riad shrugged, smiled wryly. 'It's your ugly mug I missed,' he countered, 'and that piss you serve up as coffee. How about a cup now?'

Other heads were turning, smiling faces getting up from behind desks with outstretched hands as he was ushered over to his hastily vacated old desk. 'Please, *modir*, sit down! *Esteri!* Welcome, welcome.' The warm greetings quickly followed by concerned enquiries as to his injuries and when he was expecting to be back.

A soft cushion was quickly found to prod up his back as he sank into the desk chair with its familiar protesting creak and wafting smell of old leather while a young newcomer was gruffly ordered to bring the lieutenant a cup of coffee and put enough sugar in it.

Quickly a cluster of familiar faces crowded around him, everyone talking at the same time with enough gesturing of hands to put an Italian to shame. The loud chatter was sure to draw the attention of Colonel Omar but no-one cared and Riad realised with a warm feeling that yes, he was back where he belonged, even if just for a few minutes.

The lines from Henry V coming back to him as he shook hands and endured gingerly pats on the shoulder, *'We few, we happy few, we band of brothers...*

Hushing the others with a held up hand he fixed Waleed with a stern look, 'Sergeant Waleed!'

'Modir?' came the muted reply to stifled giggles behind Riad's back.

'That day in Fahaheel when I was attacked by the woman, you shot her, correct?'

A solemn nod indicated the correctness of the statement, also confirmed by the general nodding of heads.

'Shot her in the chest as you were taught at the Academy, a double tap in rapid fire?'

'*Aiwa!* Saved your life.' This to a general murmur of consent, little doubt amongst the assembly that the next lunge of the crazed woman's kitchen knife could well have been fatal.

'Then why, Sergeant Waleed, was the second bullet between her eyes? A kill shot, so to speak?'

'It all happened so fast, Lieutenant, with you falling towards me and...'

'And to think you are the best shot in the department, taking the prize at our last competition.'

The giggles at his back now more pronounced as eyes glittering with excitement studied the two men. Waleed spread his hands in a gesture as old as the dunes, 'I thought it best, boss. Just think of the paperwork I saved us both.'

General laughter now, Waleed the recipient of good natured banter and playful jostling.

Justice Kuwait style, Riad mused as he shook his head, had he not taken that liberty himself not that long ago?

'Very disappointing, Sergeant,' he said in his best imitation of the Colonel's voice. 'Some remedial training I feel is...'

He was stopped in mid sentence by the large head of Colonel Omar appearing behind the shoulders of the group, dark eyes focusing on him with a mix of displeasure and yet, a hint of softening. 'Ajmi! In my office, now.' With that he strode away with the others rolling their eyes at Riad, one or two making gestures indicating he was in for it now as they laughingly returned to work.

8

CHAPTER

I t was two minutes past three in the afternoon when the gates to the school were flung open and the first horde of excitedly chattering kids came rushing out. Teenage girls, all dressed the same down to the school tie and domed broad rimmed hat Riad had only ever seen look good on Maggie Smith in Travels with my Aunt.

A private girl's school that still maintained the legacy of earlier colonial times and only cost him an arm and a leg. Still, worth it. No *madrissa* for his daughter. Just like there would be no wearing the penguin suit *abeya* and certainly no headscarf.

Except, of course, for those rare occasions when she accompanied him on a visit to the family in Saudi Arabia.

He spotted Rania as she came through the gates at the tail end of a small group of classmates, all by now having tugged loose the neckties with the white shirttails partially hanging out over the skirt and the long grey socks slovenly uneven. One or two shaking loose tied up hair while guiltily glancing back to see if any disapproving teacher was watching.

A studied look, he decided. A little gesture of defiance or perhaps trying to be like the American sisters they would watch on their iPads later. Was he the only one who noticed that it was always the sock on the right that was pulled down?

In silence he watched as his daughter walked right past him studiously avoiding a look at the Cherokee as she made an effort to keep up with the other girls, most of whom had their mobiles out by now and working it with that rapid one handed dexterity that Riad's generation could only dream of copying. It did not escape his attention that while the girls were chattering amongst themselves Rania was largely ignored, her slender shoulders hunched as she kept her eyes downcast.

He watched as she gradually fell behind, then stopped, turned and headed slowly back towards him.

He said nothing as she got into the car, carefully stowing her backpack between her feet. Waiting for a gap in the traffic he drove heading for their apartment in nearby Salwa. An uneasy silence was broken only by the steady whirr of the car's air conditioner and the squeal of the brakes when he spotted a large pothole at the last moment.

After a while, still looking straight ahead, he said, 'Want to talk about it?'

Rania did not reply, just sat there unseeingly looking at a piece of ribbon she was rhythmically twisting in her hands.

'That bad, eh?' he said while returning a wave from an elderly neighbour as he swung the car into his rickety undercover parking spot. In late November it was still pleasantly warm but thankfully no longer humid and he noticed that some of the men in the street were wearing jackets over their dishdashas. Exchanging a greeting with Ali, the Bengali houseboy who was enjoying a quiet cigarette on the doorstep of the building, he followed Rania into the dark coolness and into the elevator.

Wasn't it strange, he thought, how people automatically assumed their elevator mode the moment the doors closed and the cage gave its first lurch. Eyes straight ahead, no eye contact and each party shrinking into the smallest space that could be claimed as personal. All parties standing quite still, no conversation, as ears were pricked to the sounds of ascent while watching the passing floors light up on the control panel.

Always the same he thought, be it New York or Kuwait City. The only thing missing was the elevator music softly wafting through some hidden recess in the ceiling.

Different smell though. Normally there would be the faint hint of the antiseptic Ali used when mopping the floors but to-day there was the distinct hint of curry powder which had him wonder if Mrs Burud in Flat 2 was having another go at her famous fish curry which, not that long ago, led to a minor outbreak of Salmonella food poisoning with the place being quarantined for a while.

Inside their apartment on the top floor they were welcomed by the cat rubbing against their legs, tail on end and purring softly. Rania seemed not to notice, going straight to her room leaving Riad to absently stroke the feline while wondering what to do.

They had been there before, of course, with teenage girls in the house who had not? But previous moods had lasted a day or two at most but things had been this way now for going on a whole week. Something was wrong. When questioned she fobbed him off with some vague hint of homework or wanting to be alone so she could spend more time with her friends online.

Two days earlier he had a phone conversation with her teacher, a Miss Johnstone from Manchester, who had reassured him that there was nothing wrong with his daughter's schoolwork while agreeing that she did seem unusually aloof and not expressing any interest in the after school activities organised by the school. There was the promise that the teacher would have a chat with Rania.

Ambling over to the kitchen he took a bottle of home brew from the fridge while idly wondering what dinner would be. It was the maid's off day so no prepared meal and it looked like it was going to be tuna and salad again. Not that he minded, although Rania had hinted that "goat food" was not necessarily health food. Apparently the occasional burger and fries from Burger King down the street had been shown to be quite healthy when taken in moderation.

Like not more than once a day.

Still, his customary glass or two of home made white wine went down quite well, thank you, with the tuna and salad. That was if you poured it carefully from the spring topped bottle so as not to get too much sediment in the glass.

The beer was different. No matter how carefully you poured there was always that yeasty taste but, what the hell, after years of putting up with it he had actually acquired a taste for the foul stuff.

Taking his beer over to the small window looking out on the deck of the next door neighbours he wondered who was living there now. Never saw anyone, not like the time the English teacher was living there with some housemates. It felt like yesterday they would be tanning themselves on the baking cement, providing something for Riad and the old man with his pigeons on the opposite rooftop to enjoy.

Or to perve at my arse as Miss Teakle had teased him that time they had been together. But that was a while ago now, Jenny having gone back to the UK as did her fellow expats.

For a moment he thought of the little sparrow that had once nested on the windowsill and what a caring parent it had been despite battling with a huge swelling in its neck and finally being found dead one morning shortly after the nestlings had flown.

A good parent… Was he a good parent? Shaking off the thought he moved to the lounge and sank into his chair, switching on the TV. Idly surfing through the channels he watched a bit of news on Fox before turning the sound down low and reaching for the folder the Colonel had given him earlier that day.

After the customary enquiries regarding his recovery from his injuries and dutifully expressing his own appreciation of the Colonel's praise for the extremely valuable service he was rendering for the force, all the while wondering what the old scoundrel wanted from him, Omar came to the point. 'It is good of you to visit but, as you know, I cannot allow you to return to normal duties until you are cleared by the doctors.'

Riad had nodded his understanding thinking it was uncommonly civil of the Colonel not to mention the psychology bit.

The drone of the man's sonorous monotone had jerked him back to the present as the Colonel made a show of studying his fingernails, 'There is perhaps something you could help us with, that is if you feel strong enough –'

Leaving it hanging up there while studying Riad under lowered eyelids. Riad thinking the old bastard knows me all too well, knows that being idle is not my strong suit. 'I am always ready to help, sir,' he had replied a trifle wearily, the truth being that he could have done with a few days off, perhaps spend some quality time with his daughter.

'At the time of his death, Captain Abdullah Farsi had been working on the case of the disappeared girl –'

'Maddie Green,' Riad offered as Omar searched his paper strewn desk for something that would give him the child's name.

'Yes,' he said retrieving a thick file with a grunt of satisfaction. 'Four years old and belonging to Hasan Abdul-Karim,' adding after a moment's hesitation, 'the child of his wife before known as Green.'

And, yes, Riad had concluded at the time, it was the kind of weird utterance that could do with an explanation. "Belonging" to Mr Abdul-Karim just a little bit awkward. He knew the story, of course, the society pages had fully covered it at the time the wealthy businessman had married the English model who had a then three year old daughter from an earlier marriage. The child had been dramatically abducted while the family was holidaying in Australia several months earlier with no clue as to the motivation for the kidnapping or who was involved. The case had drawn international interest and equally so locally as international businessman Abdul-Karim was one of the wealthiest men in Kuwait.

'You want me to take over the investigation?' Riad had asked as Omar handed him the file.

'No, it's not a homicide so far but at the moment I don't have anyone senior enough to take over, Yaseer Hussein has been put in charge but he is on two weeks sick leave after an emergency gallbladder operation and the minister phones me every day to ---'

'I understand,' Riad had said without feeling it necessary to add that the Colonel had to be seen to be doing something about a case as cold as a Siberian winter because some very important people wanted that assurance. 'You want me to go over the case notes while Hussein recovers, see if I can come up with any ideas?'

'It would help,' Omar had said stiffly as he reached for a packet of cigarettes lying on his desk and lighting up with a sigh of satisfaction. Leaning forward he pointed at a loose leaf of yellow paper attached to the inside cover by a paper clip. 'That is the name of the Australian detective in charge of the investigation in Melbourne, the city where the girl disappeared. Also his contact phone number and email. The day before he was killed Abdullah came to see me for permission to travel to that country to meet with this detective. Apparently there has been new information regarding a possible paedophile ring. Something about computers. I agreed but now, of course –' his voice trailed away as he stared wistfully out of the window.

Riad said nothing and after a while Omar sighed and stubbed out his cigarette. 'Anyway, see what you think.'

With that Riad was dismissed without the offer of joining the chief in the mint tea and biscuits the Bengali office boy had just wheeled in.

Coming back to the present Riad heard Rania's bedroom door open followed by the sound of a flushing toilet. Then she was in the lounge and asking about dinner which he took as a good sign. 'What do you feel like?' he asked resisting the impulse to add apart from fast food.

He watched as she made a show of checking the contents of the fridge before declaring with a sigh that it looked like tuna and salad. Adding with some emphasis, *again.*

'Yvette called,' his daughter said offhandedly as she started preparing a salad. 'She says you never phone her and that she has not seen me in ages and wants me to visit. She said it would be nice if you came as well.'

Not looking up from the Maddie Green file he grunted while thinking *Yvette.* Mother to him. And was it not typical that the prima donna, a legend in her own mind, would want her only granddaughter to call her by her first name, not grandma. Vanity, woman is thy name.

'Was she speaking in French?'

'*Oui.* She says my French is getting quite good now.' A note of pride having him think perhaps not everything his mother touched always turned to dust.

Beirut, he thought. Paris by the sea and the home of the famous actress and television personality, Yvette Ayoub. Quite pleasant this time of year so why not? Perhaps a few days enjoying the beaches and the food would be good for both of them.

Then he thought of his uncles, Vytas and Francois "Bubba" Ayoub and all enthusiasm faded like the desert fog before the sun. Quite enough crime in his daily life thank you.

9

CHAPTER

It was a few minutes past ten the next morning when Waleed picked him up outside his apartment, the detective sergeant chewing on an egg roll while leaning over to open the passenger door. Exchanging the customary elaborate Arab salutations Riad wondered how the man managed to be constantly eating something yet stay as thin as a greyhound.

Good genes, he decided, staring ruefully at his own expanding waistline. It certainly wasn't through exercise, a gym in his partner's vocabulary being akin to a torture chamber.

Perhaps if the man would visit his own gym where you could idly pedal one of the exercise bikes in the backrow while studying the rhythmic movement of the young expat ladies in their spandex while the overhead TV screens ran a never ending stream Victoria's Secret models displaying their wares?

He was jerked back to the present by Waleed's sudden braking to narrowly avoid a delivery van, the driver's face a fleeting scowl as he worked the horn while simultaneously blessing them with a raised middle finger. The manual dexterity of some of these drivers never ceasing to amaze Riad who sighed and asked a cursing Waleed where the fire was they were racing to.

'Didn't you see what that pig just did?!' came the snapped reply, Waleed still hitting the horn in angry staccato bleats. 'Son of a goat herder just swung and---'

Silencing him with a raised hand Riad asked where they were heading and to remind him why he had been invited along.

'Tony Evan,' Waleed said as he gunned the Caprice through a red traffic light that had a split second earlier still been amber with those drivers waiting at the lights as usual jumping the green to already be halfway across.

No wonder, Riad thought, that Kuwait motorists killed more of their own yearly than homicides and other accidents combined. With an inward smile he thought of how in Riyadh they had bulldozers parked next to the six lane city highways, any vehicles involved in traffic stopping accidents simply bulldozed to the side as life went on.

Always practical, the Saudis.

'The computer expert?' he asked.

'The grandfather of computers in Kuwait,' Waleed answered, 'I spoke to him yesterday and he's willing to help regarding some questions Captain Farsi had encountered in his recent work.'

'The Maddie Green file?'

'Yes. And as the Colonel has asked you to look into it I thought it a good idea you came along.'

'And here I thought it was just because you missed me,' Riad said to be answered by a grunt from Waleed who was busy unwrapping a stick of gum he had dug up from a shirt pocket.

Tony Evan lived in a rundown three storey apartment block in downtown Jabriya, flats as they call them in Kuwait. A densely populated commercial area of the city and home to mainly the poorer expat workers it had hundreds of small shops selling everything from cheap kitchenware and clothing to pirated DVDs and endless mobile phone outlets.

And computer outlets as well as internet cafès and money changers where the mainly Indian and Filipino locals could send money home to families even poorer than themselves.

The buildings resembled an assortment of stacked harmonicas with their small windows and smaller balconies festooned with colourful washing on sagging lines, the flat roofs a maze of TV dishes and pigeon coops as well as assorted neon signs that would flicker and fizz at night in a mix of Arabic and English. Some of the latter would occasionally boast the kind of spelling acceptable to the Oxford Dictionary but most would need a bit of liberal interpretation.

As usual, at that time of day, the place was a beehive of activity with honking traffic, double parked cars, a swarm of pedestrians and all the noise and chaos that came along. A school day the only thing missing was the children, for Kuwait did not tolerate street urchins, at least not during school hours.

Waleed parked in a loading zone silencing a protesting shopkeeper with a flash of ID while asking the man to keep an eye on the car there's a good man.

The building, which could do with a coat of whitewash – the whole street could – had no elevator and by the time they had climbed three sets of stairs Riad had a burning pain in his chest and a faint hint of nausea.

Two minutes of loud knocking produced apprehensive faces peering around several doors but nothing at number fifteen and with a shrug Waleed produced a set of skeleton keys and, after a brief experiment, found one that opened the door.

A well directed scowl at those peering faces quickly led to the inquisitive going back to their own business.

Inside the place was a mess of discarded clothing, dirty cutlery and more empty beer cans than Riad could recollect ever having seen before in such a small space.

A quick check confirmed that these were real alcoholic beers, not the usual "malt beverages" sold in Kuwait. The man had contacts. While he was still looking around taking in the scant worn down furniture and the myriad posters pasted to the walls, mostly of video games scenarios, Waleed had gone through to the bedroom followed by seconds later a sleepy voice asking what the hell he wanted.

More protests followed and then a bleary eyed Tony Evan stepped into the lounge while blinking at the sudden brightness streaming through the uncurtained windows. The American was wearing a Coca Cola emblazoned T shirt which was at least a size too small exposing a ballooning gut with an impressive umbilical hernia. A pair of gym shorts were partly hidden by an apron of flesh while short stubby legs ended in calloused feet that could do with a wash. And a nail trimming.

'What the hell?' he uttered again as Waleed propelled him towards a corner table where elaborate computer equipment was set up.

'Who the hell still sleeps at noon?' Waleed countered, rolling his eyes at Riad who was struggling to deal with the fresh smell of body odour that had come into the room.

'I work at night!' Evan protested as he detoured to the kitchenette that occupied one corner of the room, selecting one of the cleaner looking glasses from the stack of unwashed to pour himself a soft drink from the fridge.

'When I spoke to you yesterday we agreed to meet here at twelve,' Waleed said while glancing around for a place to sit, finally moving some magazines to clear a space on the sofa.

Grunting Evan sat down at the computer control board which Riad noticed was in standby mode and much more than the standard equipment one would expect in your everyday household.

'What do you want?' Evan said thumping his gut to produce a burp.

'Remember that I told you about the policeman who was murdered recently by a kid while at a *diwaniya?* Well, we are trying to pick up from a case he was working on. Recently he was looking into,' here Waleed checked an item on the file he had opened on his lap, 'First Person Interactive Shooter Games. He mentioned a game called Scorpion Sting. What can you tell us about that?'

'Kids stuff,' Evan said as his fingers danced over a keyboard, 'it used to be avatar games where the player would control a computer generated figure moving through a scenario. Now that has been superseded by the player being the shooter himself, much more realistic.'

'What's an avatar?' Waleed asked as he idly scanned an assortment of unopened letters and bills scattered across a table.

'Jeez, don't you guys ever watch movies? The one where Sam Worthington is ---'

Silencing him with a gesture Riad said, 'it's the concept of a human taking on the form of another being in another world, a fantasy character.' Adding, 'he's right, Waleed, you should get out more.'

'Speak for yourself. At least I've got a love life.'

Riad said nothing. Thinking how the computer age had brought with it a whole new vocabulary. Thinking that, in spite of a bachelor's degree in English, had he not watched the movie he would probably not have known the meaning of avatar.

His thoughts were interrupted by Evan drawing their attention to the computer screen. 'This here is Call of Duty Black OPS, the latest version,' he said moving aside so they could follow the action on the big screen computer. 'It's one of the dozens of first person shooter games now available.'

They watched in silence as a gun barrel moved from side to side as Evan manipulated the shooter with easy dexterity, adjusting height and sweep as the shooter dodged and weaved through the combat scene, his assault rifle dealing death with enough realism to have Riad grip the back of the chair as he watched spellbound.

'Amazing,' he said in a whisper, 'it's as if I'm holding the gun myself –"

Evan grinned inviting Riad to place his hands on the twin control handles then pressing a key that had the assault rifle erupt in fire blowing away a hapless opponent in the process. The action was accompanied by a wild jerking motion from the controls which had Riad stare down at his hands in amazement.

'Haptics,' the computer boffin explained, 'recreating the feeling of the gun in your hands.'

'Must be an expensive game?'

Evan sniggered, 'Oh yeah, if you *buy* games.' The tone suggesting he didn't.

'The FBI might be on to you.'

'Great guys, they come here now and then as you know, mainly to trap the DVD pirates,' he said, inclining his head towards the shops across the street. 'I helped them once when someone jammed their computers. We've been mates ever since.'

'By someone you mean you.'

Again a shrug, 'I am a businessman after all.'

A sudden alarm from the computer had Evan lean over and quickly tap a series of commands before leaning back with a sigh of satisfaction as he took another gulp from his drink. 'Amateurs,' he said, 'trying to attack my empire.'

With Waleed busy making notes Riad felt obliged to ask. 'Empire?'

'Another game. This is a world wide multi-player one where you piece by piece build an empire of many cities, castles and armies. You do this by attacking others and taking over their assets while defending yours. This alarm was some bastard out there trying to capture one of my castles, I quickly sent him off!'

'Fascinating,' Riad said feeling more and more like a computer ignoramus by the minute.

'You can either take other players' assets by gaming them or you can buy or sell assets.' A gleam in the man's eyes hinted that he knew Riad was fascinated by this startling disclosure. 'This is how I make my living, selling off assets I take from others. Well, that and some work I do for the government.'

'The government? You mean you work in an office?'

Evan shook his head, 'I have ADHD meaning I can't work with other people. I do assignments, usually when their computers get hacked. That's how I came to Kuwait, brought here on a contract by the ruling family after I helped one of them out in New York with a little embarrassing problem.' A look in his eye suggested don't ask don't tell.

'Scorpion Sting,' Waleed reminded, looking up from his scribblings in the file.

'Never heard of it,' Evan said his attention once again back at the screen. 'Many games are private ones that don't make it to the public domain, rich guys setting up their own websites and games.'

'Like the paedophile rings?'

'Uh huh. But, if it's out there I can find it. Might just take some time.'

'How much time, Evans?' Riad asked, glancing at his watch.

'About two hundred KDs worth of time. And it's Evan, not Evans. We were too poor to afford the S.'

'You live like a pig,' Waleed countered, 'what do you need that kind of money for.'

This seemed to offend the computer man who pushed back his chair and glanced at each of them in turn, finally asking Riad to bring him a beer from the fridge, get one for themselves. 'I have a life, you know. In fact, I'm getting married again.'

'Oh yeah?' Riad said handing him the Budweiser and deciding he and Waleed would forego the generous offer.

'Good stuff,' Evan said taking a deep tug of the golden liquid and holding the cold can to his face and neck. 'I get my supply from the boys over at Camp Matilda, do some work for them. You know, being a fellow patriotic American and trustworthy.'

With a shared glance at Waleed Riad decided to let that one go.

'Married?' he said.

'Yep, nice lady I met on a dating site. American, of course, divorced like me with grown up kids. I'm meeting her next week in Dubai where I've booked a two bedroom suite at the Hilton.'

'Why two bedrooms?'

Evan looked at him with a frown, 'You can't just jump into these things! This is my next wife, for Chrissake! Not some hooker. First you have to properly meet each other.'

A dreamlike look settled on his face as he stared at the ceiling, 'At first we're going to be in separate rooms with an open door between us. Then we're going to smell each other. Just a smell --'

This startling disclosure had Riad hope the man was going to take a shower first, not kill the romance right there.

' – then I'm going to hand her one end of a piece of cotton thread while holding on to the other end, still in separate rooms. Then we're just going to talk for hours, get to really know each other. If the string breaks or she lets go it will be a bad sign for any relationship –'

Deciding now might be a good time to leave, before the narrative, exciting as it was, proceeded to the next phase, Riad looked at a grinning Waleed while pointing at his watch. 'I've got an appointment in an hour,' he reminded him, 'and I still have to pick Rania up from school.'

Gathering up the file Waleed told Evan he'd be back the next day and that he was thinking more along the lines of a hundred KD and not mentioning to the Vice Squad about the pile of porno magazines he'd seen in the bedroom.

Three miles away across the city, in a penthouse overlooking the marina at the fashionable neighbourhood of Sharq, the man known as the Scorpion Master pushed back from the computer screen where he had just watched the two detectives exit Evan's apartment.

Flitting in and out of the screen and in close up was the features of Tony Evan as the man dialled up Skype, the idiot quite oblivious to the fact he had been hacked for almost two weeks now. A grim smile crossed the Master's lips as he thought of the man's moniker of the grandfather of computers in Kuwait. That he might be but he was no longer the smartest mind in the city. Arching his stiffening back he rose from the chair and walked across to the large plate glass windows looking out over the yachts and the glittering Gulf beyond while sipping at a martini he had mixed earlier.

He had been right in suspecting that the dead police captain might have stumbled onto Scorpion Sting. Now the American was digging and, weird as he might be, he was still scarily good and would find him in the end.

Tony Evan had to die.

10
CHAPTER

They met in a spacious room leading off from Ameera al Quarashi's consulting rooms, ushered inside by a young receptionist in a too tight short skirt with enough makeup to discourage smiling in fear of cracking up. Beautiful eyes though, Riad noticed, Middle Eastern women have the most beautiful eyes and for the love of him he could not fathom why they had to wear all that mascara.

And ridiculously long false eyelashes. More American than the Americans but then, deprived of so many other liberties taken for granted by their western sisters, why not? A sudden absurd thought had him smile, perhaps the long eyelashes served to break their fall should they tumble from those nine inch high heels?

He was snapped from his reverie by the psychologist welcoming all and, starting with a middle aged woman in a black abeya seated next to her, suggesting they introduce themselves to the group. Five of them, seated in a circle on cushioned office chairs with al Quarashi, pad and pen on her lap, part of the circle.

Three women and two men. And their interrogator as Riad had come to think of the smartly dressed young lady.

Black abeya started off haltingly, speaking in such a low voice that Riad missed the name. Encouraged by Quarashi she started again, Bushra Ibrahim. This time she lifted her head and from under the headscarf Riad saw eyes meeting his with an expression of infinite sadness.

In a lifetime of witnessing crime and what it did to people he had seen enough to recognise unspeakable sadness.

Next came Amina Jasem, a morbidly obese woman of indeterminate age in a layered floral outfit that clung to areas of her body in awkward ways. She spoke in a husky wheeze while small eyes flitted between members of the group. Without a pause for breath she went on to state that she was here to let others know of the *jamarat* dwelling amongst them that had claimed the life of her only son. She was about to elaborate when the psychologist gently interrupted, suggesting they talk about that later, after everyone was acquainted.

Great, just great, Riad mused as he fought the growing feeling of being trapped, so the devil was amongst them and he without even a string of prayer beads like the man seated next to him who was feverishly counting off as silent lips recited the ninety nine names of Allah.

'Ali…Ali? Do you want to tell the others your name?' came the gently persuasive voice of the team leader, her expression betraying a hint of anxiety not missed by Riad. One to watch, this Ali, he decided.

'Major Ali al Ruqbah,' came the listless reply, 'from the Palace Guard.' The last words added as an afterthought while Riad noticed that the hand that held the prayer beads was shaking uncontrollably.

He was next stating his name in a flat monotone and turning to the woman next to him who was as out of place in that grim setting as he had ever seen.

'Sarah Green, the wife of Hasan Abdul-Karim,' she said softly, speaking in English with an accent Riad placed as the product of middle class English exposed too long to the chattering classes of the New York City soy lattè light sipping society. Seeing his frown she added with a wistful smile, 'At least I was Sarah Green before marrying again.'

The realisation of who this stunningly beautiful woman seated next to him was went through Riad in a series of unnerving tingles. Not only was she the supermodel wife of one of Kuwait's richest men, she was also the mother of Maddie Green. The disappearance of the little girl he was investigating.

What were the chances?

And why was he, an educated man of the world, suddenly feeling like a starstruck schoolboy sitting next to this renowned beauty dressed in the type of designer suit his own Fareeda had worn with equally stunning effect and was that a hint of Chanel on the air?

'Adel Rajab,' a voice said as all eyes turned to a handsome young man in a neatly pressed tailored dishdasha and carefully piled on high white guthra held in place by a top quality black iqual and wearing shiny patent leather black shoes he stared fixedly at. He was seated on the other side of the Englishwoman and had earlier moved his chair a foot further away from hers as if afraid of being placed under a spell by this apparition that could not possibly be of the real world.

A soft clap had them all look at the group leader. 'Excellent! Now that we all know each other we can begin,' the psychologist said, reminding them that she was just there as a facilitator and that they would be doing the talking. She had brought this particular group together as they all spoke English while aware that for most of them it was a second language. This with a pertinent look at Riad who had hitherto insisted on using that language during their previous sessions.

'Each one of you are here because of a very traumatic incident in your life, something so shocking, so sad, that it has changed your life forever. During individual sessions in my office we have, I think, made some progress in learning how to deal with this major upheaval in our lives but sometimes that is not enough. So often we tend to internalize things, crop it up inside while we should be sharing it with others. Only then, when we realise that we are not alone in our agony, do we begin the long process of healing.'

While saying this she looked at each of them in turn, finally settling her gaze on Riad. 'As a newcomer to our group, Riad, would you like to begin? Tell us a bit about yourself?'

Wait a minute, Raid thought. Shouldn't this be like Alcoholics Anonymous where the new guy gets up only after all the others had stated how long they had been sober, only to then in a burst of virtue signalling and with encouraging smiles from the others, hesitantly bringing out his own confession?

'I…I –' he began only to freeze as he became aware of *her* hand on his arm, of that beautifully modulated soft voice saying, 'It's OK, Riad, we're all friends here –'

Managing a weak smile he began, telling them about his profession as a homicide detective while keeping it sketchy, finally divulging the bit about the stabbing that had him hospitalized and how it was departmental procedure that after such an incident the officer should attend psychological evaluation. He wanted to add that he was fine, just fine but lapsed into silence instead.

There was a few seconds of silence before, still speaking in a low soothing voice, Ouarashi said, 'But that is not all, is it Riad? Don't you want to talk about the death of your wife, the very traumatic events surrounding that?' Something in her voice told him it was not a request.

He nodded and with an effort leaned back in his chair to fix his sight on a small painting on an opposite wall. It was of two tiny songbirds on a twig, a watercolour he thought, the male with beautiful multicoloured plumage, the female a drab beige and white. It seemed so familiar and it bothered him that he could not name the species. Maybe he thought, if aliens ever visited, they would find the male of the human species the pretty one and the female nondescript?

Then he thought of his Fareeda and how beautiful she was. And how she died… 'We knew each other since our childhood in Saudi Arabia,' he began, wanting to add that no, it was not an arranged marriage but decided, what the hell, let them think whatever they wanted. 'She trained as a gynaecologist in the USA and upon returning to Saudi Arabia worked at the Al Hada Hospital in the mountains near Taif. This is where we met again after not seeing each other for years. I was working in Jeddah at the time and had come to visit family in Al Hada. We married there and our daughter, Rania, was born there. In 2001, during the November Ramadan and while I was visiting – I was working in Kuwait at the time – Fareeda was murdered by her crazed jihadist brother. Someone who is still to this day on the terrorist wanted list of both America and Saudi.'

Here he paused to take a sip of water from the bottle each of them had been handed earlier.

'How did that make you feel, Riad? That you were not able to save her?'

This woman was like a fucking honeybadger, he thought as a sudden bitterness welled up inside him. Straight for the groin! *The Honeybadger* a distant corner of his mind said, long ago novel of Africa by Robert Ruark. Why did this crap always come up in your mind, Riad? Was it your way of dealing with stress? Was Waleed right, was all this flotsam of a Cambridge education just so much chaff that clouded your mind at the times when you should connect with the real world?

'I loved my wife,' he said simply, 'and after all these years still miss her. I did however manage to save our daughter who was also a target of Fareeda's brother.'

'Why was that Riad, why did he want to kill them? Did he want to kill you too?'

There was a sudden quiet in the room as all eyes studied him. The man next to him had stopped playing with the prayer beads but his hand was still shaking.

'He was, is, crazy,' Riad lied. 'He believed she was not only a sorceress but also an American spy. The people who were trying to kill him. As her daughter, Rania was tainted and also had to be killed. Me? Perhaps he did want to kill me too but did not get the chance.'

And what a good story it was, he thought grimly, making a note to commit it carefully to memory – a false memory – should the shrink decide to go over it again. The truth? That was his and his alone. How could he tell them that he had married Fareeda in a rush as she was pregnant to an American womaniser and that had it become known would have led to unspeakable consequences in the Kingdom? That to this day twelve year old Rania believed that he was her father and that he would die before ever divulging that secret? That her jihadist uncle had found out the truth and vowed to kill both mother and daughter and erase the blot on the name of the family?

That he had killed the child's father on that same compound during that terrible Night of Power?

'You were separated from your wife at the time, Riad. Want to talk about it?'

In a nutshell, no. But realising that this interrogator was not going away. That she *knew* things. '

'It was because of work. I had to leave Saudi because of a problem at work and took up my current post here in Kuwait. The plan was for the family to follow as soon as Fareeda could find a suitable job.'

'Hmm.' It was plain she did not quite believe him, after all how hard would it be for a female Arab gynaecologist to get a good post in Kuwait and two years?! Deciding it was something for another, private, session, Quarashi prepared to move on. Leaving Riad to wonder how he could ever tell this group that his wife had been lesbian, at best transsexual. That her lover had been a nurse on the compound, that it had taken him years to conclude that simple truth.

Years of sleeping in separate rooms while wondering what was wrong. No way he could ever confess that in front of two Kuwaiti males from a culture that could not care less whether a woman was otherwise inclined or not. The choice was never hers so what kind of male would that make him?

More so, what chance of keeping that choice bit secret outside this little circle of intimacy?

'Bushra,' the group leader prompted,' last week we spoke about the events at your hospital during the Iraq invasion. You told us about the atrocities you witnessed and specifically how one of the young doctors had been brutally murdered in front of you by the soldiers. I gave you a copy of the official war crimes of the time compiled by our government in which the events you experienced are fully discussed. Did you find solace in reading about it?'

Again the almost inaudible voice as the woman kept her gaze cast down. 'Yes. It was sad but I think it helps.'

'Was there anything that stood out? Any one of the many atrocities listed, that made you feel you are not alone in this? Perhaps a name you recognise?'

'There is – a nurse at Adan I think I knew from long ago. She is mentioned.'

'Perhaps we can try and find her and you can talk to her. Would you like that?'

A slow nod.

Quarashi scribbled something and smiled at the woman, 'I will get the name from you afterwards and we'll talk about it at our next session.' Turning her attention to the woman in the floral dress she asked how she was. Was the work she was now doing at the nursery in Shuwaikh helping her to find inner peace?'

'By the grace of Allah I feel better when I walk amongst the plants and smell the flowers and the green leaves. Especially the baby palms still in their plastic pots when I water them. I think of how one day they will grow big and ---' Here she broke down in sobs digging a crumpled handkerchief from amongst the folds of her dress to dab at her eyes while the psychologist put an arm around her shoulder.

'Just to remind us, Amina's son died from a drug overdose only three months ago. He was just sixteen years old. I sense you have come a long way in your lonely journey of grief, Amina but there is great mercy from Allah and He will fill your heart with joy again.'

A general murmur as the group nodded in solemn confirmation accentuated by a mix of "Inshallah" and "Hamdillah" with Riad's oh God *please* a silent prayer.

'Let us move on to Ali,' the group leader said, passing a box of tissues to Amina and turning to the major who had resumed his nervous fingering of the prayer beads. There was no sign the man had heard her and raising her voice a fraction Quarashi repeated the prompt, adding that he was amongst friends, safe.

'Ali al Ruqbah,' he said after what seemed like a minute. 'Major in the Palace Guard. ID number SR 369 X.' His voice trailed off as he continued staring at the beads in his hand with a puzzled look, as if seeing it for the first time.

'Now remember, Ali, there is no need to state all those things. There are no Iraqi soldiers here and nobody is going to attack you. I, we, want you to tell us about how your week was. The things you did yesterday, your family, your friends. Things that made you feel happy.'

As the man visibly struggled to form a sentence, the psychologist got up from her chair to come up behind him and gently massage his shoulders while uttering soft words of comfort. Raising her eyes at the group she reminded them that their friend Ali had been a prisoner of war in one of Saddam Hussein's notorious camps for several years where very bad things had been done to him. But, as a strong man, he had survived and in fact returned to his duties in the military until a recent personal crisis had brought about severe depression and anxiety.

'PTSD, Post Traumatic Stress Disorder can sometimes manifest in this way, leading to a psychological crisis even years after the traumatising events. The worst is a feeling of being all alone in this with nowhere to turn and everyone out there a potential enemy.' Turning to the man she said, 'I want you to think of one nice thing that happened yesterday or even as you came here today. Something you saw or heard that made you feel good. I will give you a minute to think while we listen to Sarah, OK?'

A numb nod from Ali was answered by a note of approval from the leader who resumed her seat while the psychologist turned to the Englishwoman inviting her to pick up the session.

11
CHAPTER

Sarah Green spoke in a soft voice with sentences ending in a lilt creating the impression of inviting contradiction or possibly questioning her own statement. With eyes downcast she studied her painted nails which, as expected of a supermodel, were immaculate. 'My daughter, Maddie, disappeared six days after her fourth birthday.' Adding, after a brief pause while she fiddled in a tiny bag for a tissue, 'It is now one hundred and ninety six days with no word, no clue and it's very very hard for me –'

It was hard for Riad too, witnessing this beautiful woman pour her heart out, sharing the unbearable grief. As she hesitatingly revealed details of her everyday life, how she was struggling to find ways to deal with the constant anxiety and feelings of helplessness Riad sought escape from a growing feeling of depression by letting his mind wander over what he had read in the Maddie Green file, Sarah's voice fading into the background.

The coldly clinical documented facts of the suspected kidnapping floated before his inner eye interspersed with countless equally coldly clinical photographs of the crime scene. The child disappeared from the family home in a fashionable Melbourne suburb, one of the many homes Abdul-Karim owned around the world, while her parents were at a restaurant down the street. It was early evening, still light outside, and in that quiet Carlton street there was light traffic only with the occasional pedestrian strolling past on their way back from work.

The child's nanny on leave and unable to find a babysitter at short notice the mother agreed to accompany her husband for a quick meal at a nearby Italian restaurant in Lygon Street arranging to phone Maddie and check on her every half hour. They would be back in time to tuck her into bed, in the meantime she would watch a kiddies program on TV.

At the restaurant they were warmly greeted by another couple, the man a business associate of Abdul-Karim, who insisted they join them at their table ordering champagne as it was an anniversary celebration. Excusing herself to phone Maddie at the pre-arranged time she received no answer, the mobile she had left with the child going straight to voice mail. Inwardly cursing herself Sarah mulled this over for a minute as her anxiety grew, finally apologising to the others that she would just go and check on the little one, be back before they knew it.

To order her a banana split in her absence and yes, one of those nice Galliano liquors.

Hailing a taxi she was back at the house ten minutes later only to find her daughter wide awake and mesmerized by an animated movie. No, she had not heard the phone and as long as mummy returned soon she would not be scared.

When Sarah and her husband returned home an hour later Maddie Green was gone.

'—so I lie awake at night and listen to the noises in the house, the chimes of the grandfather clock in the hallway counting off the hours, the rhythmic tap tapping of a leaky faucet somewhere or the little noises my husband makes as he tosses and turns in restless sleep. And I lie there, eyes open and I can hear her voice in the sighing of the wind outside and I see her smile as if she is right there beside me and I reach out to her and touch only the empty coldness of crumpled bedclothes.' There was complete silence in the room as she paused to dab at her eyes with a tissue before glancing at them all in turn.

' So I lie there in a netherworld halfway between sleep and hallucination until the daybreak prayer call from the mosque tells me another empty night is over. Day after day I miss her more than ever.' At this she lapsed into silence, staring at some unseen object on her lap and after a while the team leader asked in a soft voice what it was she found the most difficult.

'Not knowing,' Sarah Green Abdul-Karim said, 'not knowing—'

After a while they went on to the last one in the group, the young man known as Adel Rajab. Thirty five years old he was from a wealthy family and a successful businessman in his own right. He did not declare the nature of his business. In excellent English with just a hint of an American accent he stated his problem as one of anxiety that in turn led to episodes of obsessive compulsive behaviour. Riad wondered whether this was the usual case of not stepping on the cracks in sidewalks but it transpired it was an obsession with shoes, to be more specific, ladies shoes. This was divulged without the slightest hint of embarrassment and if he noticed Sarah Green recrossing her slender legs to move her own stilettoes a trifle further away he did not let on.

No, he did not collect them or wear them, simply liked the smell of them, especially when a beautiful young woman took them off. Especially red ones. It would sometimes lead to the embarrassing situation where he would, during one of his frequent overseas business trips, arrange for a private meeting with such a young lady in his hotel room for no other reason than for her to remove her shoes. This had led to several misunderstandings culminating in that tragic day when a woman had panicked and in a rush to leave had slipped on her smooth nylon stockings knocking her head against a table and sustaining a fatal head injury. Even though in the end he was not accused of causing her death he had been plunged into grief with a deep seated feeling of guilt ever since.

As he listened Riad tried to decide which phase of grief the young man was still struggling with. Was it still shock or was he only now going through denial not yet proceeding to anger? It bothered him that he could not recall which phase came next, was it bargaining or depression?

Come to think of it, had he ever proceeded to the final phase of acceptance when it came to the loss of his wife or were those sudden bursts of anger, even rage, that so often led to him dispensing his own form of justice proof that he had never made the transition?

The soothing voice of the psychologist brought him back to the present, 'But you no longer have this obsession with the shoes, do you Adel?'

A shake of the head, 'No.'

'What do you do now when you feel a sense of anxiety coming on, want to tell us?'

'I retreat to my computer room where I play games.'

'Are these interactive games, where you compete or team up with other players?'

'Sometimes.'

'And the anxiety, does is still wake you at night?

He shrugged, 'Sometimes, when I'm on an overseas business trip but I don't do the shoe thing any more.'

'Just the games?' Quarashi asked as she made a note on her pad.

'Yes,' Adel Rajab said while still not making eye contact. For Riad, who was studying him with interest there was something else here but what? What personal tragedy had befallen this patient, surely not the accidental death of a young call girl that he could, if he was telling the truth, not be held accountable for? No, his instincts told him there was something more and quite possibly the psychologist knew but was not divulging.

'Thank you all for coming to-day,' Quarashi said as she shoved her pad into a slim leather bound file. 'I feel we have made some real progress here and will arrange for another group session next week. My secretary will be in touch.'

The meeting over they filed to the back of the room where refreshments had been laid out. As Riad accepted a glass of mint tea he became aware of the presence of Sarah next to him, the perfume a giveaway. 'I listened to your story Riad – may I call you Riad?—and in a way your loss reminded me of my own. At least you know what happened to her – That is the hardest for me.'

Not knowing what to say he waited for her to continue. 'You are a detective, here in Kuwait. You would have seen in the papers that, at my husband's insistence, the local police are also searching for Maddie, helping the Australian police look for any connection as to who might have –' here she broke off, taking a few sips of tea while studying him from under lowered eyelids.

Riad said nothing.

'I know she might be dead,' she said in a listless tone, as if stating a cold matter of fact and it was unexpected enough to have Riad catch his breath. She was looking at him now, twin sapphires boring through to the back of his skull, 'I can deal with the despair of that horrible possibility. It's the hope that kills me –'

A sudden tingle had him realise she had clasped his hand in both of hers, a cool soft touch so unexpected his impulse was to pull away while knowing he never could. 'What do you want from me?' he said hoarsely.

'You are not only a detective but also someone with experience of the wider world. You also have some time off now, leave from your work with the local police. I want to hire you to go to Australia and find her.'

And there it was, just like that, even before she added, 'I can pay you, I have plenty of money.'

Crazy! Thinking on his feet now he said, 'You mean be a private detective? Do you know how many homicides to date have been solved anywhere by a private detective?'

She shook her head, 'No –'

'To date, none.'

'I see –' she said helplessly, her hand falling away from his arm. He was saved by his mobile vibrating in a pocket. It was an overseas number and he recognised the code as Saudi Arabia but not the caller. Excusing himself he stepped into the corridor and took the call.

'Riad? It is Mohammed.' His brother, speaking in Arabic which was the only language he knew.

Aware of a faint tinge of anxiety as to the nature of this wholly unexpected call Riad went through the customary exchange of pleasantries quickly establishing that his elderly father was well, before enquiring as to the reason for their conversation.

'It is Talal, he is in trouble.'

Talal? Furiously casting about in his memory for a Talal, presumably a family member as no outsider would have merited this call, he was spared embarrassment by his brother adding, 'Our young brother by Fawzia. He went searching for his sister, Yasmin, who is fifteen and has been taken.'

'What!?' Still struggling to put a face to Fawzia, one of his father's later wives, he realised he had never met her during one of his infrequent visits to the family compound in Al Hada. Talal, half brother number three, he vaguely remembered as a gangly shy youth who barely spoke, overawed by the presence of the first born son and head to be of the clan.

It was a shock to realise he had not even known of the existence of the sister but then, had he ever really cared?

'Taken?,' he finally managed, realising Mohammed had been talking and he had not taken in any of it.

'By the Jezail, a tribe from near Khamis Mushyat. They took her from the sea near Jeddah. Talal has gone off to find her and bring her back.'

Desperately casting about for a chair Riad paced about instead. 'What beach, what --?'

'She went swimming, with English family, they could not stop the Jezailis.'

Suddenly Riad could see the whole picture quite clearly. He even remembered the fourth wife as being educated overseas and bringing with her some liberated ideas that would still be frowned upon in the more conservative circles of the Kingdom. Had this licentiousness by Saudi standards been transferred to the daughter? Swimming? What, while wearing anything but a formless full length abeya and in the company of strangers?!

'Why tell me this?' he said lamely, knowing the answer.

'Our father says you are the eldest son. The honour of the family has been touched. You must come.'

The honour of the family ... And instantly he was back on that mountain in Saudi in that terrible month of Ramadan when life changed for him, for all of them, forever. Was there ever anything more disastrous than a family matter of honour...

12
CHAPTER

In the old days, Riad mused, the *good* old days, it would have taken almost two weeks to make the journey from the Gulf to Al Hada in a camel caravan. Enough time for this whole family issue to have been settled amicably or more likely violently, without him having to get involved. Now, less than twenty four hours after receiving the summons, he was driving into Al Hada's Valley of the Princes at the wheel of an Avis rental wondering just what the hell he was supposed to do.

The Saudia Airlines flight into Taif was as usual jam packed with families laden with shopping bags, the black clad headscarf wearing ladies talking all at once, some showing amazing mental dexterity in sustaining a conversation with a fellow traveller while simultaneously berating an unfortunate spouse on a mobile phone.

The much vaunted female multitasking, he decided, reflecting how the one task always seemed to involve talking in a loud voice. He had tried to discern which of the women would be a local young *sheikha,* usually one surrounded by a gaggle of others acting as a protective shield of sorts while the real chaperone, a brother, would be sitting across the aisle enduring the mind numbing boredom of a chore he had no way of escaping from.

From bitter experience Riad had put all essentials into a carry on bag, fully expecting his luggage to once again be bumped off the plane to accommodate the voluminous excess baggage belonging to those aboard that drew the most water. He would be lucky if his luggage turned up two days later, usually with no attempt at any explanation.

A drink would have been nice too but, alas, the soft drinks or tea on offer did not hold much appeal. Not much prospect of anything more bracing being available at the family compound either. Good old Saudi Arabia he thought bitterly, officially dry and with the alcoholics to prove it. He would probably have to swing by some old expat friends on the Al Hada Hospital compound to get hold of a bottle of home distilled *sedique* and that compound, with all its memories, was a place he had vowed never to set foot in again.

The journey had been tiring and he was fighting drowsiness as he tried to concentrate on the winding road now taking him through the hills and valleys with elaborate high walled palaces everywhere to be seen. The summer retreat of the Saudi princes in the days before air conditioning the establishments were now mainly staffed by servants and the rapidly dwindling number of ancient royalty, mainly women, who still preferred the quiet life in the mountains to the hectic hubbub of Jeddah.

Mothers of princes whom he knew from experience still wielded enormous power over their sons and grandsons, capable of overturning local government decrees with a single phone call if wont to do someone a favour.

Approaching the Al Ajmi family compound now, his father's trellised vineyards dotted amongst the rocky outcrops with conifers interrupting the blue skyline, he returned a wave from a pedestrian herding a scattering of goats, recognising the man as one of his father's workers. Then he was driving through the open gates and into the spacious courtyard to be instantly surrounded by a small group of excitedly chattering urchins, all dancing around the car and excitedly calling out to one another. Wearily getting out from behind the wheel he stretched his back while doing a slow three sixty of the place, ignoring the crowd that had now fallen silent, staring at him with expectant upturned faces.

Children, the boys in short cut dishdashas with the young girls in colourful embroidered dresses and bows in their hair, chickens milling about with a tethered goat and several cars and pickup trucks parked under a trellised area off to one side.

No adults about until a manservant came running up with an apologetic smile to take his bags (his suitcase had been on the flight after all) and lead him into the main house with the children trailing silently behind.

It was cool inside the house and he was glad to accept a glass of iced water from a servant girl who had hastily been summoned from the kitchen.

Indicating that he wanted to see his father at once Riad was led through to the rear section of the house where Ebrahim al Ajmi sat in a chair with a blanket spread over his knees. It was a reception room off the main bedroom where his father received guests and Riad recognised many of the trappings. From the wall mounted artworks collected over a long career as diplomat to some of Europe's greatest cities to several hunting trophies, the pride of place taken by the stuffed head of a magnificent maned lion, its features forever captured in a snarl of defiance.

It had long puzzled Riad how his father, a devout Muslim, would have these stuffed heads of animals he had killed during many an African safari whereas it was forbidden in the culture to portray any of Allah's creatures sporting a head, something to do with not having any false gods before Him. The reason why all those wrought iron human figures on the roundabouts of Jeddah were headless?

Vanity thy name is hunter was Riad's conclusion.

'*Salaam aleikum*, my son,' the old man in the chair which Riad now saw was a wheelchair, said in a soft voice without turning his head. '*Ahlan was sahlan.* Welcome.'

Stepping up to grasp the outstretched hand Riad was shocked to see how old his father had become in a short time. (Short time? It has been five years Riad!) Old and frail with no more the strong grip of the warrior of yesterday, no more body heat...

'*Was aleikum salaam,* my father,' he replied with a catch in his voice while accepting the chair the manservant had brought up.

'It is good of you to come,' his father said motioning the bowing servant to bring refreshments. 'Did Mohammed tell you what happened?' Nice, Riad, thought; no enquiry as to how he was, the trip, little Rania back home, just straight on to business. At least the old man was making eye contact now, watery eyes studying him with interest as if seeing him for the first time.

'Only that Yasmin had been taken by Jezaili tribesmen and that Talal has gone after them, that both are in trouble.' And how medieval it all sounded, like a chapter from a Walter Scott novel. Hopefully, he mused, with a happier ending.

'Talal is safe,' a voice said behind him, 'but Yasmin is still missing.' It was Mohammed, the thick pile carpets masking his entry. Grasping Riad by the shoulders and holding him at arms length, a smiling Mohammed looked him up and down with a smile of approval. 'You look good, my brother. We had heard that you were injured.'

'Rumours of my death have been greatly exaggerated.' Somehow it did not sound as pithy in Arabic as in English which explained the other man's puzzled look.

'You look good too,' he offered, noting that Mohammed had beefed up a trifle, the loose fitting dishdasha not quite hiding a pot belly. 'How many children have you fathered by now, a dozen?'

This was met by a loud guffaw with the old man nodding sagely, 'You have many young family now, Riad. Something you must start taking care of now.'

Oh God … Changing tack he asked about the situation that had summoned him.

'Talal is in a hospital in Jeddah. He was injured in the attack but is alright.'

'What? You told me he had disappeared, gone after the Jezaili.'

Mohammed sighed as he pulled up a chair. 'That was what he told us initially. It now turns out he was with Yasmin and another girl on a boat belonging to an English couple. They had been snorkelling off the boat and picnicking on the beach when attacked. The English were not hurt while the two girls were taken. Talal tried to stop them and was beaten badly. The others took him to the hospital.'

'Wait! Hold it for a minute,' Riad managed, his voice rising as incredulity took hold, 'you mean to tell me he was with this party and they were then attacked by strangers coming out of the desert like that?'

Mohammed said nothing, just nodded numbly.

'And there has been no word of Yasmin? No contact from the kidnappers?'

'No.'

'Who is the other girl?'

'Talal won't say.'

Oh he will, Riad decided grimly, he will once I get to him. 'And the English couple, are they husband and wife?'

'Yes. They are friends our brother and sister made in Jeddah, from the university where they were studying. They have a sailing boat and were just going sailing for the day when—'

Cutting him short with a motion of the hand Riad said, 'Let's go,' rising from his chair.

Startled Mohammed asked where to. 'To Jeddah. I'll drive.'

'But you have not had time to refresh, have some tea—'

'No time to lose. Every minute that goes by makes it harder to find our sister.' He wanted to add "alive and unmolested" but decided that went without saying.

'Just a moment,' an old voice said as they made to leave, Ebrahim al Ajmi rising from his chair with a helping hand from a manservant that had seemingly appeared from nowhere.

'Father?'

Walking across slowly with the aid of a cane his father stopped to face Riad who noticed with a tinge of shock how the man had visibly shrunk in physical terms. The voice, however had regained a hint of strength. 'I know you, my son, all too well. You may not realise yet but you are an Ajmi and although you are soft, like your mother, the blood flows in you and can be stirred. I knew you would want to leave at once to find these people and have made preparations.'

An impatient motion from a raised hand had all heads turn to the door where two men had appeared. Young and bearded wearing Bedouin headscarves they sported crisscrossed bandoliers over their torsos and each had a rifle slung over a shoulder.

'Yusuf and Hasan. Two of my best men that I trust with my life. They will go with you. There is a Land Cruiser parked outside and loaded with supplies. Also a powerful radio that I will man on this side should you run into trouble. Also this,' reaching for something the manservant had retrieved from a corner of the room he handed a stunned Riad a silver plated AK 47. 'You will take this. It is my personal weapon and is now yours.'

Knowing that protest would be futile Riad nodded while appraising the two newcomers. Hard men of the desert was the inescapable conclusion which had him wonder just what kind of business exactly the old man was in.

Asking Mohammed and the others to leave them, the old man waited until they were alone then turned to Riad. 'There is something I once told you when you were very young, perhaps too young to understand. So I tell you again. Long ago there was a great and powerful king of our people. He was a fair but ruthless man who ruled by strength over a savage people. When it came time for him to die he realised that his son was not like him, that he was not strong and ruthless, that the people would take him and kill him.

So he called him to his bed and said, son, I ask just one thing of you. And this you must promise me to obey. When I die I want you to take me in a straight line to the royal graveyard. Straight. You must not deviate one foot from the line. So when the king died his son gave the order that all buildings, all houses, all animals, everything that was between his father's death bed and the grave be destroyed to make a straight road to the king's final resting place.'

'So it was done and the people were shocked and said, the king was a hard man who reaped where he had not sown and ruled us with a cruel hand but this son is an even harder man and his hand and his eye will be upon us. And so he ruled and was happy.'

Taking Riad's hand he smiled wanly and, lowering his voice, added 'Soon you will be the chieftain of this family. I want you to think about that when you go on this mission and then do for me this one thing.'

Riad said nothing as he gazed at his father with a feeling of growing dread.

'I want you to bring me the head of the man who took your sister—'

13
CHAPTER

As usual the twenty minute journey down the winding Al Hada mountain pass ending two thousand feet down and into the heat of the desert left Riad with a faint tinge of nausea. Also with memories long suppressed, like the time he had kicked open the door of the toilet to find his young brother, Abdullah, shooting up. Abdullah long dead now and as they sped past the service station where it had happened he wondered if Mohammed felt it too, for like now he had been driving them that day.

Telling his brother to take the bypass route through the desert as he did not have the stomach of going through Mecca with its traffic jams and pious pedestrians with nary a smile between them. Better to use the roundabout route compulsory to all non- Muslims even if it was in poor condition and in parts blown over by the shifting sands.

There was little conversation, each man busy with his own thoughts. The two men at back sat upright in their seats staring straight ahead and if anyone was bothered by the ping ping from the dashboard when Mohammed exceeded the seventy miles an hour speed limit they kept it to themselves.

A strange beauty, the desert, Riad reflected as he gazed at a distant group of camels with the small frame of the herder barely visible as it danced and wove in the shimmering heat waves. He knew that his father had a camp in the desert that he liked to visit from time to time to appraise the goats and camels but probably more to reconnect with a deep nostalgia for the days of his youth. It made him wonder if he, the reluctant scion of the family, would ever be obliged to make those sentimental trips.

Knew he would and forcibly put it out of his mind.

After a while they joined the six lane highway linking Mecca and Jeddah and were immediately confronted by endless giant billboards advertising anything from Rado watches to Givenchy perfume to LG television sets and fridges. The setting sun was dead ahead now and blinding and it was stuffy in the car, even with the air conditioner going full blast.

The occasional buildings were coming up now, scattered with nothing that could be seen as a village. Traffic was busier than Riad remembered it with many trucks, each sporting yet another ad. Plenty of truck stops too, each with an adjacent mosque and then the sun was down and they pulled in at one to refuel just as the prayer call went up from the mosque, the metallic voice of the recording crackling with static.

Indicating to the others that he would tend to the fuel while they went to pray, while fully knowing he would not be joining them for the brief sunset prayer, he motioned over a Bengali attendant who set about filling the Land Cruiser's tank. Idly watching the numbers roll by on the register he exchanged a greeting with a young man in a light grey business suit who had pulled up at the next pump in a blood red Ferrari.

The fashionably trimmed beard and carefully coiffed hairdo coupled with the wraparound Oakley sunglasses as well as the dazzlingly white high collared shirt worn open at the neck to show off the chunky silver chain and the expensive Italian loafers spelt money. Serious money, Saudi prince kind of money.

'Your car sounds like it's running a bit ragged,' Riad remarked, 'you might need it tuned.'

'Damn low octane fuel,' the other man sighed, 'it's supposed to run on high octane but try and find that in this place. Sooner or later the engine is damaged.'

'Here one car is the same as the other and most are used up before long so never buy a used car from an Arab,' Riad affirmed, watching the pump attendant return the hose to the bowser and fumbling in his pocket for his wallet.

'Never buy a used woman from an Arab either,' came the reply punctuated by a little giggle.

All too true Riad reflected and thought again of his little half sister and what could have happened to her by now. And then he thought of Maddie Green but that was someone else's concern, his was family business. Suddenly in a hurry, he paid the Bengali pump attendant then got behind the wheel and blasted the horn three times.

In Jeddah he drove straight to the New Mowasat Hospital and with the others waiting in the car went up to Talal's room with Mohammed. They found the young man propped up in bed watching a movie on a laptop. An eyepatch covered one eye with several plasters on his face and shaven scalp not quite hiding the bruises. The hand that greeted them was swathed in a bandage. 'Marhaba,' he said through swollen lips as he glanced somewhat anxiously at Riad who had pulled up a chair.

An attempt at small talk by Mohammed was cut short by Riad who had cornered a young doctor at the nurses' station and had been updated on the young man's condition. Several facial lacerations, a bruised eye, some loose teeth and three fractured ribs with a small pneumothorax that needed observation only.

'Tell me what happened,' he said simply pulling over a box of chocolates from the nightstand to carefully select a soft centre.

'We, Yasmin, the other girl and I drove down to Ras Mosheikh along the beach road, about twenty miles south of Jeddah, where there is a good snorkelling spot. We met up with an English doctor and his wife who had anchored their boat there and was scuba diving. Then suddenly four men, Jezaili by their red smekh wrapped around their faces, came over the dunes in a jeep and attacked us, taking the girls and beating me and the English doctor. It was his wife who brought us back on the boat.'

'Where is he now?'

Talal shrugged, pushing himself up against the pillows and   thus further away from this menacing older brother whose voice had taken on an edge, 'I don't know but he works at the National Guard Hospital and might be there. He was not so badly hurt.'

'Who is the girl?'

'I think her name is Leila.'

'You think?'

'She is a friend of Yasmin's. They are together in the class at university.'

'You drive hours through the desert with this girl and yet you want me to believe you do not know her name, or where she comes from?'

Looking helplessly at Mohammed and finding no relief in the other man's features he turned back to Riad who seemed pre-occupied with the chocolate box. 'I... she, she is from Qataran, Leila al Thani. She is working on a research project at our university, marine biology of the Red Sea.'

Leila al Thani. From Qataran. Princess Leila al Thani of the royal family of Qataran. Resisting the impulse to wring the recalcitrant young man's neck Riad moved his chair up to bring his searching gaze closer to the young man's nervously blinking eye.

'Do you realise the implication of this, Talal?'

A whisper, 'Yes—'

Looking at a silent Mohammed Riad sought confirmation that no ransom demand had been received, also that there had been no mention of the kidnapping in the local papers or on the news. He was met by a shake of the head, no.

'This is a *sheikha,* Talal, a princess. She would have a minder at all times, one or even two older women. Where were they?'

'We did not tell them about the trip,' came the soft reply, eyes downcast.

'You stole away with the woman, knowing full well the consequences –' It was a statement, not a question and was met by a wall of silence.

And suddenly he could see the whole picture. 'You and this girl were planning to run away together, the English with their boat was to be the means. The Qatarans would have been looking for her within hours and because it's a private family matter they are taking care of it themselves, not notifying the Saudi police.' Which meant, he thought grimly, that things were about to get ugly very quickly.

Silence from the man in the bed was all the confirmation he needed. 'Where is your 4x4?'

'Still there. In the desert.'

'Come,' Riad said, indicating they were leaving and Talal was coming along.'

'But, I can't. I'm injured, I—'

'Shut up before I do it for you,' Riad snarled, grabbing the young man by his pyjama front and dragging him out of the bed to fall in a heap at his feet. 'Get dressed,' he said motioning Mohammed to bring his clothes over from a cupboard. 'You are no longer safe here. To-morrow we shall go and find the vehicle, in the meantime I'll think of what to do.'

'I'm sick, hurt. I cannot travel,' came the wailing reply, pleading eyes darting between the two older brothers.

'You'll live,' Riad replied, ripping the drip line from the young man's arm with enough force to leave blood spattered on the carpet, tossing him a tissue to stem the bleeding.

Half an hour later they checked into a Jeddah hotel with Talal and Mohammed sharing a room and instructions to the latter not to let the young man out of his sight. The two armed companions elected to stay with the car and camp overnight in whatever vacant lot they could find. Over a shared meal in the hotel dining room a plan of action for the next day was put together. They would leave at four a.m. and take the coastal road heading south. According to Talal the site of the ambush was two hours drive away and after locating the abandoned vehicle their two companions, both expert trackers according to Mohammed, would lead them on the spoor of the kidnappers.

'What about the police?' Talal asked while looking anxiously at his eldest brother, half expecting another slap.

'What about them?' Riad replied, calling over an Indian waiter to bring more hummus.

'I…I phoned the Jeddah police yesterday and they put me through to an officer, he…I was told they would send someone but no-one came—'

Motioning for the young man to pass him the jug of flavoured ice water, Riad said wearily, 'Did this officer perhaps ask you for the name and number of Yasmin's father, our father?'

'Yes.' Hesitant now, a look of puzzlement in his gaze Talal fiddled with his napkin.

'For a Saudi you are amazingly ignorant how things work in our world,' Riad sighed. 'The moment the officer, a Captain Husseini by the way, learned this was the daughter of a well known Saudi his first reflex would have been to hush the whole thing up. After discussing it with father the arrangement was that we would try to find her first with the good captain ready to render official assistance the moment it was requested. The reason we are here now.

Sensing the question in Talal's eyes he said, 'You've been living in the world of Facebook and YouTube for too long now, this is not the western world, not for a young woman from a prominent Arab family. If it were to become known that your little sister had been a captive of strange men with no chaperone the scandal will be terrible. Enough to ruin her chances of marriage forever.'

Suddenly overwhelmed with a sense of bitterness he went on, 'I know Captain Husseini from the time I was a rookie cop in Jeddah, a long time ago now. He's a good man held prisoner by a corrupt system. Do you know what happens in Kuwait City when an expatriate's wife, a white woman, visits the police station to lodge a complaint of physical abuse by her husband?'

Shaking his head he leaned closer as the others looked on in silence. 'Nothing is what happens, Talal. Nothing. She poses a potential embarrassment, lots of confusing paperwork and possible repercussions and not even a dead body to show for all the fuss. So they have the crazy woman sit outside in a stinking sweltering waiting room amongst the hopeless, the dying and the unspeakable, an object of curiosity, you could almost say a white elephant. And when she steps up to the desk to enquire what's happening she is fobbed off by the clerk with the suggestion perhaps she could come back to-morrow? Perhaps speak to her husband, be nice, patch things up?'

Met with a wall of silence he pushed back his chair. 'The real question is why the disappearance of Sheikha al Thani has not been reported to the authorities.'

'Perhaps they spoke directly to the minister,' Mohammed offered tentatively.

Riad shook his head, 'No. Word would have gotten to Husseini, who does not know of the identity of the second woman and is not to know, understood?'

His two brothers nodded in unison as they watched the retreating form of the two bodyguards heading for the exit and the parked car. 'Why would the Oatarans not notify the police?' Mohammed asked.

'Because by now they're searching for little Leila,' Riad said grimly, 'searching hard and not taking any prisoners.'

14
CHAPTER

They reached the abandoned Land Cruiser at twenty minutes past eight by Riad's watch, the sun already high and the car's air conditioner at full hum. Highway 55 had run straight as an arrow only taking the occasional lazy deviation when forced by a rocky outcrop amongst the mostly soft featureless desert.

With nary a blade of grass in sight, or a shrub, let alone a tree, it was the most desolate landscape on earth. Just barren desert as far as the eye could see with half formed mirages dancing on the horizon and glimpses of a glittering Red Sea in the distance. No villages, no people but nevertheless plenty of traffic on the narrow two lane road. Mainly trucks doing the run down to Najran near the Yemeni border, also lots of small pickups driven by ageless bearded Bedouin often with livestock on the back tray, even camels. As well as families travelling in large American saloons and SUVs.

No oil here so no industry, no jobs and no settlements. Just barren desert yet all these people. Where did they come from and where were they going?

Riad vaguely recalled a speed limit of seventy miles an hour being in force but clearly not enforced. Here the driving was to the conditions of the road which, to Riad's jaundiced eye considering the potholes and the sections of thick sand washed across the tarmac would be a cautious fifty miles an hour but in practice was somewhere close to a breakneck eighty or ninety. And then there was the inexplicable hurry of the motorists as they rode each other's bumpers working their horns and passing with all the gay abandon of a death wish maniac at the most impossible sections.

Mohammed was driving with Riad sunk in thought when a suppressed curse next to him had him look up to see a large black Suburban truck off road and parallel to them bouncing wildly over the uneven sand as the driver, by all appearances a twelve year old boy, made to pass them. Through the tinted windows of the truck he could make out veiled faces staring back at them while a small child waved from a back window.

Seeing the child's smiling face made him think back of the phone call from his mother when he had got back to his room the night before. Dispensing this time with the usual treacly niceties she had asked in her clipped disapproving mother's voice whether he realised that his daughter, her beloved only grandchild, was desperately unhappy at school. That Rania was being bullied and what was he going to do about it? Protesting that it was the first he had heard of it while silently admitting to himself that she had been very standoffish lately, something he had put down to possibly hormonal changes in a girl growing up (what did he know?) he sheepishly agreed to talk to Rania and try and be a father to the child.

For once the subject of his own father did not come up and mercifully also no details regarding her own decidedly bohemian lifestyle, something to be grateful for. Clearly Yvette Ayoub was upset and so was he when, after repeated attempts, he could not get his daughter to answer her phone.

Here he was two hours ahead of Kuwait time and on a Thursday, weekend in the Arab world, she would still be asleep. He would try again later he decided, forcing the thought to the back of his mind as he concentrated on the scene that met them.

Driving by the GPS co-ordinates Talal had provided they had left the highway driving along a rough track to reach a small secluded bay hidden amongst several high dunes. A spot favoured by many European expat scuba divers for the spectacular coral reefs as well as an old WWII wreck lying in sixty feet of water, several tyre tracks could be seen with a partially sand covered pile of trash visible at one end of the small beach.

No sign of life now but it being weekend Riad thought the chances good of some others turning up. At his instruction Talal described the scene of the attack and as half expected there were no clues to be found that would point to the direction the assailants would have taken with their two captives. Once again he asked the young man to describe their attackers, a description that fitted the wild desert dwellers all too perfectly.

Jezaili. Tough nomadic desert dwellers, non-Muslims who followed a poorly understood pagan religion and whose women dressed in ornately embroidered deep red abeyas while displaying elaborate tattoos covering their hands and faces. Women who, like their males, wielded a mix of ancient rifles and AK47s and who spoke a language that took a modern day Arab some concentration to decipher.

Living in areas of the Rub al Khali, the most inhospitable domain on earth, their actual numbers were unknown as were most of their customs. The Saudi authorities had long ago and wisely decided to leave them to their own devices seeing as they were almost never encountered by anyone and posed no real threat to the regime. To find them this far from their normal habitat was unusual and had Riad wonder if it had been a disguise. But why?

He was still standing at the lapping edge of the water drinking sweet tea from a thermos flask and running his eyes over the flat blue sea out to where the yacht would have been moored when a shout had him turn to see Yusuf, one of the trackers, wave from the top of the nearest dune. The man was beckoning them to follow and Riad shouted at Mohammed who was back at the vehicle asking what the man was saying.

'They have found something,' came the answer,' a few miles that way.' He pointed towards where the man was standing, impatiently waving. 'He says we should bring the car.'

Shortly after arriving Riad had instructed the trackers to take the other 4x4 and head south but off road, see if they could pick up any tracks. It seemed they had.

Fifteen minutes later, after the kind of side slewing high speed dune driving much favoured by tourists in Dubai but which did nothing for Riad's stomach, they reached the spot where the other man was waiting.

'What tracks?' Riad asked while leaning against the side of the Land Cruiser and wishing he had not skipped breakfast after all. Gazing around he saw nothing but a flat stretch of featureless sand, dunes to one side and the sea the other.

A rapid discussion between the two trackers led to Yusuf following his brother over to the other vehicle where an object was retrieved and handed to Riad. 'What is it?' he asked turning the flat piece of lightweight ribbed metal over to look at a stamped inscription on the side. In Arabic it was a series of numerals and letters ending in QT.

'Hasan, he find this in sand, there,' Yusuf said, pointing to a nearby glistening section of beach where the incoming tide was lapping. Hasan who did not seem to speak at all, nodded, pointing at a spot and standing on it to slowly sink down to knee level, water swilling around him.

'Car come past here. Go down in soft sand,' Yusuf said. To illustrate Hasan who had extricated himself moved six feet to sink into a parallel trough of quicksand.

'And they used light metal ladder strips to get out, this piece breaking off?'

'Aiwa!'

Examining the object again Riad concluded that, rust free, it was recently lost and he did not need the confirming comment from the others crowding around to know the lettering indicated property of the Qataran government.

'What made Hasan come down to look on this beach?' Riad asked, handing the piece of metal to Talal who looked at it in puzzlement.

A rapid discussion between the two trackers, in a dialect Riad was only able to follow in snatches, led to the explanation that it being prayer time Hasan had gone down to the water's edge to perform ablutions. That was when he came across the object.

Riad, who did not much believe in co-incidences or luck for that matter, had to bow to this one even before Yusuf, feeling some sort of better explanation was needed, added 'It was the will of Allah—'

To which Riad could only accede. Raising his gaze to the surrounding soft sand dunes the conclusion was that the abductors – he no longer thought of them as Jezaili – thought the beach would be a quick safer transit to the beckoning distant hard desert stretch, only to become stuck in the quicksand. There was the faint possibility it could have been someone else, mad Englishmen out for a spot of sunstroke baiting, but he did not think so. Nor did he think the Qataran military, if the tiny Gulf nation even had more than three men and a dog, would be into selling off surplus equipment.

No, this was their quarry and they had been moving south.

'How many cars?' he asked leading the way back to their vehicles.

'Hasan think only one,' came the reply, 'and he say very light. Not like Land Cruiser.'

The mystery of how these desert men could so confidently come to that conclusion once again escaped Riad who nevertheless knew from experience that they were usually right. 'Let's go!' he shouted, getting into the front passenger seat wincing as he bumped his shin against the silver AK47 resting against the dashboard.

Two hours of rough riding through a stone strewn section of hard desert including a brief stop to swop a punctured tyre had them reach the crest of a shallow wadi where the lead vehicle, driven by Yusuf, slew to a sudden halt. Along the way they had come across sporadic vehicle tracks, fresh and with no attempt to obscure them, all heading parallel to the nearby sea while resolutely heading south.

Every now and then, when about to crest a section of high ground, Yusuf would call a halt while they scoured the area ahead through powerful binoculars. This time there was something to see.

The helicopter, a commercial eight or ten seater by Riad's judgement, was lying at an angle with its nose partially buried in the sand and the tail section at an unusual angle. Even at a distance of several hundred yards he could see that all identification markings had been roughly painted over in dull grey. There had been a fire for the engine compartment and most of the rearmost cabin was blackened and still smoking.

A long deep furrow in the ground indicated the shattering impact of the crash landing.

A short distance away lay two canvas covered oblong object which, judging by the shape and size, could reasonably be expected to be the bodies of the hapless pilots. A further one hundred and fifty yards away and closer to the beach was a small four poster tent with a white Volkswagen Beach Buggy parked next to it.

Two men in brown dishdashas with Bedouin headwear were leaning against the car smoking. Both were clean shaven and Riad could make out the shapes of rifles resting against a seat.

No sign of life inside the tent which had its sides lowered. At the entrance flap and placed on a flat rock was a military style radio, much like the one in the back of Riad's Land Cruiser.

Moving back down the slope while taking care to keep low and out of sight Riad held a brief conference with the others. 'The women are inside the tent. The men are not Jezaili, they are Qataran, sent to take back the sheikha. The helicopter was sent to take them off to a boat and that must still be the plan.'

'But it was Jezaili! I saw them!' objected an agitated Talal earning himself a withering look from his brothers. 'That was what you were meant to think, Talal. For Qatarans to operate illegally in our country would be to invite repercussions. That's why those two down there are wearing dishdashas, not uniforms.' Waving away further questions from the young man he went on, 'One vehicle means only three, possibly four men.' Turning to Yusuf he ordered him and his brother to perform a wide sweep of the surrounding area to check for any sentinel and with a nod they scurried off, taking their weapons with.

'What do we do now?' Mohammed asked as he passed the binoculars back to Riad.

A good question, he decided. The last thing they wanted was a shoot out and with all of several hundred yards between him and the opposition there was no way they could sneak up close enough unseen to stage a surprise. Another factor was time would be running out, surely these men, he could only think of them as professionals, would have a Plan B activated by now.

Radio for help? Captain Husseini perhaps? But it would take time for the police or the military to get there and somehow he did not think time was on their side.

Make a decision Riad! Don't be like Mr Micawber waiting for something to turn up, it's bound to be something unpleasant. Your little half-sister (whom you hardly knew existed until a day ago) is down there in that tent, in the hands of strangers and the honour of the Ajmi is on your shoulders.

Act man, act! As usual in times of crises the legacy of a wasted education threatened to overwhelm his senses, having him retreat into comfortably familiar much loved fiction such as the completely irrelevant the play's the thing from Hamlet which made no sense at all.

Maybe it was the hunger gnawing away at his stomach, perhaps they should eat something, brew some tea, give themselves time to think things over?

'No other men outside,' it came from Yusuf who had crept up next to him carefully putting down his weapon before slowly creeping up to crest to peer down at the camp below.

'Good. You and Hasan move two hundred paces to opposite sides but remain unseen. Mohammed and I will slowly drive down there with the car and pretend to be Bedouin coming to see what was going on. Their attention will be fixed on us and give you chance to move further around and slowly come up behind them. But do not come up until you see at least one more man come out of the tent.'

'What about me?' Talal asked, a hint of a tremor in his voice.

'You stay here. With the radio. If things go bad you contact Captain Husseini.'

'B...bad--?'

Sighing Riad said nothing, rolling back onto his stomach for one last look through the binoculars. Which was when the third man stepped out of the tent and stood there for a minute, lighting a cigarette while scanning his surroundings. Dressed in a pair of light blue chinos and a Calvin Klein tee shirt he wore Italian leather sandals, a chunky gold watch glinting on a slender arm.

Stunned Riad worked the focus of the powerful field glasses for a clearer view. There was no mistaking the man's identity.

Well how about that? A *deus ex machina,* just when you need it. The old Greek playwrights could not have written this one better he said under his breath.

And suddenly it all made sense. Who would you send when your daughter is about to run off with some nobody other than a son and a brother. Good old family honour once more.

'Change of plan,' he said with a grin climbing to his feet and dusting off his pants. 'It happens the man down there, the leader of that little party, is an old friend. I'm going to drive down there alone and talk to him, sort things out. All of you stay up here until I come back. Yasmin will be with me.'

And with that, protests ringing around his ears, he got behind the wheel of the car and drove over the top of the ridge heading for the party below.

The terrain was uneven and rock strewn and it took him several minutes to wind his way down to where the men had by now spread out, their assault rifles at the ready. Finally coming to a halt yards away from the tent where the third man was still standing and watching him intently, Riad got out while being careful to keep his hands in full view.

'Hello Chunky,' he said amiably, spreading his arms in a welcoming gesture. 'Long time no see!'

Frowning, eyes narrowed, the other man hesitated then lightened up as recognition came. 'Riad? Gigolo, is that you?!' he replied in English, 'Well blow me sideways! Here of all places!'

'In the flesh,' Riad said as they shook hands then, after a moment's hesitation, embraced in the Arab fashion.

'How long has it been?' Chunky, more commonly known as His Highness Prince Suleiman al Thani of Qataran, asked while apologizing for the less than salubrious surroundings greeting his unexpected but most welcome friend.

'Since our days at Harrow? More than twenty years my friend and I still have not forgotten the time you ran that pair of ladies knickers up the flagpole and had me take the blame.'

'More than made up for that time during the rugger game when you and your team mates gave us that mud bath then turned off the hot showers in our dormitory.'

'Happy memories,' Riad agreed as he declined the offer of a cigarette. 'Now we seem to have ourselves a bit of a situation here, Chunky, wouldn't you say?'

'"Chunky—"' the sheikh repeated with a shake of the head, 'nobody calls me that anymore, ever since leaving school.'

'You have lost a lot of weight,' Riad agreed, 'do you work out?' While thinking "gigolo?" Was I really that much of a lad amongst the ladies?

'I gather the young lady is family?' Chunky asked, a sudden thought having him recoil in horror, 'Surely not a *wife*?'

'A sister, well, half-sister. With her companion no doubt your sister?'

Chunky nodded, 'A strange business, not?' He turned to wave at his companions to lower their guns. 'And then the young man, this Talal, is a brother?'

'Alas, yes. How did this all happen?'

Leading Riad over to the buggy, a long wheelbase six seater Riad now noticed, he indicated they got inside it being the only seats available. 'We learned of the growing friendship between the two from Leila's chaperone. Of course we did not know it was someone from your family. Leila refused to return home saying she was close to finishing her studies but our father suspected what was happening so sent me to be ready should she try to run away to somewhere it would be embarrassing to retrieve her from.'

Retrieve, Riad mused. Like a parcel.

'I had a small GPS tracker planted in the lining of the bag she normally carried which is how we could track her when the word came of her escape. I had been staying on a yacht of ours now waiting just over the horizon. We landed by that helicopter over there together with this buggy.'

'What happened?' Riad asked, indicating the chopper.

'Our pilot thought it safer to return to the yacht and wait for a signal to return. He was not sure whether Saudi radar had picked us up earlier although we were flying very low. Sadly he crashed on coming back.'

'Not family, I hope?'

There was a moment's silence as Chunky fiddled with an ornately engraved cigarette lighter, his gaze resting on the two covered bodies in the distance. 'A younger brother. Also a friend.'

'I'm sorry. If only we, my family, had known perhaps all this could have been avoided.'

Chunky shook his head, 'Very difficult,' he sighed. 'Leila had been promised to another, already when she was fourteen.'

With an effort dismissing the thought Riad asked what Plan B was, adding that perhaps he could help.

'A launch will come across from the yacht as soon as possible.'

Riad frowned, 'why the delay, isn't the boat nearby?'

'A Saudi coastguard ship is out there, we have to wait for it to move on but it seems to be patrolling, perhaps looking for smugglers.'

Or a lost helicopter, Riad thought. 'A nice touch, the Jezaili disguise,' he said with a chuckle.

'Glad you liked it, old boy,' Chunky said, 'items we picked up during an earlier falconing trip near the Yemeni border. Never thought it would come in handy one day.'

Glancing at his watch Riad decided it was getting late and he really did have to eat something now with the prospect of a meal not looking good at his present location. 'OK if I take Yasmin back with me now?'

'Of course,' Chunky said with an apologetic gesture, 'we only took her because the women refused to be parted and in the heat of the moment my men were not sure which was which.' Turning he entered the tent and following a brief conversation in rapid Arabic re-emerged with two young women in tow.

'You are Yasmin?' Riad asked looking at the more likely of the two while realising with a detached sense of shame that he did not even know what his sister looked like. The Ajmi nose, he decided, that clinched it.

No reply, just a nod with eyes downcast.

'I am Riad, your brother. Talal is waiting back there, over the ridge. You will come with me now.' He was about to say something to the other man when the second women darted forward and in a pleading tone asked if Talal was alright.

They stood in silence for a while then Riad spoke, 'You really do love Talal?'

Hands wrung together she said simply, 'We love each other---' Hearing the hopelessness in her sob, seeing the moisture glinting at the corners of her eyes something broke deep inside Riad. Something that had been festering inside him for so long now. This, this *thing* about their women, this condemnation of their women. How could this be? Why did it always have to be like this? Had it not already cost the life of his wife, of Rania's mother? When would it end?!

'Perhaps we could arrange something?' he said at length, meeting Chunky's gaze and seeing something there, a spark of compassion perhaps? All those years of a British public school education must have installed some liberal western values in the man after all, Riad knew it had certainly in his own instance.

'It will take money,' Chunky said flatly.

Riad nodded, 'Perhaps if we arranged for my father and my young brother to visit the emir, discuss matters?' Translation: agree to a price.

'That will be good.'

'We'll be off then,' Riad said, opening a passenger door for Yasmin who got in with a last pleading look at a softly crying Leila. 'My people will be in contact with your people.'

He had always wanted to say that.

'Be hearing from you,' Chunky called out as Riad put the car in gear. A thought had him hold on to Riad's hand a second longer, 'I say old boy, you wouldn't mind not ratting on me being here, to the Saudis?'

'Of course not. *Stet Fortuna Domus.*' The old Harrovian motto always sounded weird to Riad, even more so now.

Chunky grinned, 'Always thought that old school tie stuff would pay off one day. And don't forget, next year is our twenty fifth anniversary at Harrows. I expect to see you there!'

The trip back to Jeddah was largely in silence. There was not much to say.

15
CHAPTER

Fear had the boy in its icy grip as he became aware that the alien was behind him, no! Right *above* him! He could hear its rattling breathing, louder in his left ear and there was something wet and cold at the back of his neck and he thought it might be sweat but could not be sure. Careful now! Pivoting and at the same time raising the gun he saw only the forbidding bleakness of the tunnel with its tubes and wires everywhere and the only light from a low set green glowing wire mesh covered portal.

Debris on the ground and, ten paces away, the torn and blood spattered remains of what had been the last of his squad, the soldier's upturned helmet slowly filling with moisture dripping from the ceiling.

The rifle was heavy in his grip but it was new and he had been warned at the start of the mission that it would be different but so much better against the alien.

A sudden glimpse of a moving form from the corner of his eye had him whirl only to see the tail of the lizard like monster slither around a far corner. Swallowing hard and gripping the weapon tighter he set off in pursuit.

In the next room The Master clicked on the headset mounted microphone and said, 'Mission terminated, Sergeant Khalid. Abort. Repeat, abort.'

Leaning back in his swivel chair he watched the images on the console screens as the boy stiffened, then slowly, reluctantly, removed the fully encasing helmet, his pupils dilated and oddly staring on a close up view from one of the many monitors dotting the games room.

'You are back at base, Sergeant. Stand down.' With that he switched on the overhead lights as he watched the boy, how old was he -- fourteen?—glance in awe at the replica AK47 now propped up against a wall before peeling off the combat suit that trailed wires connected to a variety of biological monitors.

This one showed promise, The Master thought, not the slightest rise in pulse rate, no measurable sweating, no increase in respiratory rate, not even when he had to kill a comrade the alien was using as a shield.

A natural born killer? No, he decided, a *programmed* killer. But there was still a lot of work to be done before the boy would be ready. He had been tempted to introduce the LSD laced Coke today but the timing was not yet right. That would have to wait for a weekend or school holiday in case there was unexpected side effects that even the minuscule dosages he used could sometimes bring about.

A glance at his watch gave the time as three minutes to two pm. Time for the boy to return home from the extra science class his parents believed he was attending after school. Would it not have been so much easier had he been able to work with street urchins, kids without caring families that would not know, or care, what little Khalid was up to?

But there were no street urchins in Kuwait City. At least not belonging to citizens. And the odd abandoned expat waif would before long be rounded up by the police and speedily deported back to whatever hellhole they came from.

This particular boy had been with him going on two months now. First starting him on basic shooter games like Call of Duty and Red Dead Redemption and watching him hone his skills, more importantly studying his choices, he had finally decided he was ready for the next phase. The Game. The final test for this one was when he chose to blow the head off the farmer just to test his new shotgun.

Not all had been suitable, of course but two out of five was pretty good. Of course it helped enormously that the school psychologist helped him recruit, part of her PhD project apparently. Useful idiots he believed is what ISIS called them. Not that he was a jihadist, where's the money in that?

No, this was a commercial venture and one, should his plans become realised, that would make him a very rich man indeed.

He watched as Romi, his Filipino manservant escorted the boy down to the basement garage, carefully blindfolding him first. Like the others the boy would never know the location of the games room or indeed, the identity of The Master. Romi picked them up after school in his nondescript Corolla and dropped them off close to their homes afterwards. All part of the big adventure these boys shared and, under strict instruction, never mentioned to friends or parents.

The first rule of The Game was never to talk about The Game.

After the pair had left he poured himself a generous measure of Chivas Regal on the rocks then resumed his seat at the control panel that took up most of one wall of the large lounge area. From here he could monitor the whole of the penthouse including the spacious reality room where his projects received their final preparations, the next phase for young Khalid.

Idly watching a rerun of the performance he had just managed while sipping the whisky he turned his mind back to Evan, the so-called "grandfather of IT" in the city. It was time to retire the man and he knew just how to do it. Had another soldier all trained up and ready to go and, just for fun, he had this boy conditioned as a ninja assassin, a master with a broad bladed katana.

A thin smile hovered on his lips as the warm and familiar soothing of the whisky coursed through his blood and he switched channels bringing a website up on the large central screen. Going through a series of cutbacks and running a circuit through three continents it took a full minute before the face page of the paedophile porn site came up. Fingers moving lightning fast over a keyboard he bypassed the numerous sections he had previously engaged until he found the reality streaming site he wanted.

The girl was four years old yet already a woman. She was dancing all the while staring up at the man seated in the chair from behind a half mask of a black whiskered cat. The camera angle showed him from the shoulders down only, no face but The Master could see from the hands resting on the armrests that the man was quite old. He even thought the insignia ring on a pinkie looked familiar and was mildly surprised the man had not thought of removing it.

The girl was wearing a pretty party dress with lots of frilly petticoats of stiff nylon ballooning out and a large black sash around her tiny waist and tied in a bow at the back. She had on elbow length black silk gloves that went surprisingly well with the flat heeled patent leather shoes and white bobby socks. A sparkling tiara rested amongst golden tresses and the makeup had been skilfully applied by no doubt an adult hand.

He was glad that the knees were not showing under the dress, that always bothered him. The knees of a four year old always seemed to be so knobbly, not streamlined like the rest of the little legs. Of course, soon when she changed into her sweet itsy bitsy sequined pink bikini, so much more would show but that was also OK.

He watched as the little body gyrated and contorted, the wiggle movements of the hips they had only recently taught her – not quite Shakira but getting there – and as always the sheer suppleness of the very young, the smooth firmness of that faultless flesh excited him. And all the time those pale blue eyes stayed fixed on the man in the chair while the knowing little smile hovered around the deep red of her painted lips, tiny white teeth showing in flashes.

Now, as the music built to a climax she was advancing steadily, writhing and drawing figures in the air with doll like hands and – oh God! She was darting out her little pink tongue, running it across her slightly parted teeth and as the man reached out for her his hands were trembling.

Aware that he was sweating, his own breath coming in short sharp bursts, The Master fought unsuccessfully to tear his gaze away and suddenly it was over and he fell back in his chair, the glass forgotten in his limp grasp. God she was good! She had learned so much in just a few weeks. She was a star.

16
CHAPTER

The phone call came at nine, Colonel Omar, a meeting set for ten with his presence required. No details but the suggestion he shaved and be in uniform. For a moment the uniform bit puzzled him, as a plainclothes cop he seldom wore it and this order suggested the presence of a high ranking official, perhaps the minister. Or could it be the press, about his most recent case that had elicited some coverage, mainly about the supervision of schoolkids? Shrugging off the thought he showered and shaved then rummaged through his closet to find the desired item, which now seemed to be two sizes too big, a reflection of the weight he had lost since his injury.

How did Big Ray Chandler put it again? *His clothes sat on him like a shack around a horse.* The thought made him smile.

The Maddie Green file, he decided as he finished dressing, studying himself in the mirror and adjusting polished leather belt and holster to the correct angle. Having read the file and returning it to the station earlier he had not yet had the opportunity to report back to Omar on his thoughts. And what exactly were those thoughts, Riad? Over a leisurely breakfast of freshly made temeze flatbread from the Iranian bakery downstairs, honey and goat's cheese washed down with lots of coffee, he ran over in his mind what had been discovered to date.

Not much, was the inescapable conclusion. Four year old white girl snatched while on a visit to Australia. Taken during a brief window of opportunity with no traces left behind of an intruder. Nothing else taken, no clothing, no toys. Nothing. Both parents in the presence of witnesses when the abduction took place.

No ransom note. This a surprise as the father is a very rich man.

Correction: step father. Real father deceased, no details stated.

Case being investigated by Melbourne based Victorian police who fear it might be the work of a paedophile ring.

Recent report from the investigating officer, a Detective Inspector Reed, that an undercover agent had come up with evidence of a new blonde white girl being touted on the paedophile circuit but nothing concrete to date.

That the case was still receiving regular news coverage in the western world, not so much in Kuwait.

A brief internet search had revealed just how many similar cases had been recorded in the past but also the number of small children killed by parents and carers, often in the most horrific ways. And how few of these cases ever got solved, usually because no body was found.

Pausing to wipe away a coffee stain with a dishcloth he considered knocking on his daughter's door to see if she was awake and perhaps wanted to join him for an ice cream and some shopping down at the Mubarak Street Virgin Store Arcade later that morning. But, it was school holidays and she had been a bit lethargic lately, so let her sleep in.

'Bye, darling!' he called half heartedly, adding, 'I'm off to the office and will be back at twelve!'

No response other than the cat rubbing up against his leg. Staring down at the inscrutable face he realised she had not been fed yet and, with a sigh, went into the kitchen and opened a tin of cat food. It was a task his daughter normally did first thing in the morning and one more sign that the poor child was overtired.

Gathering his keys he went down to the car.

The traffic was light that morning, something he ascribed to a sizeable number of Kuwaitis having gone abroad for the holidays, and he reached the Salmiya Police Headquarters twenty minutes later.

After exchanging pleasantries with the staff at the front desk and accepting a handful of mail, as well as one of the Egyptian typist's home baked cookies, he headed up the stairs to the detectives common room and the colonel's office.

For once he managed to transit the open office space without the usual barrage of greetings, mainly because at that hour most of the detectives were out and seconds later was waved through to the big man's office without the hijab wearing little secretary bothering to glance up.

Sarah Green was dressed in a floral summer dress, her long slim legs elegantly draped to one side, a double string of pearls on her neck and a smile on her lips. 'Hello Officer Riad, so nice to see you again.'

The voice was soft, languid, with a hint of the melodic. Lowered under lashes sapphire blue eyes mocked him to respond. She was languishing in one of Omar's uncomfortable visitor's chairs and making it look comfortable.

The man in the chair next to her was wearing a gleamingly white neatly pressed dishdasha of expensive material. It was buttoned at the neck with a clerical style collar fastened with a mother of pearl stud. His lean features were cleanly shaven with a pencil thin moustache and capped by a white guthra draped at the sides over a wide shiny iqal. The cufflinks were jade and gold and from under one peeked a rose gold Patek Philipe wristwatch of a price tag that would cover a police lieutenant's salary for a year.

'Pleased to meet you, Lieutenant, my wife speaks highly of you,' Abdul-Karim said as he rose to extend a limp handshake. He was tall and lean, at least six two, Riad thought and the brogues were hand tooled and quite exquisite.

You can always tell a man by his shoes, Riad reflected, cheap suits could still look good but cheap shoes never.

He muttered something in reply and turned to Colonel Omar as he waited for the Bengali porter to bring up another chair from the corner of the room. Squatting behind the oversized desk the Colonel looked like a big fat toad dressed in the uniform of a New York bellhop. He was wearing all his medals again, Riad noted and by looks of it one or two new ones. Staring hard he tried to spot a Coca Cola button before pulling himself together.

'Salaam aleikum, modir,' he said as he sank into the chair only to be informed by the man that for the sake of the lady – this with an awkward bow of deference to said lady – they would be speaking English.

There was a moment's silence as they waited while the porter placed a silver tray of tea and biscuits on a small table, going around behind the desk to place Omar's within reach of a pudgy hand.

'Please,' the Colonel said, indicating the refreshments, 'and do try the honey, it's from the family farm at Jahra.' The last with an ill concealed hint of smugness, small eyes all but disappearing under heavy jowls as he smiled. Turning to Riad he said, 'Mr Abdul-Karim has requested this meeting to be updated on progress made on the search for his daughter. It seems new information has come to light. There is the possibility of a child trafficking ring being involved. Mrs Abdul-Karim, er Green, has asked that you be present, she was aware that I had you look into the case.'

As Omar reached for a file on the cluttered desk – normally there would be ample space but when VIPs called the man made a note of looking busy – Abdul-Karim spoke. The voice was soft, the English with a hint of an American accent. East coast, Riad thought and was that a Harvard fraternity ring on his little finger? 'Sarah is understandably most upset at how little progress have been made, it's been four months with no word and, and—'

There was a catch in his voice and a strange look in the dark eyes and, placing a hand on her husband's sleeve, Sarah took over. 'I heard from a detective in Melbourne yesterday, an Inspector Reed. They have found the body of…of a small girl. In a suit…suitcase—' Here she broke down in sobs as shivers ran through her slender frame. Abdul-Karim put an arm around her shoulders as she gratefully accepted an offered handkerchief, skilfully dabbing at moist eyes so as not to disturb the mascara.

Colonel Omar gazed at his fingernails, Riad gazed at the woman. Curious, he thought, so much pain, so much tears, yet not the ravaged sunken eye look he had seen on so many faces over years of studying life's underbelly.

Abdul-Karim made to continue but was stopped by his wife with a firm shake of the head, 'It's OK. I'm alright now.' With that she tucked the handkerchief into a small purse and fixed Riad with an intense look. 'The body has not been identified. They want me to travel to Melbourne. Also to test DNA. I want you to be there as well.'

And there it was, just like that. Glancing at Omar the only help Riad got was a raised eyebrow. It seemed the matter was settled. 'Why me?' he said, deciding he needed some tea after all, spooning in extra honey.

'My wife informs me she has discussed the situation with you when you met at a certain social function. That you are familiar with the case and that you are also currently on special leave from your police duties. She trusts your judgement.' After a moment's hesitation and injecting an apologetic note, he added, 'I will be travelling with you, of course. Business in Melbourne,' he said with a smile.

Riad, who was still digesting the nice touch of "a certain social function" – sounds so much better than a psychology therapy session – nodded. 'I see,' he said glancing at the Colonel who was idly flipping through the file and clearly not seeing anything of interest there. The matter was settled. It went without saying that it would be an all expenses paid trip, probably in a private jet and with champagne to spare. What's not to like, Riad?

'Will I have time to pack a toothbrush? He asked, rising and shaking hands with the businessman who took Riad's hand in both of his and staring intently at Riad's face as if searching something there, 'Maddie is not my own child, Lieutenant,' he said hoarsely, 'but I love her very much and I want her back, safely.'

There was a tear in his eye and this one Riad thought was real.

'There is one more thing—' the woman said, her eyes downcast. As they waited she hesitated before speaking, 'I—I have been in contact with a psychic, a lady in Melbourne who is a forensic psychic. She has been of great help in solving so called cold cases, mainly in America.'

'Yes?' Riad prompted as she hesitated again.

'She has heard from Maddie,' she said in a small voice, 'I want to meet with her and I want you to be there.'

I see dead people... A flitting image of the Sixth Sense movie flitted before him and when his eyes met those of Abdul-Karim they were unfathomable; dead.

Great, he decided, just great.

It was late afternoon when Riad got home, he had stopped off at The Police Beach Club for a planned gym session, exercise he felt his body could now really do with, only to be waylaid by two colleagues who insisted he share a cold drink with them and provide details of his recent adventures in Jeddah.

And why did that not surprise him? The fact that they seemed to know so much about what he considered a private family matter? He could only guess at where they had got their information from, a family member, possible the idiotic Talal, loading it onto Facebook, pictures and all? A darker possibility that emails had been hacked.

It did not seem to matter, there were no secrets in Kuwait.

So they had sat around telling each other lies and after a while he had managed to extricate himself and now he was home and looking forward to another cold drink, this time with alcohol in it.

As usual his daughter's bedroom door was closed with what he supposed was music faintly audible. Once again his "I'm home!" elicited no response but that was something he had become used to of late. Like the closed door, the mono syllabic response to his efforts at conversation, he had put all this down to the travails of teenage blues. He had even gone as far as discussing it with one of her teachers, a young woman he had somehow got the impression Rania liked, again coming away with a not altogether reassuring "she's OK, they're all like that at this age."

But this time there was something wrong. For starters the breakfast table had not been cleared, something Rania had always been meticulous about. And then there was the cat, on the outside of the glass balcony door, meowing and pawing, wanting in from the merciless heat outside.

'Rania! Are you alright? Come out, I want to talk to you.'

No response and, moving to just outside the closed door, he asked again.

So things had been a bit awkward recently and maybe he had not paid enough attention but this was not normal. With a mounting feeling of anxiety he turned the knob and went inside.

It was dark inside the room, the heavy curtains drawn with the only light from a flickering vanilla scented candle on her desk. The music was from an iPod plugged into small speakers and fell silent as he approached. Lying next to it was her mobile phone and he could see there had been several unanswered calls.

Something was wrong! 'Rania?!'

She was lying on her bed in a foetal position, face turned to the window. As he came closer he could see she was asleep, a small wet stain of drool on the pillow but what was that blue tinge around the lips? Suddenly alarmed he shook her roughly by the shoulders and encountered no response, just a limpness one would expect in a small baby. No moan – my God! She wasn't breathing!!

Desperately fumbling for a wrist he detected a thready suggestion of rapid pulse which was when the small plastic pill container slipped from her hand. A glance was enough: Rohypnol and by the looks of things she had swallowed the whole contents.

Stumbling over discarded clothes on the carpet he reached the lounge and his own mobile lying on the dining room table within seconds, running back to Rania while feverishly dialling for an ambulance. Kneeling next to her icily cold body, something he prayed was due to the full on air conditioning, he tried to recall CPR. Airway, that was it! Hands shaking he parted her lips and teeth to check that her tongue was not blocking the throat then, after a moment's hesitation, placed his mouth over hers and started blowing.

The exercise was abruptly terminated when she suddenly convulsed and vomitus filled her mouth running down a cheek. Dark eyes fluttered open and after a few seconds focused on his as recognition slowly flooded back.

'Daddy,' she managed hoarsely after a false start, 'I…I—'

'It's okay, baby,' he said in a whisper, 'I'm here now. Things will be alright.'

Nodding numbly she dropped back against the pillow and closed her eyes. For the next twenty minutes, while waiting for the ambulance, he sat by her bedside coaxing her to breathe as her pulse steadily improved and a hint of colour returned to her cheeks.

While the medics, with a doctor in attendance, took her downstairs to the waiting ambulance, Riad gathered up her desktop computer and mobile as well as the empty pill container. The doctor had instructed him to check her bathroom for any other medications before following them to the hospital. During a quick search Riad was relieved not to find any drugs but dozens of bottles and jars of cosmetics,

most of which he would have no clue as to their function and in a way shocked that his little girl would even possess.

Where have you been, Riad?!

Then he saw it. A spidery scrawl across the mirror in red lipstick, the message painfully cryptic: Love you Daddy. Sorry...

17
CHAPTER

'**Y**our daughter will recover fully,' the man in the white coat said, 'the toxicology results are still pending but she has responded to the reversal agent we use for tranquilizers and there is no evidence of opiate poisoning. Her blood gases are back to normal and early tests show no liver or renal damage.'

Nodding Riad looked up dully and stared at the face before him. The man, Egyptian he thought, was smiling uncertainly, stubby fingers with coarse black hairs clamped around the reassuring touch of a pocketed gold plated stethoscope. The chunky watch on his wrist was gold as was a pinkie ring and Riad thought it went nicely with the gold tooth.

'Thank you,' he said.

'We will keep her in the High Dependency Unit overnight, Dr Agarwal said, 'just a routine thing.' He nodded towards the laptop Riad had open on the small coffee table he had dragged across from the far side of the waiting room, bringing it to where he had a view of the open doors to the HDU, 'Your daughter's?'

Getting no response from Riad the doctor wiped a shiny brow with a neatly folded handkerchief and tried again, his voice taking on a sympathetic tone, 'Any idea why she would have done this? Something on her laptop perhaps?'

'No.'

Excusing himself with a promise to be back he headed for his parked car, taking the laptop with him. Truth was he could not open the device at all, there being a code required. All attempts at trying the most likely combinations had quickly resulted in the thing shutting itself down.

The industrial suburb of Jabriya was as bustling as ever and Riad was lucky to find parking across the road from Tony Evan's building. Clutching the laptop he found the ancient elevator disgorging a batch of hyperactive kids with an audible hiss and, after a moment's hesitation, decided to chance it, stepping inside and pressing the button to the third floor.

At least to what he thought was the third floor, the lettering on the black buttons long having worn off. After a brief sagging sensation the elevator creaked into motion with agonizing slowness while Riad tried to decide whether the smell was urine or disinfectant.

It took a full minute of incessant hammering on the door for Evan to open it, peering suspiciously from behind the security of a safety chain. 'Oh, it's you, Detective. I—'

'Open up,' Riad said, 'I need your help with this laptop.'

It took Kuwait's grandfather of computers exactly seven minutes to break Rania's key following a few questions regarding family names, pets and important dates. 'It's all bullshit, these passwords,' Evan said as he leaned back in his padded chair reaching for an open beer. 'All this business of random letters and symbols interspersed with upper and lower caste letters. Pah! A basic robot code breaker will solve them in a matter of hours. Your daughter's password was pretty predictable.'

Glancing at Riad he said, 'Know what a good password is? Any four random unrelated words strung together. Like biscuit, Ferrari, surf, inchoate. Know how long it would take a robot computer to break that? Two years. That's why business sites won't accept it, makes it hard to spy on you.'

Riad, who was still trying to work his mind around "inchoate" nodded. 'I'll make a note. Now, can you get me into her Facebook or Twitter or whatever she was using.'

Deciding to accept a beer after all Riad grew silent as he read through his daughter's Facebook page. Stupid bitch! featured more than once from different contacts, as did Bedouin filth! and You're so ugly your dad has to tie a dead mouse around your neck so the cat will play with you!

There was more, the postings becoming more frequent just recently. The last one dated the day before brought a sudden flash of rage welling inside him, Why don't you just kill yourself, you fat slag? She isn't even fat, he thought shaking his head, was that why she hadn't been eating lately?

'Cyber bullying,' Evan said looking over his shoulder. 'There would be even more on her phone I'd say.'

'Could you trace these, these *people*?'

Evan shrugged, scratched at a stubbled chin, 'Sure but what's the point? It won't stop anything. I'd say take her off social media and perhaps change schools. Have you checked her phone SMS messages?'

Riad admitted he had not, he'd left her phone at her bedside thinking she might want to contact him.

Studying Riad's worried features for a moment Evan shrugged, not having kids himself he could not quite connect with the agonies of parenthood. Virtual characters moving across a well designed virtual world of the game were so much easier to interact with. And, should you get bored with that, there was always the web to surf.

Which had him think of something he'd seen the night before. 'Say,' he said turning to face the detective, 'you know how you sometimes surf the net, just sort of *surf*, you know?'

Riad who wasn't much of a surfer nodded numbly.

'Well, sometimes, out of the blue you find yourself inexplicably looking at a porn site. Not that you ever *look* for these things, understand?'

Riad whose thoughts with his daughter nodded again, 'I suppose,' he said softly.

'Maddie Green, the little girl who went missing, I think I saw her on a porn site. Here, I'll get it up for you.'

Instantly back in the present, a flutter of excitement replacing the numbing feeling of gloom of just seconds earlier,

Riad was about to ask Evan for details when there was a knock on the front door. 'Who's there?' the programmer shouted, his eyes still fixed on the computer screen.

No answer, just more knocking, more insistent this time.

'What happened to the surveillance camera I saw mounted above your entrance?' Riad asked as the other man got out of his chair with visible effort.

'Some idiot spray painted the lens last night. Also did the peephole. Probably one of the idiot kids infesting the place. Bloody rats!'

Shuffling across while stifling a yawn Evan reached the door, yanking it open with a curse that died on his lips. Standing before him was a man wearing a helmet, a matt black face covering Perspex and plastic oversized apparatus, a tiny red laser light shining steadily and pointed at him. Too stunned to move Evan watched as the black scabbard the visitor held in one hand transformed into a shining steel samurai's katana in the other. Then there was a flash of light on steel and Evan found himself staring numbly at the broad red and yellow gash that seemed to divide him from shoulder to waist.

He never made a sound as he died on his feet.

Witnessing it all in a flash and reacting purely on instinct Riad went for his sidearm, cursing as it snagged on the holster. As the killer calmly stepped over the fallen Evan to advance into the room, sword at the ready, Riad leapt up and flung the chair towards the menacing form. Ignoring the object with no effort the killer was three paces away and raising the katana when Riad shot him.

Momentarily halted the man stopped to stare down at the spreading red pool on his chest before, as the second bullet struck home, toppling slowly to the carpet to lie there motionless.

Ears ringing from the loud explosions, his senses numbed with shock, Riad moved as if in a trance, kneeling down next to his would be assassin to remove the helmet.

Staring down at the sightless eyes Riad found himself gazing at the face of a mere boy.

In another part of the city the man known as Scorpion Master leaned forward excitedly, his pulse racing, as he watched the unfolding scene on a large monitor screen linked to the desktop camera on Tony Evan's computer. Excellent! He could not have hoped for a better endgame, both target and hitman dead.

No comebacks. No need now to dispose of the boy but, this with a tinge of regret, for the boy was good. One of the best so far and he could have been useful later. He sat there for a few minutes longer, watching the detective phone for assistance while ushering frightened onlookers out of the open front door and shutting it. Leaving the streaming running he went over to the corner cocktail bar to mix himself a drink then resumed his seat to watch the unfolding scene.

Eight minutes by his watch and still no police response. This he decided was appalling, no wonder crime was spiralling out of control. Finally the front door crashed open revealing a uniformed cop crouched in the ready position, his firearm at the ready, with visible behind him other faces. He could hear the detective call them inside and for the cop to put away his pistol. He watched as the troupe filed into the room, Colonel Omar he knew and Sergeant Waleed he had seen that previous occasion when he had visited in the company of Riad.

No scene of crime investigators yet and no forensics team but he knew they would not be far behind. That was when they would remove the dead man's computer for analysis and, careful as he had been to erase his tracks, he could not be sure.

Silently watching and listening for a further twenty five minutes to ascertain that the poor fools had nothing on him and with a white overall clad SOCO about to take an interest in the computer he sighed and, reaching for his mobile, dialled a number. Instantly his view was gone while several street blocks away a technician reeled back as a small explosion destroyed the hard drive he was about to examine.

In the Evan apartment it took the best part of a minute for total panic to settle down to mere chaos and Riad felt safer when Waleed reluctantly stopped waving his service pistol about and holstered it. Having regained the power of speech Colonel Omar extricated himself from under a table angrily shaking off the helping hand of a young cop to bellow at the technician who had landed flat on his back. 'What in the name of Allah?!! What have you done?!'

Arab kneejerk reaction Riad thought as the rigidity of shock flowed from his body. When something goes wrong someone, a minion, must be to blame. No such thing as shit happens.

'An autodestructing device,' he said with a motion for the visibly shaken technician to carry on. 'He had not touched anything yet which means it has been triggered from outside. Someone has been watching or perhaps listening in.'

He pointed at the oversized helmet Waleed had picked up and was studying with interest. 'Just like the case of the shooting in Salwa the helmet is the key.'

'See here,' Waleed affirmed, showing the others the inside of the headpiece, 'Here is the aperture where the bolt that would kill the boy would fire from, just like the one the other boy was wearing.'

Riad nodded, 'Except this one was already dead, no need to trigger it.'

Someone had found the Colonel a chair into which he sank gratefully, wiping his neck with a handkerchief. His broad face was suffused as he pushed back his cap and loosened a top tunic button and drank from an offered glass of water. 'A terrorist attack!' he exclaimed hoarsely. 'We must notify the Security Branch at once!'

Riad who was thinking more along the lines of a series of well planned assassinations thought it prudent not to contest this for the moment. Clearly both hits were orchestrated by the same puppet master but why? Both targets were ordinary people, not VIPs. Security Branch would stomp over all of this, claim access to all their files then come up with the dreaded "confessions" which was their way of solving things.

They would muddy the waters forever in what was essentially a homicide case.

His kind of case.

Was this a serial killer at work? Somehow he did not think so. Too elaborate, serial killers like to do their own work, directly interact with their victims.

It was all about control and sadism, not murder by proxy. No, there had to be a motive for this. Find that and he would have his man.

He was about to speak his mind when Waleed, who had been on his phone, came over saying, 'That was Farook, from Forensics. It seems the young boy from the earlier shooting had LSD in his blood.' He pointed at the body on the floor, now being examined by a SOCO who was careful not to move it in case of a booby trap. 'What are the chances we'll find the same here?'

An earlier call had been sent out for an explosives sniffer dog which was now at the door having the others move aside to make room for it. The Colonel was clearly petrified of the animal, a rather cute Beagle and had taken up refuge in a far corner while searching his mobile for what would be the number of Security Branch. Coming to a conclusion Riad decided it was now or never.

'Colonel?' he said, joining the man while indicating to Waleed to back off with a subtle motion of his hand.

Omar looked up with a frown, his face was still red, a patina of sweat glistening on his forehead, 'What?'

'Sir, I think I know what is behind this.' Adding, after a moment, 'It is not terrorism.'

This was enough for the Colonel to lower his mobile and glance at his lieutenant suspiciously. 'How do you know that?'

'Everything points to both killings being orchestrated by the same unknown controller. The targets were not random, there is something linking them.'

Omar stared at him incredulously, 'What?! The first target was half a dozen ordinary citizens on a pavement diwaniya, how could –'

'The target was Captain Farsi, sir. The scenario was carefully picked to picture him as someone who was just in the wrong place at the wrong time. I suspect the case he had been working on was behind it, he was getting too close to the truth, something he discovered on the internet. When Sergeant Waleed took over and I got involved we decided to seek the help of the dead man, Tony Evan, a computer expert. Which was why he had to die.'

The Colonel frowned, glanced down at his phone as if seeing it for the first time and slowly returned it to a pocket. 'A case,' he said slowly, 'what case?'

'The Maddie Green File.'

———

18
CHAPTER

Ameera al Quarashi recrossed her legs, the silk fabric of the culottes making a soft swishing sound. Topping off the shiny black and yellow polka dot pants was a white silk top with a wide black belt separating the two. The shoes were needle pointed black stilettoes and today's jewellery a collection of silver bangles on a wrist and an oversized ruby on a finger.

As always the makeup was skilfully applied in the Arab fashion of accentuating the eyes and the long black hair was piled on high and kept in place with a silver and tortoiseshell clasp.

Riad thought the clasp went nicely with the oversized tortoiseshell spectacles.

'There is blood on your uniform,' she said, pointing at a spot on his sleeve Riad had not noticed before.

'I cut myself shaving.'

'You must be a fast healer,' she shrugged, 'I was somewhat surprised at your earlier call, Lieutenant Ajmi, our scheduled session is only for the day after tomorrow.'

'It's about my daughter, Rania. And call me Riad.'

'OK. I can see something has upset you, your daughter is not well?'

'Firstly, thank you for agreeing to see me at this late hour but I did not know where else to turn to. Rania is in hospital. Earlier today she tried to kill herself.' How banal it all sounded, he thought to himself, like discussing a daughter's first period. Was this something fathers often went through or was it women's business, the mothers taking over?

'She is alright?'

He shrugged, 'The doctors say she has not suffered any lasting damage.' Deciding to come to the point he went on, 'We found disturbing messages on her Facebook page as well as some SMS messages on her phone which my colleagues are in the process of tracing. Abusive messages calling her all kinds of demeaning things including telling her to kill herself.' Here he hesitated for a moment as the full horror of that last bit came back to him. Forcing himself to continue he said, 'We think it is from classmates at her school.'

'How do you feel about that?'

Jesus Christ! What was this, a knee jerk reaction from a robot shrink?! 'This is not about me!' he snapped. 'I came to you as the only person I know who could hopefully give me some advice on how to handle this.'

The psychologist was about to enter something on the pad she had reached for when something she saw in Riad's eyes had her gingerly put it back. 'I do have some experience with children' she said, and edge to her voice. 'Mainly early teens. I do sessions at a Jabriya school, dealing with often gifted children who have behavioural issues. Perhaps I can arrange to see your daughter, how old is she now, twelve?'

He nodded numbly, struggling for a moment to arrange his thoughts in orderly fashion. 'There's a problem, I'm due to fly out on a police matter the day after to-morrow and am thinking of leaving Rania in the care of my mother – she's in Beirut – until I'm back. It's just that my mother is, well different, and I'm in two minds. Perhaps you could see Rania to-morrow, at the hospital? See what you think?'

It sounded lame to him even as he uttered it. Would Rania even wish to see anyone, even him?

'It's not a good idea,' Ameera said. 'Not in that setting and not at this early stage.'

A sudden thought made her frown, 'What police business? Aren't you still on probation, until such time as I sign you off?'

'Orders of Colonel Omar,' he said, wondering whether he should tell her about the boy he had shot and killed earlier that day. Deciding not to, it would only bring up the old PTSD issue again and he didn't really have anger management issues, did he?

'I gather you will not be attending our next scheduled group session then?'

'No.' Neither will Sarah Green he thought but let the shrink find that out for herself.

'In that case there's not much I can do at present. I would like to see Rania when she is back home but in the meantime I can give you something to read.' With that she rose and, excusing herself, left the room. He could hear her giving instructions to the secretary and after a few minutes she came back and handed him a printed article in a slim manila folder. 'This is an article about teenage angst and suicide ideation.' A thought had her add, 'has Rania ever shown signs of harming herself?'

'God, no!'

'Good. There is a syndrome but we won't go into it now.' She glanced at her watch and said something about another engagement and Riad promised to reschedule an appointment as soon as he was back from his trip.

After he left she went behind her desk and sat there thinking for a while. Then, using her mobile, she dialled a number from memory.

The other side picked up after five rings, 'Yes?'

'We have a problem –'

Once outside the heat was stifling and pausing on the sidewalk to remove his jacket, toss it in the back of the car, Riad's mobile rang. Was there a different ringtone when it was his mother? He knew it was absurd but somehow he always knew when it was Yvette without even glancing at the caller ID. A kind of negative telepathy he thought wryly as he fished out the phone.

'Hello, *maman*, so nice to hear your voice, I trust you are well?' he answered, aware of that familiar feeling of faint apprehension.

'Not that you care,' came the reproachful reply, 'and don't call me that, I'm Yvette, remember?' She was speaking in French and as usual Riad had to concentrate to keep up. He wondered if there was a man present, she liked to phone when there was a new gentleman caller as Riad thought of the seemingly endless array of shysters, actor people and gigolos that was her world. The trick was to subtly introduce the new man, who was invariably world famous in Beirut, in the hope that Riad would mention this to his father. How sad that two old people who had loved each other that much could never reach that little bit of compromise that would have ensured lasting happiness.

'*Qui ma* – Yvette, I was meaning to phone last night but things have been so busy at work that –'

'I have tried to phone Rania several times now. She is not answering and her Facebook page is down. Even my emails go unanswered. I want to know what is wrong!'

Aware that passing motorists were staring at him standing in the blazing sun he got behind the wheel and started the air conditioner, opening a window to let the hot air out. As always he could not decide whether it made sense to initially open or shut a window but then he would usually be driving, wouldn't he? With an effort banishing the irreverent thought, the phone suddenly slippery in his grasp, he decided to plunge right into it.

'There has been an accident, an incident. Rania is in hospital, she took some pills—'

He was cut short by a loud wail on the other side followed by a few seconds of stunned silence when he could hear her breathing and traffic noises in the background. Then a barrage of questions. Patiently warding off countless interruptions he told her all he knew which now seemed not much.

'I was thinking of sending her over to stay with you in Beirut for a while, just for the school holidays, give me time to decide what to do.'

'Well– there is a small problem--' Yvette Ayoub replied which startled him, normally she would be delighted to see her only grandchild.

When he was silent she went on, 'You see, I'm planning to leave for a holiday in Australia, in ten days.'

'In Australia—'

'Yes! I'm visiting Vytas and Bubba! They live down there now. Big businessmen and making lots of money.'

Uncle Vytas and Uncle Francois "Bubba" Ayoub. Brothers of Yvette and what some police forces would refer to as well known

Lebanese underworld identities. How on earth could they have been allowed into Australia and how come he only learnt of that now?

For a moment he thought of asking as much, decided he did not have the energy.

'Where in Australia?' he asked.

'Melbourne!' she gushed dreamily, 'such a beautiful city! The restaurants along the river, the snow topped mountains in the distance, the young men in striped blazers rowing their ladies along the banks while music wafts across—'

'Yes, yes. Quite,' he said hastily before the narrative became even more bizarre. By a quick calculation there was at least three different cities in that picture, not to mention time periods, but what the heck, she was an artiste after all.

Instead he told her of his own impending trip and after a short discussion it was agreed that Rania would fly over to Beirut where Yvette would look after her, at least for the next week or so until other arrangements could be made.

There was just this one thing he had to ask and, as always it wasn't easy. 'You don't perhaps have a guest staying over at the moment? I mean-- well, you know?'

There was an iciness in her voice when she replied, 'It is not natural for a woman of my status to go about in society unescorted, Riad. My private affairs is none of your business!' Adding, after a moment's hesitation, my friend Pierre visits often and, besides being a highly sought after ladies hairdresser, is a very nice and handsome young man.'

Another "beard" as Shakespeare would have termed it was the inescapable conclusion but, at least, harmless in a sense, Yvette was far too astute to be fleeced financially by any of the passing parade of escorts.

'That's fine, Yvette. I just don't want Rania to be in the way, you know?' he offered placatingly.

'My Rania is always welcome to visit and I wish you would come along, wouldn't it be nice to have a family reunion at last?' With a feeling of mounting trepidation he agreed.

There followed a further five minutes of discussion regarding arrangements culminating with the promise that he would get Rania to speak to her later that day if she was better.

When he tried to start the car the battery was flat.

———————◆———————

The Colonel had insisted Riad file a report on the day's events – just another way of covering his own backside – and on his way down to the station he swung by the hospital to see Rania.

She was awake and smiling wanly when he came into the room. The ashen features were accentuated by the raven black tresses draped around her head against the white backdrop of a pillow and the hand lying on the sheet was icily cold when he stroked it.

'I'm sorry…' she whispered, dark eyes looking at him but not quite meeting his.

'It's OK, darling,' he said stupidly, placing the chocolates he had bought in the hospital foyer next to her.

She had been moved to a private room on the eight floor and he was pleased to see that flowers he had sent up earlier had been neatly arranged in a vase on a small table. The room was light and airy with cheerful prints on the walls and a view of a purple sea in the distance, the light of day fast fading.

From the corridor wafted the sounds of a busy place and he thought of closing the door but had been told not to by the nursing staff.

Words did not come easy and he kept it to the mundane. The cat was good and he would remember to feed her. No, he had not spoken to Miss Johnson (a lie.) Her own response was lethargic, monosyllabic and Riad realised now was not the time to talk about what had happened. Nor about the planned trip to Australia.

He saw her eyes resting on the blood stain on his sleeve and hastily covered it with a hand. As he stared at his daughter he marvelled at how much she looked like her mother and, as always, it hurt. More than when he strove to see something of himself there knowing full well that he never would.

She walks in beauty, like the night.

———————

Of cloudless climes and starry skies
And all that's best of dark and bright
Meet in the aspect of her eyes...

The lines of Byron's classic poem was still in his thoughts when a soft voice behind him said, 'Rania and I had a quiet talk just a while ago. She is feeling better now and we've agreed to talk again later.'

Glancing up he saw it was a young nurse, Irish judging by the accent and with shiny auburn hair tied in a bun. The green eyes were kindly, the even smile somehow highlighting the faint freckles on her cheeks. He thought she looked quite beautiful.

No ring on her finger.

What is wrong with you, Riad?! Why does this sexual thing always pop up at times of extreme stress? Was it the organism's instinct to procreate when staring death in the face? But what death?

'Thank you. I guess she needs to talk to a woman sometimes. Her mother is –'

'I know,' the nurse whose name tag read Sr Mary McInnes, said gently, 'Rania told me.'

'Yes. When will she be ready for discharge?' he said, hastily adding, 'there's no hurry. I'll have to make some arrangements you understand.'

'Speak to Dr Agarwal to-morrow, he does a round at eight and I'm sure will have news for you then.'

And with that she was gone, leaving behind the hint of an exquisite perfume. It was a specialty of Riad's and it bothered him that he could not identify the brand.

19
CHAPTER

It was after dark when he arrived home. On the way over he had stopped off at the neighbourhood branch of the Sultan Centre Food Mall to buy a few essentials and a smiling Ali helped him carry it from the car.

The elevator was still working, had been for more than a week now and he decided to take this as a good omen. Another positive was that Suleiga, the maid, had been in and had left a chicken curry on the stove as well as cooked rice.

Deciding he wasn't hungry after all he fed the cat then opened a beer and sat in a lounge chair to watch TV. Idly channel surfing he stayed with LBC long enough to watch his mother interviewing some gushing Lebanese starlet. As usual she was showing her good profile angle and as always the makeup was skilfully applied. Still a good looking woman at, how old was she now? He wondered whether she still sang, he knew she did the odd cameo role in drama productions, the sickly sweet sentimental stuff of Arab television, the kind he never watched.

Finally settling on a movie channel showing an old western featuring a swaggering John Wayne, he let his mind drift back to the events of the day.

The Maddie Green case. It seemed he was now formally assigned to it, working with Waleed. Over a coffee earlier the sergeant had brought him up to speed as to where they were with the investigation.

Captain Farsi had covered a lot of ground in a short time and Riad had been impressed. He had known the man as a dedicated professional with a degree in criminal psychology from a lesser American university who had a serious scholarly disposition but nevertheless loved to share a joke with colleagues.

Just what had he uncovered to lead to his murder?

Some of the work had not been included in the file Riad had been studying earlier and Waleed had found extra material from the dead man's locker after gaining access to it.

Consisting of no more than a dozen pages in the captain's sprawling handwriting it was cryptic with many abbreviations and it was all about Maddie Green. Except, when it was about Sarah Green Abdul-Karim.

Born in London's East End twenty seven years ago to a heroin addicted streetwalker mother Sarah never knew her father. At the age of two years and three months she was placed in foster care, the mother dying not long after from suspected AIDS. Over the years Sarah rotated through a number of foster homes, all in the district of greater London, finally graduating from high school and, on a government grant, enrolling for a law degree.

Six months into her studies she was spotted by a talent scout in the crowd at a football game. A modelling contract followed and she never looked back.

Her stunning good looks coupled with a classic A frame dress size ten and correct height made her a no-brainer for the kind of ramp model the haute couture houses were looking for. The haughty look in those startlingly blue eyes didn't hurt either.

Nine months later she was living in Paris and a supermodel earning millions. There followed the usual flurry of affairs with influential men and movie stars until, six years ago, she married the multi-millionaire hotelier, Ross Green.

Two years later a daughter, Madison (Maddie) was born by caesarean section. Withdrawing from the modelling scene to care for Maddie the baby girl proved to be a sickly child from early on. There were multiple hospital admissions under a variety of diagnoses and over a period of two years the opinions of a number of Paris's prominent child specialists as well as their London counterparts were sought.

No specific underlying cause for the child's presentations of myriad aches and pains as well as apparent gastrointestinal presentations was ever found. By all appearances the child seemed to meet the required milestones for a normal age related girl.

There was never any suggestion of trauma or injury.

After a period of absence Sarah returned to the modelling world and was often photographed with her baby daughter, usually with a nanny in attendance.

Often the gossip magazines would be eager for snippets of news from the life of the glamour couple and quite often the discussion would turn to Sarah's agony over the ill-health of Maddie.

Three years into the marriage Ross and Sarah Green consulted a Dr Lorna Willoughby, a family counsellor in London. No details available.

Two months later Ross Green died during a boating accident on his luxury yacht in the Mediterranean. Sarah, who had been on board in the company of half a dozen guests, was overcome with grief and withdrew from public life for five months. When next seen on the circuit she was on the arm of financier Hasan Abdul-Karim who had been a family friend and business associate of Green.

Abdul-Karim had been one of the onboard guests the night Green was inexplicably lost overboard while at sea, his body never found.

After a six month period of mourning during which the model was seldom seen in public and then always dressed in black, Sarah and Abdul-Karim were married and she gave up modelling fulltime to accompany her husband on his frequent business journeys which took them from Europe to the USA to the Middle East and Kuwait City where Abdul-Karim had extensive business interests.

During these trips, often lasting two to three weeks, young Maddie would sometimes be left in the care of a nanny at the couple's London home. These trips away appeared to coincide with periods where Maddie's general health improved with less frequent visits to the doctors.

There followed a brief note on Abdul-Karim who hailed from a wealthy Kuwaiti family with interests mainly in construction. A financial wizard the young man studied at MIT before taking a position in Silicon Valley where he proved to be a genius programmer involved in developing software. After two years he left and disappeared from view, emerging a year later with an innovative software system that revolutionised online financial transactions. He sold it to a major company for four hundred million US dollars and entered the world of finance becoming, at the age of thirty five, one of the most prominent businessmen of his generation.

An earlier arranged marriage to Sana Jassem, daughter of a wealthy Kuwaiti businessman, ended after two years when she filed for divorce citing the husband's refusal to have a child. A dowry settlement was reputedly negotiated, no details ever disclosed.

When seen about in public with young Maddie present she was often seen hand in hand with her stepfather and by all appearances the two seemed close.

When Maddie was three she once again went through a period of poor health leading to frequent visits to medical specialists including three hospitalisations. Multiple special investigations were carried out but no surgery, this despite the mother's insistence that something was wrong and that exploratory surgery should be considered.

Four months later and six months before Maddie disappeared, Abdul-Karim arranged for the family as a unit to be seen by renowned child psychologist, Dr Richard Turner, at London's Great Ormond Street Children's Hospital.

Following three sessions the psychologist suggested Maddie be admitted for a period of observation. Sarah refused and terminated all further appointments.

There are no records of the child falling ill between then and the time of her disappearance.

There followed a list of contacts, some of which had been in the file originally handed to Riad.

The question was, why did Farsi not include this in the official police file? And why was it handwritten and not typed on the captain's office computer? Was it because he suspected he was being hacked?

His instinct told him Farsi had formed a theory regarding the case and was following it up, also that he was working alone, not sharing the findings with anyone which was a worry in itself. After a while Riad decided to give it a rest and padded off to the kitchen in search of another beer.

While heating up a plate of curry and rice in the microwave his thoughts turned to the imminent trip to Australia. What exactly was expected of him? More specific, why him when he had only met the child's mother the once and how did she even find out that he was looking into Maddie' disappearance?

The Colonel, he decided. When pressed the man, eager to please when *wasta* was the name of the game, had ratted on him, no doubt with enough spin to brand him as his top investigator.

Reclaiming his chair in front of the TV he switched channels while picking at the curry. He finally found what he was looking for on Sky News UK, the tail end of an update on the Maddie Green case. The discovery of the body of the little girl in the suitcase was big news in Britain and there was growing public demand for Scotland Yard to be involved in the investigation.

The Assistant Commissioner was on camera explaining that his department was in regular contact with the Melbourne Metropolitan Police and was being of assistance with investigating certain aspects of the case of a sensitive nature.

He declined to comment further, promising for an update at a later date.

The newsreader moved on to an interview with Sarah Green conducted during a recent visit to London. The ex-model was waif-like in appearance, her hair tied back in a bun and spoke in a hesitant soft voice as she pleaded to the kidnappers to please be in contact with the family. The blue eyes were larger than ever with dark circles faintly visible.

She looked more beautiful than ever and Riad wondered whether she had ever considered an acting career. She would have been good.

20
CHAPTER

The man in the navy blue pinstriped suit walked through the main entrance of the vast Los Angeles Convention Centre at exactly ten minutes to ten o' clock on the second morning of the E3 International Gamer's Convention.

He knew it was ten minutes to ten o' clock without glancing at the expensive watch on his wrist because that was how he had timed it. Exactly ten minutes would be required to make his way through the massive throng of gamers in the main foyer, all moving from console to console like so many rats in search of a byte that would satisfy that insatiable need for just a minute or two.

The meeting with the Russian was scheduled for ten o' clock, it would not do to be early or to be late. The potential buyers had been adamant on that. The transaction would be delicate and there would be eyes and ears about, electronic spying equipment even, and the small meeting room had been carefully chosen and swept for bugs that very morning.

Unlike many of the mostly young people milling about he was not shouldering a backpack but carried a slim black leather briefcase. When the security detail checked it they found an Apple laptop plus two small solid state electronic devices that the man explained was to do with a new game his company, Al Jumaih Electronics Pty Ltd with its headquarters in Kuwait City, was introducing. On checking his credentials and confirming he had an appointment at the Sony stall he was let through with a cheerful Have a Nice Day.

Tall and handsome he was noticed by more than one of the young ladies as he moved with graceful ease through the crowd, politely exchanging nods and greetings from gaming representatives who instinctively sensed this was no ordinary kid out spending their pocket money.

Had anyone managed to engage him in conversation they would have noticed that, despite his Arab or possibly Pakistani appearance, he spoke beautifully modulated English with the slightest trace of a foreign accent. The eyes remained hidden behind designer shades yet one knew they were intelligent eyes, perhaps slightly mocking as was the hint of a smile on wickedly cruel lips.

The fragrance was Versace and just subtle enough to arouse interest.

If he noticed hungry eyes looking him over as he passed one would be blonde starlet after another he shook it off with no more effort as would a thoroughbred an annoying swarm of flies. His thrills lay elsewhere and, as he headed for the broad staircase to the first floor, he felt his pulse racing as excitement built. This was it! Two years of unceasing hard work and now he was about to pitch his product, his genius.

Passing through a second large hall he paused for a few seconds to gaze at the newest first person shooter game playing out on a huge screen with the large crowd on the main floor as well as two balconies watching in rapt silence at the latest magic on offer from the world of virtual reality.

The graphics were fantastic, he had to admit, but how could it ever compete with the images from the real world, what he was offering? The unrivalled thrill of the real kill?

Smiling to himself he checked his watch and walked quickly to the stairs taking them two at a time while silently miming the words of a Leonard Cohen song that had come into his head for no reason at all.

The smartly dressed young woman hovering at the doors to private viewing room number 67B stepped forward as he approached, smiling as she studied his business card before handing it back and motioning him inside with a Welcome Mr Masters, Mr Ruslan is expecting you.

A discreet sign taped to a door informed the viewer that this was where Hazelton Enterprises Incorp could be found.

Once inside a small anteroom his briefcase was checked by a non-smiling man of indeterminate age with a shaved head and the suggestion of a tattoo just peeking out from under his crisp white shirt collar. The man calling himself Masters stood still as he was expertly patted down finally being handed back his briefcase and being ushered through to an inner room. No words were exchanged as none were necessary.

Two men rose from where they were seated at a table to shake hands, the fat Russian introducing his companion as a Mr Walsh, a New York based lawyer and business associate.

Both men were smartly dressed in sober business suits with the lawyer adding a touch of flair sporting a diamond studded tie clip and cufflinks to match.

If Mr Ruslan was aware of cake crumbs down the front of his necktie and barrel chest he chose to ignore it.

The handshake was firm and fleshy, the small grey eyes speculative. 'Welcome. Please be seated.' Turning to the hovering young woman he indicated she should bring over some refreshments for Mr Masters. They were enjoying a fifteen year old single malt and he should join them.

Masters knew this was not an invitation, a request even. The Russian did not do requests. Accepting the tumbler with a gracious bow he made a show of taking a sip while trying not to grimace as the raw liquor burned its way down the back of his throat. He was not a drinking man and could never understand how anyone could stomach this stuff but nevertheless made a brave show of it.

'Shall we get down to business?' Ruslan said as he motioned the girl to refill their glasses, adding, 'How you Americans say, talk chicken?' The latter with a guffaw and a friendly jab at Walsh's sleeve.

'Turkey. Talk turkey,' the American said impassively as he watched Masters unpack the laptop connecting it with a cable to the large screen at one end of the room.

'I take it you have studied my demonstration tape?' he asked hoarsely, the whisky fumes still there and choking him.

Ruslan nodded, 'We find it most interesting. Which is why we invited you here, to-day. To ask for a demonstration.'

Walsh nodded, 'If what you showed us is genuine, not something faked in a digital lab, there could be some interesting uses for our organisation.'

Interesting choice of words, Masters thought, "organisation" rather than company. But then he already knew that, did he not?

'Then let me show you,' he said. Taking a small removable hard drive from an inside pocket he slotted it into the laptop and quickly brought up the images stored there, including a short video clip.

The first was a standard Farpoint VR head and face covering helmet as used in the latest virtual reality shooter games. 'From all outward appearances this apparatus is standard, as can be purchased anywhere. I have however made some changes, such as the 120 degree forward viewing camera which connects by radio link to a console with a range of three miles. Secondly, via the same radio link, the controller can talk to the gamer – I prefer to call the person a gamer,' he added with a slight smile, 'for that is what they think they are doing, just a game.'

The next image showed the inside of the helmet and here he pointed to a small barely noticeable aperture set to one temporal side. 'This is a recessed three inch steel bolt which, when fired by remote control, is propelled by a small compressed air cartridge penetrating the skull and killing the gamer.'

'I like it!' the Russian shouted, thumping the table and grinning like an excited schoolboy. 'No more worry about the hitman being caught. What you say, Walsh?'

His eyes hooded, the lawyer said nothing.

A sudden look of suspicion clouded the fat man's features, 'How you make the kid wear this mask? He does not notice this, this sharp thing?'

'During the early phases of his conditioning I have him use a standard VR helmet. For the actual event I tell him this is a new model, specially modified for use in the next phase of the game.'

'The video we have seen is very impressive, I take it this one you are now rolling is another hit?' the American said, the voice unexpectedly soft, almost speculative as he watched the graphic scene unrolling.

'This was recorded only days ago, in Kuwait City. Here the boy was playing a samurai game I designed. Note the graphic detail. The target was a local computer hacker who had been threatening to stumble onto our other business.'

'The girls—'

'Yes. Rest assured, I stopped him before he could do any damage.'

The American stirred in his chair, produced a slim silver cigarette case from an inside pocket and accepted a light from the young woman who was doing the rounds, refilling glasses. 'Ah, yes, the hacker. Tell us about your dealings with him.'

Masters hesitated, this was the one weak spot in his setup. Eyeing his refilled glass with a degree of apprehension he pressed on, 'Early in the development of this program, when our business was still only with the pornography and trafficking, I needed some help with certain technical aspects this man was of help with. Even then I realised that he was a security risk and may have to be eliminated later, so I gained access to his computer while he was called away for an hour—something I organised – and tapped into his desktop cam as well as installing a small remotely controlled explosive charge.'

'Hmm,' Blowing a smoke circle at the ceiling Walsh sounded sceptical, 'and you are quite sure there is no trail leading to you, to us?'

'Yes. No comebacks.' Did he sound a bit too self assured there? He thought not.

'Who were those two men in the room when this computer guy was killed?' It was the Russian who had dug up a large cigar from somewhere and was now puffing away steadily, acrid plumes of blue drifting across the table.

'The older one is a detective, a Lieutenant Ajmi. The other one I suspect is a colleague. I do not know the nature of their business with the dead man.'

This merited a minute of silent meditation during which the two business associates exchanged glances while Masters brought up more images on the screen.

'Arab detectives,' Ruslan snorted, 'camel herders only good for beating up little people. They pose no risk to us.'

His associate seemed less certain but said nothing. Finally a decision seemed to be made, 'We will want to see first hand the preparation involved in such a hit, the programming of the boy.'

'Of course. I at this very moment have a boy in training, he should be ready soon. If you would care to visit—'

'I will come myself,' Ruslan said as he reached for his glass, downed the contents in a single gulp. 'I love this idea of using young boys, never before! No-one will see it coming!'

Walsh looked at his watch, 'I have another appointment, a new product Atari wants us to look at promoting.' He pointed at the laptop Masters was placing back in the briefcase, 'This is all very exciting and there is certainly a market for something like this. But let us not forget our main business, the playgirls. I for one am very pleased to see our latest little star being such a sensation.' Stubbing out his cigarette he rose and turning to their guest said, 'How much do you want?'

Meeting his gaze Masters said, 'Twenty million US dollars now, another twenty million on successful implementation of the program.'

'The money will be in your account by to-morrow,' Ruslan said, rising to shake hands with the parting comment that they would be in touch.

The meeting was over.

Following the American out the door Masters paused to check a new SMS confirming his flight out later that day. From the corner of his eye he saw the young lady going through another door to a room beyond where the outlines of a couch was visible. She was undoing her top and followed by a lumbering Ruslan who clutched the whisky bottle in a ham like fist.

Had he been that way inclined he might have been jealous but his pleasures lay elsewhere. Suppressing a chuckle he followed Walsh out the door which the bodyguard closed before taking up his position once more. The man's unblinking gaze was as deadpan as before.

21
CHAPTER

The other girl had arrived the night before last and she only became aware of her being there the next morning when Martha told her. The girl's name was Minnie and she was only three years old. Her mommy also had to go away and would also come back soon to fetch her.

Minnie was a scared little girl as she had not been away from home before and that was why she cried so much. They had met that morning when Martha had fixed them breakfast and this time there was extra treats, pancakes with lots of syrup and a yummy milkshake too.

Minnie had not wanted to eat hers but Martha said that was alright, she would soon feel better and why did they not all go into the living room and play with all the toys there?

It would have been nice if they could go outside and play in the shadows of the big old tree but Ken had locked the doors although she knew Martha also had keys she carried in her apron pocket.

She asked her and Martha said Minnie was still new and could easily wander off and get lost and there were snakes and spiders out there. Bad things that could hurt her.

But, she knew, the bad things that would hurt Minnie was inside this house, when the uncles came.

Minnie's skin was dark and her hair was black and very curly. Her frock was ugly and too big and Martha said she needed a good scrub and Ken said she was an Abo kid and they had better check for lice as well.

Even the next day Minnie was still crying for her granny and when asked about her mommy she would cry even more.

By the afternoon of the third day they started Minnie's lessons and Maddie was allowed to sit and watch as long as she kept quiet. Minnie looked different now with her thick hair all fluffed out and shiny and a pretty tiara on top. The stones in the tiara would sparkle when she turned and the light caught them. Gone was the dirty old frock and in its place a nice party dress with lots of stiff petticoats that had it stand out just like a princess, also with the lace up ballet slippers.

Martha had placed a silvery bracelet on her wrist and Minnie would look down at it in wonder every so often.

First they started with the dancing steps. Just taking it slow with Ken putting on the music and nodding his head in approval when, under the patient coaching of Martha, she started getting it right.

At times, when Minnie would sit down and cry and refuse to practice any more, she wanted to go up to her and show her how easy the moves were and tell her that there would be ice cream but Ken would give her a stern look and once again remind her that once the camera rolled they were not allowed to use any names.

Minnie had her own room down the corridor and so far no uncles had come to visit her. Ken seemed to be growing more restless and moody by the day and in the evenings, after the girls had been fed and were allowed to play together in the lounge for a while before bed, she could hear him arguing with Martha in the kitchen.

There was a man coming, they did not seem to know when but Ken was worried about this and so was Martha.

It was on the morning of the fourth day that she and Minnie first played together with the camera on them. No dancing this time, just the two of them lying together on the thick pile carpet and dressed in their nighties. At first they were told to just talk to each other and to giggle a lot but Minnie did not want to so Ken told Maddie to rub Minnie's tummy and slowly run her hands down her thighs.

Minnie went all rigid when she did this but Maddie just smiled at her and said it would be OK, she would see. Then, while she was caressing Minnie Ken said she should put her free hand on her own tummy then into her knickers and make low moaning noises.

This reminded her of when the uncles came and she did not like it and Martha stepped up and told Ken it was enough now and time the girls had a break, suggesting a walk outside while it was still nice and not too cold.

Ken scowled at her but said nothing. Later that day he went into town leaving Martha to look after them. This time Martha did not send them to their rooms as before but let them play in the lounge with the television on the Cartoon Network channel. Spongebob Squarepants was on and Maddie loved it but Minnie wanted to see what movie was on the Disney channel so Maddie went over and changed the channel, although she knew this was not allowed.

Scrolling through the channels she suddenly found herself frozen, the control dropping from her grasp. She was staring at a photo of herself, taken at her last birthday party with her smiling at the camera and waving. A man was talking but the blood was rushing in her ears and she could not make out the words. Then the picture was gone to be replaced by two people sitting opposite each other with the logo of a TV news station in the background, the man asking a question. The camera shifted to the face of the woman and a cry escaped from Maddie's lips.

It was Mommy and she was crying and---

'What the hell are you doing?!!' Martha screamed as she roughly yanked her away from the television screen, scrambling for the control and quickly turning the TV off.

Staring up at Martha in shock Maddie could see the woman's face had gone quite white and her whole body was shaking. From the corner of her eye she could see that Minnie had recoiled to the far end of the room and was staring at them with widened eyes.

Then something unexpected happened. Martha sank down in the nearest armchair and, still holding onto Maddie, put her arms around her and waved for Minnie to come over as tears ran down her cheeks. 'Oh you poor poor babies,' she said softly, over and over again.

22
CHAPTER

Detective Inspector Josh Reed sat back in his chair and stretched, yawned, gazed out the window. A dreary Melbourne winter's day outside, wet and windblown, it was warm and stuffy in the small room he shared with three other members of the Sexual Offences and Child Abuse Investigation, North West Metropolitan Branch (SOCIT)

His fellow officers were out on a case, the visitor's chair now occupied by a burly man in a raincoat that looked a size too small. Clean shaven with ruddy features above generous jowls that moved when he spoke, or in his case growled, he had small watery eyes that looked disapprovingly down a pitted nose that looked like it had been punched once too often.

'How sure are you she's the girl in the porn video?'

The vice cop who went by the name of Doyle shrugged, 'We're pretty sure the footage was shot in Oz, in one of the frames our technical boys reckon they saw a flock of corellas reflected in a glass fronted background picture. Amateurish but then these bozos usually are amateurs. The girl looks about four, the age of Maddie Green, and she's blonde.'

'Could be dyed, of course. Or a wig?'

'Sure, or a fucking thirty five year old midget with no tits and no bum.' Seeing something in the other man's eyes Doyle spread the shovels he used for hands in a placatory gesture and added ' Okay,

okay! Why bother? It's not like the punters are looking at the hair colour, for chrissake!'

Sighing Reed turned back to the desk and pulled over the file the vice cop had brought over. It was slim, no more than half a dozen pages and in silence he read through it once more.

Marked confidential, it was a transcript copy of a report by a Scotland Yard detective regarding a break-in at the Great Ormond Street Children's Hospital, London, two years earlier.

Detective Inspector John Williams was called to the scene, the office of a staff child psychiatrist Dr Richard Turner at five minutes past midnight where a burglar had been apprehended inside the office by security personnel. The man sustaining a head injury in the ensuing struggle and dying twenty four hours later from a severe brain injury.

He was subsequently identified as Stanley James, an elderly low rate private investigator with a run down office in a seedy part of Soho. There was no secretary and perusal of the man's files, stacked in open faced cardboard boxes, revealed a client's list of life's rather sadder battlers.

One name did stand out. A Mr Ruslan with the address given as the Connaught Hotel. The date was two days before the break-in. Next to it, scribbled in pencil, was the amount of five thousand pounds. Nothing else.

Subsequent enquiries had confirmed that Mr Ruslan had stayed for three nights, no forwarding address given. A copy of his passport had shown him to be a Russian citizen. He did not appear on police radar, no recorded interest.

The hapless Mr James had been disturbed by security officers within minutes of the alarm being triggered and when confronted he appeared to be ransacking through an open filing cabinet drawer. During the ensuing struggle a patient's file slipped from under his jacket and was retrieved and placed on the consultant's desk. When DI Williams arrived he flicked through the file only to be confronted by an out of breath Dr Turner, the psychiatrist shivering in an old dressing gown, who snatched the file away, stressing that all information stored there was strictly patient confidential.

The name on the file was Madison Green, daughter of Sarah Green.

There followed a list of technical aspects regarding routine police work related to the case, nothing of interest being discovered.

Then came the interesting bit, added in handwriting at the bottom of the last page. Doyle had confirmed that the writing was his, the fruit of a telephone conversation between himself and DI Williams (ret.) Speaking in strict confidence to Doyle the inspector had revealed that he had been ordered by no less than the police commissioner to delete any reference to the Green file in his report. He was not to contact Ms Green or her husband. The case was essentially closed.

Pressed by Doyle the Scotland Yard inspector could recall only one term that stuck in his mind. It had been added as a footnote on an inside flyleaf and, scribbled in red and accentuated, it read MS? FDIA?' He was not positive that he recalled it exactly and a medical acquaintance had wondered if the MS referred to multiple sclerosis? Williams had not followed it up as another high profile case demanded his attention.

Closing the folder Reed pushed it away and ran his fingers through his hair, 'what made you contact the poms regarding Sarah Green?'

'As you know this has been viewed as primarily the kidnap of a rich man's kid. That's why it came to Vice and not Child Protection. It's only now that no ransom is forthcoming and these porno videos turn up that things change. In kidnap cases we have learned to investigate the family as well. Just to make sure it's not one of those weird family games between parents we see now and then. It took a bit of effort to track down DI Williams, he's retired now, but I was lucky to get a tip off from a police clerk who remembered him fondly.'

A whirring noise from the big man's inside jacket pocket was followed by Tina Turner singing "You're simply the best. Better than all the rest--"

Retrieving the device with a grunt Doyle mumbled something about being there in ten minutes and pushed back his chair. 'Gotta go,' he said, straightening his loosely knotted necktie and reaching for an overstuffed briefcase. 'Keep the file and, oh, you might be interested to know that I looked into that incident on the Green yacht, the time the husband disappeared?'

Small eyes twinkled as he studied Reed for a reaction. None forthcoming he shrugged, adding, 'One of the guests on board the pleasure palace that night was a certain Mr Ruslan—Knock yourself out!'

And with that he was gone leaving behind a faint hint of Old Spice cologne and a thoughtful Detective Inspector Reed.

23

CHAPTER

lancing over Riad saw that Sarah Green was still asleep, stretched out on the extended First Class seat, the thin blanket pulled up to her chin and not quite hiding those legs that seemed to go on forever but probably stopped at her hips.

She was beautiful. Even after more than eight hours flying following a two hour layover at Dubai Airport she looked as fresh and flawless as always. The startling thing was that, unlike so many of today's young celebrities, everything about that famous face was real. No trace of silicone, no signs of Botox yet, none of the ridiculously long false eyelashes so much in vogue with the young set these days.

Just the slightest hint of cosmetics, subtle yet there just like the expensive perfume that teased his senses when she turned in her restless sleep.

She was dreaming now, he knew that from the twitching and the rapid eye movement just visible under fluttering eyelids, the quickened breathing. And she was saying something, the words too faint for him to make out. Papa? Could that be? A small child's voice yes, but "papa?"

What secrets hid behind those beautiful sapphire eyes? He could only wonder but there was this growing, nagging, feeling that the ultimate clue as to what happened to Maddie Green, lay with beautiful, enigmatic, Sarah Green.

Laying his head back against the softness of the cushion and returning the smile of the hovering airline hostess while accepting an offered glass of orange juice, the words of the Peter Sarstedt song came to him,

But where do you go my lovely
When you're alone in your bed?
Tell me the thoughts that surround you
I want to look inside you head, yes I do...

A glance at his watch showed there was an hour to go before landing at Melbourne's Tullamarine Airport and any moment now they would be serving breakfast. Easing himself into a more comfortable position he adjusted the reading light and picked up the lever arch file resting on his lap once more.

Unable to sleep on planes he had read through its contents during the night, every little scrap. It had been handed to him by Hasan Abdul-Karim at the Kuwait Airport with the explanation that it contained all the information he had gathered since the disappearance of his stepdaughter. He had once again apologized that he would not be joining them for at least the next five days as urgent business matters in Los Angeles dictated his immediate presence.

Sarah would show him around the city which had become their second home and he was eagerly waiting to hear Riad's opinion once he had met up with the investigating police officer in Melbourne.

Flipping open the lid he idly paged through the contents again. Most of it were newspaper and magazine clippings, the latter invariably including a photograph of the anxious mother, often posing with a sweetly smiling little Maddie. The occasional family photo with Abdul-Karim looking slightly uneasy while baring his evenly matched teeth without really smiling. It was the picture of a shy man more than anything else.

A lot of the cuttings were from the Australian press as expected but also from their London counterparts, especially the tabloids. One photo from *The Guardian* stood out, a paparazzi shot taken with a long lens of Sarah crossing a Chelsea street, her features for once looking haggard and visibly upset. It was the only picture of the model Riad could recall where she did not look ravishing, as if the camera had caught her in that one unguarded moment when the mask fell away.

You talk like Marlene Dietrich
And you dance like Zizi Jeanmaire
Your clothes are all made by Balmain
And there's diamonds and pearls in your hair...
But where do you go my lovely
When you're alone in your bed?

There were interviews of the couple by the police and lots of backstories mainly of Sarah but also of Abdul-Karim and their jet set lifestyle.

Some articles speculating on where Maddie could be now if she was alive and some of where she would be if not.

There was an interview with the nanny who had travelled with the family but had taken ill with food poisoning the day before and had been a patient at the Epworth Private Hospital on the night Maddie was taken.

There was even a transcript of a tape recording made during a session with a clairvoyant, a Madame Revetcky. Abdul-Karim had been present and presumably made the recording, probably clandestinely, having it typed out later.

The mystic had told them that Maddie was alive and being well looked after but that trouble was not far away. That there was a journey waiting, not a physical one but emotional, and that the key to finding Maddie, before it was too late, was closer than they thought.

They only had to look, also inside their own hearts.

All in all there was more about Sarah Green, the supermodel, than about the daughter. Even a magazine piece about her earlier life when married to Ross Green and the tragic events that night on their luxury yacht when the businessman was lost overboard, the body never found. "Sarah Green's endless nightmare. How much more punishment will fate heap on the darling of the fashion catwalk?"

The cuttings were filed according to their release dates, the gaps widening as the timeline progressed and the case went cold.

Life, indeed, went on.

The house in Drummond Street, Carlton, was a semi-detached double storey with a tiny front garden and steep steps leading up to the front porch. As he helped the taxi driver retrieve the luggage from the trunk Riad looked the street over. Number 36 was one of a series of identical houses, some with others without wrought iron balconies. Compared to its neighbour it was well appointed with the outside walls painted in a light shade of blue-grey with the imposing stained glass panelled front door in glistening black lacquer and sporting a gleaming polished brass knocker.

Well pruned red and yellow standard roses lined the fashionably worn brick steps. No garages fronted on the street and at a guess those would be at back. Across the road were more of the same Victorian era homes with a modern low rise apartment block on a corner slightly incongruous.

It was a quiet street with little traffic although the CBD was only a few blocks away and downhill. Up the other end and equally close by was busy Lygon Street with its Italian restaurants and city trams.

He stood aside as a young mother pushed a baby stroller past on the sidewalk and reflected that this was the first passer by he had seen and this on a normal Monday morning.

A nice quiet upper middle class neighbourhood. A safe place to raise children. And yet—

Sarah was at the top of the stairs impatiently waiting for him to join her. Chrissie, her personal assistant who had travelled with them, was fiddling with the keypad on the front door, the mobile phone for once not in her hand.

Paying off the cab Riad joined them inside the cool confines of the old house. The immediate impression was that the place had been extensively renovated and modernised. Still there remained the feeling of a more genteel era when the pace of life was slower and people actually received friends at home and sat in lounges and admired bric-a-brac as they talked about children and schools and church bazaars and quite likely the weather.

The ceilings were high and ornately carved, the staircase leading up to the first floor narrow and steep, the planking well worn ancient yellow wood scrubbed down and well polished. A wide corridor led to the back of the house which featured a modern kitchen with sliding glass panels opening onto a tiny walled off courtyard with a rattan couch and a small palm in an oversized earthenware vase. The walls were eight feet high with a neighbour's side window overlooking and a black steel security gate visible to one side.

A back door led to a small pantry and beyond that a single garage opening onto a narrow service lane.

Abdul-Karim's Audi was parked here, the lane empty of any pedestrians.

His bedroom was to be what he reckoned was the original lounge, the first door to the right as one entered the house with a large old style sliding wood framed window looking out onto the street. The solid looking wrought iron burglar bars would have been a later addition. There was a beautiful old Adam fireplace against the back wall, painted white and at a guess no longer in use seeing as the whole place was reverse cycle air conditioned.

Next to the fireplace a connecting door opened to a second, smaller bedroom. Unlike the king sized bed in his own room this one featured two single beds. At a guess it would have been the original dining room.

Apart from the beds and a solitary wing backed armchair in Riad's room the place was sparsely furnished. Spartan almost, which at a guess went with the modern abstract paintings and the artificial flowers in the large weaver basket next to the door.

Built in clothes cupboards lined a wall and like the rest of the room they were painted white.

The whole effect was one of light and airiness.

There was a small downstairs toilet and shower which he presumed was for his use while upstairs Sarah showed him the main bedroom which led out onto the balcony. It shared a modern bathroom with a second bedroom at back which was where Maddie and her nanny had stayed. Normally her personal aide would stay in the other downstairs bedroom but she would now use Maddie's old room.

While Sarah took a shower and freshened up, something that to his surprise took no longer than half an hour, Riad who had showered and shaved on the plane, went over the house with a critical eye. All windows were securely barred offering no point of entry and were possibly an escape hazard in the event of a fire. The back door was solid with a Yale lock and deadbolt whereas the garage had a roll up electronic door and opened up to a short corridor via an access door. The one end led to the back door while the other led to a second door which opened to the outside lane. Both could be locked.

The house was protected by an elaborate alarm system with a panic button strategically place in the kitchen, main bedroom and inside the front door.

The inescapable conclusion was that whoever took Maddie had a key, or at the very least knew the security code to the alarm should the lock on the door somehow have been bypassed.

Or the child had opened the door. But why would she? Surely she had been cautioned regarding strangers, besides judging by the height of the spyglass fitted to the front door, she would not have been able to reach and peer through it.

The more he thought about it, the more it pointed to someone the child knew taking her. But who?

And why?

24
CHAPTER

They breakfasted at one of the many restaurants on the Southbank side of Melbourne's Yarra river, Sarah insisting on an al fresco table next to the public walkway although the day was windy and overcast with light squalls rippling the slow moving water. Dressed warmly in a tweed jacket and corduroy trousers Riad nevertheless felt the odd shiver as a draught whirled amongst the mostly deserted tables. He made a mental note of buying a hat at first opportunity.

Sarah was wearing an ankle length light grey dress over shapely soft leather black boots topped by a maroon bolero jacket and a slim belt from the Gucci collection.

Riad knew it was from the Gucci collection because Sarah, noticing his interest, told him so. The knotted silk scarf was from her own designer collection, the black beret a little something she had picked up during a visit to Paris.

The makeup, as always, was flawless and was it his imagination or had she gone for a slightly paler look that morning?

I might have something to do with their appointment later that morning with DI Reed or perhaps it was just the stress taking its toll.

Beneath the oversized Garboesque shades the eyes were inscrutable as she idly scanned the few passers by. At that early hour these were mainly groups of young women, mothers with babies in prams and the occasional smartly suited young man hurrying along clutching a briefcase and anxiously glancing at his watch.

Seagulls were sunbathing on the cement while keeping a wary collective eye out for any morsel a careless pedestrian might drop. Was it not amazing, Riad thought, how they seemed to line up, all pointing in the same direction. The wind perhaps? Or was it simply a matter of watching your neighbour should someone try and steal a march?

Across the river loomed the impressive skyline of the city with the central Flinders Station bright yellow in the pale early morning sun, the tall skyscrapers at back struggling to break free of their own deep cast shadows.

A bustle of traffic on the distant St Kilda Road bridge, the sounds of the city faint over the water while sparse river traffic moved slowly and seemingly aimlessly by. What a beautiful city, he thought with a sudden hard to place pang of nostalgia for what he knew not. Was it because it reminded him of Paris in a way? It had been said that Melbourne, with its fine cafès and restaurants, its passion for the arts, its cosmopolitan populace, was the most European of Australian cities. He could see that, yet somehow it reminded him of a New York he knew well from his young days.

Was it just the central theme of the river or was it something deeper, a sense of quiet unease that was gnawing at him, a foreboding? The policeman in his genes wondering what this city's underbelly was like and knowing that to be the reason he was here in the first place.

Their food arrived and discovering he was hungry Riad set about demolishing his eggs Benedict with avocado and salmon, delighted to find the Hollandaise sauce done just right with the tangy aftertaste he liked. Chrissie had ordered a poached egg and smashed avocado on sourdough and was idly picking at it while frowning over whatever was occupying her attention on her iPad. The young woman was dressed in a sombre black business suit with white open neck blouse, her shoulder length hair tied back in a tight bun.

Sarah's green salad lay untouched as she exchanged a wan smile with two passers by, elderly ladies and tourists at a guess, who had recognised her and were excitedly waving as they worked their mobile phone cameras.

Riad was thankful that they did not deign to approach while wondering how long it would be before the paparazzi swooped.

Conversation at the table had been sparse and was interrupted by Chrissie pointing out that their appointment at the police station was due in twenty minutes. After a moment's hesitation Sarah daintily lifted a sprig of celery from the salad bowl, frowned as she nibbled at it before tossing it back and declaring herself ready to leave. Drawing back her chair Riad watched her get up and for a moment seem unsteady on the six inch stiletto heels which brought them eye to eye. Steadying herself on his arm as she stooped to retrieve her bag she smiled and said something about a moment of truth and he wasn't sure whether it was about their impending meeting with Detective Inspector Reed or something more personal.

Chrissie had dialled up an Uber driver and, efficient to the minute, she had them ushered into the Melbourne detective's cluttered office at the appointed time. Reed had met with Sarah on previous occasions and the latter did the introductions. If Riad was somewhat bemused to be introduced as "Kuwait City's Finest Detective" he managed to hide it behind a smile and handshake.

Chairs were found and then they were clustered around the detective's desk.

Moving some piled up files to clear a space on his desk Reed reached down for a thick file which he placed in front of him without opening it. 'I tried to contact you yesterday, Miss Green,' he began, apologetically spreading his hands, 'but unfortunately without success. I was hoping to spare you this trip.'

'We were on a flight,' she replied, 'and please call me Sarah.'

'Yes. You see we have identified the young girl whose body was found next to a remote stretch of highway—'

'—In a suitcase—' she added with a visible shudder, eyes suddenly wide.

Reed nodded, went on, 'The good news is it is not your daughter. No need for us to take that DNA sample after all.'

He paused for a moment to allow her time to dab at the corner of an eye with a tissue before continuing. 'The girl was murdered by the boyfriend of her mother, whom he had killed weeks before, afterwards traveling with the child. He was still collecting the dead woman's Centrelink payments and using her bank card, that's how we traced him. He confessed giving us enough details about the child and the crime scene to clinch the case.'

Riad said, 'Centrelink?'

'Australian Social Security.'

Sarah said, 'How dreadful, the poor little thing—' More tissue dabbing followed by a quick glance at a small vanity mirror passed over by Chrissie.

Leaning back in his chair which creaked in protest Reed sighed, 'A not uncommon matter of the parents or carers being responsible for the death of a child. We even have a word for it, filicide. According to a newly released report by the Australian Institute of Criminology a child is killed by a parent about once every fortnight in Australia.' Opening the folder he read from a the top page, 'Between 2000 and 2012 there were 238 incidents of filicide, involving 260 offenders and the deaths of 284 children. In most cases a motive was not known. But where there was a motive two thirds related to a domestic argument. Of those a quarter related to the upbringing of children and 18 percent related to custodial arrangements.'

'How horrible,' Sarah said softly but Reed was not finished yet.

'Filicides accounted for 18 percent of domestic homicide incidents and 7 percent of all homicide events. New South Wales had the largest number of cases with Victoria, including Melbourne, not far behind. Almost a quarter of the victims died by a beating. Others were strangled or suffocated and ten percent were stabbed or drowned.'

'However we have reason to believe that Maddie is alive?' Riad said after a stunned silence where the only sound was Reed's stertorous breathing.

Nodding Reed produced a photograph from the folder which he handed to Sarah, 'I do apologise if this upsets you, Mrs – Sarah – but we have reason to believe this might by your Maddie.'

'Wh...where did you get this?' Sarah asked in a small voice as she studied the photograph of a small blonde girl in a cat mask striking a dancing pose.

'It was forwarded to us by colleagues from the FBI's Child Exploitation Task Force who captured it from a child pornography site. We have been able to access the site and have graphic motion footage that I would rather not show you, it is quite shocking.'

'The child is wearing a mask,' Riad said, 'how can we be sure it is Maddie?'

'There is a program called Image Analysis. It uses different mainly digital tools to study provided images, in the case of the girl in the video clip we are currently comparing it digitally to home videos of Maddie provided by the parents. Our computer enhanced system compares body features including movements and posturing as well as obviously speech patterns. Unfortunately there had not been any of the latter.'

'When will we know for sure?' Sarah asked. Seemingly in control of her emotions again she had moved forward in her chair, white knuckled fists clenched in her lap.

'I expect a report within the next forty eight hours.'

'I want to see the video,' Sarah Green said, a note of determination in her voice.

'Madam I... I would not advise it. It's, well, it's very *graphic* and—'

'I want to see it.' This time her voice was steely, something in the blue eyes having Reed lower his.

'I will need special permission from the chief, the viewing would be in a secure environment and limited to who can be present.' After a moment's hesitation he suggested a time the next afternoon to which Sarah agreed.

'I take it you don't have any further information regarding the search for Maddie?' she asked.

'Nothing so far but we are looking, of course.'

'I suppose no news is good news,' she said wearily. 'Thank you, Mr Reed, until to-morrow then.' With that she rose, stating that, if that's alright, Lieutenant Ajmi would like to stay to hopefully clarify some issues he might be of help with.

Having earlier received Riad's credentials from Colonel Omar in Kuwait Reed had no objection.

In silence they watched the two women leave before resuming their seats. 'Why exactly are you here, Lieutenant?'

'Call me Riad. Firstly, I'm here as a fellow policeman and not in the employ of Mrs Green or her husband. In Kuwait City the family have considerable influence in high circles, to the point where the Minister of Police felt it necessary to instruct my own boss to get involved in the investigation.'

Seeing the incredulous expression on the other man's face Riad held up an apologetic hand while smiling, 'I know, I know! There is nothing to indicate this crime has any connection with my own jurisdiction, other than the individuals involved. However I suspect your office would be as short staffed as we are. Another pair of eyes looking over ground already covered might just suggest a fresh lead, no harm in looking.'

Studying him in silence Reed said nothing. Not for the first time Riad noticed the other man's peculiar habit of every so often blowing on the cupped fingertips of his right hand, a soft almost spitting motion of which Reed seemed totally unaware.

After another moment's staring at his visitor under hooded eyes Reed sighed and pulled over the file. 'It's all in here. All fucking one hundred and forty seven pages of it. Knock yourself out, you can use the desk over there but none of this leaves this office.'

Nodding his appreciation Riad had a few questions. 'Firstly, was there any CCTV footage of the house, perhaps from a camera across the street or a neighbour?'

Reed snorted, 'This is not London where every square metre is covered by camera, my friend. We checked, nothing. I guess in an upmarket quiet neighbourhood like that people didn't see the need.'

'And I suppose no witnesses seeing anyone with a small child get into a car that evening?'

'Unfortunately, no.'

'The nanny checked out? No suspicious contacts, her hospital stay verified?'

'Of course.'

Reaching for the file Riad had one last question, 'Who do you think took Maddie?'

Swivelling his chair to look out the window Reed said, 'It was the stepfather, Abdul-Karim. A case of jealousy, not wanting to share his glamourous wife with anybody, not even a little four year old daughter. This is a man who divorced his previous wife because he didn't want children. A man who has all the money in the world to orchestrate something like this.'

Which, Riad thought, still did not explain why Maddie surfaces in a child porno racket, why she wasn't simply disposed off. Permanently.

25
CHAPTER

It was past three that afternoon when Riad left the police station having had a meat pie and coffee from the downstairs canteen earlier. Reed had introduced him to a few fellow cops and one suggested while he was there he should come along to an Aussie Rules football game – footy he called it. Then he could taste the national dish of a "pie floater" after the game which apparently was a cheap meat pie tossed into a cup of soup and tasted better when consumed after a dozen or so beers. This led to much laughter and Riad made a note to skip the pie floater if possible.

They were a friendly enough bunch and he left with a warm feeling that wherever you went, the world of the enforcer was essentially the same.

The women had gone shopping proving to Riad that when the going gets tough the tough go shopping. Or was that the rich? Same thing he guessed. Deciding to walk he headed up Flinders Street before catching a tram heading into the CBD. Getting off at Elizabeth Street he walked the short distance to the lower end of the Bourke Street Mall where he found a small coffee shop in a side street and ordered a ham and cheese croissant and short black coffee.

The city centre was bustling with foot traffic, everyone seemingly in a hurry with lots of schoolkids in uniform and carrying backpacks. The trams were everywhere, all of them packed and he marvelled at the efficiency of the inner city transport system, also that it was for free.

A truly cosmopolitan city he decided, in a matter of minutes spotting pretty much every race or ethnic group he could think of. And quiet. The traffic flowing smoothly with no-one leaning on a horn and no-one shouting or waving a finger.

Not New York after all was the inescapable conclusion. Yet, like any world city now, people minded their own business. No eye contact with fellow passengers on the trams when everyone appeared engrossed on whatever flitted across their mobile phone screen.

Eyes averted as they passed by the occasional beggar hunched against a wall while careful not to bump into anyone coming the other way which, he thought, was a miracle of sorts seeing they never looked up from the phones.

His mind whirling from scanning the police file he decided to give it a rest and do something he had been putting off ever since arriving the day before.

Phone Uncle Vytas.

An hour later when the Number 96 tram pulled up at St Kilda's Luna Park stop and Riad disembarked his uncles were waiting. Parked close to the grotesque clown's head façade to the theme park the car was easy to spot as no doubt it was intended to be. A small model sedan of no longer youthful vintage it had DEBT COLLECTOR painted down the sides in letters three feet high. The writing in bold black against a garish orange paint job.

Spotting Riad Uncle Vytas got out of the passenger side. This was an exercise in itself due to the man's substantial bulk and the little car rocked and settled slightly to the driver's side when finally freed of its passenger.

'Riad! Little brother! I so happy to see you!'

Wearily accepting the bone crushing handshake and none too gentle slap on the back Riad mumbled something suitable in reply and let himself be led back to the car where he could see a bearded and widely grinning Uncle Francois, better known as Bubba, behind the wheel.

'Welcome, welcome!' growled the younger brother, 'we all so happy to see little nephew! Much happy!' At least, Riad mused, this one got the family connection right.

'Nice to see you again, Uncle Bubba,' he said mechanically as the little car ground into motion with the meshing of protesting gears. With two virtual gorillas jostling for space in the front he was amazed to find that Bubba seemed to have no difficulty working the manual shift although a little more finesse might have been helpful.

'Pliss,' Vytas said over his shoulder, 'no more this "uncle" business now, OK? You big now, no longer boy.'

'Mother told you why I'm here?' he asked as he braced himself for a looming crash with a delivery truck that by some miracle never came.

'Sure, Yvette she tell us. Police business, we understand. Just say we help. We have, how you say, contacts.'

I'm sure you do, Riad thought grimly and some of them might even be on the right side of the law.

They had turned off the main road now leaving the beach behind and minutes later pulled up at an apartment block that had seen better days and probably dated back to the sixties.

'Here we are,' Vytas said proudly as they got out of the car. He pointed to one of the small shops that fronted the ground floor of the building as Bubba led the way. 'Family business. Good money too!'

With no pleasure Riad studied the sign painted on the plate glass window. V & F Ayoub, Private Investigators, Security Consultants and Debt Collectors. In smaller case letters there was a phone and fax number as well as the rejoiner that discretion was their motto.

Then they were inside, the secretary who looked no older than sixteen put down her nail file and without looking up from the glossy magazine she was reading said, 'That Brown woman phoned again. She's pissed that you haven't been around yet to sort out her shitbag tenants.' As she spoke she artfully moved a wad of chewing gum from one cheek to another and Riad hoped she wasn't going to get confused and chew on what looked like a safety pin stuck through a lower lip.

Waving this little technicality away Vytas told Skye, that was her name, to take money from the till and go down to the bottle store on the corner, bring back a bottle of Jack Daniels. The sweetener being a Vodka Cruiser alcopop for herself. As she rose from behind the desk with a sigh and headed for the door Riad wondered for the umpteenth time why the ornately tattooed individuals always seemed to find it necessary to wear as little clothing as possible, show off those tats no matter how freezing the weather outside.

In the surprisingly spacious inner office Riad took one of the fake leather visitor's chairs while Bubba sank down in the other and Vytas claimed his own chair behind the desk. Reaching down with a grunt he opened a drawer and produced a half full bottle of whisky and two none too clean looking glasses. They watched in silence as Vytas poured generous measures, Bubba having fetched a teacup for his share.

'Hair of dog!' Vytas said as he threw back his head and downed his drink in a single gulp.

Running his eyes over the windowless surrounds Riad took in the series of filing cabinets, the desktop computer, the threadbare carpet and the framed picture on the wall that he recognised as a view of Beirut's beachside. 'I didn't know you were living here in Melbourne,' he began after taking a tentative sip at his drink.

'Bubba and I come here twenty years ago already!' Vytas said with a laugh, 'We be refugees. Escape from civil war in Beirut, Muslims make much trouble for us. Too much dangerous.'

Riad nodded, thinking while you being good Christians of course. There would be a backstory for sure, most likely one involving the Lebanese police who would have been only too glad to see the back of these two. Note to self: be nice, Riad, this is family and we all know you can't pick those. Besides, you're here because you need their help.

'So you started this business,' he said while wondering what other "business" there was.

'Good no?' Bubba agreed, adding 'we also have car yard in Fitzroy suburb, fix up and sell used cars. Good business!'

'We bring little money with when we come Australia, enough to start business.'

'Sometimes Vytas do a little business, like time you see him in Kuwait,' Bubba said emphasising this statement with a broad wink.

'Yes,' Riad said vainly trying to suppress the memory of when, during the Gulf War, his uncle surfaced in Kuwait City as an arms dealer, a matter only resolved when the Americans, seeing the potential of a tame lord of war, intervened. Nobody wanted to go there again.

Watching anxiously as Vytas refilled their glasses Riad asked about the debt collection business, 'Isn't there a bit of intimidation involved, I mean when confronting people who owe—'

'What this "intimation?"' Bubba asked, frowning.

'Intimidation. It means threatening people into paying.'

The two brothers exchanged glances of sheer incredulity. Clearly the very idea that their little nephew could think this of them! 'No!' Vytas finally managed, almost choking on his whiskey, 'Nothing like that! We never haff trouble, just ring doorbell and often people already have money right there, don't even haff to open door all the way, just give cash. No problem.'

Riad could picture the scene, a narrow street in a built up poorer neighbourhood and the orange debt collector car rolls up. Neighbours' faces peering from behind lace curtains to see who had been living beyond their means this time. Then out get these two huge gentlemen, a bearded barrel chested Bubba sporting that ridiculous pork pie hat he was wearing now, while the taller and equally generously proportioned Vytas with his bald head, pig's eyes and perpetual cherubic smile rang the doorbell.

No trouble at all.

Skye was back, dumping the brown bag wrapped bottle on the desk and stating that it was her afternoon off and she had a nails appointment. 'Nice to meet you, Mr Riad,' she said pulling the door closed behind her.

They watched as Vytas unscrewed the cap before tossing it into a waste basket. Clearly there would be no need for it again. 'Yvette tell us Rania iss staying there now. Some problem in Kuwait?'

'Anyone make trouble for you or Rania, you tell us, OK?' Bubba said, leaning forward and balling a fist. 'You family. We sort out.'

Suppressing the vision of that horror Riad reluctantly accepted a refill before coming to the reason for the family reunion. 'I have a job for you,' he said, instantly wondering whether he was crazy to get these two buffoons involved. Deciding it was too late to stop now he pressed on, 'There is a lady I want you to follow, find out who she meets, where she goes. This must be discreet, she is not to know. I will pay you your regular fee plus another thousand dollars each as a bonus. The job should only take a few days, while we, I, am here in Melbourne.'

Handing over a photo of Sarah Green taken from the face page of a fashion magazine he watched his uncle's face break into a slow smile. 'What beautiful lady! Famous, no?'

'She haff boyfriend?' he asked hopefully.

'She's married. To a millionaire.'

Bubba had the photo now and seemed equally impressed. 'Sarah Green,' he said in awe, 'supermodel. I see her on TV, something about her small girl taken.' He frowned, looking at Riad, 'You want us find child?'

'No, I'll do that. I have a growing suspicion that the mother knows more than she is telling me. I need to know if she is in contact with anyone that might lead me to the girl.'

Over another round of drinks they settled the details of the shadowing of Sarah Green which would start the next morning.

26
CHAPTER

Sitting at the kitchen table enjoying a breakfast of scrambled eggs and toast washed down with orange juice and lots of strong coffee Riad watched Sarah Green being interviewed on a local TV station's breakfast program. Dressed in a sleeveless floral silk dress with a high clerical collar to lend it an oriental look she looked fresh and even a little chatty. Gone was the pale and weary Sarah of the previous evening when the three of them had enjoyed a meal of pasta and wine at an Italian restaurant where Sarah had been instantly recognised and fawned over by hovering waiters that got in each other's way in their eagerness to please.

The Sarah of old was here this morning, flirty and chatty and with just the right touch of melancholy and soberness when the subject of the missing Maddie came up. Delighted at how the camera just loved her the producer switched from camera to camera while the interviewer, an attractive brunette, managed just the right tone of reverence and sympathy while trying to elicit that something special, perhaps some news about the investigation?

Perchance catch her in that unguarded moment of naked vulnerability?

No chance of that. This was classic Sarah Green, supermodel and international socialite, back in her natural environment and on with the show.

With the interview drawing to a close Riad switched off the TV and cleared the table. The previous evening Sarah had, over a glass of wine, enquired about what, if anything, he had learned from going over the official police file. One or two ideas that merited looking into, he lied, the truth being that the investigation until now had been pretty thorough. Enough to point to an inside job and it was now just a question of who, why and how much time they had to find Maddie before the inevitable happened.

For he knew, as did Detective Inspector Reed, that once Maddie had outlived her usefulness, she would be far too dangerous to ever release.

The dead stay dumb.

Glancing at his watch he reckoned Sarah and Chrissie would have reached the street outside the studio by now with Vytas ready to pick up the trail. Sarah's stated plan had been to go shopping promising to meet up later for lunch. He, in turn, would follow up on those leads. In reality he would be on the internet, digging up every bit of information he could find about Sarah Green's earlier life, including the death of her first husband. Also Mr Hasan Abdul-Karim.

Two hours later Baker saw them exit the Myers store on Bourke St and set about following at a discreet distance. Pedestrian traffic was heavy with lots of tourists milling about and he had little trouble in staying undetected. Except for Vytas, who spotted him ten minutes after Baker first started shadowing his own quarry.

The man was good, Vytas decided, either a cop or possibly a private detective. The trench coat and trilby perhaps a little over the top, like an old gangster movie he thought.

Shunning the omnipresent jampacked trams, most likely to avoid being crowded by enthusiastic fans, the women were easy to follow as they made their way—via a coffee and cake stop—to Elizabeth Street and started heading uphill to distant Spring Street and the Parliament Buildings.

Sweating in his black Northface quilt jacket, the day had turned out warmer than expected, Vytas kept a steady fifty paces behind the other man, relying on him to keep the women in sight at times when they rounded a corner. Not for the first time he marvelled at how women could walk that far and that fast on those thin six inch heels, deciding it had something to do with youth and the fact they carried a little less weight than he did.

Earlier inside Myers, at the vast perfume section, Sarah had been instantly recognised by fawning attendants who swarmed from all around leaving other customers bemused as they searched for someone to serve them.

The fact that her face was staring down at them from a huge lit poster advertising a new range of lipstick might have had something to do with it.

But out here on the pavement, hair tucked under a slouch hat and wearing oversized sunglasses, Sarah Green was incognito, never turned a head. Which, Vytas thought, did not say much for the men of Melbourne for nothing, not even her Burberry coat, could quite hide those curves and the seductive way those hips moved as she did her catwalk stride.

Fifteen minutes later they entered the mall housing Dymocks, the city's largest bookstore and as he descended the elevator to the main floor Vytas could see that the place was crowded. It was a good place for a clandestine meeting, a maze of sorts between high bookshelves with scores of shoppers milling about. Something was about to happen, he could feel it in his bones, for at the entrance to the shop Sarah had sent her companion off on a mission, the other woman hailing a cab.

Baker had reached a similar conclusion and fingered the mobile in his raincoat pocket. This could be it, the client had said that Sarah would sooner or later be meeting with a stranger, someone who was not on one of the photographs he had provided him with. It would be a one on one meeting, possibly in a public place and with her companions absent.

The client, who had given him a most generous retainer, wanted him to photograph this person and follow him or her and get a name and address. The client had provided him with exact details of where Sarah was staying, who her traveling companions were and an outline of her scheduled engagement making the business of following her a piece of cake. Browsing through the crime section he could keep an eye on the woman where she was idly paging through some photographic volumes.

Vytas, in the meantime, had taken up position near the rear of the shop where there was an elevated section from where he could keep an unobtrusive eye on Sarah. Baker was temporarily out of sight behind a bookcase but Vytas was confident he would spot him if the man decided to leave and take the up escalator. Having not previously perused much other than what could be found in glossy plastic covered issues of Playboy and Mayfair, Vytas was fascinated to see all these people, pretty girls too, all so serious and quiet and paging through books and buying them. Why, with TV and DVDs, anyone would want to read a book was quite beyond him. More so, why his nephew, an Ayoub for chrissake, would go to university to do nothing else than read more books. What good was that?

Increasingly aware of a thirst coming on, he hadn't had as much as a beer all day, he groaned inwardly and set about listlessly paging through a historical volume again. At least it had pictures.

The man in the dark pinstriped business suit stood at the top of the escalator while pretending to scan through his mobile phone. In fact he was casting an eye over the shoppers below. As previously agreed Sarah was at the wildlife and photography section, visible from his position and it took him no more than three minutes to spot Baker, the private detective just stealing a furtive glance at his quarry once too often. For a moment he considered the possibility of a paparazzi waiting for an opportunity but where was the long lens camera? No, this man was following her, the question was why?

Glancing at his watch Ruslan realised the agreed time had arrived and rode the elevator down. Moments later he was strolling up Sarah's aisle pretending to scan the displayed titles as he went along. Seeing him approaching she kept her eyes focused on the book she was studying while instantly aware of a quickening of her pulse, the catch of the breath in her throat.

'Hello Sarah,' he said softly, stopping two paces from her to lift a volume off the shelf, started paging through it. 'Don't look now but do you know the man in the beige raincoat over on your left?'

Alarmed she looked anyway, 'What? No, why?'

'Never mind. How are you?'

Ignoring the question she asked how Maddie was in a strangled voice that ended in a sob.

'Shh. Keep it down. She is fine. I saw her just two days ago.'

Unable to stop herself Sarah was rocking on her feet, a keening motion that had the man touch her gently on the shoulder checking her. 'I want her to come home now—' she said, turning pleading eyes to meet his.

At the far end of the store Vytas had produced a small monocular viewer and, withdrawn into the shadows of a stand of audiobooks, was studying the conversation. He couldn't make out the words but clearly the two knew each other and the woman was visibly upset. Cursing inwardly he watched the idiot in the raincoat slowly sidling up while still pretending to browse.

'She will be back soon, I promise.' Smiling while replacing the volume to pick up another Ruslan said soothingly, 'have I ever lied to you?'

'No,' she said in a small voice, 'It's just—it's been a long time now and—'

'You're not back to cutting up people's clothes again, are you Sarah?' he asked in a suddenly stern voice. 'You know that was something the police wondered about the time they investigated your first husband's disappearance.'

Shaking her head vehemently, 'No!'

'Shh! You remember why we're doing this, Sarah, to help you? To help Maddie?'

She nodded numbly, pleading eyes still fixed on his, the photo book dropping out of her hand with a dull thud. 'Wh... where is she? Please you have to tell me!'

Aware that people were staring at them and that any moment now she would be recognised he made a soothing noise, gently removing her hand from his sleeve. 'Close. She is close and—'

'Tell me!' she growled in a voice threatening enough to startle him.

'The house --' It escaped him before he could check himself and he hastily moved away from her to head for the exit with the parting words that he would phone.

Turning away and producing his iPhone Baker scrolled back the photos he had taken, pleased to find that at least two showed the man's face clearly. To keep it unobtrusive the device had been hidden under the trench coat filming through a small strategically placed aperture with the flash deactivated.

It had however not fooled either Vytas or Ruslan for a moment, mainly because they were expecting it and because there was a certain way a man stood, square on, when taking a photo. It did not apply to selfies but Vytas, never having taken a selfie in his life, would not necessarily know that.

On the outside sidewalk Ruslan paused to light a cigarette before, satisfied that Baker had followed, set off on a brisk pace for what turned out to be the nearby Elephant and Wheelbarrow pub. At that hour the place was already busy, the lunch hour traffic drifting in. Stopping at the bar counter he ordered a pint of draught while asking where the toilets were. It proved to be up a steep flight of stairs and off a second lounge area that was not in use at present.

Perfect. Taking a deep tug at the beer and leaving it on the counter he headed up the steps and, pausing for a second checked that the small lounge with its Olde English style nooks and crannies was deserted, he quickly checked the men's toilet to find it unoccupied.

Better and better. Then, treading quietly, for the bare floorboards were creaky, he took up position behind a pillar and waited. Fifteen minutes went by while two customers, one male one female, visited the ablutions before Baker's head showed at the top of the stairs. Ruslan kept under cover as the private eye scanned the lounge area before deciding to head for the toilet. This was the moment Ruslan stepped out from behind the pillar and knocked him viciously across the back of the head with a brass knuckleduster, lowering him gently as he collapsed.

Dragging him behind the cover of a chesterfield couch he quickly located the phone pocketing it. He was about to go for the wallet when a voice behind him said, 'Iss not nice thing to do, no? Bashing man then robbing?'

Getting slowly to his feet Ruslan studied the newcomer, deciding in an instant this was not someone to tangle with and backed away before quickly descending the stairs and heading outside where he managed to hail a cab on an opposite street corner.

Watching him go Vytas knelt by the fallen man who was groaning softly but showing no signs of wanting to come round. The wallet was in an inside pocket and the driving licence identified him as one Samuel Baker, forty five years of age. A calling card gave his profession as private investigator, citing a downtown office address. A small amount of cash and some credit cards, all of which Vytas ignored. He found what he was looking for in another pocket, a slim notebook which, at a quick scan, revealed scribbled notes on the movements of Sarah Green over the past twenty four hours.

Of more interest was the name of the client on page 1.

Downstairs Vytas beckoned over the bartender informing him that there was a man passed out on the floor of the upstairs lounge. He wasn't sure whether drunk or perhaps some medical emergency but someone had better take a look, call an ambulance perhaps. As a waitress was despatched to investigate Vytas made his way outside then decided it was time for that drink and perhaps a steak and fries on the side.

He quite liked the Elephant, would have liked to have partaken it there but no doubt the police would show up before long and that would not be good. So he went to the nearby Boiler Room instead.

Fifteen minutes later and onto his second pint of Carlton Draught Vytas pulled out his mobile and dialled Riad's number. It was answered after three rings.

'You OK to talk now?' while chomping on a handful of peanuts.

'I'm alone, Vytas.'

'Good, iss good.' There was a moment's pause as Riad listened to the sound of a man slurping a beer followed by a burp. 'Sorry. Now, I follow lady, no problem. She meet man in Dymocks bookshop. They know each other, take care not be spotted. The lady gets very upset, begs man who shakes head and leave again—'

'Did you get a photo of the man?' Riad interrupted, aware of a sudden flutter of excitement. This could be it!

There was a snort on the other side of the connection, 'No, I plan to follow, take photo when closer to man, but, also more. Another man, following the woman when she leaves TV building, his name Samuel Baker and he private detective. He take photo in shop and other man spot him. Baker follows the man who traps him, takes phone before I could stop him—'

'So we don't have a photo of the man she met?'

'No. But I see his face.'

'How do you know about this other man's identity?

In a few words between gulps of beer and a side grunt of appreciation to the waitress who brought across his steak, Vytas told him.

There was a moment's stunned silence as Riad took this in. So Hasan Abdul-Karim had hired a private investigator to follow his wife. How about that. And who was the stranger in the bookshop?

Once again everything pointed to Sarah Green as the key to this case.

'Thank you Unc—Vytas. You've done well. I will phone you this evening.'

Which left Riad wondering just how he could find a way of transposing the image of a face stored in the memory bank of Vytas Ayoub to something useful, like a photograph.

27
CHAPTER

Early for the lunch date with Sarah and Chrissie Riad ordered a glass of Oyster Bay Chardonnay and set about scanning the morning's edition of *The Australian*. The front page was all local politics, a subject of little interest to him and it was only on page four where something caught his eye. An article on the craze of video gaming taken from the *Wall Street Journal* it described the lengths gamers would go to in order to get better at competitive online games, the current most popular one being Fortnite. Never having been a gamer he was fascinated to read about more than 125 million people playing it worldwide, mostly in free mode with up to 100 players competing until one is left standing. Winning bestows the kind of bragging rights once reserved for local sports stars.

A game for all ages, a new development was how parents, worried that their kids were not able to keep up with classmates and losing social standing in the process, were engaging online coaches, paying up to $US 60 and hour for the services of a professional gamer. The article went on to mention the fast developing world of first person shooter games, headlining the new Red Dead Redemption 2 as an prime example of how moral ambiguity had replaced the old values of good against evil, revenge once only tolerated when it followed a great wrong. The reviewer stated how moral issues don't enter the arena here as he blows off an innocent bystander's head just to test his new shotgun.

He goes on to question whether it is just a means of letting off steam or is there something worrying about the ease with which we resort to extreme violence?

Riad's thoughts went back to the recent random killings Kuwait City, both instances involving juveniles wearing an interactive gaming headset. Were they taking lessons in how to get better at killing, a case of being desensitized and programmed perhaps?

Everything pointed to it except the seeming lack of motive.

He had raised this aspect with Waleed when his Kuwaiti colleague had phoned the previous evening, then morning in the Middle East. After the usual banter about exploiting the lax morals of the ladies of Melbourne and making a detour to the Gold Coast where the lifestyle was apparently especially exciting, the sergeant had updated him on the progress in the investigation. Both the kids had been gamers but then so was most of their schoolmates. The boys had been from the same school but being in different grades was not thought to have known each other. Both had been described as loners and had been counselled by the visiting school psychologist as had many other troubled or underperforming students.

The name of the psychologist quite familiar to Riad.

Interviewed by Waleed she was at a loss to explain what could have led to the violent behaviour of the boys. Apparently both had been normal enough but experiencing a degree of social alienation which she ascribed to their adolescence. After a few sessions, conducted at school after the end of the day's lessons and with the full permission of the parents, both had shown good progress and could be discharged from follow up.

One boy, the younger of the two, had bragged to a classmate about how he had been receiving lessons in gaming and was also trying out a new game and would be the first amongst them to play it. Questioned he clammed up and wouldn't say where he was receiving the instruction or by whom.

The inescapable conclusion was both boys were being manipulated by some unknown figure with an agenda as yet unclear. One thing clear to both Riad and Waleed though was that they were dealing with a new kind of serial killer. Death by proxy.

To date Waleed had been fruitless in searching for a gaming coach of any description in Kuwait and while online coaching was possible there was the question of money which neither of them had. Also their respective laptops had been devoid of anything along those lines.

No, the boys had been coached, and brainwashed, locally and in person. The real question being how they had been put in touch with the master killer and where the training took place. Not all boys would be suitable subjects and he had a feeling the master would not want to waste his time on someone who was not going to respond to his subtle ministrations.

Someone was doing the recruiting, someone with the skills and training to know what to look for. Once again the question loomed, why?

Seeing the women entering the restaurant Riad folded away the paper and rose to beckon them over to his table, signalling a waiter in the process. The place, chosen by Sarah, was an upmarket Japanese seafood restaurant in the city's Docklands and he had to take a taxi to find it. Only open on certain days for lunchtime fare the place catered mainly for late afternoon and dinner clients who enjoyed the exotic food and spectacular sunsets over the bay.

An earlier glance at the prices was enough to convince Riad that (a) it was the kind of place where he, not being much of a sushi guy, would have to swing by a McDonalds on the way home and (b) he couldn't afford it anyway. Luckily the Platinum Amex card nestling in his pocket would take care of things as before. It was compliments of Mr Abdul-Karim who explained that Sarah had expensive tastes and would be obliged if Riad would pay for everything using the card, no expense too great. She was not used to carrying any money herself and besides would be embarrassed to be seen paying a restaurant bill and expected her male companion to take care of such mundane things.

Riad had said he understood and promised to let the businessman know if the latter had to transfer any more cash to the generous amount already deposited in Riad's personal account.

Sitting down with a grateful smile at the waiter who held the chair and had the man all but slobber all over her, Sarah declared a healthy thirst and asked Riad what he was drinking.

He told her and she wrinkled her nose, 'Surely this calls for champagne? I mean a beautiful day like this?'

But the măitre d', who had magically appeared from nowhere, was way ahead of them, proudly displaying a magnum of chilled Bollinger while the waiter hovered with an ice bucket and stand.

'Oh Maurice, you remembered!' she exclaimed offering him a limp wrist which he gratefully took ever so gently to almost brush it with pursed lips.

The manager, whose name was actually Alphonse -- but who cared about such trivialities when dealing with a world famous celebrity— simpered, 'A pleasure as always, Miss Sarah. And may I state that you are as lovely as ever!' With this he bowed away motioning the waiter with a backhand signal to open the bottle while another rushed up with champagne glasses.

'I'm starving!' Sarah exclaimed, scrutinizing the imposing oversized and ornately embroidered menu and turning to Riad with a sigh, 'Oh, I don't know. You order for me?'

Sure, he thought, how hard could it be to decide for someone who ate like a sparrow and was probably vegan not forgetting gluten sensitive. 'She'll have the salad,' he said to the waiter, handing back the menu. 'Easy on the vinaigrette. And I'll have this fish,' unable to pronounce the Japanese word he pointed at the item.

'We don't use vinaigrette on our salads, Sir,' the waiter sniffed as he snatched the menu turning to Chrissie who giggled and ordered a selection of sushi.

'You did that on purpose, you wicked man,' Sarah said when the man moved away but she was smiling.

'What? Like you were going to have a 500g T bone steak with a side of fries and garlic bread?'

'I mean the waiter, silly!'

Riad shrugged and took a sip of the Bollinger, 'So, how has your day been? I watched your interview on TV, of course and it seemed to go well as always. Meet anyone you know while out shopping?'

She looked at him strangely, 'What do you mean?'

'Your face is plastered on billboards all over town, Sarah. Surely someone must have recognised you, asked for an autograph perhaps. Or a selfie?'

She shook her head and glanced uncertainly at Chrissie who was occupied with her iPad as usual. 'No. Well, the girls at the Myers cosmetics department, of course, but no—'

'Sarah had no further appointments,' Chrissie volunteered without looking up from whatever was streaming on social media, 'so she gave me time off to do a bit of my own shopping while she went to a bookstore.'

'Yes,' Sarah affirmed, not meeting Riad's eyes as the waiter arrived with their meals.

Oh my poor lovely, Riad thought sadly, how well you play your role but I can see inside your head and, before long I will know that one big secret which holds the key to this charade you insist we play. He was about to start picking at whatever the dish on his plate was when his mobile rang.

It was his daughter. 'I have to take this,' he said rising and going over to the deserted front section of the restaurant.

'Hello Rania. How's daddy's girl doing?'

'I'm OK, dad. Yvette has been taking me everywhere with her and it's been fun to be allowed into the backroom of the LBC Studio and see how TV shows are made. Gran—Yvette, is a real star here and she is even going to have me as a guest on one of her programmes!'

Lovely, Riad decided, no doubt without announcing you as an actual grandchild of the ever youthful star.

The line was bad and he had to strain to make out the next sentence, something about when he was expected back in Kuwait. Also reminding him that his mother had been planning to visit her brothers in Melbourne and had suggested Rania come along while Riad was still there. A family reunion of sorts.

'I'm only here for another few days, darling. Less than a week tops. But I promise that as soon as it's summer down here again, you and I will visit Australia, you will love it.' A thought had him ask whether Yvette had any special gentleman friend at the moment, someone who visited frequently, stayed over sometimes? His mother's passing parade of colourful lovers a constant worry and a source of more than one spectacular emotional meltdown.

'Only Pierre. He's quite old, almost like grandpa, but he's funny and makes her laugh. He's also very rich.'

What a surprise he thought but kept it to himself. Decided to change tack, 'Are you remembering to take your medicine, the pills the doctor gave you in Kuwait?'

'Yes dad! I told you I'm OK now.'

'As soon as I'm back I'll look into a new school for you, perhaps the new private one in Salmiyah.'

'Yvette thinks I should go to a boarding school in Europe like she did, an all girls school. She went to La Rochelle in Switzerland and—'

'Yes, yes,' he said hurriedly, thinking and we all know how that worked out for her, declaring, 'We'll talk about that when we're both back home. I have to run now, sweetie but I'll call you back this time to-morrow, OK?'

'Love you, dad,' she said followed by a kissing sound before the line went dead.

Love you too, he said softly to himself reflecting on how she sounded more upbeat, no longer depressed, while feeling guilty that he was so far away.

When he got back to the table an uncharacteristically aloof Sarah had eaten two salad leaves and drained a second glass of champagne while Chrissie ordered dessert.

CHAPTER 28

ustralian Federal Police Commander Zena Michaels, attached to the Centre to Counter Child Exploitation, was an attractive middle aged woman whose dress uniform was tailor made sporting several medals while her blonde hair was tied up in a bun which fitted nicely under her officer's cap. Dark eyes stared back at them, narrowing slightly as they settled on Sarah and highlighting the small creases that Riad thought would be quite attractive when she smiled.

Not that she would smile that often he decided. Those penetrating eyes would have seen too much in her call of duty to warrant that. For a moment he wondered whether the blonde hair was real or was she that black eyed blonde Raymond Chandler was always so fascinated with?

No ring on that finger.

It came as almost a disappointment when her voice was flat and brittle rather than the husky deep throated growl conjured up in his imagination. Too long, Riad, he reflected, too long without a woman in your life. Concentrate, dammit!

Her manner was smart efficient yet friendly as she invited them into the small office where the viewing would take place. They were back at the Flinders Street Police Station, Michaels having flown in from Canberra an hour earlier bringing with her the video footage as agreed.

After introductions she had explained that child pornography footage was securely stored at the Federal Police Headquarters in Canberra where only two approved officers were allowed to view it as required and both had to be present. They could imagine how deeply disturbing some of the imaging was and how delicate the nature of investigating these crimes were.

The blinds had been drawn and all phones and computer equipment removed from the room, the only furniture now three hardback chairs facing a deal table with a scarred top on which sat a laptop computer. The only light was from a single bulb set high in the ceiling and covered with a steel grid, its shadows casting a spider's web over the room.

Before entering the room and while being encouraged to partake of the hot drinks and sandwiches on offer, Michaels had laid out the rules. 'Detective Inspector Reed will wait here as will Miss Green's assistant. Miss Green, Lieutenant Ajmi and myself will be the only persons to go inside and view the tape, understood?'

Shifting her glance from person to person as they nodded in unison Michaels declared herself satisfied. 'Before we start allow me to give you some background on how we obtain this kind of data and of recent developments in the field. Recently the Australian federal and state police have helped to capture a global paedophile ring, leading to the arrest of 63 suspects and the rescue of 18 young children. This followed the arrest of an Australian man who had filmed his sickening sexual assaults on a child which he then shared worldwide.'

'For two years the world's leading victim-identification experts had tried to identify the offender as well as the young girl, the FBI taking the lead on this. The material was known in law-enforcement circles as the Magenta Heart series and we managed to narrow the search down to New Zealand or Australia. The breakthrough finally came when a man in Seattle was arrested in 2016 for the possession of child pornography and examination of his computers and encryption devices revealed he was corresponding with another man who was boasting of his abuse of a young girl.'

She paused to take a sip of water as the rest of them watched on in silence. 'Interpol found that the photo images of this young girl matched that of the unidentified child in the Magenta Heart videos and checks turned up an IP address for an Adelaide man. The case against him was clinched when we found an incriminating unedited copy of a related two minute video on his mobile phone. The man, who was known online as "Heartbreaker", handed over passwords to his online accounts enabling us to take over his identity and ensnare other offenders. This was known as Operation Sampson and working with the US Department of Homeland Security we found he had been involved with more than 50 separate child-exploitation groups on an encrypted messaging service.'

'Several of these offenders were arrested and jailed for prolonged periods in the USA while the Adelaide man, as well as a local associate, were also convicted and are serving long sentences. I mention this to illustrate how much combating this has become an international phenomenon requiring the resources of worldwide police organisations.'

Turning to a very pale Sarah she said in a softer tone while gently touching her arm, 'I know how hard all this is for you to hear, Miss Green but we have reason to believe your daughter has fallen victim to such a ring with indications that it is operating locally. It would help tremendously if you could positively identify her as the girl in the short clip I'm about to show you.'

'I'm ready,' Sarah whispered, lifting her chin and striding purposefully through the door with Riad and Michaels exchanging glances before following.

What happened next was hard, brutal and mercifully short. Michaels waited for them to be seated then, without further comment, slotted a disc into the side of the laptop while remaining standing. 'This is an edited extract of the video loaded off the relevant child exploitation site. Just three minutes in length but enough for Miss Green to identify the subject if indeed it is Maddie.'

She typed in a password and seconds later the images started rolling. A small child was dancing, gyrating around a vertical pole, spider thin limbs with seemingly too large knees twisting into near impossible positions, the slender neck and back arched back in rhythmic jerking motions.

Golden blonde hair was piled on high in a bun held in place by a clasp with a single lock dangling seductively down over a cheek. She was heavily made up with rouge, powder and thickly laid on mascara and glimpsed between the vividly red lipstick the small teeth were very white as her tongue darted between them.

She wore only a tiny pair of sequined knickers and the oil on her body glistened under the harsh overhead lighting. As she came close to the camera she smiled and blew a kiss, the nails on those little fingers every bit as red as the lipstick. The blue eyes twinkling or was that just the lighting?

The music was Bolero by Ravel, and as haunting as ever. Music from the movie "10" and to fuck by as Bo Derek so vividly described it. Riad wondered if he was the only one in the room who knew that.

One minute and twenty seconds into the clip Sarah started screaming. Piercingly sharp it cut through Riad like a razor as he felt a vice closing over his heart. Instantly Michaels was by her side, snapping shut the laptop lid to cut off the streaming images. Still too stunned to move Riad watched numbly as the policewoman pressed a sobbing Sarah to her breast, stroking her hair while making soft soothing noises.

The door opened at a crack and Reed peered in, his eyebrows raised in a question. A glance from hard black eyes had him quickly scurry away, closing the door.

Michaels had pulled up a chair to face Sarah whose face was still buried in her hands as her shoulders jerked in now silent sobs. After a while she said, 'Is it her, Sarah? Is it Maddie?'

Unable to speak the answer came in a series of nods finally punctuated by a soft 'Yes—'

29
CHAPTER

The building in lower Brunswick Street, Fitzroy, dated back to Victorian times and had originally been office space but in recent years had been extensively renovated and now served mainly as low rent accommodation for students. The outer façade was Heritage Foundation protected which was hard to fathom seeing how ugly it was while inside it was now faux art deco without the class of the real thing. They took the elevator, modern and mirror panelled, to the fifth floor and with Sarah leading the way found themselves in the offices of Madame Revetcky, Clairvoyant, Medium and Spiritualist.

The lettering on the frosted glass window to the office door added, Group Séance Sessions available.

Inside there was a small front office with an antique writing table serving as a reception desk and three matching chintz covered chairs. Dark French style wallpaper lent a somewhat gloomy atmosphere as did the oriental carpet in shades of faded red and blue. There were no pictures on the walls and the telephone on the desk was modern and hence out of place.

Nobody occupied the desk but an unseen buzzer must have announced their arrival for the inner door opened to reveal a stocky woman dressed in a multi coloured ankle length kaftan with green silk headscarf, oversized spectacles hovering uncertainly on the end of a stubby nose.

Behind the thick lenses small eyes peered at them for a moment and then recognition came, leading to a broad smile baring blackened teeth.

'Miss Sarah!' she exclaimed in a sharp voice that had a distinct roll of the "r" and stretched out the last syllable in Oriental fashion. Pudgy liver spotted hands grasped Sarah by the shoulders followed by a hug while over Sarah's shoulder Riad could see calculating eyes studying him with interest. Chrissie, hovering in the background as always, merited barely a glance.

'So nice to see you again. Of course I knew you would be calling, even before you phoned earlier.'

Of course, Riad observed under his breath, which made Madame Revetcky ask who the gentleman was. Introductions followed and Riad was mildly amused to hear himself introduced as a friend of the family.

'Come, come,' Madame Revetcky wheezed as she led the way into the room which was surprisingly spacious and decorated in the Oriental style complete with heavy drapes covering the windows and oil paintings on the dark green and maroon walls of stern looking men and women, all wearing ornate headgear and exotic looking garments. The men were all bearded and with dark eyes accentuated by kohl to give them that look of the mystic.

The women were all in reclining positions and wearing flowing dresses of flimsy material and showing plenty of jewellery with tiaras being especially favoured. The look decidedly waif like yet mysterious.

Soft lighting was provided by several low set table lamps around the room and it took a moment for Riad's eyes to adjust to the gloom before making out an octagonal table in the centre on which stood an opaque crystal ball on an ornately carved silver base. Two high backed chairs sat at opposite sides of the table and facing the crystal.

In a corner he could make out the shape of a hookah with a sliver of smoke from the top mounted clay receptacle betraying its recent use. It explained the heady aroma of apple and spices in the room and, quite possibly the lady's blackened teeth, although Riad reckoned that was more likely from marijuana.

Bringing up a third chair Revetcky invited them to take their places at the table. Chrissie had preferred to wait in the anteroom. Moving noiselessly across the thick pile Persian carpet Riad became aware of faint music wafting from an unseen source. A sitar he decided and suitably moody and relaxing at the same time.

'You want to talk to the child,' Madame Revetcky said without further preamble. 'As always we have a medium present, to transport us to the ethereal world where all our spirits dwell.'

Lifting an arm, slowly for dramatic effect, she pointed at a dark corner of the room where only now Riad was able to discern the shape of a small figure seated there. The person had been so still as if asleep and as a soft glow from a hidden source gradually highlighted the outlines it was clear that she—it was a young woman dressed in contemporary blue jeans and a simple white tank top – was indeed in an altered state. Long flowing blonde hair partly obscured the lowered face while slender wrists were folded motionlessly in her lap. Straining his ears Riad could just make out her shallow rhythmic breathing.

A small braided bracelet graced a wrist and in the new light Riad could make out the shapes of colourful flower charms threaded through it. The kind he had seen on the wrists of so many young women in the city.

'Leila is a natural medium,' Madame Revetcky said, 'a very rare phenomenon. I hypnotized her earlier.' Her sonorous tone became businesslike as she directed them to first hold hands as she completed the circle, then focus their full attention on the girl. Then, turning to the medium and speaking in a lowered voice she asked to speak to the spirit of Maddie Green.

There was a moment's silence during which Riad was intensely aware of the increasing pressure in Sarah's grip, long nails biting painfully into his palm. So slowly as to first suggest a trick of lighting the crystal ball between them began glowing, a soft green-blue effect that, just for a moment, reminded Riad of a mechanical swami in a glass cubicle he had once seen somewhere, the type that for five dollars tells you how rich and how famous you will be. One day.

The figure in the corner remained motionless and, after a further minute of complete silence, Madame Revetcky said, 'What is your name?'

'Maddie,' the medium said in a child's voice. 'Is Mommy there?'

A sob escaped from Sarah's lips as she stared intensely at the shrouded face across the room while Madame Revetcky motioned her not to say anything, to let the spirit explore the room.

'I see Mommy now,' the voice said with the hint of a little laugh. 'She looks sad but I'm alright. I will come home soon.'

'Where is she?' Sarah hissed, still not taking her eyes off the medium.

'Shh—' the clairvoyant cautioned, 'she hears you. Wait for the answer.'

It came a moment later, 'I'm close, Mummy, so close I can almost touch you. A big house with a garden and nice trees. I can hear the sea, all around me and at night I can see many lights far away over the water. I feel safe here, two big lions are keeping danger away. Please come soon, Mommy—'

The light in the crystal ball started fading and as the faint music returned Madame Revetcky indicated the session was over. It seemed even spirits needed a break. Over the last few seconds Riad had become aware that Sarah had been studying him intensely while he had been keeping his own gaze steadily on the clairvoyant's throat, searching for those subtle signs even the best ventriloquist could not quite hide on close study.

And this one was good but not good enough.

'Is—is she gone?' Sarah asked in a hushed voice.

Madame Revetcky nodded, then added in a soothing voice that Maddie was happy and expected to be united with her mother soon. As Sarah nodded numbly Madame Revetcky turned her attention to Riad who was about to rise, 'I find you most interesting, Mr Ajmi. Would you be willing to have your palm read?'

He was about to decline when Sarah, without glancing up, said she too was interested in what secrets were hidden there. Defeated, Riad reluctantly allowed the madame to study the palm of his hand.

Apparently it did not matter whether it was the right or left, no hiding from the eye of the all seeing mystic.

'It is as I suspected,' Madame Revetcky said with a nod of satisfaction, 'most interesting. A complex man who has seen much, suffered much pain. In many ways a man torn between two worlds. Also a dangerous man, someone who would not hesitate to take matters into his own hands, even the law.'

Raising her eyes she studied Riad with interest then added, a touch of wonder in her voice, 'I see a dark secret, something close to your heart that has caused you much anguish,

something you have never told anyone. Perhaps something that only a loved one, a good woman, could ever erase.'

Sighing softly she traced a finger over the skin of his palm to indicate a long lifeline before coming up with the startling revelation that, in a previous life, he had been a priest or, as she phrased it, a man of the cloth. 'Father Henry,' she said firmly, 'that is your real name.'

Which proved to be a conversation stopper of sorts and seconds later they filed out returning to the anteroom. In the far corner the medium was still asleep.

As he watched matters being settled Riad was mildly amused to learn that even clairvoyants and palm readers had not been bypassed by the modern world as Sarah settled the bill by means of a credit card swipe. A sideways glance at the amount had him decide it would keep Madame Revetcky in the gin he had smelled on her breath for a good while. Maybe leave something over for the medium.

Out on the sidewalk it was raining again, the soft sifting rain that was so typical of a winter's day in Melbourne. People hefting colourful umbrellas were hurrying by and the traffic was busier than earlier with lots of uniformed schoolkids about and alive with energy as they shouted and played chicken with the trams while others were lost in the flickering world of their mobile phones.

Chrissie had produced a tiny umbrella from somewhere with just enough cover for the two women as they crossed the street. The water streaming down his neck Riad wished they were still in that yesteryear where men wore hats and city gents had umbrellas of their own. While waiting at the tram stop he struggled for shelter under the crowded corrugated iron canopy and checked his phone. There was a message from DI Reed and with no tram in sight and the women engaged in muted conversation he returned the call.

'Lieutenant! Nice of you to call back. Any new leads so far?' Reed sounded strangely upbeat which had Riad ask him the same. 'Nope, but there's someone I want you to meet, a journalist. He has been investigating the earlier case of the still unexplained death of Ross Green three years ago. As I told you earlier, I feel the clue to solving this one might just lie in the past. This bloke works downtown at *The Age.* If OK with you I've arranged to meet him over a few drinks at his pub. Will five o' clock suit you?'

Riad said it would and made a note of the venue, a small bar close to the offices of the newspaper on 655 Collins Street in the city's Docklands. A glance at his watch showed he had less than twenty minutes to get there.

'I've just spoken to Detective Inspector Reed,' he told Sarah who stared at him blankly, her face white and pinched against the cold as she huddled in her Burberry greatcoat. 'I have to meet him at five. Where shall we meet up later?'

It was Chrissie who answered, 'Miss Sarah wants to go to Naked for Satan, it's just up the street here. We'll get a table at the rooftop bar. They serve light meals too.'

'Give me an hour,' Riad said while making a mental note of the name while wondering what fresh lunacy might await him there.

Minutes later he caught a tram heading downtown while the women were still waiting patiently.

The tram was full, standing room only and as he watched the different stops pass as they turned down Elizabeth Street heading for Southern Cross Station he thought back of the events of the afternoon. Shortly after leaving the police station Sarah had declared her intention of visiting the clairvoyant and insisting Riad come along.

Understandably she was still visibly shaken after what had happened earlier and seemed totally unaware of the appraising stares of passers by. Riad had thought of taking her arm as they exited the building to cross to the waiting cab but decided this would be the kind of photo any lurking paparazzo would relish.

And now this last all too smooth transit from the macabre to the bizarre. Just what had transpired in that aroma saturated darkened room minutes earlier? Did Sarah really believe all that mumbo jumbo? Had she not noticed the ventriloquist act as he did? Why did he feel the whole thing had been an elaborate setup and for his benefit?

As the tram rumbled over the points turning into Spencer Street the suspicion that had been lingering at the back of his mind for a while became clearer. It *was* for him! The big house and garden by the surrounding sea, a peninsula of sorts; no way a fraudster clairvoyant would ever be that specific unless she had been briefed and by who else but Sarah Green?

Sarah Green who knows a helluva lot more than she had ever divulged. Sarah Green who had brought him all this way from Kuwait to find a Maddie where the Australian Police with all their resources have so far been unsuccessful.

A nice clean cut brave detective from a corrupt part of the world where he would have learned to bury certain things and come up with that alternate truth that all could live with. An Arab yet not an Arab but a man of the world with just enough time spent in the fleshpots of a decadent Europe where he could be trusted to take the broad view of things.

Sweet! How clear it now all seemed. Riad Ajmi, prostitute policeman for hire. Oh so discreet and educated to boot. Someone who would move easily in her world and could be trusted not to embarrass.

Someone who would bring home Maddie Green.

30
CHAPTER

The Hightail Bar and Grill on Collins Square in the Docklands was only twenty minutes walk away from the Southern Cross Station where Riad had disembarked but it was raining hard and he took a cab which dropped him outside the place a few minutes later.

A large modern open plan venue sporting a long U-shaped bar the place was packed at that hour, mainly office workers and businessmen taking advantage of happy hour. Threading his way through the throng Riad spotted a waving Reed at a table and headed across.

'Meet Jerry Wheeler,' the detective said, 'an old mate from that excuse for a newspaper down the street. Jerry, meet Riad Ajmi, the Kuwaiti cop I've been telling you about.'

They shook hands and Riad pulled up a chair. 'What's your poison?' Reed asked indicating they were having beers, several empty stubbies on the table suggesting Riad had some catching up to do.

'I'll have what you're having.'

'Righto,' Reed said rising, 'I guess it's my shout. It always seems to be when drinking with this hack.'

Wheeler shrugged as they watched the retreating back of Reed fighting his way through the crowd that were now four deep at the bar, 'What does he expect for nothing? Information don't come cheap.'

That did not seem to merit comment and Riad leaned back in his chair and studied the room. Loud music was coming from somewhere but against the general noise of the clientele it was fighting a losing battle. Was it his imagination or was it especially the women that were the loudest?

The back of the long bar was lined with mirrors fronted by a kaleidoscope of assorted liquor bottles and the light cast from a fluorescent section made for a pleasing mellow effect. Off to one side several large TV screens were mounted high on the wall all of which were turned to sports channels.

The peculiar game of Aussie Rules Football seemed to be prevailing. 'The Saints,' Wheeler said, tilting his beer towards the screen Riad had been watching, 'playing Collingwood. Hard to say which side sucks the most. I'm a St Kilda man myself, got a few bucks riding on The Saints.'

'There doesn't appear to be an offside,' Riad ventured.

Wheeler looked puzzled, 'Why would you want an offside?'

Riad, whose sole experience with team sport was soccer, shrugged, left it at that. As the other man tilted his head back to suck the last dregs out of the bottle Riad looked on, deciding he could just about do with a cold one himself now.

At a guess the newspaperman was in his late thirties with a wiry frame and a three day stubble that was a trifle too unkempt to be designer, more likely just a matter of not caring to shave that day or the previous few. A good head of wavy brown curls could do with a haircut but that was just Riad's opinion. The handsome features were deeply tanned, the smile ready and showing too large white teeth that vaguely reminded him of the keys of a piano. He was wearing an olive windcheater over a polo top, an ornately carved jade clasp on a threaded black horsehair string around his neck.

Slender fingers were nicotine stained.

Reed was taking his time getting back to the table and Riad decided it was time to get things going. 'I take it you're a journalist,' he stated the obvious, 'and that you have some information about the Maddie Green case?'

'An investigative journalist,' Wheeler corrected him. Riad detected the hint of an accent, something in the way he pronounced the "a's" like a flat "e." 'Three years ago I investigated the disappearance of the millionaire businessman Ross Green, the then husband of supermodel

Sarah Green and the father of her child, Maddie. It happened during a Mediterranean cruise on his luxury yacht, the Fairy Knowe. Apart from a crew of three several guests were on board, Jean Martin, a model and friend of Sarah's, Irina Sakharov the companion of Russian businessman, Dimitri Ruslan and Hasan Abdul-Karim an old family friend and business associate of Green's. together with the Greens a total of six guests.'

Wheeler withdrew a packet of cigarettes from a pocket, stared at it in puzzlement then, with a sigh, shoved it back. 'Force of habit,' he said ruefully, 'No smoking anywhere in this bloody country anymore. Anyways, soon fags will be so expensive I'll have to stop eating. Now, where was I?'

'The people on the boat,' Riad prompted.

'So here's what happens. They sail out of Cannes on a planned seven day cruise of the Mediterranean heading for the Italian Amalfi coastline. Partying all the way as you do. Baby Maddie is left in London in the care of her nanny, she had been ill the week before the trip and it was thought best she didn't go on the sea trip. On the second night out there is a big party on board, it's Sarah's birthday and the booze flows. The sea is calm and the yacht is cruising at a steady fifteen knots with barely a breeze stirring – I get this from an interview with the skipper, a Yank called Troskie – at this point they are about fifteen miles from land and heading southeast.'

He paused as Reed returned with the beers, three Corona longnecks expertly cradled in one hand while the other created a passageway through the pushing crowd. Wheeler created a space on the table and the detective sat down with a grunt.

'Cheers,' Reed said, raising his bottle to his lips and Riad, who had since learned that using a beer glass, even in the poshest of environments, was an un-Australian thing to do,

followed suit. The beer was pleasantly cold and he took another sip before setting it down.

'Jerry's been telling me about the Ross Green disappearance case,' Riad said.

'You mean the murder case.'

'What?! The coroner's verdict was accidental drowning at sea,' Riad said.

'I'm getting to that,' Wheeler said, holding up a hand. 'After dark the party moved inside from the sundeck to the main lounge. By this time it was going on midnight and everyone had had a lot to drink. The two female crew members, Danish and fresh out of high school and on a working holiday, had retired to their cabin with the skipper alone in the wheelhouse. As the night wore on the music downstairs grew louder and the party noise more riotous. At ten minutes past midnight he heard a woman scream and, alarmed that someone might have gone overboard, he placed the yacht on autopilot and went down to investigate.'

He paused to take a sip from his beer then continued, 'in the lounge he found himself walking into the midst of a loud argument, a very drunk Sarah shouting abuse at her husband who appeared quite angry while a shaken Abdul-Karim, being the only sober one there, tried to intervene. Sarah had tossed a drink in her husband's face and on the couch at the other side of the lounge Ruslan and the girl he had been smooching laughed loudly. Jean Martin, Sarah's friend is passed out stone cold on the other couch.'

'Spotting the skipper a furious Sarah shouts at him to mind his own business and storms off to her cabin, the master cabin at the stern, with a stone faced Ross Green in pursuit. Regretting the earlier decision not to pull into one of the many marinas along the way for the night, Troskie cautioned the others against going out onto the deck alone and headed back to the wheelhouse. Once there he cut the boat's speed down to ten knots and switched on the powerful side spotlights used when fishing and also when anchored with guests swimming off the deck at night. This enabled him to keep an eye via two CCTV cameras for anyone going overboard, a real concern of his now.'

'At fifteen minutes past five in the morning the intercom phone in the wheelhouse rings. It's Sarah and she's hysterical, Ross has disappeared and he's not in the lounge and she's worried as he had an hour earlier slipped and fallen in the en-suite bathroom and cut his head, bleeding profusely. Still quite drunk he had staggered out of the cabin to look for the first aid kit stored near the bows. Concerned when he didn't return she went looking for him, in the process rousing everyone on board. Green is not on board. So Troskie starts a search of the area and radios the Italian coastguard for help.'

'Now comes the good part! *Shit!*' an excited Reed interjected, while Riad noticed he was once again going through the strange motion of dry spitting in the palm of his hand. Noticing Riad's puzzled look Wheeler smiled, 'He's got OCD, wait till you see him lock and unlock his car five times while everyone stands around waiting.'

'It's Tourette's, you idiot, and still better than you crossing yourself whenever you show up at a murder scene.'

'So I'm Catholic ain't I? For God's sake can't—'

Taking on the role of the adult in the room Riad held up a restraining hand, suggested they get back on topic. 'So what happened next?'

Taking a deep gulp of his drink while still glaring at Reed the reporter picked up his tale, 'So the final conclusion is that in his drunken state Green fell overboard and was lost at sea. Traces of his blood was found in the main cabin but nothing on the side of the basin where Sarah alleged he had hit his head. On questioning she claimed to have wiped it clean immediately after he left. A coastguard patrol boat arrived within an hour to help with the search but Green's body was never found. Subsequent questioning of the crew and guests by the police failed to come up with anything. No-one had seen him after he and Sarah left the main lounge, no-one had heard anything suspicious. All had gone to bed soon after the Greens had departed, only to be woken when the alarm was sounded. Now, here comes the puzzling part--'

Leaning closer while cradling his beer, Wheeler lowered his voice forcing the others to come closer, the background din as intrusive as ever. 'Misfortune at sea was the conclusion. Drunk man falls overboard at night and tragically drowns. Open and shut, yes?' He shook his head solemnly, 'but not to this investigating reporter who can smell a story a mile off. You see there's just one or two unexplained anomalies here. Firstly, a heavily bleeding man leaves the cabin but no traces of blood is found outside of the cabin. Secondly, the CCTV footage of the blind spots on the sides and rear of the boat fails to show anyone entering that space. Facts disregarded by the police who, ludicrously, suggested Green might have emerged on the front deck from a hatch at a time when the skipper was distracted, gone overboard from there.'

Noticing a passing waitress Wheeler called her over, ordering another round plus a plate of fries with ketchup. As the young woman moved away he studied her departing form with an appreciative eye before turning back to his story. 'So, just how did Green get off the boat? Well, I managed to get hold of a copy of the plans of the Fairy Knowe and, what do you know, it turns out the stern stateroom, the Green's cabin, has a large picture window at the rear end and projecting partially over the water. A window that can open and large enough to accommodate a man's body. Six feet below there's a four foot wide wooden platform for swimming purposes with a steel ladder leading up to the rear deck. A body going overboard through that window and off that platform would not be spotted unless someone was standing directly above the stern deck and peering down.'

'So Sarah Green lied?' Riad asked as Wheeler paused to take a sip of his beer.

'What else? But there's more. How come the man's body was never found? The Mediterranean is hardly a shark tank and most drowned bodies float sooner or later. So, old Wheeler decided to investigate and chats up one of the little Danish sweeties that were on board that night. Not that it was exactly a chore, you understand,' he added with a suggestive leer, lewd enough to have Riad decide the man was well on his way to being stoned.

'Go on,' he said.

'Well, little Anita, that was her name, tells me that when she cleaned the cabin after the police had left she found that a matching pair of marble statuettes the Greens had bought the day before departure in Cannes was missing. She thought it strange but dismissed it at the time thinking it might have been stored elsewhere or even taken away by the police as part of their investigation.'

'Weights used to sink the body,' the ever helpful Reed added, in case Riad wasn't able to figure it for himself.

Well into his tale now Wheeler pressed on, 'Another thing the girl told me, earlier that day she had taken a cheese and fruit platter to the Green's stateroom and this included a paring knife, a rather sharp six inches of steel. A knife that was not listed amongst the items taken away by the police for forensics and its absence noticed by Anita when she cleaned up afterwards.'

'So Sarah stabs her husband, kills him, then tosses him overboard through the stateroom window, unseen by anyone? But she weighs in at about a hundred pounds top and Green, by all accounts, was a big man. How did she manage to heave him up and over?'

'Simple. She had help; two big boys on board, one married to her now. Take your pick, perhaps even both?'

'Fuck!' Reed said loud enough for both men to stare at him as, seemingly unaware, he did the blowing in the palm of the hand thing again. Wheeler rolled his eyes.

'Still leaves the question why?' Riad said.

'DNA.'

'What?!'

Wheeler smiled, took another tug at his beer, 'Got you now, haven't I? Yep, you heard right, DNA. More precisely a DNA paternity test. You see, when the skipper, this Troskie bloke, came into the lounge to see what the ruckus was about he overheard Green shouting something about a DNA test at Sarah, the daughter's name in there somewhere. It was all he heard as they clammed up when seeing him but it was enough to make me think.'

'Yous having another round?' It was the little waitress, clearing away empties from their table, her false eyelashes at least an inch long with the tattoos down a bare arm colourful in the soft lighting.

'Pardon?' Riad said.

'Are yous having another round, same again?'

Yous, presumably the plural of "you" in Newspeak. The image of Professor Higgins in My Fair Lady flashed before his inner eye to be quickly dismissed. *Why can't the English teach their children how to speak?*

But Wheeler already had his hand up and wearily Riad realised he had no choice but to follow suit. 'One for the road,' he said lamely, wondering what the time was but not wanting to look at his watch, break the spell. 'So you checked on the DNA angle?'

Wheeler nodded, 'Sure did. I found out that, while they were in the USA where these things are legal without court orders, Ross Green did a paternity test. I suspect without Sarah's knowledge, must have gotten a buccal mucosa sample somehow – you can get this simply from the rim of a drinking glass – and likewise tested himself and Baby Maddie. Well, surprise! He's not the father! The results were posted to him, in personal mail forwarded from his London office shortly before they left Cannes, and found by the police when they removed his personal effects from the yacht for analysis.'

The packet of cigarettes had magically appeared in his hand again and once more he stared at it in puzzlement, checking himself just in time from lighting up. The printed image on the packet was that of an oral cavity horribly deformed by cancer and had Riad wonder how anyone could still smoke when confronted by that every time you lit up. 'Filthy habit,' Wheeler said, producing a fruity cough to illustrate the point.

'How did you get hold of that information?' Riad asked, the image of the cancer still at the back of his mind.

Wheeler laughed, 'Let's just say money changed hands, a few thousand euro to be exact.'

'I don't recall seeing that in the newspaper reports.'

'Editor quashed it, didn't he? Decided to publish only the straight up story and never bothered to tell me why.'

Riad shifted in his seat which was becoming uncomfortable. He was also aware of a growing hunger and wondered whether he would get a decent bite at this bohemian sounding place he would have to head for soon. Wheeler and Reed were digging into the fries that had arrived earlier, slurping it down with dripping helpings of ketchup but he was in need of something a bit more substantial.

'Why the sudden interest now? I mean how does this connect with the disappearance of Maddie Green?'

'Did I mention that I'm an investigative journalist?' His eyes were sparkling now, his slender frame tensed with excitement. 'In my line of work it's essential to have contacts inside the police and, through them other international sources. So when I learned that Sarah was being asked to submit for a DNA test, the case of the baby girl in the suitcase, it made me contact my source. I was amazed to learn that when pregnant with Maddie Sarah had a paternity test done, this time in London and submitting the name of the potential father. This was done via one of the many private companies now offering this service. Well, they found a match and the next thing the FBI is onto them, it seems the father's DNA came up on their own list of underworld figures. It seems they somehow pick up on these privately done tests.'

Sensing Riad was bursting to ask a barrage of questions Wheeler silenced him with a gesture, 'But here's the really good part, it seems the man in question is not only the father of little Maddie, he's also Sarah Green's father—'

'*Sweet Jesus Christ!*' Reed managed, saying it for all of them. Riad was too stunned to speak, struggling to find words.

'Who? *Shit!*' Reed exclaimed breathlessly, furiously spitting in his hand.

In answer Wheeler produced a photograph from an inside pocket of his jacket and placed it on the table. Taken on the deck of a large yacht it was of five people, all smiling at the camera, none of which were the Greens. 'This was taken by Anita's friend the day the guests came on board the Fairy Knowe. That is Anita in the middle and to her right is Abdul-Karim and Jean Martin and, to her left, Irina Sakharov and Ruslan.' Placing a dirty fingernail under the smiling face of the Russian and tapping it he said, 'And here we have the daddy of little Maddie Green.'

The magnitude of what he had just heard had Riad's senses reeling and as if from a distance he heard himself ask what was in all this for Wheeler.

'I have a deal going with one of the glossy weekly gossip magazines, the ones you find at the supermarket checkouts. Only this one is a spinoff of a very prestigious New York based monthly fashion magazine, no names no pack drill. They are bankrolling me feeling when this breaks it will be big. What I want from you, Detective Reed, is the promise of an exclusive when there's any news on Maddie or, for that matter, the mother. In exchange I'll pass onto you anything new I dig up.'

Turning to Riad he said, 'As for you, I'm not sure where you fit in but the same applies.'

But Riad knew where he fitted in, had finally figured it out. Now it was simply a question of formulating a plan to find the girl, fast, before it really became a case of a stone for Maddie Green.

'May I keep this photo?' he asked, rising. 'I'll make a copy and return—'

'Keep it,' Wheeler said with a dismissive wave, 'I have copies.' He glanced around for the waitress, 'Let's have one more for the road.'

'One more,' Riad cautioned, 'and the road might just rise up to meet you.' With that he tossed some money on the table, enough to cover the tab and bade them good evening, promising to call Reed the next day. Over his shoulder he could hear Wheeler shouting a curse at the game on TV, sounded like The Saints were losing again.

Outside the night air was bracing and he had to pause for a moment to steady himself before hailing a cab. Resting in his shirt pocket was the card Commander Michaels had given him earlier that afternoon. It was time to give her a call.

31
CHAPTER

The rain had stopped raining when the cab dropped him off at 285 Brunswick Street, Fitzroy, a few hundred yards up the road from where they had met earlier with Madame Revetcky. A three storey nondescript building near the corner there was a bouncer at the door who barely spared Riad a glance and then he was inside, a long bar to his left with the barman polishing glasses. The high ceilinged room in shades of purple and black. Two couples were at tables off to the side and in deep conversation, apart from that the place was empty. Noticing his puzzled look the barman pointed a finger at the ceiling, 'Upstairs,' he said, 'Second floor, lift's over there.'

Thanking him Riad took the elevator and stepped out into a noisy crowd of mainly young people clustered around a bar with a roped off dining area to the left and glass sliding doors leading off to a rooftop balcony. There was music, nothing that he recognised and mercifully not overwhelming. The décor was shades of ochre and yellow with lots of brass paraphernalia and, on a wall, a collage of photos of naked and semi-naked women. Tastefully done the hairdos suggested the good old days of yore while two settees in an alcove were from Victorian times or possibly early French.

Lighting was subdued but not to the extent where diners couldn't read the menu and most of the tables were filled. Pausing to glance around he was faced by a young waitress in a black tee shirt sporting the place's logo and asked whether he was dining. Shaking his head he explained that he was looking for a party of two women, one wearing a colourful Burberry coat, the other—

'You mean Sarah Green, the supermodel?' she said not quite managing to hide a starstruck expression.

'Yes.'

'She's out on the deck,' she said, pointing in the direction of the open glass doors, 'but she doesn't want to be bothered, the manager had to shoo some fans away earlier.' This with and appraising frown. Resisting the impulse to straighten his necktie, run a hand through his hair, show due deference, Riad explained that he was with Miss Green and she was expecting him.

Still dubious she stepped aside to let him pass and all the way across the room he was aware of her eyes on his back.

Outside he was instantly buffeted by the chilling breeze that had sprung up which explained why the only others standing there were two young men, businessmen judging by their suits, nursing beers – in glasses this time, it was that kind of place – and studying something on an iPad.

Making his way between tables he rounded a corner and spotted Sarah and Chrissie at a table in the shelter of a large potted plant, the remains of a meal evidence they had been there for a while. An ice bucket cradled the inevitable magnum of Krug and if Sarah noticed his approach she paid no attention, just stared ahead into space or possibly at the tall buildings across the street.

A cigarette was between her fingers and several butts on the tiles where she had stamped them out.

'I didn't know smoking was allowed in restaurants,' he said, pulling up a chair.

Sarah snorted and a nervously smiling Chrissie said that after some customers had complained the manager suggested they move outside and found this secluded spot on the rooftop balcony. She found it necessary to explain that in the warm summer months that area would normally be very crowded. Miss Sarah was a regular customer and—

Riad said nothing, placing his hands on the steel topped table he leaned forward and stared hard at Sarah, willing her to meet his gaze. She flinched slightly and looked away.

'Miss Sarah is not herself this evening,' Chrissie said hesitantly, adding, 'she's feeling sad and missing little Maddie and wants to be alone.'

'Look at me Sarah. LOOK AT ME!'

Slowly, moving like an automaton, she turned to face him, blue eyes dulled and unseeing. She was quite drunk which had him ask how much she'd had.

'The whole bottle,' Chrissie said in a barely audible whisper, 'and a few dry martinis before that.'

'No drugs?'

Chrissie shook her head vehemently, 'Miss Sarah doesn't do that.'

'So peaceful here,' Sarah said dreamily as she turned to stare out over the city, the flickering neon of the CBD but a few street blocks away. 'All those pretty lights, winking and calling. Do you think Maddie sees them too?'

But Riad was thinking fast now. A glance over the balcony rail down at the street below had confirmed the paparazzi had arrived as he knew they would. Festooned with cameras and warmly dressed against the cold, three of them were in conversation with the bouncer on the pavement, no doubt the one who had tipped them off in the first place. He had to get Sarah out of here without being photographed in her current state for tonight he wasn't just Maddie's searcher but Sarah's keeper. Beckoning at a waitress through the large picture window he ordered a pot of strong black coffee as well as the check.

Getting up to move out of earshot he dialled Vytas' number, got him on the third ring. 'Uncle Vytas, I need a favour.'

'Sure. Iss no problem, you say.'

There was noise in the background, faintly familiar but not typical city sounds, 'Where are you?' he asked.

'Vytas at airport, drop off Bubba.'

Riad was about to ask why but decided that could wait, 'I need you to come and pick me and the two ladies up, right now. We're at a place in Brunswick called Naked for Satan, know it?'

There was a moment's pause during which Riad pictured the big man frowning, scratching his head. 'I think but, no problem, I put GPS.'

'Another thing, I want you to come in a taxi, not your little car, OK?'

'My car good!' Vytas protested indignantly.

Riad thought of the debt collector sign on the side and supressed a shudder. 'Just do as I ask you, I will pay you well. Another thing, there's a few paparazzi outside on the pavement, think you can handle them? I don't want any photographs, the lady is not feeling well, understood?'

The voice on the line chuckled, this was indeed the kind of thing Vytas savoured, the standover business. 'Punks!' he growled, 'Vytas take care.'

Which left Riad to ponder his next move while they waited. At Chrissie's suggestion he ordered a focaccia which took the edge off his appetite. Gazing through the picture windows at the scene inside at the bar while eating he marvelled once again at what appeared to be modern day Australian society, at least where the young people were concerned. Not a blue collar venue the girls were all dressed to go out, short skirts and impossibly high heels the norm. many with bare arms and seemingly oblivious to the cold weather.

All wore their hair long and loose with carefully applied makeup, false eyelashes the fad of the day. All drinking vodka cruisers in a variety of colours and straight from the bottle, the conversation lively, the laughter loud and just a little forced.

The striking thing was they were in a tight gyrating circle, pointedly several feet away from a group of young men of a similar age. The men were noticeably quieter, less animated, and were drinking craft beers. Less dressed up they wore mostly smart casual with a smattering of young businessmen and office workers.

Here the discussion was footy and cricket and never women. And during all the time Riad studied them nobody in either group ever glanced in the direction of the other sex. Clearly the girls went out in groups and dressed up for each other. The few mixed couples were mostly of an older age group and Riad thought wherever they had hooked up, it couldn't have been here.

What was going on? Was this the new feminism? If so it didn't look good for the country's future population growth.

As he watched Chrissie coax more of the sweet black coffee into a reluctant Sarah Riad's thoughts drifted back to the earlier conversation with Zena Michaels. He had phoned the Federal Police Commander while in a cab on his way to Brunswick and arranged to meet her the next morning at nine. She had been scheduled to fly back to Canberra but was intrigued at his suggestion as it might just be the way to find Maddie. She would think it over and come up with some ideas of how they might play it.

So why did he feel she had been waiting for his call all along, the reason she hadn't left town yet. Had he been set up? First Sarah Green and now the policewoman? And why did that thought arouse him just a little?

Vytas arrived three quarters of an hour later, having phoned to let Riad know he was pulling up outside the place and what did he want him to do?

A few minutes earlier, after some thought, Riad had asked the waitress to please call the manager, it was about Sarah Green. There was something to be said for celebrity status, he mused as he saw the man hurry over, you never had to stand in line, everyone always eager to help, bask in that glowing spotlight that followed life's beautiful people.

Taking the man aside he had explained that Miss Green had unfortunately taken ill, and would have to be escorted to her waiting car but that there were photographers at the front entrance and it would not do to have her picture taken under these circumstances.

Perhaps they could leave discreetly by a back entrance?

Glancing uncertainly at Sarah who was now leaning her head on Chrissie's shoulder the man, Riad judged him no older than about mid twenties, weighed his options. On the one hand it was good advertising to have the lady snapped leaving his elite establishment, on the other hand she was clearly inebriated which raised the spectrum of Melbourne's licensing laws. Serving alcohol to a drunk person was a serious offense and questions might just be asked.

It turned out there was indeed a back entrance and he would be happy to escort them.

'Where does it lead to?' Riad asked.

'An alley that opens to the side street around the corner.'

'Excellent. I'm sure Miss Green will be most grateful for your kindness.' As an afterthought he added 'and professionalism.' People tended to like that touch.

Signalling to Chrissie to get Sarah ready to leave he phoned Vytas. 'We're coming out the back way, an alley around the corner. Take the cab around there and ask the driver to wait. You walk up the alley, I might need you to block anyone trying to follow us, no photos, OK?' A grunt indicated it was and Riad turned to the hovering manager who was helping Chrissie steady a very wobbly Sarah whose features had turned a deathly pale.

'One more thing, no paparazzi inside this place, right?'

The young man shook his head, 'they're not allowed to take photos inside here.'

'Good. Let's go.'

Following the manager, Sarah firmly supported by both Chrissie and Riad, they took a route around the rooftop balcony to enter the main bar area on the opposite side they had entered, away from the crowd and next to the elevators. Minutes later they were in the foyer and heading for a door marked as private, the manager's office. Ushering them in he indicated another unmarked door and then they were in an alleyway amongst a collection of overflowing trash cans with darting shadows and scurrying sounds suggesting a family of resident rats.

It was dark and there was a step and Riad cursed as their charge stumbled and proceeded to do precisely what he had feared all along, vomit all over his shoes.

It came as no surprise to Riad that the three paparazzi on the front pavement had a spotter inside the place all along, the man suddenly appearing in the doorway behind them and bringing up a camera from under his raincoat in a swooping motion.

Seemingly from nowhere a large hand appeared out of the gloom and took the camera away from the stunned would be photographer as one would candy from a baby. No force needed. 'Come along,' Vytas said affably, encircling the startled man's shoulders with a friendly arm, 'let's take walk, to taxi. I give back camera there.'

Minutes later they were in the cab and pulling away, the hapless photographer alone on the sidewalk and furiously waving his arms. 'Shouldn't you give back his camera?' Riad asked.

Cursing, Vytas ordered the driver to stop, then opened his door and placed the object in the road while shouting at the man to come and get it.

At the house Riad asked Vytas to wait in the cab while he helped Chrissie get Sarah up the stairs and to her room. Returning he paid off the cab adding a generous tip plus the fare to take Vytas back to his car. Then he took the big man aside and showed him the photograph taken on the Fairy Knowe. 'Is the man who met with Sarah Green in this photo?'

Taking the photo for a closer look Vytas nodded and pointed at a smiling Ruslan. 'Him,' he said emphatically, 'I recognise bastard anytime!'

Declining to comment, saying he would explain all later, Riad cautioned against approaching Ruslan. Thinking just another chip of a jigsaw puzzle slotting into place he instructed Vytas to follow Sarah the next day, not let her out of his sight. She had an appointment to shoot some or other television ad, the location not known to him, but the agency would pick her up at this address at nine. Vytas would wait, in an unmarked car, down the street and follow. Satisfied that the man understood Riad peeled off twenty one hundred dollar bills promising there would be more the next day.

heading back up the stairs he wondered whether he should have added the unmarked car should preferably not be a stolen one but shook off the thought. Vytas was a force of nature, no point trying to teach him his business. It was only when reaching the front door that he realised he had forgotten to enquire about the emergency business calling Bubba to Beirut.

32
CHAPTER

H e stood under the piping hot shower for all of fifteen minutes, letting the water wash away the grime and despair of the big city, feeling the heat slowly dissipate the tension in his shoulders and neck to be replaced by a pleasant sensation of bone tiredness. Towelling himself dry he studied his reflection in the mirror taking in the tousled hair badly in need of a cut, the faint yet definite bags under weary eyes and, finally, settling on the scars of a thousand yesterdays.

They were all there, some now fading white lines, others like the recent nephrectomy scar, still red and raised and throbbing at the end of day. Each one a wound that came with its own story, own memory and all of them bad.

And all our yesterdays lighten fools the way to dusty death was how Shakespeare had put it. Which yet to come scar would be his own fatal wound? For there would be more, of that he was certain. Perhaps even as soon as the next few days, for he was about to enter the den of the dragon once more to find Maddie and bring her home.

And a certainty was that whoever had her would not give up that prize easily. There would be blood.

Back in his room he pulled on a tee shirt and climbed into bed, taking his laptop with him and checking his emails. One from Colonel Omar requested an update on the situation regarding the missing child, something he would deal with later. Another from Waleed stating they had traced the source of the AK47 used in the first attack but so far nothing leading to the puppet master. The man had been very good at covering his tracks. Following Riad's suggestion he was interviewing the other students at the killers' school as well as teachers, a painstaking task with so far no clues.

For the second day in a row nothing from Rania. Equally odd that his mother had not phoned. For the first time he could recall that troubled him. Glancing at his watch he decided he would phone the next morning, still evening there. Right now he had another important call to make.

Dialling the number Riad listened to a series of clicks and buzzes typical of the long distance call before being connected to the rooms of psychologist Ameera al Quarashi. Did he wish to make an appointment? asked the receptionist after taking down his name.

Maybe later, right now he had to speak to the therapist rather urgently. Yes, his own health, mental health that was, had taken a downturn, hence the urgency.

It turned out the doctor was in the middle of a consultation but would return his call as soon as she finished, perhaps another five or ten minutes she added in an attempt to cheer him up. He said he would hold and spent the next five minutes listening to the Arab equivalent of elevator music and then the familiar voice of the psychologist came on the line.

'Lieutenant Ajmi! So nice to hear from you, I presume you are overseas at the moment?'

Riad said he was and confessed that he wasn't really going through a personal crisis but would appreciate her help in clearing up something, the case he was working on.

'Is that the Maddie Green case, Sarah's little girl?'

'Yes,' wondering how she knew but then presumably Sarah would have told her. Pressing on before she had a chance to enquire about everyone's mental wellbeing and how things were in Melbourne – an easy bet she knew that bit too – he came to the point.

'We, the Australian Police and myself, are currently retracing Maddie's earlier years, specifically her many visits to what turns out to be amongst others, child psychologists. A curious bit of information came up, something one of the analysts had question marked.' He paused, wondering how to phrase the question without giving away too much.

'Yes--?'

There was nothing for it but to plunge on, 'The term "MS" – presumably an abbreviation for a medical term. Initially it was thought to perhaps indicate possible multiple sclerosis but subsequent tests and examinations had definitely excluded that diagnosis. I want to know from you, in the field of psychology, what could this "MS" possibly refer too?'

'Hmm…' There was a moment's silence during which Riad could hear a phone ring in the background. He also became aware of a crossed line, someone speaking rapid Spanish and fading in and out.

She was speaking and he had to strain to make it out. 'Can you say that again?' he asked, pressing the mobile closer to his ear.

'Munchausen Syndrome. It is where a patient presents to doctors repeatedly often demanding invasive procedures. Also known as Factitious Disorder it involves mainly women who act out sickness to gain sympathy and attention. There is a variant, called Munchausen syndrome by proxy, where the mother makes the child appear mentally or physically sick to gain—' She paused, suddenly aware of what she was saying.

'You—you don't think, I—I didn't mean to suggest—'

'No!' Riad said quickly, 'of course not. Besides there may be other, even non medical, terms the doctor could have been thinking of.'

'Yes!' al Quarashi said quickly, relief in her voice. 'Like Meniere's disease, for instance. Or Mediterranean fever, the rich travel a lot, you know?'

Deciding to change the subject Riad asked whether she was still doing counselling at the school where the two juvenile killers originated from.

'Oh yes, so many children there that need therapy, you wouldn't believe it. Often it has to do with the parents suffering from severe PTSD as an aftermath of the Kuwait Invasion and passing the stress on to the kids. I also offer counselling at two other schools and, God be praised, none of those kids have turned into a sword wielding killer!'

Riad thanked her for help, once again expressing the reassurance that the information was confidential and simply a matter of leaving no stone unturned in the search for Maddie. And, yes, he would be in touch the moment he was back in Kuwait to complete his own therapy.

After ringing off he lay there for a while thinking about what he had just heard. Then he rang Waleed, the detective still at his office and eating a meal at his desk. After the usual banter about the good life in Melbourne Riad asked about what information regarding the second killing had been released to the press or anyone outside the immediate circle of investigation, pointing out that the decision had been made to keep that information under wraps for the time being. No-one had leaked his sergeant reassured him which led Riad to issue a set of instructions, taking the investigation down a new route.

'In my absence, who's leading the investigation?'

'Omar,' came the prompt answer, accompanied by a soft laugh. 'The fat man sees some political advantage in this one, maybe even another medal!' Adding, on a sombre note, 'Cut short your holiday and get back here, *modir*. Things are going nowhere fast.'

After ringing off Riad padded over to the kitchen and fixed himself a cup of coffee, taking it back to the room. The house was quiet and for a moment he wondered whether he should check on Sarah but decided the ever vigilant Chrissie would call him if there was a cause for concern.

Settling back in bed he reached for his laptop and Googled Munchausen syndrome by proxy. Wikipedia had a long article and it made for fascinating reading. At the time of diagnosis the average age of the victim was 4 years with half aged younger than two. By the time of diagnosis up to 6% of those affected would have died, mostly from smothering by the abuser, infection or physical injury. Seven percent suffered long term injury including permanent psychological damage. The mother was the perpetrator in more than 76.5% of cases, the father in 6.7%

There followed a long list of medical problems, often a combination of several and many of these easy to fake as they are subjective, based on the abuser's testimony.

Aside from the motive, which is to gain attention and sympathy for the abuser, another feature that distinguishes Munchausen by proxy from typical physical child abuse where the perpetrator lashes out at a child in response to something like crying, bedwetting or spilling food, is the degree of premeditation involved. Assault on these children appear to be planned and unprovoked.

The article went on to describe how often doctors can become unwitting accomplices in harming the child with batteries of tests and often invasive procedures, also how the abuser – once again typically the mother – would tend to switch medical providers until finding one that will satisfy their ongoing needs. So called "doctor shopping" and "hospital hopping."

His interest was pricked by the statement that many Munchausen Syndrome patients are thought to have been MS by proxy victims themselves, the disease becoming a lifelong and multi-generational disorder in some cases.

Laying aside the laptop he conjured up the smiling face of Maddie Green captured on one of the many family photos he had been shown what now seemed a long time ago. Was this what had been staring him in the face all along? Was the little girl a victim of this terrible syndrome? But to *this* extent? It hardly seemed credible and yet...

Deciding to raise this with Zena Michaels the next morning he switched off the bedside light. His mind a whirl of thoughts and theories it was past midnight when he finally drifted off to sleep. A deep and troubled descent into a netherworld of darkness and raging storms and running through the clawing undergrowth a small blonde girl, barefoot and naked, long hair streaming, blue eyes widened in fear and glancing back at the monsters snapping and snarling in pursuit. Very red lips were parted in a silent scream and tiny arms and hands reaching out to him.

Except he couldn't move. A curious state where he was half awake, conscious in a way of his surroundings yet not there. And paralysed, his limbs heavy and unresponsive no matter how hard he tried to marshal them into moving, to help the girl.

At first he thought it was part of the dream, the flaxen haired young maiden now close and taking shelter in his protective embrace as the demons chasing her closed in. But there was something new in his dream, a heightened sense of touch, of closeness, of someone breathing on his face.

Slowly surfacing from a state of sleep paralysis, something he had experienced in many a previous nightmare, he became aware he was not alone. Snuggling up to him was another being, the warm and soft unmistakeable form of a woman, long legs entangled with his own, hot breath down the side of his neck and a sense of moistness where the mouth rested.

Still half asleep it took him a while to realise it was Sarah Green, the lingering fragrance of her perfume the giveaway. She was moaning softly in her slumber and the hand resting on his belly was as cold as ice.

Instantly awake now he lay there as if carved from stone, his mind racing to form a picture of what had happened. Nothing was the conclusion. At least nothing he had done,

Sarah must have woken from her drunken stupor and come down the stairs without waking Chrissie to climb into bed with him, promptly going back to sleep.

A restless sleep where she kicked and shuddered while softly moaning over and over, 'Help me. Help me—'

Not knowing what to do he raised a free arm and softly stroked her hair which was soaked in perspiration and plastered to her cheek. Gradually, after what seemed like an hour, she drifted into a more peaceful sleep but still he did not dare move, afraid of disturbing her.

His eyes now long adjusted to the dark he found himself staring at the ceiling fan as it slowly revolved, casting moving shadows on the wall. Somehow it brought back the words of a long forgotten song, the haunting theme achingly sharp in his mind: "Like a circle in a spiral like a wheel within a wheel. Never ending or beginning on an ever spinning reel... Like the circles that you find in the windmills of your mind—"

With the lyrics of the Legrand/Marnay song looping through his mind, immortalised in the voice of Dusty Springfield, he turned his head to stare down at the sleeping face nestled in his arms.

And once again he wondered, where do you go to my lovely when alone in your bed? How I wish I could see inside your head…

Sleep for him was impossible now and as he lay there he thought of the irony of his life. Here he was in bed with one of the most beautiful women in the world, after much champagne had flowed, and powerless to do anything about it.

Oh Riad, where did it all go wrong? The thought brought a wry smile to his lips.

He must have dozed off for the golden colours of early morning was streaming through the blinds when he woke, aware of the bedroom door slowly swinging open. Blinking as, still weighed down by the dead weight of the sleeping woman, he unsuccessfully tried to raise himself up on his elbows he became aware of a man standing in the open doorway.

It was a motionless Hasan Abdul-Karim, his face an expressionless mask, dark eyes staring, taking in all. Meeting those of Riad and showing nothing, no emotion, no anger. Just nothing. Then, moving slowly, he retreated closing the door softly behind him.

It was seven thirty on Riad's wristwatch.

33
CHAPTER

Getting out of bed carefully so as not to disturb Sarah he stood for a minute staring down at the sleeping woman whose face was partially covered in tousled locks of blonde of hair as she moaned softly and stirred restlessly. Why? He thought, why go through this charade, this amateur display of Cluedo when the evidence was mounting that Sarah Green knew exactly what had happened to her daughter, knew who had taken her and most probably knew where.

Why could she not simply bring it to herself to tell him the truth and maybe, just maybe, save Maddie before it was too late?

Deciding against shaving he used the bathroom to complete his ablutions before dressing in a clean shirt and selecting a pair of blue corduroys and comfortable trainers, topping it off with an old quilted casual jacket he had bought once on a trip to New York. Then he went through to the kitchen where an unusually quiet Chrissie was seated at the breakfast table listlessly chewing on a piece of toast and not deigning to meet his gaze.

There was no sign of Abdul-Karim and he wondered whether the man was upstairs or had left on some or other business. Somehow it didn't seem to matter.

'Sarah is not well,' he said, pouring himself a cup of coffee from the percolator bubbling on a shelf. 'I suggest you go and wake her and get her ready for this shoot. The car will be here before long.'

Wordlessly she got up and left the room and minutes later there was the sounds of feet in the hallway and then the creaking of stairs as the two women made their way upstairs.

It was still early for his meeting with the Federal Policewoman and he decided to take a walk up the road to a small café two blocks away and get a morning paper. Outside it was cold and blustery but mercifully not raining and the few pedestrians about were swathed in warm winter wear and hurrying along, bent forward against the swirling wind as they weaved to avoid the puddles of the night's storm. A low slung winter's sun was struggling to peek out between buildings and in the distance he could just make out the hum of busy morning traffic.

It was a pleasant sound, a beautiful noise as the song went and made him think of other big cities he had known and once more raised the question of why he was here right now, in this one.

He was about to enter the shop, a 7 eleven franchise, when his mobile buzzed. Taking shelter under the shop's awning he answered. No caller ID but the number displayed an overseas one. 'Hello Gigolo! How's tricks?'

It was Suleiman al Thani, the man sounding as cheerful as always and with all the money in the world, why wouldn't he be.

'Chunky,' Riad said, turning his back to the wind and cupping the phone, 'what a surprise.'

'I got your number from your old man, been speaking to him quite a bit lately, in fact.'

'Let me guess,' Riad said as he strove to inject a note of enthusiasm into his voice, 'there is talk of a wedding arrangement?'

'You bet, brother! You'll have to be there at the final negotiations, of course.'

'Of course,' Riad sighed.

'But this is not the reason I phone. Do you remember Pudding Johnson? Well, his old man has finally passed and our boy is now Lord Hailwood and throwing a mighty party to celebrate. All the old classmates will be there for a whole week of shocking debauchery. The relaunch of the old Pudding and Pie Dining Club! Shooting, wining, dining and wenching. He wants you to come, please say you will!'

For a moment the long suppressed memories of a brief period of recklessness spent in the midst of a collective madness that clearly never ended for some flashed before him to instantly be repressed. 'Uh—yes,' he said dully, while desperately trying to find a way out. This was family to be and apparently an old school friend to boot, not something to be dismissed out of hand. 'When is this party?' he managed finally.

'Next month, the weekend of the thirteenth. At his pile in Norwich. You know the place, we all went down for a weekend in our senior year. That was when Lady Hailwood discovered you starkers the time we streaked down the—'

'Yes, yes,' Riad interrupted hurriedly. Another painful memory to suppress. 'I'll try my best to be there.' A sudden thought had him ask where the caller was at that moment.

'In London, old boy. Been banging about at Annabelle's last night, got the most godawful hangover I don't mind telling you.'

Riad was thinking fast now, his friend was no doubt a wastrel and playboy but he was also a successful businessman in his own right, someone with extensive contacts. 'I have a favour to ask of you.'

'Anything for family. What is it?'

'I need all the information I can get about a certain Dimitri Ruslan, a Russian businessman. It has to do with a case I'm working on.'

There was a moment's silence on the other side then Chunky came back, suddenly sounding more sober, 'This is a dangerous man, my friend. Someone to be careful around. I do know him from a deal we once did, a casino in Macau. That was before I knew he was Russian Mafia, I was lucky to walk away. What exactly to you wish to know?'

'What is his relationship with Sarah Green, the supermodel, where did they meet for the first time and what was his connection with her first husband. Also what connection does he have with Abdul-Karim, her current husband. Think you can ferret that out for me? I'd be most appreciative.'

'I'll see what I can do. Give me a day and I'll get back to you.' And with that the conversation was over. Collecting a copy of *The*

Australian Riad phoned for an Uber car and minutes later was on his way to the meeting with Zena Michaels.

The Sirocco restaurant was in the foyer of the Flinders Lane Holiday Inn where Michaels was staying. She was seated at a window table and waved him over. On the way over he had glanced at the paper's headlines and remarked to her about the case of a four year old boy that had been snatched from his foster grandmother's front garden just days before. 'Another one for your unit?'

She sighed, nodded, 'Yes. At least it will be. Currently it's still a police matter but I have a bad feeling about this one.'

Glancing around Riad saw it was the usual hotel buffet, the kind of place you make your own toast and fix your own coffee from a machine offering four choices. A passing waitress placed a small slip at his elbow which offered the option of an omelette made to the individual's taste. Taking the offered pen he ticked a few boxes and handed it back to her.

'Good choice,' Zena said, handing over her own slip and settling back to study him over the rim of her orange juice. 'You look shit,' she said with a grimace, 'bad night at Hanging Rock?'

'What?'

'Never mind. How is the Ice Queen this morning?'

For a split second he wondered if she knew about the events of the past few hours then shrugged it off, 'She's had a bad night and this morning she's booked for some photo shoot or other. Why do you ask?'

She shook her head and motioned over a waitress, asking her to bring over some orange juice. Also some fresh croissants. There was a note of authority in her tone and the young girl went quickly over to the buffet. Fixing Riad with a businesslike look Michaels leaned over placing her elbows on the table, 'Let's talk turkey,' she said evenly.

'Let's.'

The nearest other guests were two tables away but she dropped her voice nevertheless. 'You recall that I mentioned yesterday about the paedo we caught and has handed us access to his different online contacts, including the site where we saw Maddie? Well, we have so far kept all this secret, you are one of only four, together with Sarah five, people who know this. Taking over his identity we have been onto this site with purpose of gaining access to the little girl, arrange a meeting. Progress has been made to the point of a price being arranged, three thousand dollars for two hours with Maddie, four if they include a second four year old whom we have not identified so far.'

None of this surprised Riad, he had seen it coming. Knew why he was there. 'You want me to be this person,' he said softly.

She nodded, 'There is the fear my department could have been infiltrated, the members known. But you are an outsider and less likely to be exposed when the contact is made.'

Turning to stare out the large picture windows at the street scene outside he saw that it had started raining again, lingering for a moment on a well dressed middle aged woman who was simultaneously trying to juggle her umbrella while gathering up a toy poodle on a red leash. It had baulked at crossing a puddle and now hung like a miserable rag doll under a clutching arm as water dripped from the umbrella's rim and onto its head.

He felt for that poodle, knew exactly how it felt. 'You saw me coming,' he said as a man in a chef's apron stepped up with their omelettes. 'That's the reason you didn't fly back to Canberra last night.'

'Maybe. Or maybe I just wanted a change of air. Let me tell you something about this Miss Sarah Green of yours, something we only discovered a few days ago. As a young child growing up in London she was taken away from her mother, a druggie prostitute, and placed in foster care. It turned out that not only did mummy dear turn tricks, she offered threesomes featuring little Sarah. It seems her clients included some very disturbed gentlemen, we might almost say paedophiles. You may well ask how we know this? As with cases involving minors this was all suppressed by the British courts until we, working with our London counterparts, managed to get a look in.'

There was a pause as she took a few bites from her omelette, declaring it yummy and smearing some marmalade on one of the croissants that had arrived. 'Would you like some coffee? I'll be mother and get some.'

As she strode over to the espresso machine he watched her, taking in the way she moved in the dark grey trousered business suit she wore that morning, the black stiletto heels making her look even taller than the six feet that had her look him straight in the eye, the unflinching stare always just that little bit challenging. Like the day before her hair was tied up in a bun and just for a moment he visualised it shaken loose and tumbling down. Not for the first time he realised there was an animal magnetism there, wondered if it was because they were both predators in a way, hunters of men if perhaps in different ways.

Then she was back with the coffee, swivelling in her seat to stare out the window, 'I love this city,' she said sipping her drink. 'It's the most European of all Australian cities and it's not just the cultural scene or the restaurants, sidewalk cafes and rooftop bars but the atmosphere of the place. The cosmopolitan crowd, the multitude of trams and, of course, the river.'

Riad nodded, he knew what she meant, had felt it too. Not a bad place to live he mused, to raise a child. With a pang of guilt he thought of Rania and wondered what she was doing. He'd have to phone her later and once again he wondered about the family business Vytas had alluded to the night before.

Far away for a moment he realised Zena was speaking, '— interesting that she had been on one of those websites that, for a fee, trace you ancestry. This one was called Guardian Angel and still operates. This snippet also courtesy of London colleagues who have put a lot of work into the Maddie Green case. Well, it turns out that Sarah had provided a name her dear mommy had given her and as this Lothario proved to have his DNA on file with no less than Interpol and the FBI a match was found. He is indeed Sarah's father.'

She turned to gaze back at him, a look of triumph on her face.

'Let my guess,' Riad said wearily, 'it's Mr Dimitri Ruslan.'

If this stunned her she hid it well, 'How did you know?'

Riad shrugged, 'I also have my sources but the clues were there all along. He is here in the city right now, the question is why and how is this connected with Maddie's disappearance if at all?'

'It seems we have a lot to discuss,' Zena said, rising. 'Shall we take a trip down to my office at Federal Police HQ on La Trobe Street? We can take a tram.'

Returning the smile of the waiter she led the way only to pause at the foyer elevators. 'I have to go to my room and powder my nose. Feel like coming along?'

'Maybe later.'

'Whatever you say, big boy,' she said coyly and stepped into the elevator leaving him to study his newspaper and seeing nothing.

33
CHAPTER

'**A**nd you are sure it was him?'

'Baker nodded. It hurt to nod his head and he made a mental note not to do it again. 'The bastard who sucker punched me? Sure I'm sure. Can't wait to get my hands—'

Abdul-Karim silenced him with an impatient gesture, 'Do you know where he is or was staying?'

'No. I've checked all the hotels – a bigshot like him would only stay in the five star ones but I checked all the others anyway; no luck. I do have something to go on though—'

'Yes?' Abdul-Karim said eagerly, moving his chair closer. They were in the lounge of a boutique hotel in Little Bourke Street with the only others nearby a small tour group, suitcases at hand, waiting for their bus.

'His company, Hazelton Enterprises, an offshoot of Rospolites Komersk, have been manning a stall at a current computer software convention at the Melbourne Exhibition Centre in downtown Docklands. He was spotted there yesterday by my associate. To-day is the last day of the convention. With a bit of luck I can pick up his trail there, at the very least find out where he's heading if no longer here in the city?'

'Oh he is here in the city, alright,' Abdul-Karim said softly, 'his business, his real business, is not quite settled yet.' His face darkened for a fleeting moment then he seemed to come to a decision 'I want you to follow him but not confront him. I want to know where he goes, who he sees.' His eyes narrowed as another thought struck him, 'This associate of yours, is he a handy man in a tight spot?'

Baker nodded, winced and gingerly touched the back of his head, 'Ronnie? Sure, man's a journeyman light heavyweight, isn't he?'

'Take him along, I'll put some more money into your account. But remember, don't confront Ruslan, just let me know once you find out where he's going.'

'May I ask what the purpose of the whole exercise is?'

Abdul-Karim had risen from his seat and was reaching for his coat, he paused to stare into the open space of the distant lobby and when he spoke his voice was soft, almost wistful. 'It's about a little girl, a very frightened little girl, someone dear to me—'

'Shouldn't the police be involved?'

'It is a very delicate matter, a family matter. The future wellbeing of more than one person is at stake here, not a police matter at all.'

With that he placed a black fedora hat on his head, buttoned up his overcoat and strode for the door, leaving a slightly bemused private detective wondering at how it was always this way, the client telling you one half of the story and that being the half full of lies.

If he didn't believe Abdul-Karim's story he believed the five thousand dollar retainer nestling in his bank account and that was good enough for him.

At that moment Dimitri Ruslan was staring at the caller ID on his mobile before, with an impatient sigh, answering, 'Sarah, *tovarisch!* How is my little angel?'

There was a sharp intake of breath then silence on the line until she spoke, the voice soft and audibly strained, 'This has to stop now, you bastard! Where is she?! I have to see her now!'

'Sarah, Sarah,' he answered placatingly, 'such passion! Did you forget our little arrangement, my dear? So soon? Was it not exactly this that made you the strong woman you are today?'

But she was crying now, soft shuddering sobs, sounds of the phone being lowered enough to pick up background noises. Enough traffic to be somewhere in the central city. He waited for her to blow her nose and come back to the phone, her voice now monotone and tired. 'It was not to be this,' she said hopelessly, '*Please* Ruslan, just tell me where she is and I promise you nothing will happen to you. I just want Maddie back!'

A sudden thought had her ask if it was money he wanted, warming to the idea as she spoke. 'We can make it a ransom payment! A kidnapping and you took money and...'

She was stopped by Ruslan's laugh. A nasty laugh that scrunched her insides into a ball of pain. 'Stupid woman. The whole fucking world knows this wasn't a kidnap for Mickey Mouse ransom. The police will never buy it.'

'W... what are you saying?' She asked, the words catching in her throat.

'Little Maddie has real talent, my dear. She's already a star and with the correct management will be a great investment as the years go by. After all, she comes from a great bloodline doesn't she? Grandmother a whore, mother a whore, what's not to like?'

'You raped me!' she shouted, 'when all I wanted was to find my father and you took me and abused me and—' a sudden thought had her hesitate, then ask hesitatingly, 'Is she, is she at the place where you took me that time when—Yes! That's it! I know it is! The big house on the beach...' His silence was enough to confirm she was right.

'Maybe we can work something out,' Ruslan, suddenly worried, said in a placatory tone. 'Perhaps if the ransom was tempting enough. I'll tell you what, meet me at Yuri's Bar at two, remember where it is?'

'I think so.'

'Come alone, if I see anyone with you I will disappear, understand?'

'Yes, yes, can I just—'

But the line had gone dead.

———◆———

'Let's go over it again,' Zena said as she rose from where she had been perching on the edge of the table to go back to the large whiteboard. Turning to fix Riad with a schoolteacher's look she tapped at the board, 'Name?'

'Ernest White. My friends call me Ernie.'

'Online handle?'

'Nightcat17.'

'Dark Angel login?'

'Catchtreefourdancer.'

She stared at him dubiously, 'Say what?'

'You heard me.' He repeated the sequence, faster this time.

Sighing she flipped the board over to confirm he was right. 'Who the hell chooses a random four word password anyway?'

'More secure than any combination of numbers and symbols,' he replied thinking of the Kuwait computer geek or, as he preferred to think of him, homicide number two.

Grunting she flipped the board over and took Riad through another twenty minutes of gruelling personal ID theft as she called it. Satisfied that he could, with a bit of luck, pass as Ernie the paedophile, she called a break. 'Christ, I'm as dry as a nun's tit; let's go and get a drink. There's a pub just around the corner.'

Whatever Zena Michaels was, she was no nun, Riad thought with a smile.

From a corner where he had been patiently watching the rehearsal DI Reed rose with visible effort and stretched out. Despite a chill in the room he was sweating visibly and his shirt was rumpled and stained at the armpits. The necktie was loosened to button number three and Riad thought deciphering its food stains would be an exercise in itself.

'We have to go over the logistics of the backup one more time,' he said, 'We'll have a SOG team on standby and I will be in a separate car with two detectives. Riad will be in a rental – the real Mr White doesn't own one, something the mark might be aware of – which leaves the question, what do we do with you, Commander Michaels?'

At the start of the sessions there had been a short but terse difference of opinion as to who would be in charge of the mission, for the moment won by Reed who pointed out that the retrieval of the girl was still a Melbourne Metropolitan Police matter. A matter of who pisses on whose patch the Detective Inspector had put it.

'I'll be in the trunk of Riad's car,' she said firmly, crossing her arms.

Reed had anticipated this, 'What if they search it?'

'If they're that suspicious we'd be stuffed anyway, don't you think?'

'Well, at least you won't be driving,' Reed snarled nastily having Riad glance at him sharply.

'What's the matter, Reed, bad hangover?'

The detective smiled ruefully, rubbed the back of his head, 'Lack of sleep, bloody kid's been playing up again and I've just about had it.'

Riad was about to sympathize about a newborn in the house when something he saw in Zena's eyes had him hesitate. 'Reed's been having a bit of a rough ride lately,' she said softly, 'They adopted a boy years ago, what is he, twelve now?'

'Fifteen,' Reed said sourly, dry spitting a few times in his palm, 'we couldn't have kids and it's fucking impossible in this bloody country to adopt an Aussie kid, bloody stolen generation and all that shit, so we got this Korean orphan. *Whore!*' More rapid spitting. 'A nightmare from the start, mainly because of my crackpot wife. Had to tell him he was adopted didn't she, then catered to his every bloody whim.

Now he's a full blown psycho, refuses to go to school, says we can't tell him anything as we're not his real parents and just behaves like a cunt all along.'

Warming to the theme now he took a swig from a bottle of water and, still staring at something outside the window, went on, 'First it was PTSD, the brat from a slum or something, then came obsessive compulsive hyperactivity disorder and more shrinks. Wife tells everyone he's on the autism spectrum, like it's some kind of achievement. Kid eats Ritalin for fucking breakfast. Worse is, he's quite clever, a bloody computer wizard but knows nothing else. Beth's gone psycho herself now, accuses me of all kinds of shit and last night – well, last night I just lost it, walked out.'

'Maybe you should take some leave, once this is over,' Zena offered with surprising gentleness.

'Forget it,' he said wearily, 'let's go and get that drink. The date with little Maddie is set up for six tomorrow afternoon, gives us time to run over details again before then.'

Reaching for his jacket Riad was brought up short as his mobile rang. It was Vytas. 'Lady in bar on Spring Street now, having lunch. They finish the meeting at Elaine's Studio one hour ago and Sarah took Uber to here, other side of city. I follow on motorbike. The other woman, she was here but left half hour ago, walking. Maybe shopping. When she gone Sarah gets on phone and talks long time, also getting very upset, crying.'

Supressing his rising excitement Riad asked whether she had met anyone at all, while silently cursing the fact that Bubba, a potential second "cut out" tail, was away on some family business which would almost certainly mean some or other less than legal venture.

'No. One more thing, a man is following Sarah. I only spot him later, when she get to bar. He goes inside, but careful, no want to be seen. When he sees her he sits on dark corner and watch, orders drink and make like reading paper but he watching her OK.'

'Most likely just another reporter,' Riad offered, 'any camera on him?'

'You no understand,' Vytas sounded like he was chewing on something and Riad waited patiently as the man briefly choked then continued, a trifle hoarsely, 'This is man on photo.'

'You mean Ruslan?' Riad said quickly.

'No, other man on photo.'

Abdul-Karim.

Thinking fast he asked if the man was still there.

'Yes. Watching lady. What you want me do?'

Dammit! Where the hell was Bubba when you needed him? He asked as much.

There was a moment's hesitation and when Vytas came back there was a change in his voice, 'Something I must tell you. I don't want, you busy man on special job so I try protect but sometimes…'

'What is it, Vytas?! Is it this family business? Where is Bubba?!'

'Iss Rania, at Yvette's. Her friend, he try it with our little sister, she very upset, go complain at police. They say he good man, important man in Beirut, she must go away –'

Jesus Christ!!

'What the hell?! When were you going to tell me, it's my daughter you idiot?! Did Yvette tell you this?' It was all beginning to make sense now, his mother being strangely uncommunicative and Rania not answering calls.

Vytas was speaking again, a note of hurt in in his voice, 'Yvette phone me, she very upset. This man very nasty, tell her he make trouble for them. So I send Bubba, no want to worry you, busy man and—'

Feeling clumsily for a chair Riad sat down. He was only faintly aware of the others staring at him, aware that his hands were shaking. 'So what did Bubba do?' he asked dreading the answer.

'Bubba, he how you say, no *sensitive* man, you know? He go to man's house and hurt him little, hang him outside window by legs and man fall too much far. Lucky he alive, only some bones no good. Problem now is man's family want to make trouble for us.'

'No you worry, Vytas take care already; we put Yvette and Rania on plane to Kuwait. They already in your house and safe. Soon I go Beirut, finish problem.'

I'm sure you will, Riad thought grimly, I'm sure you will. In the meantime what to do? If only his daughter had an Australian visitor's visa, like presumably Yvette did, he could bring her over but that would take time.

'I want you to phone Yvette right now, tell her to get a visa for Rania to come here. I will speak with her later and she had better answer the phone this time.'

'But iss still dark there,' Vytas protested, 'they sleeping.'

'I don't care, wake them up. And stay with Sarah, I want to know where she goes. Don't let the other man see you.' With Vytas' protests dying in his ear he killed the call.

'Family problems?' Zena asked as they headed for the door.

Riad nodded wryly, 'You could say so.'

'Happens in the best of families,' Reed said sombrely.

In the worst too, Riad decided.

'Nobody's perfect,' Zena added. It was a statement sufficiently out of place to have the others glance at her before shrugging it off.

'Let's walk,' Zena said as they came out on the busy sidewalk, 'Relax, Reed, I won't let you step on any cracks.'

'Cracks don't worry me,' Reed said as he turned his collar up against an icy wind, 'It's the crackpots I can't stand.'

34
CHAPTER

Opening her hand slowly she glanced at the small red object nestling there. There was a cross on its flat surface, now shiny with sweat from her tightly clasped palm. Slowly, gingerly, she opened one of its blades and ran a fingertip lightly over its sharp surface. The point was sharp too as she pressed it down on her arm until it raised a small drop of red blood.

It didn't hurt at all, not compared to the other hurts when the uncles came visiting. She had spotted it lying on the lawn outside earlier that morning when Martha had taken her and Minnie for their walk. The grass was long and Ken was busy mowing it at the bottom end where the cliff ran down to the beach and the sea. Martha had left the girls for a moment to pick up the carcass of a dead rabbit Artos had killed the night before, tossing it in the garden bin and Maddie knew she had not noticed the object.

Minnie saw her tuck it in her knickers but said nothing. She knew it belonged to Ken for she had seen him cut cheese with it but now it was hers and that brought a strange feeling. Of power.

Back in her room, after the morning's lessons were over, she hid it under the mattress, planning to find a better hiding place later. After lunch Martha said there would not be any dancing lessons that afternoon, an uncle was visiting later and he wanted to play with both of them. He was a very rich man and would bring them presents and Ken wanted them to be nice to him.

Maddie was disappointed because she was getting very good at dancing now and Ken had even let her watch some of the videos he made, saying that she was already famous and would be a great dancer one day. Some of the new moves they were practising now was not really that difficult, more like gymnastics she thought, where she would show off how supple she was.

Minnie wasn't nearly as good and she still cried a lot, especially when they were alone in the big lounge after dinner when Martha left them to wash up. She would put the TV on Cartoon Network and take the control with her, warning them again not to touch the set or Ken would get angry.

They had pancakes for lunch and Martha let them have all the sweet syrup they wanted and also some Coca Cola. Afterwards she watched them brush their teeth and then they both got into the bath and she washed them with bubbles in the bath and all. She said they had to be nice and clean and smelling nice for the uncle for he was an old man and liked things to be neat and clean. Then she dressed them in their best party dresses and dabbed perfume behind their ears.

This time they did not put on makeup as the uncle did not like that, Martha said as he liked things pure and unspoilt. Martha had laughed softly and in a strange way when she said that and Maddie thought there was something sad in her eyes.

Just before the uncle was due to come Ken put the dog away. Artos was a guard dog and very dangerous and she and Minnie had been warned to stay away from his pen which was at the back of the house. When they were allowed outside he was always locked away first and at night he would roam the property.

He would never bark, just growl softly when he did not like something and sometimes she wondered if he was also a prisoner, just like she and Minnie was.

The uncle arrived later that afternoon in a big black car with a long hood that had a pretty shiny angel on its front. A man wearing a suit was driving the car and he got out and opened the door for the uncle who was sitting in the back. Although her window was off to the side and a distance away from the front of the house she could see the uncle was very old just by the way he walked.

The other man who was much younger got back into the car and stayed there.

A few minutes later Martha came to fetch her and Minnie who had been in her own room next door. The old man was sitting in the lounge when they entered and he smiled and asked them to turn around. One by one Martha brought them up to him and he would smile and run a hand gently up their cheeks and stroke their hair. He would smile while doing this and his teeth were very yellow and he seemed unaware of the spittle on the side of his mouth.

Maddie had never seen anyone with as many fine wrinkles as this uncle. They made his skin, which was very pale, move very much like that of a lizard she had seen once at the zoo and underneath his watery blue eyes there were bags showing pink flesh that looked strange. Large brown freckles were dotted around his temples and his wispy hair was unkempt and ashen grey.

The hand that touched them was bony and ice cold, the nails long and yellow.

After a while he took a fat brown envelope from his pocket and handed it to Martha who gave it to Ken. Maddie saw Ken take what looked like a lot of money from the envelope and count it. Then he looked at Martha and nodded.

As always they used the room with the large mirror behind which was the video camera. Maddie said she had to go to the bathroom first and Martha told her to hurry. Inside her own room she went to the bed and took the pocket knife out from under the mattress and tucked it into her knickers. Then she flushed the toilet and washed her hands and went back to where Martha was waiting.

Inside the special room the uncle had taken off his clothes and was only in his underwear which was white and baggy with black elastic suspenders that held up his long socks. His legs were very thin and very white and had lots of knobbly blue veins crisscrossing them. He had hung his jacket and pants over the back of the chair and his neatly folded white shirt and necktie lay on the seat, his hat and gloves placed on top.

Shiny black shoes were tucked under the chair.

When he saw Maddie he smiled and went to sit down on the bed, motioning her to come and sit next to him. Minnie was already on the bed and huddled in the corner, her back up against the wall as she studied the uncle with wide open eyes.

Maddie was only vaguely aware of Martha leaving and closing the door quietly behind her as she went across and sat on the edge of the bed. 'Did you have a nice day at school, Charlotte?' the uncle asked and stroked her hair.

Martha had told them that the uncle was very old and sometimes forgot names or they might remind him of someone else. She wanted them to play along as this would make him happy. She had also told them they had to call him Uncle Ted as that was his name.

'Yes, Uncle Ted,' she said gaily, accepting the small package he handed her with the demure expression they had practised.

'Is your teacher pretty?' he asked, 'what is her name?'

'Miss Johnson,' she lied as she unwrapped the gift, a small porcelain figurine of two ballet dancers in embrace, 'She is very pretty.'

Turning the object from side to side she knew instinctively that it was quite expensive, for had she not seen others like this in their big house in Kuwait and had mummy not cautioned her against breaking them by accident? She wondered what Minnie's gift was.

'You are so clever,' the uncle said as he slid a folded sheet from an envelope and opened it. 'So young still and already you write so well and such beautiful handwriting.' Holding the letter at arms length he started reading in a croaky voice that faded at the end of each sentence. *My darling papa, I long for those warm summer days to come again when we can go down to the yacht again, just the two of us and enjoy once more those endless days of sunshine and the warm smell of coconut oil on our bodies. And glorious food and a nice cosy nap in the afternoon as the boat rocks gently on the swells and you cuddle me and say sweet things to me as I drift off to sleep. I love you so much and I miss you and I want to be with you again soon. All my love, your Charlotte.*

Underneath was a line of crosses and Maddie thought the perfume was nice too. She recognised Martha's handwriting, of course, had seen her practising it at the dining room table on more than one occasion.

'The letter is good,' Uncle Ted said in a voice suddenly gone stronger, 'The bit about the warm oil is a nice touch. Maybe next time you can add something about the dog, your little spaniel, Peaches, remember him?'

'Of course, Uncle Ted. He was such a pretty little dog.'

He nodded then with a sigh lay back on the bed and beckoned for Minnie to join them.

Minnie wanted to take her frock off but the uncle shook his head, said that would be naughty and her mommy would be cross if she found out. It was alright just to cuddle for a bit though and perhaps she could rub his tummy just a little? His hand was under and around her now and cradling her buttock as his free hand ran up and down the insides of Maddie's thighs.

He was making strange noises now, almost like the purring of a kitten, she thought and the hand on her thigh was warm now, warm and sweating. Then his hand had moved away and he was clumsily fiddling with Minnie's knickers while telling her softly in a hoarse voice that she was a very bad girl and that he was going to punish her. As she had been trained Maddie rolled over to lie on top of the uncle and make soft moaning noises while shoving a hand down her own knickers.

Minnie was writhing now, not liking it and it was then that Maddie saw it, the thick looking cigar in the man's hand that he was trying to shove into Minnie's special spot. And as she saw the terror on her friend's face as she tried to move away, little arms powerless against the new found strength of the uncle, something snapped inside Maddie.

She had the pocket knife in her hand now, the big blade snapped open and then she was pushing it violently inside the body of Uncle Ted.

Again and again.

The scream was so unexpected, so penetrating it had her recoil in horror to the point where she rolled off the bed onto the carpet. The sound was not human she thought in that instant, more like that of a farm animal, a pig maybe, as it was slaughtered. The man was up against the bedstead now, as if moving away from the object that was still protruding from his belly. His face a mask of horror he stared numbly at the knife that was rocking to and fro in time with his rapid breathing while bright red blood trickled out beside it, a sticky wet pool slowly spreading out on the sheets.

Shaky fingers hovered uncertainly and darted away every time he moved to touch the knife's handle, his eyes fixed on the thing inside him and seeing nothing else. His lips moved but no sounds came and then the door crashed open and Ken was standing there, momentarily froze, his face slack with shock. 'What are you doing?!' he shouted, suddenly regaining function of his limbs to rush in and roughly yank Maddie away to viciously slap her across the cheek with enough force to leave an instant raised weal as tears sprung from her eyes.

His rage was out of control now and as he prepared to slap Maddie again Martha was in the room and stepping between them, her arms raised. 'Ken, Ken!! Don't mark her! Remember what the boss said. Please!' But Ken had already let go of the girl who slumped at his feet and was staring up at him with something akin to sheer hatred in the blue eyes.

There would be no crying. Maddie Green was long beyond crying.

With nary a glance at Minnie who had moved away from the bed and was crouching in a corner, Ken knelt on the bed next to the stricken man and did a quick assessment. 'He'll live,' he said over his shoulder to Martha, 'A flesh wound mainly, probably didn't penetrate to his guts, the blade is pretty short.'

Without further ceremony he pulled out the knife in a single rapid motion, so fast the old man hadn't time to yelp. Staring critically at the wound for a few seconds Ken decided no major vessel was involved and ordered Martha to fetch some bandages. The other man was on his feet now and gingerly touching his side, staring in horror as his hand came away bloodstained. 'I—I, what do—'

'It's probably OK but get to a hospital and have it checked,' Ken said as Martha returned with gauze dressing which she expertly applied holding it in place with strips of Micropore.

'Wh—what do I tell the doctors?'

Ken shrugged, his attention back on Maddie who had risen to her feet and was glaring at him defiantly, 'Make up something, tell them you cut yourself shaving. Now go!'

Seeing something in Ken's expression the visitor hastened to don the rest of his clothes while muttering something about reporting this to the police.

'You might think that one through a little bit, what were you going to tell them about you and the underage girls? That you're Father Christmas making an early visit?' Turning his back on the hapless man he added, 'Piss off,' then to Martha, 'See him out to the car and tell the driver there's been an accident and he's to take him to a hospital. Stress that under no circumstances does he give this address, get it?'

Nodding she left, supporting the softly groaning visitor who winced with every hesitant step. As the door closed behind them Ken sat on the bed and carefully wiped clean the blade of the pocket knife before shoving it in his pocket. While doing this he was staring at Maddie, his expression one of deep thought. 'Now Maddie, Maddie, Maddie... What are we going to do with you, my lovely?' he said at length. Shaking his head he left them, locking the door behind.

Back in his office he poured himself a generous measure of Jack Daniels before dialling a number from memory. Dimitri Ruslan answered on the third ring. He listened in silence as Ken told him what had happened. When he finally spoke it was to ask who the customer was. Ken told him and Ruslan shrugged it off, 'I know him, there won't be trouble. The girl, she is OK?'

Thinking back on the angry weal marring the side of Maddie's face Ken decided against mentioning it, 'Sure,' he said smoothly, 'no worries. What do you want me to do?'

There was a moment's silence while Ruslan thought before saying, 'She is still our most valuable asset ever. Her followers now number well over a thousand, this business of having her turn tricks is a sideshow, good money but a sideshow and it's too dangerous now. How are the bookings?'

'A client tomorrow afternoon, Nightcat17. A regular on Dark Angel but never here to date. Paid in advance.'

'Hmm. Alright, let him come, the usual safety precautions only this time search the girl and make sure no bullshit happens, savvy?'

'Sure. What then?'

'Sadly I think Maddie is fast coming to the end of her usefulness. I think a suitable ending for her would be a snuff movie, there's a big market and so far it's been adult pros, never a kid. It could make us a fortune.'

Suppressing a shudder Ken rang off and leaned back in his chair, taking a deep sip of the liquor as he thought back on what he had just heard. In a life of crime he had seen and done his share, even the occasional killing. *But a snuff movie!*

His hand shook slightly as he downed the drink in a gulp. Maddie Green was about to die.

35
CHAPTER

arah Green paid off the cab then stood for a moment surveying her surrounds. To one side was the Frankston tramline, opposite a seemingly continuous row of small houses dating back to pre-war years, some semi-detached and most in need of a coat of paint. Cars were parked everywhere, many of the them in front yards and fighting for space amongst children's bicycles, rickety looking swing chairs and rusting barbecues.

To one end was a long flat roofed building housing a number of small shops, the signs on the plate glass windows advertising a butcher, a dressmaker and an auto spare parts shop amongst others. Yuri's pizzeria and bar was around that corner if she remembered correctly and if the cab driver thought it unusual that a classy woman such as Sarah should be in this kind of neighbourhood he kept it to himself while making sure she had his number for the ride back.

Avoiding the many puddles from that morning's rain she made her way to the corner. Schools were not out yet and nobody seemed to be about, the only noise that of the traffic and the occasional tram rumbling by. And of course the dogs, every front yard seemed to have one and try as she might she could not pick a clear pedigree amongst the bunch. They barked incessantly as all eyes followed her progress.

On the sidewalk outside Yuri's she hesitated for a moment taking in the place's cheerless façade while remembering this was where she had first met the man she was about to confront once more. This nemesis that somehow had this terrible hold on both her and Maddie.

Sitting on his Harley Davidson a hundred yards down the road Vytas watched her push aside the vertical plastic flycatcher strips to disappear inside the darkness of the place. He studied it for a moment longer, noting the handful of plastic chairs and tables outside and the absence of any customers. A worker's waterhole he decided, a place the boys would use as a pitstop before heading home. There was only one logical reason she was here and at this time, to meet someone and his guess would be the same man as in the bookshop that day.

Then he turned his attention to the man in the other cab who had finally alighted and was now walking briskly down the road and heading for the bar. It was the man he had spotted earlier stalking Sarah in the hotel lobby, the one Riad had identified as Abdul-Karrim. He had instructed his cab to stop a distance away from where his wife had alighted and clearly did not want to be spotted.

He was still watching, uncertain as to his next action when another man got out of a car parked down a side street diagonally across from the bar and went quickly over to the approaching Abdul-Karrim who seemed to recognise him.

'Are you sure this is the place?' Abdul-Karim asked as he turned his collar up against the cold breeze.

Baker nodded, 'She's inside there alright, meeting someone I'm sure.'

'What happened to the backup you were going to bring along? You know how dangerous Ruslan is.'

'House arrest,' Baker said with a shrug, 'you know how it is.'

Abdul-Karim did not know how it was and for a moment thought of asking whether Baker was armed but then presumably the man would have learned from previous experience.

As the two men withdrew into a recess next to the butcher shop Vytas could see the newcomer was the private detective he had encountered in the Elephant and Wheelbarrow days earlier.

A safe bet that Abdul-Karim was his client and the meeting of the three players witnessed so far could only mean a shared focus of interest inside that bar and that would be Mr Dimitri Ruslan. Switching off the bike he prepared to follow. Pausing in the lee of a corner house to allow the others to enter the bar he drew an automatic pistol from an inside pocket of his leather jacket and checked the clip. He slid one into the breech and eased the hammer back down before tucking it into the back of his belt.

Once inside the darkened front room of the bar Sarah saw that the proprietor, Yuri a thin as a wire individual with the features of a rat and small darting eyes, was the only one there. He was busy wiping down tables and in the background she could see a dull glow coming from the open clay oven.

Spotting Sarah his first reaction was to shoo her out, the place not yet open for business but then recognition flowed and he halted in midstride, lowering his hands to his sides.

'Where is he?' she said flatly, placing her umbrella on a table and glancing at a drawn heavy curtain that she knew led to the back section. 'In there?' She inclined her head in the direction.

Yuri nodded and licked his lips nervously, 'Yes.'

There was no need to mention a name, they both knew who they were referring to.

Drawing aside the curtain she went through into a short dark corridor and entered the only room that had a light shining through an open door. Ruslan was sitting at a table smoking a cigarette, an open bottle of vodka next to him with two glasses. He did not get up, signalling her to take a seat. Hesitating she decided to remain standing.

'I now know you are keeping my daughter in the big house down at Portsea, the same house where I---'

She could not bring herself to say it and laughing Ruslan said it for her, 'You mean our little love nest, my sweet. And what a night that was! After all we created our pretty little girl there, did we not?'

'You raped me, you bastard!' she cried out, her voice choked with tears. 'We met here, you were going to tell me about my mother and where you met and then you took me to that house and you raped me again and again!'

'Tch, tch, tch. My poor little innocent girl. You want to hear about your mother? She was a cheap whore, just like you. Just like little Maddie. And you all belong to me! It was you who came to me about

Maddie, in your sick mind you wanted to use her to erase your own nightmares wasn't it?!'

'But—but you're my father!!'

Kicking back the chair with enough force to send it crashing against the wall he grabbed hold of a shaking Sarah pushing her back up against the wall while ripping open her blouse and violently hitching her skirt up and over her waist while fumbling with the front of his pants. 'You're a whore,' he said in a voice gone low and hoarse with lust, 'you've come here because this is what you want!'

A sudden noise at the door had him whirl around to see Abdul-Karim stand there, a look of shock on his face. The man next to him had a gun and it was pointed at him.

'You scum!' Abdul-Karim screamed as Ruslan wheeled around swinging a helpless Sarah in front of him while at the same time bringing his own automatic up in one single fluid motion. The explosion in that small room was deafening as the Russian fired first, dropping Baker with his first shot before traversing and catching a rushing forward Abdul-Karim in the chest with his second to send him crashing down in a heap at his feet and staring helplessly up at him and Sarah who had recoiled in horror.

Grinning cruelly, his teeth bared in a snarl Ruslan lined up the smoking pistol at his victim's forehead when a voice from the door told him to drop it. In that fleeting second he could see it was a big man and he had a gun in his hand and it was pointed at him. But Ruslan was in the moment now and still grinning he raised his pistol and Vytas shot him.

Staring for a moment in unbelief at the blood pouring from his side as the gun dropped from his grasp Ruslan turned and stumbled through a second door that led to an open area at the back of the place. Moments later there was the sound of a car revving then speeding away with screeching tyres. Vytas let him go, turning his attention to a sobbing Sarah and seeing she was unhurt, knelt next to the two fallen men. Baker was dead, shot through the heart, his expression one of eternal surprise. Abdul-Karim was still alive but breathing heavily with pink froth bubbling on his lips. His pulse was rapid and thready.

Fumbling for his mobile Vytas saw that Sarah had disappeared, presumably out the back as well. Dialling 000, the Australian emergency number, he called for an ambulance and gave them the address. Then he went back to the main section of the bar, stepping over the prone form of Yuri in the process. The man had been unconscious when Vytas had entered close on the heels of the other two men and presumably had been knocked out by one of them. Either way he would not have seen Vytas.

Pausing for a moment to check that he had not left any fingerprints he remembered his bullet casing and went back to retrieve it. Peering through the front window he saw that a small crowd had gathered, no doubt drawn by the gunfire. Crossing to the backroom he peered through the open back door to find it led to a narrow service road with several garages opening on to it. There was no-one about and predictably no sign of Sarah Green.

He set off at a slow trot for where he could see the road open onto another where cars could be seen driving past. Once there he paused to check he had not been seen before heading back by a roundabout route to where he had parked the Harley.

It was only when he had put several miles between himself and Yuri's Bar that he pulled over at a kerb and phoned Riad.

'What?!!' There followed a second's stunned silence while Riad, who had just come away from a terse conversation with his mother in Kuwait and was yet to talk to Rania, struggled to digest this latest news. Forcing himself with some effort to calm down, he asked Vytas to go into detail. As he listened with growing incredulity he realised the endgame was upon them and things were about to come to a head very quickly. Now more than ever the life of Maddie Green was at stake.

'Did anyone see you?'

'I don't think. No.'

'Your gun, is it licensed, I mean can it be traced to you?'

There was a pause, 'Well...not exactly. Iss gift, you see—'

Riad saw all too well, 'Get rid of it, immediately. Toss it in the river after wiping off all fingerprints as well as those on the bullets, OK?'

A sigh, 'Sure, no problem. I pick up shell, no touch nothing.'

And what else would you expect from a professional Riad thought glumly while his mind raced. So Ruslan was wounded and on the run while Sarah was missing somewhere and hopefully not with him. One man was dead and Abdul-Karrim possibly as well. *Dammit!*

'What you want I do now?' Vytas' concerned voice jerked him back to the present. 'Go home,' he said after a moment's reflection, 'and stay out of trouble. I'll phone you later.'

Having arrived back at the Docklands police HQ a short time earlier for the scheduled afternoon's briefing session, Riad had excused himself when the call from Yvette came through, stepping into a corridor away from the others. As expected there were tears interspersed with her usual protestations that she too was allowed to have a life and could she help it if men were bastards? He seemed such a nice man, beautiful hands (God knows how that was relevant and Riad decided he'd rather not know) and always so polite and generous too. How could she know he would do such a thing? And with a young girl at that when a beautiful woman like her was there making him the envy of Beirut?!

Was it Riad's imagination or was there just a hint of jealousy there? Truly a sad day when a grandmother was envious of a granddaughter but then she was an *artiste* after all.

Ascertaining that they were safely ensconced in his Salwa apartment Riad asked about Rania. 'She's good now, good girl. She was so angry! Just like you Riad! But no crying and strong, you know?'

'Why does she not answer when I try to call?'

'She is ashamed, Riad, afraid you will blame her for what happened. I will talk to her, she will phone. Her teacher came over, from her school, nice lady. She is very kind and spent long time talking to Rania and afterwards she seemed more relaxed, you know?'

'She is not to be left alone, mother, remember?'

'Yes. The lady teacher, her name is Mary, she wants Rania to talk to a professional person, a psychologist, to help her. Rania told her that you have been and now we have appointment to go as well. OK?'

He nodded absently, 'Good. I have to go to a meeting now, I'll speak to you again later.' As an afterthought he asked about Uncle Bubba.

'Francois had a little trouble leaving from Beirut airport so he went to visit my cousins who live near Saint Michel in the mountains, you remember where we went to ski many times? It is close to the border with Syria and, you understand?'

'Yes,' he understood only too well. A quick hop over the border and Bubba would be back in Melbourne before you could say "police file."

Commander Zena had peered around the door looking for him and he was about to follow when Vytas called.

It was only much later that he thought about asking just who this psychologist was Rania was seeing.

36
CHAPTER

The meeting started at three and with the Head of Detectives, the lieutenant in charge of the SOG team as well as the Assistant Commissioner of Police present the small room was crowded, leaving Riad to find a seat at the back.

'What is this "SOG"? Riad asked as he studied the man in black combat gear.

'Special Operations Group,' someone whispered, 'like the American SWAT teams.'

'The death and glory boys,' came another whisper and someone tittered.

'DI Reed had the floor and was going over the operational details of the next day's raid. Quickly covering previous ground he reviewed what was known at that point.

'Lieutenant Ajmi, seconded to us from the Kuwaiti CID (a lie but close enough) has agreed to assume the identity of Nightcat17 and is scheduled to meet with Maddie Green to-morrow at 18hoo, the venue to be announced by the persons of interest by phone contact close to the time. We do know it is somewhere on the Mornington Peninsula, an area well known to most of us. Starting from here the furthest point is no more than an hour away, traffic permitting.'

'I take it we are in possession of the mobile of Nightcat17 and that is the number the perps have?' The question came from the SOG officer, a small compact man dressed in black down to his combat boots and with a crew cut to complete the picture of the action man.

Reed confirmed adding that the paedophile in question was kept in isolation at the Remand Facility while Commander Michaels from the Feds was maintaining his dark website so as not to arouse suspicion.

'Lieutenant Ajmi will be wearing a GPS enabled wristwatch allowing us to track him to a range of one kilometre.' He held up the bulky item for all to see, adding, 'See this button here? By pressing it he will signal that he is in the presence of the girl and Lieutenant Casadio's team will close in.'

Moving to a large whiteboard and grabbing a marker pen from the table Reed drew a rough outline of the Mornington Peninsula. 'At its base and on the outskirts of the city is Frankston. It's a big place with many possible locations where the victim could be held. Then, as we move along towards the apex we have lots of smaller towns dotted along this central highway leading to the Nepean Nature Reserve at the tip. A popular holiday destination scores of Melburnians flock to the beaches all along here over weekends and, as we all know, to-morrow is a Saturday.'

Pausing to take a sip of water he went on, 'Now we have reason to believe Maddie is being held in a secluded house, probably with a large garden and there is also some suggestion close to the sea. Most such homes are at the pointy end, places like Sorrento and beyond that Portsea. Needless to say many of these properties are the domain of the rich and influential and we'll have to take care not to inadvertently tread on any toes while out there.'

This was met by a mumbled comment and a wry smile from the SOG officer evoking a disapproving raised eyebrow from the Assistant Commissioner. Hesitating for a second Reed pressed on, 'As stated earlier, at this end a single beach road runs all the way terminating at the nature reserve. Buildings on one side and a long line of beaches lining the bay. At Sorrento the distance between where the Queenscliff Ferry docks and the opposite Ocean Beach is less than a kilometre. Sure, there are smaller cutback roads but by and large the access route is along this here beach road.'

'What about access by the bay or the open sea on the other side?' the SOG man asked.

'Possible from the bay side but not on the ocean side where the breakers are treacherous. Some of the older homes do have boathouses. As the water is shallow no large vessels are usually found there.'

'Nevertheless, it might be a good idea to have one of ours out there,' the lieutenant said, 'the same reason we are having a police chopper on standby. I need not remind you we will only have one bite at this apple.'

Idly wondering what other clichés the man might come up with Riad found his thoughts drifting back to the events of an hour or two ago. When was the news going to break and would it influence this plan at all? Should it?

'Thank you for your insight, Lieutenant,' The Assistant Commissioner said dryly, 'but may I remind you that the less people we let in on this operation, the smaller the risk of it being penetrated. This being the main reason we have our colleague from the Middle East as our agent. We will however have a helicopter.'

'Who is your sergeant, Reed?' The Chief of Detectives asked, 'shouldn't he be here?'

Taken off guard Reed looked uncomfortable, 'No-one at the moment, sir, DS Jenny Momberg is on maternity leave at present and, well we're short staffed and—'

'You should have told me, Reed. It's not right for a DI to work without a sergeant. I'll send Jones over, she's a good detective.'

The meeting then went over the communication details and halfway through this the Assistant Commissioner's phone rang. If anyone thought Tina Turner's *You're Simply the Best* was an odd ringtone for a senior policeman they kept it to themselves. The meeting paused while he took the call, all watching as the colour drained from his normally ruddy features while he nodded numbly before asking whether the wife had been informed. 'The Alfred you say? Very well, I'm heading over, meet me there.'

With that he rang off then sat there for a moment before reaching for his cap and getting to his feet, 'There has been a shooting in Camberwell. One man dead, a second seriously wounded and taken to The Alfred. The wounded man has been identified as a Mr Hasan Abdul-Karim who is the husband of Miss Sarah Green as I'm sure you all know. The incident happened inside a pizza parlour just off Burke Road and we are at present trying to find witnesses.'

Turning to face Reed and Michaels who had now joined him at the table he added, 'The question is obviously whether this connects to our present operation. According to ID found on the dead man he is a registered private investigator named Baker, presumably hired by Abdul-Karim. Two sidearms were found at the scene, one which has been fired. There is also a blood trail leading towards an exit door and presumably belonging to the shooter. No trace so far of him. DCI Summers is the senior man down there and is checking hospital casualties. Hopefully we may lift some useful prints off the pistols, both CZ 9mm, and the brass shells.'

He frowned, 'The wife is not answering her phone, would you be able to get hold of her and bring her to the hospital, Lieutenant Ajmi?'

'Yes, Commissioner. I think I know where to find her.'

Pausing with his hand on the door handle the Commissioner added, 'For now Operation Bluenight remains active. I will schedule a briefing for later today when we have more information. Hopefully Abdul-Karim can be interviewed.'

With that he was gone, audibly calling for his driver as he headed down the corridor at a fast pace and leaving Riad to ponder the elephant in the room. No mention of the person who had wounded the shooter or perhaps they just hadn't thought it through yet.

'Operation fucking Bluenight,' Zena Michaels said with a sigh, 'who the hell comes up with these codenames?'

'Probably Sadie the cleaning lady,' the SOG officer noted laughing at his own joke to general murmurs of weary assent.

As the meeting filed out Reed drew Riad aside, 'Michaels and I feel we three have to get together later to run over what the hell is going on here without Captain America from SOG being present. Let's say six at my place in Collingwood, it's close by.' He handed Riad a card with his home address scribbled on the back. 'I'll get some beers and a barbie going. 'In the meantime see what you can get out of Sarah Green, the beauty queen must know more than she's letting on.'

'Sure,' Riad said, pocketing the card, 'I'll be there, just throw another shrimp on the barbie.'

'Here we say prawn,' Zena corrected him but his wink had her smile.

There was a traffic jam on Flinders Street heading towards the central Federation Square and as Riad sat in the back of the cab watching the scenes of a big city pass by he wished he was a private eye. Like his favourite, Philip Marlowe, who could retire to his admittedly seedy office, put his feet on the desk, pour himself a generous one from the office bottle and light a pipe.

And think. Think as you watch the afternoon shadows grow long with no client in the waiting room and the phone off the hook. Just study the changing pattern the sunlight through venetian blinds make on the opposite wall as you let your thoughts run free.

That was what he needed now more than anything else. Over the past few days a pattern had formed in his mind and he reckoned he knew what had happened to Maddie Green. Even knew why it had happened, knew who was responsible. What he did not know was exactly where she was.

And, more important than anything else, how much time they had left to find her alive.

God, he needed a drink! 'Is there a bottle store on our route?' he asked the cabbie, a Sikh sporting a powder blue turban and flowing beard.

Glancing uncertainly at him in the rear view mirror the man took his time thinking this over, finally saying he would find one on the GPS. 'No parking anywhere right now, sir. I will have to double park while you go inside.'

Approaching Flinders Station they were barely moving now, the crossing swarming with what seemed like thousands of pedestrians, all hurrying along, many unfurling umbrellas as the rain started again. Glancing around at the myriad other cabs moving in both directions he noted once again how many of the solitary passengers occupied the front passenger seat rather than sitting at back as he was. He asked the driver about this.

'It is an Australian thing, sir,' the driver said chuckling. 'Australian males will always sit in the front with the driver, sometimes even if they have a lady present. Tourists, no, they sit in the back.' He refrained from adding *like you, sir.*

Mulling this over Riad decided it was this curious thing called mateship that he had heard so much about. A truly class free society, a gesture of endearment almost like the omnipresent "mate" that seemed to be the norm.

He decided he liked that. Yeah, he could live here.

'Where are you from originally?' he asked the driver who was now carefully coaxing his way over the intersection where the light had long since turned against the pedestrians but without much success in clearing a pathway for the piled up cars. The patience of the drivers once again striking, nobody blasting away on a horn.

'I'm from the Punjab, sir. Five years I live here now. Before that I was in Adelaide.' Narrowly avoiding a collision with another driver that had cut in he asked where Riad was from.

'Kuwait.'

The driver thought this over for a minute then nodded to himself, 'Ah well,' he said, 'nobody's perfect.'

Smiling to himself Riad let that one go. They were heading into the heart of the CBD now, the river at their back and the traffic becoming less hectic. Riad began to recognise some landmarks as they approached Carlton when they pulled up in a loading zone, the driver pointing to a liquor store across the road. An elderly man was standing at the corner strumming a guitar. He was wearing a type of oilskin coat, a battered Akubra hat and a week's growth of grey whiskers. An impressive belly suggested he wasn't short of what the locals called a feed. Lying on a blanket at his feet was a Kelpie of advanced years who paid little attention to the passers by who tossed coins into a bowl.

'How much is that doggie in the window?' the old man sang with no consideration for melody or tone, smiling at all comers, 'I do wish that dog was for sale –' At this point the dog would wearily raise itself on its front legs and howl. It was a well rehearsed combo and Riad felt for the dog.

'Why don't you rather have the dog sing and you bark?' a man suggested as he tossed some coins into the bowl, 'it can only be an improvement!' Both parties laughed as the dog slumped down once more, until its next performance.

A wise man had once remarked that it was always a sign of a free and democratic society when you could see weirdos and eccentrics on the streets and being accepted as part of society, something quickly suppressed under a totalitarian regime. Here everyone was free. Except Maddie.

Ten minutes later he was at the house, clutching the brown bag wrapped bottle of Glenfiddich as he wearily climbed the stairs to the front door. It was unlocked and pausing for a moment in the hallway he listened for any sounds of others being present. He must have been heard for there was the sound of creaking floorboards above his head and the Chrissie peered over the balustrade. Behind the spectacles her large eyes looked even larger than before and there was a hint of incipient hysteria in the reedy voice when she asked in an urgent whisper where he'd been.

Ignoring the question he asked whether Sarah was upstairs.

'She came back an hour ago. She was in a terrible state, her clothes dirty and a nasty cut on her hand. She must have walked for miles because there were blisters on both heels. She was in a state and I couldn't get anything out of her so I called the doctor, you must just have missed him. He bandaged her hand and gave her an injection and some pills. She's in bed now, sleeping.'

'Mr Abdul-Karim has been shot,' he said deciding whichever way he phrased it would still sound brutal. 'He's been admitted to the Alfred Hospital in a critical state.'

Chrissie gasped and grasped the balustrade for support, 'No!'

'I suspect Sarah may have been present so I want to speak to her.'

'I – The doctor gave her a sedative and said she would sleep for hours. I don't think we should wake her right now.'

Thinking this over Riad decided there was no pressing urgency as the police were unlikely to share his suspicions. 'I'm going out for a while and should be back by eight. Then Miss Green and I are going to have a chat and go over to the hospital to see her husband. If anyone calls, the press or even the police, do not answer the door. I will deal with it later.'

Fetching a glass from the kitchen and scooping it full of ice cubes he went to his room and poured himself three fingers of the scotch. Sinking into the chair he switched on the television and turned to the news. Two overseas hikers were missing in the Blue Mountains for the third day and a major search was underway. A student led protest march against the opening of a new coal mine had caused major disruption in Sydney and questions were being asked in parliament. A shooting in Melbourne made it just before the weather report. No details yet but thought to most likely be another incident of the gang violence gripping the city.

After a moment's hesitation he poured himself another, the scotch settling nice and warm and slowing down the jangle of his nerves just enough to collect his thoughts. Mainly why the women in his life always seemed to be that complicated, starting with his long dead wife, his mother, his daughter Rania and now Sarah Green and little Maddie.

Most of all he thought about Maddie.

Phoning for an Uber ride he was about to leave when his phone rang. It was Chunky phoning from London, the man surprisingly awake for that early hour. 'Riad! It's me, Chunky, what's up?'

Sighing softly Riad returned the pleasantries while trying to recall what the nature of their business was. Hopefully not the negotiations regarding a marriage between the families again, right now he could not stomach that.

'Noo –' his friend chuckled. 'that business is still in the pipeline, you know how long these things take!'

Yes, Riad thought grimly, money matters always do.

'It's about this guy you asked about, Dimitri Ruslan, remember?'

Riad said he did.

'Well, he has properties all over, many listed to his companies and hard to trace but of interest to you is that he has a large ocean going yacht, the MV Elena II and she is presently moored in a Melbourne marina...'

37
CHAPTER

'Wife's doing a night shift at Werribee Hospital,' Reed said as he turned the sausages on the barbecue before wiping his hands on an apron that had the slogan "I can fix most things but I can't fix stupid" down the front. He lifted his beer in salute and Riad followed suit while reflecting on the Aussie practice of always having the can inside a stubbie holder even when it was freezing out there on the deck, the wind lifting the edges of the canvas and flicking the rain on the Weber adding to the sizzle.

Wrapped in a fleece lined bush jacket Zena was sipping a second large vodka and tonic (no ice, no tonic) and had slumped into a moody silence as she stared at the flickering flame of the barbecue. After a while he asked her about her day to be told that earlier that day her team had received notice of another two cases of reported underage child grooming online. One had been only five years old, luckily the parents had cottoned on and reported it.

'It's like the war on drugs,' she said, pressing the glass with its cold liquid next to her forehead. 'We're losing it. You know how many case of underage child grooming we dealt with over the past year? Twenty six; enough to make you sick to the core.'

Riad said nothing, what was there to say? They had been going over the plans for the next day and the more Riad thought about it, the more potential loopholes there seemed to be. After the call from Chunky Riad had phoned Vytas asking him to find out where the boat was moored.

His uncle was at a get together of the Lebanese community in nearby Soutbank and promised to get right on to it. The call came as he was onto his second beer and excusing himself he took it in the lounge. Vytas' voice was muffled by a buffeting wind and at a guess he was in the open at the Docklands. Contacting an old friend at the Harbourmaster's Office – no names no pack drill – he had quickly established that the MV Elena II was lying at the Melbourne City Marina. He was looking at her right now. A seventy footer she was likely to have a crew of three. There were lights on board, did Riad want him to investigate? Maybe find arsehole, finish him good?

'*No!!* No. This man may be the clue to finding the girl.' After a moment's reflection he added, 'This contact of yours, at the Harbourmaster's, can he be trusted?'

'Sure! We do many business, good money for him too.' Realising this might not necessarily translate to reliable in the world of his policeman nephew he added somewhat apologetically, 'May need some money, you know?'

Riad sighed, he knew all too well. 'We'll square with him later, ask him to let you know the moment she leaves, then phone me.'

Which left him with the burning question of when or if he should tell his fellow officers about his suspicions and if not, why not? Just who are you protecting, Riad? He decided no, his instincts on this one were good, tell Reed and Zena and they would be obliged to share the information with the others and there was the risk of someone with Ruslan's reach having an informer inside the department.

He would play this one close to the chest. The Americans had a term for it, "Mission Creep", when focus is lost and the objective becomes blurred and as a result the casualties mount. The mission was clear, find Maddie Green, bring her home safely. Anything else was a bonus.

Instead he changed the line of conversation telling them about the case in Kuwait City, the details regarding the killer being manipulated inside a virtual reality world sounding more far fetched every time he related it. The others agreed it was bizarre indeed, Reed adding sourly that it sounded like the world his son would know about, not that the boy showed any interest in sharing it with his parents.

No-one came up with any novel ideas of how to tackle the case other than it was one for what Zena called the "tech boffins." After a while the conversation dried up and attention shifted to the aroma wafting from the barbecue grid, Riad realising he hadn't eaten since breakfast.

'These snags are just about ready,' Reed finally declared, licking relish from his fingertips. 'Just another few minutes for the drumsticks and we're ready to go. There's some coleslaw in the fridge and I think Beth bought some fresh rolls.'

Excusing himself for a trip to the bathroom Riad paused by an open door halfway down the corridor. A teenage boy was seated in front of a large screen laptop flanked by oversized speakers and a bank of smaller monitor screens mounted on a raised dais to one side. On one of the flickering monochrome screens Riad could see himself framed in the doorway, another showed the scene on the deck as well as several other sites around the house. The rest of the darkened room resembled an electronics workshop, the occasional blank space on a wall sporting a poster of some or other video game.

'You're Riad,' the boy said, removing his earphones to swivel around and study him with liquid black eyes shining in an expressionless face. It was a flat statement, the voice reedy and lilting. He seemed oblivious of a broad strand of black hair partly shrouding an eye.

'Hello Sam,' Riad said, smiling.

There followed a moment's awkward silence as the boy studied him much, as Riad thought, a biologist would a rare species of frog. 'I was watching you on the deck and I heard when you were telling them about the boys in Kuwait and the game they were playing.'

Casting his mind back to the outside deck Riad could not recall seeing a CCTV camera or for that matter a microphone. 'I know what you're thinking, Sam said, 'I have this whole place wired but it's state of the art stuff and the old fool out there wouldn't know.'

'You mean your dad –' Riad countered as he stepped into the room, getting a broader view including what looked like a workbench to one side.

'He's not my dad, I'm adopted. From Korea.'

Riad nodded, 'I know,' he pointed at scattered bits of electronics lying about the desk, 'Building something?'

Shifting his glance to the desk the boy frowned, 'I'm building a new VR headset, the ones on the market now are so primitive.'

Virtual reality Riad said softly to himself, was this Huxley's Brave New World? 'Was that why you want to talk to me?'

'The way those two gamers were, right there in the zone, cool man! And the controller, now there's a wizard.' For the first time he smiled displaying braces on baby size teeth, 'I play Fortnite and I'm a master at Red Dead Redemption, Call of Duty, you name it. But this stuff you're talking about is out there, man! I need to know more!'

A chill was settling down the nape of Riad's back as he came closer to glance at the image on the computer screen, seeing a heavily armed first person shooter frozen in time and inside a building of sorts. 'You're a gamer,' he said, stating the obvious. 'No wonder you don't want to go to school.'

'School!?' the boy laughed scornfully, 'what are you talking about man? Old Man Claasen, the IT teacher, can barely play Pacman, he types with two fingers. I could program when I was four. I'm part of a small group now that's busy designing our own VR game, I'm doing the storyboard. That's why I'm interested in this story of yours.'

'It's not a story. It's real, several people have died thus far and, unless I catch this mastermind, more will.' Suddenly feeling old, a dinosaur finding himself in a time warp, Riad felt for the edge of the bed and sat down.

'Feel like a real drink? I've got some good stuff here,' the kid said, 'Chivas Regal twelve year old, don't tell Reed though, he thinks its ginger beer in this bottle.' He dug a plastic soft drink one litre bottle out of a drawer together with two none too clean plastic cups and was looking at Riad expectantly.

'Maybe later.' Why did none of this surprise him Riad wondered, deciding the kid was probably right, nothing a school could teach him. 'All this stuff costs money,' he said, looking around, 'where do you get the cash from?'

'I play an internet game where you compete against thousands of mugs out there, building empires and attacking each other, that sort of kid stuff. You can buy and sell castles, even armies and that's how

I earn easy cash, taking money off amateurs. Unlike Robin Hood, I steal from the poor and give to the rich, me.'

Working hard at supressing his growing incredulity Riad mentioned the game Tony Evan had been playing.

This had Sam look at him in a new light, 'You *do* play.'

'A little,' Riad lied, then asked him about a game called Scorpion Sting. He watched as the kid's fingers flitted across a keyboard at lighting speed, images flashing by on the screen and being discarded one after the other.

'I've heard of it,' Sam said offhandedly but it's a closed game, invitation only. Besides it's been taken off.'

Riad's reluctant admiration for the boy was growing by the minute, he even lied well. What else could he do? 'Who would do that?'

Pushing away the keyboard Sam shrugged, 'Web police perhaps? Like, you know, the FBI, whatever?'

Deciding to change tack Riad asked how the boy took possession of his winnings and was astonished to know he owned a Bitcoin account and no, his parents did not know about that, besides it was way too complicated for them.

'You thinking of becoming a professional gamer?' he asked.

'You see that poster on the wall, the guy with the ninja turtles tee shirt and shiny red jacket? That's Web Spinner, the reigning world champion; last year he racked up twelve million US dollars in winnings. Now he does mainly exhibitions and designs games.'

'Is there any way we can block the signal coming into a VR headset, like the one the controller is using in Kuwait?'

Sam thought this over for a moment then grabbed the headset lying on his desk and studied it, frowning. 'This headgear you're describing receives its input via the internet, almost like Messenger where online you can make a call cost free. The controller is too far away for Bluetooth and short wave radio is dicey.'

'Is there a way I can block it?'

'A Wi-fi jammer,' the boy said without hesitation.

'A *jammer* –' Riad echoed lamely.

'Sure, it's a compact circuit you plug into your iPhone or a separate power source and it creates its own Wi-fi network. You can then block all other cell phones in the immediate vicinity and also set up false Wi-fi addresses that will confuse the suckers even more.'

'And you can build such a thing?'

The boy laughed, 'No need! You can buy them pretty much anywhere for as little as ten bucks. I've seen the Node MCU jammer in action, it's only about the size of a credit card. Pretty cool man, causes chaos!'

This stunning bit of information had Riad shake his head in wonder, what an asset a kid like this would be to any police force. Or, for that matter, the criminal world.

'There's a snag though –'

'Oh?'

'It's illegal to use in public, interferes with emergency calls, that kind of stuff.'

'Could you find me one?' Riad asked, 'One that's small enough to go into the pocket of a jacket?'

Sam shrugged, 'I think so, what's in it for me?' The look in the dark eyes was enigmatic, calculating.

'Credits,' Riad said, rising. 'I would make sure you'd get credit for being the gamer who stopped the Scorpion Master. How about that for a resume?'

'Cool!' Sam said, wonder in his voice, 'How soon do you need it?'

'Yesterday, but I'll settle for next week.'

'Sure you don't want a drink?' the kid asked before shrugging and returning the bottle and glasses to the drawer.

'I've got to go, the others will be looking for me. Think you can keep this deal between us a secret?'

Sam grinned, made a sealing motion across his lips.

'Say, you don't have a camera installed in the toilet, do you?'

With an exaggerated sigh the boy flipped a switch and one of the screens went dark. 'Don't know why I bother,' he said, 'It's not like cool chicks ever visit.'

Out on the deck the rain had stopped but it was still icily cold and the decision was made to eat inside. Reed had found a bottle of red wine and soon they were sitting down for what proved to be a very satisfying meal. As he enjoyed a sip of the excellent Coonawarra shiraz Riad looked around the room, taking in the framed wall mounted prints of natural scenery, most of it from around Australia as explained by Reed. A few had the family snapped with a spectacular scenic backdrop and in all of these the boy looked happy leaving Riad to wonder what went wrong.

He did not disclose his earlier conversation with Sam, something he would take up later with Reed.

It was nine thirty by his watch when Riad said he had to go as he still had to escort Sarah to see her husband and it was getting late. On the way back he shared an Uber with Zena who appeared unusually animated and was snuggling up to him under the pretext of it being freezing. Something Riad found surprising seeing the industrial amount of vodka she had imbibed.

'Is there a woman in your life, Riad?' she asked huskily as he became aware of her perfume. He thought this over, deciding there was his mother and, of course, Rania but presumably this was not quite what she had in mind.

'No.'

She snuggled closer, 'It's not natural for a man to be celibate,' she murmured softly, 'it causes all kinds of tensions. Are you feeling tense, Riad?'

'The woods are lovely, dark and deep. But I have promises to keep and miles to go before I sleep ...' he said softly, stroking her hair before kissing her.

'Whatever you say, big boy,' she sighed before kissing him again, more urgently this time.

Sarah Green was still asleep when he arrived back at the house, a worried Chrissie slumped in a bedside chair watching a cooking program on TV with the sound turned down. She looked up when Riad came into the room then glanced back at the sleeping form huddled under a thick pile eiderdown. 'She's very restless, keeps on talking in her sleep but I cannot make out what she's saying. Just a jumble of names in between sobs.'

Without comment Riad sat on the edge of the bed and started shaking the sleeping woman, 'Wake up, Sarah. Wake up!' This was met by a low moan and kicking of legs as she tried to move away from the hand on her shoulder.

'What are you doing?' Chrissie protested, 'the doctor said that -- '

'It's time to go and see Mr Abdul-Karim,' Riad said firmly, 'the police will be surprised she hasn't been there yet.'

Intensifying his efforts he finally managed a response with Sarah opening her eyes and, after a few seconds of incomprehension, asking what was happening.

'Your husband has been involved in an accident,' he said, more for Chrissie's ears than anything else, 'he's in hospital and I am taking you there to see him. Now.'

With that he instructed Chrissie to get her ready while he went downstairs to brew some coffee.

'The police did phone, about an hour ago. I told them you had broken the news to Miss Green and that she was in a state of shock and would be down later, just like you suggested.'

'Good work. Did anyone else call?'

She nodded, 'A reporter from Sky News, he knew all about the shooting. I told him she was on her way to the hospital. I took the phone off the hook after that.'

'Good work, Chrissie. Now let's get moving before the press is parked on our doorstep.'

His initial hunch had been right, there was an informer inside the police department with another possibility that a hospital employee was the media source. Either way it was a good decision to keep Operation Bluenight on a very tight circuit.

With one exception, Sarah would have to be told. It was the only sure way of keeping her at bay and away from the next day's action. By the time he returned to the room Sarah was sitting at the dresser with Chrissie brushing her hair. She stared dully at Riad, wordlessly accepting the offered mug of coffee and taking a sip.

'Hassan has been admitted to the Alfred Hospital, to the Intensive Care Unit. He's been shot but then you know all about that, don't you Sarah?'

Chrissie recoiled in shock, a small cry escaping from her lips but the only reaction from Sarah was a slight flinch as she stared straight ahead at the image in the mirror. 'I know you were there, Sarah. I know it was Ruslan who fired the shots. I even know why you were there. At present the police know nothing of this and for the moment I choose to keep it that way. For to-morrow I'm going to get Maddie, bring her home to you. We have a fair idea where she is and I want you to promise you will keep away.'

Turning to Chrissie he said, 'And that goes for you too, understand?'

Chrissie nodded numbly, the mug in her hand shaking and spilling coffee.

'Mornington –' Sarah said softly, still not looking at him, 'A big old house, next to the sea – It's where he took me that time –' She broke off, burying her head in her hands as dry sobs racked her body.

Riad wanted to reach out to her but resisted, asking instead whether she would recognise the house. Shaking her head slowly the answer was no, it had been after dark and the only thing she recalled was an old hotel they drove past, not far from the house and there were lots of parked cars and a party happening on a terrace.

Thirty minutes later a cab dropped them off at the hospital and with Sarah tightly flanked by Chrissie and Riad they managed to fight a way through the throng of waiting reporters and into a foyer where a duty policeman quickly escorted them to the elevator and heading for the ICU.

As they rode up in silence Riad marvelled at how Sarah seemed to come to life as the cameras flashed and the shouted questions from the reporters threatened to overwhelm all senses. Just showbusiness was the answer, even in tragedy there was always showbusiness with no such thing as bad publicity. Only publicity.

38
CHAPTER

The darkness was her friend, the uncles did not like the darkness, they always wanted the light on, so they could see her better. Stare into her face with that strange look, almost as if looking inside her and excited about it. Except she knew there was nothing inside her.

Nothing at all.

And they would listen and smile when she made those little noises Martha had taught her even though it *meant* nothing.

Lying on her back and staring at ceiling now where she could trace the faint outlines of tiny carved angels staring down at her she thought of how the scariest uncles were the ones that didn't say anything, didn't do anything. Just sat there and stared with slack mouths, lips moistened by a darting licking tongue. And when their time was up and Ken knocked on the door they would get up slowly and leave, without ever saying a word.

She was feeling hungry now and wondered what time it was. It seemed like hours since Ken had shut her inside her room and locked the door after forbidding her to switch on the light. He had told a weeping Martha there would be no dinner for Maddie or Minnie who had also been sent to her room.

He would deal with them later.

With the shutters closed and the heavy curtains drawn it was very dark in the room and it seemed that sounds were carrying further for she could hear Ken and Martha shouting at each other in the kitchen.

Once her eyes had grown accustomed to the dark she had cautiously gone over to the cupboard and fetched Barney, her teddy. He was now cuddled in her arms and as always his fur was soft and smelled of the perfume Martha had them put on when the uncles came.

He didn't say anything but she knew he listened. She would tell him everything, even make up stories and sometimes they would end in sadness but mostly they were happy. She was telling him a story now, of their big house in London and how her nanny always dressed her in pretty clothes when they went out shopping with Mommy.

And Albert, their driver, who would bring the big car around when Mommy wanted to go out. Albert who always winked at her and called her Little Miss Green and would always have a treat hidden for her somewhere in the car and would laugh when she found it even when Mommy scolded him saying it was bad for her teeth.

Picking Barney up she gazed into his little brown eyes that never seemed to sleep and sighed, 'Oh Barney, if only you could talk. You could tell me about your parents and the things you like.'

The sound of the tall clock in the hallway striking the hour reached her ears and breathlessly she counted the musical tones aware of a sudden feeling of unbearable loneliness.

'Where are you, Mommy?' she whispered into the darkness. 'When will you come for me?'

———◆———

'Soon,' Riad said, switching the mobile to his other ear. They had been talking for twenty minutes now and the phone was heating up. *'Maman* says the Australian visa should be ready soon and then we're all going to come down here for a holiday. But my work here is almost done and I'll be home with you before then.'

There was a silence and he thought he could hear Rania breathing but then it was a long distance call and he couldn't be sure. He had waited until they had returned from the hospital and Sarah had retired for the night before pouring himself a nightcap and making the call, figuring it would be late morning in Kuwait and Rania would be up.

As he listened to the sequence of clicks and buzzes as the connection travelled to God knew where before looping back to its destination he felt the familiar pain of a deep seated anxiety; would she take his call, was his little girl alright? The phone rang for a long time before she picked up and then the voice was almost formal, no longer that of a little girl.

And now they had spent minutes talking about everything except the elephant in the room while Riad racked his brain on how to raise the issue. Finally he asked about the psychologist they had visited. An earlier discussion with his mother had revealed that Yvette had arranged the session under the pretext of therapy for herself, taking Rania along for moral support. In on the charade the therapist had conducted a mini group session with the two, focusing on the events in Beirut.

On first hearing this Riad had offered a silent prayer of thanks for being spared the sight as he conjured up the picture of Yvette becoming needy the moment too much attention was given to her granddaughter. It was the nature of the beast that was showbusiness. Nevertheless it could only be a positive thing that Rania had someone professional to talk to and hopefully dispel some demons.

'Ameera is so nice,' Rania said, her voice brightening, 'she comes and sits right next to us and talks about other things, not just, you know –'

'Ameera?' Riad asked, 'I thought Yvette said you are seeing a doctor at Al Mowasat? What is Ameera's surname?'

'Al Quarashi. She says she knows you.'

'I see,' Riad said hesitantly, 'How did Yvette get to see her?'

'I don't know, I think she spoke to Waleed and asked him who you were seeing, you know, after your injury?'

Ameera al Quarashi whom he had been thinking about lately when he was not thinking about Sarah and Maddie Green. The same Ameera whom he intended having another discussion with on an altogether other matter as soon as he was back in Kuwait.

'Is there something wrong, Dad?' Her voice lowered now with just a hint of anxiety perhaps?'

'What? – No! No, darling, it's all good. Just curious that's all. Well, it's getting very late on this side and I have a busy day to-morrow. I'd better get some sleep, I'll phone you same time to-morrow, OK?'

'OK.' There was a pause and he sensed something else was on her mind and asked as much while trying not to inject a note of concern.

'Are – are *you* alright, daddy? You never tell me about the danger of your job and it's just that I worry. You always say we are going away to a safe place to live, like Uncle Vytas and Bubba, but it never happens. I find it hard to believe in impossible things!'

So that was it. He should have seen it coming. 'Do you remember when we read Alice in Wonderland together, just the two of us? We made it a bedtime story except you refused to go to sleep, always just one more page, daddy?'

'I remember –' The voice closer to the phone now, warmer.

'Remember where Alice says she can't believe in impossible things?

'Yes.'

'Remember what the Red Queen said?'

And unexpected laugh, 'She said Alice should try harder, she said sometimes she believes in up to six impossible things before breakfast!'

'Love you, darling.'

'Love you Dad.' And with that the line went dead leaving him suddenly feeling utterly alone and suddenly afraid that things might so easily go wrong for all of them come the cold light of dawn.

His final thoughts as he finally drifted off to sleep a vision of Lord Tennyson's The Lady of Shalott, for that was increasingly how he was seeing the lovely yet tragic Sarah Green. His dark lady for whom he was beginning to care far more than was good for him. His flaxen haired beauty who seemed forever trapped in a curse of viewing the world through a hazy mirror and into a puzzle and wanting to reach out and yet --.

Out flew the web and floated wide –
The mirror crack'd from side to side;
"The curse is come upon me," cried
The Lady of Shalott ...
Hugging his pillow tighter, he slept.

39
CHAPTER

He stood quite still for the best part of a minute, willing his breathing to slow as he surveyed his surroundings. His hunch had been right, the easiest way to get inside a large hospital like this was through the tradesman's entrance, the one spot a stretched police would be less likely to monitor. A busy place, the back entrance of the Alfred, with delivery trucks and waste disposal utility trucks and even the odd hearse all coming and going and at all hours. Dozens of private vehicles as well and likely belonging to the maintenance workers and domestic staff he could see going about their tasks in what appeared to be the laundry where he was now.

Dressed in the workman's top and trousers he had borrowed off one of the Elena's crew and sporting a black baseball cap with a car manufacturer's logo he could easily pass for one of the outside contractors in the process of making a delivery. The clipboard, once again courtesy of MV Elena, helped to complete the picture.

So much for getting this far, the nightwatchman having a smoke break and in conversation with a truckie barely sparing him a glance. The next challenge would be to get into the main hospital section where his destination lay waiting. Smiling at an elderly woman, morbidly obese and wheezing as she brushed past carrying a heaped up basked of fresh linen, he searched for and located what he was looking for. A neatly stacked shelf of blue hospital scrubs and, next to it, white medical coats.

It took but a minute to change into the scrubs and don a white coat, discarding his clothes inside the dirty linen bin behind which he had taken shelter. People were everywhere, all seemingly in a hurry and barely sparing him a glance. He had replaced the baseball cap with a linen theatre cap and all he needed now was one of those identification tags he saw everyone wearing. About the size of a mobile phone they had a photograph of the owner on one side as well as their status. The reverse was blank and the card's bulkiness suggested it functioned as an access key to different sections of the hospital.

Spotting the lady he had moments earlier encountered where she was now busy stacking a shelf he brushed past mumbling an apology and in the process lifting her tag. With an indignant cry of so rude echoing in his ears he strode quickly for the large sliding doors that led to the main section of the building. Once inside the basement with access to different service sections he headed for a battery of elevators and pushed the button for the third floor. Several people got in when the doors opened on the ground floor and over their heads he caught a glimpse of a solitary cop assisted by two security guards checking IDs while a harassed looking receptionist was trying to placate several distressed strangers who were in search of an assaulted family member.

On the way up one or two others stared at him uncertainly but he had turned the name tag now attached to the front pocket of the coat so that the photo side did not show and no-one confronted him. In the corridor leading to the Surgical ICU he paused for a moment to get his bearings then headed towards the sliding doors at the end at a fast purposeful pace as he had seen the young doctors and nurses do, while appearing to be in urgent conversation on his mobile phone.

Halfway down the corridor he detoured past a deserted nurses station where a stethoscope was procured. A set of double doors posed no barrier as the card did its job and then he was inside the unit and immediately taken aback by the sheer activity in the place. Open plan with what seemed like several dozen curtained beds, all occupied and all attached to a myriad of tubes and lines leading to softly puffing ventilators and wall mounted monitors, the large ward was ablaze with overhead lights and to one side an oblong glass fronted central control station. Several nurses were rushing about and in a far corner a white coated doctor could be seen peering over a large clipboard aided by two nurses while a third was busy changing an infusion bottle.

In a nearby bed an elderly man, seemingly confused and having kicked off his blankets, was shouting at the top of his voice for someone called Edna and judging by the pool of yellow fluid slowly seeping down the side of the bed and onto the floor he had pulled out his catheter. Somewhere close by a bedside alarm was pinging insistently but this did not appear to warrant urgent attention from the staff.

The solitary nurse manning the central desk was intently scanning the bank of monitors and urgently talking into a phone and hardly noticed him as he came up behind to study the whiteboard denoting the names of the patients in the various beds.

Hasan Abdul-Karim was in bed number three and judging by the sheer number of attachments to his body not doing well. At least two drip lines were going, one administering blood while a ventilator rhythmically breathed for him and the swathe of dressing packs covering his naked chest were soaked in blood.

Post surgery and deeply sedated or possibly in a coma he did not respond when the visitor pulled shut the curtain around the bed before stepping up to study the infusion lines. Selecting the central line inserted in a jugular vein he took a small syringe from a pocket and injected its clear contents into one of the colour marked IV access points. Potassium cyanide it was instantly lethal and by the time the visitor pulled aside the curtain to rapidly head for the entrance a clamouring monitor was announcing the patient's cardiac arrest.

'Wait! Doctor! Wha –' The young nurse was running from the monitoring station and staring after him in bewilderment as several others emerged from hitherto unseen patient bays to rush to the emergency. As he turned into the short corridor leading to the access doors he was confronted by an older nurse who had just come from what appeared to be a supplies room. Her eyes widened as she scanned his wildly flapping ID disc which had flipped around, the grim unsmiling face of Annie Wilks, the cleaning lady, staring back at her.

As she opened her mouth to shout a warning he clamped a hand around it and forcibly pushed her back into the room knocking her out with a vicious punch to the side of the jaw. But the distraction had cost him precious seconds and judging by the corridor loudspeaker announcing a Code Black in SICU he had to get out of there fast before the place swarmed with security officers. Stepping back into the corridor and closing the door behind him he had to take a step back as a uniformed female security officer rushed through the swinging doors to head for the ICU barely sparing him a glance in passing.

But he knew his luck wouldn't hold and once inside the main corridor he ducked into the nurses station where he had earlier stolen the stethoscope and withdrew from his belt the item he had brought along from the boat. The station was still deserted but there was the sound of voices coming from the other end of the corridor now and then he had pulled the safety tag off the distress flare and flinching only slightly fired it into a bank of shelves where it exploded in a bright flash of phosphorescent red, instantly staring a fiercely burning fire. Rushing out and towards the people coming in his direction at a fast pace he shouted "Fire!" wildly pointing to his rear and adding something about getting an extinguisher as they hastily parted to let him pass.

The overhead fire sprinklers came on even before he reached the stairs at the far side of the elevators accompanied within seconds by the loudspeakers now changing from Code Black to Code Red without breaking stride.

Nobody was using the stairs despite the metallic voice from the speakers instructing that the elevators should not be used and by the time he reached the basement his breathing was back to normal. Then it was simply a matter of discarding the white coat and retrieving his baseball cap before striding out through the outside gates once more. This time the security guard did glance at him but satisfied he wasn't carrying any stolen items, let him pass without a challenge.

Mikhail was waiting behind the wheel of the car where he had earlier dropped him off and thirty minutes later they pulled up at the marina where the Elena II was moored. While the crewman parked the rental car his passenger sprinted up the gangway and headed for the main lounge where he knew Ruslan would be waiting. He felt incredibly alive, even high, as the earlier adrenalin surge gave way to a rush of endorphins leading to a tingling sensation all over and a feeling of being on top of the world.

Of being invincible.

Dimitri Ruslan was reclining on the couch, a large whisky in hand. His bare chest swathed in a bulky dressing which was gingerly being adjusted by a female crew member.

'The avenging angel returns!' he said as the new arrival went over to the wet bar and dug a Coke out of the fridge. Ruslan's words were slurred, the effect of the pain killers the attending doctor had pumped into him and this seemed to annoy him for he repeated his greeting.

Slumping into a chair the man known as Scorpion Master studied his accomplice with mild amusement. 'It's done,' he said simply while tilting his eyes in the direction of the young woman and making a slight movement of his head.

Turning to the woman Ruslan dismissed her saying she would not be needed again that night. They watched her leave then the Russian leaned forward to reach for the whisky bottle on the coffee table wincing as the pain from his cracked ribs intensified.

'What did the doctor say?' his guest asked.

'He says I was lucky. The bullet only grazed and broke some ribs but did not damage the lung. He stitched my up in his rooms and gave me some shots.'

'So, no hospital?'

Ruslan wanted to laugh, checked himself just in time, 'Don't be crazy. They would report it to the cops and they would come for me. Tell me about Abdul-Karim.'

He listened attentively as his guest went over the details of the hit, smiling broadly at the culmination of the tale. 'Good!' he said, 'Good. The bastard would have given me up first chance he had. What about Yuri?'

'The police questioned him for two hours but he did not tell them anything other than a stranger, a customer, came in and asked to use the bathroom. He was busy sweeping the floor when suddenly hit from behind knocking him out. He never saw his attacker.'

'Hmm. The police found the DVD collection he was shifting for us?'

The Scorpion shrugged, 'Of course. That's why they wanted Yuri down at the station again at nine to-morrow.'

'And?' Ruslan asked expectantly, taking a deep tug at his drink.

The other man smiled mirthlessly, 'I'm afraid he's not going to make it. Ever.'

Ruslan suppressed an inner shudder as his gaze met that of his guest, the Scorpion's eyes unfathomable pools devoid of any expression. The Russian had done his share of killing but he had never met a stone killer like the man sitting opposite him slender fingers idly playing with a string of prayer beads.

'You're a cold hard man,' he said reaching for the bottle, 'All those first person shooter games must blur your perception of the real world.'

'My analyst says there is no proof of a player confusing virtual reality with the real world,' Scorpion said solemnly. 'I, of course, beg to differ.'

To this undeniable fact Ruslan could only agree. He gestured towards the bar, 'Have a real drink! We celebrate!' Met by a blank look he grimaced and added, 'I forget, you don't drink, don't smoke and don't enjoy the ladies, no?'

Ignoring the remark Scorpion Master informed him that he was booked on the morning Emirates flight to Dubai and Kuwait and that his advice for Ruslan would be to make tracks himself. 'The Convention ends to-morrow anyway and we have made all the contacts we need. Mikhail can wrap up at the stall but you should get out of here.'

Ruslan nodded as he splashed ice into his tall glass adding a generous helping of the whisky. 'I have already given instructions for the Elena to sail but the skipper says he has to take on bunker fuel first. We look at leaving maybe lunch time.'

Deciding he was hungry the Scorpion went over to where a smorgasbord had been set up on a side table and selected an assortment on a small plate before returning to his seat. 'What about the girl?' he asked between bites of salmon on mini-toasts.

'I fetch her.' He frowned, 'There is only one problem. She is booked to see a special customer to-morrow, a man who has been an agent for us, bringing us into a much wider network than we have had before. He wants to sample the wares and I don't want to disappoint him.'

'So what's the problem?'

Ruslan shrugged, the sudden unguarded movement bringing on another spasm of pain. 'I have been trying to contact him for the past three days but no luck. This is not like him. Also, three customers we got from him were arrested by the Americans recently. All this makes me suspicious ...'

'To-morrow might be a trap?'

Ruslan nodded, 'Possibly but I have to get the girl, she is valuable but also knows too much.'

'Does this client know where you're keeping her?'

'No. The problem is Sarah just might.'

There was silence for a minute, both men thinking about dealing with that particular problem and coming to the same conclusion. The Scorpion voiced it for them, 'Too risky to take her out,' he said wistfully, 'Not with that Kuwaiti cop bodyguarding her. He's a dangerous man.'

'You know him?'

The man known as the Scorpion Master smiled grimly, 'You might say I know his innermost secrets. We see the same therapist –'

40
CHAPTER

He had the dream again that night, not the one where he was trying to get away from some unseen threat while his limbs were somehow semi-paralysed and only able to move with great effort but another familiar scene from a twilight world. He was on a golf course and others were present although he never did see their faces. Everyone had played their tee shot and now it was his turn. Except somehow his ball was in an impossible position, wedged in between stones or sometimes up against a wall or even in a narrow drain.

Carefully eyeing the shot while the others waited patiently he would replace the ball in a still tricky but slightly better spot, only to find that when he was about to swing the ball was once again in that hole. And all the time he was aware of the absurdity of the situation for it was a tee shot, for God's sake! On a grass tee from where the others had hit perfect shots just a minute ago and why couldn't he?

This absurdity would normally come to him seconds before he became fully awake and still in a twilight world where he was aware of things around him while also aware he was not awake.

A police psychologist, one he saw years earlier when first experiencing the nightmares, had told him the two dreams were essentially the same. Panic attacks of a kind and always to do with a sense of helplessness. Of being unable to control things that were spinning away from him. There followed therapy sessions, he could vaguely recall some breathing exercises and eventually the nightmares became less frequent until they disappeared altogether.

So why were they back now?

The shrill clamour of his phone alarm had him wake in fright at six the next morning. Bathed in sweat he lay there for a minute as the last fragments of the nightmare slowly evaporated and he strove to collect his thoughts. Sarah! Was she alright?! Forcing himself to calm down and think rationally he ran through his mind the day ahead. D Day. The day they had planned for what seemed like forever now, going over the details again and again while looking for flaws. All the time realising how flimsy a plan it was, how easily it could all go wrong.

How easily they could lose Maddie Green forever.

Not a morning person he switched on the TV and lay there watching a breakfast show for a while before padding over to the kitchen for a coffee. Chrissie looked up when he entered and said she was about to fry up some eggs and bacon and there was fresh orange juice in the fridge. He asked how Sarah was doing and was informed she was still sleeping and had had a peaceful night.

He was on his second cup of coffee when his phone rang. It was Reed. 'Abdul-Karim was murdered in the Alfred ICU last night, by an intruder masquerading as a medic. We have CCTV footage of the suspect and the Assistant Commissioner has called a meeting for eight, at my office. He expects you to be there.'

'How, I mean, what makes you think of murder, he was in a critical state post surgery last I checked?' Seeing Chrissie's questioning gaze, Riad lowered his voice, 'For chrissake, weren't they guarding him?!'

'It was a professional hit, a IV injection of cyanide most likely. We found a discarded syringe that smells of bitter almonds and our SOCO reckons it was injected into the victim's drip.' There was a pause while Riad digested this new complication finally telling Reed he was going to, for the moment, keep this from Sarah.

'Her husband's death?!'

'No. His *murder.*'

Assuring Reed he would be there at eight he turned to Chrissie whose shocked features suggested she had overheard enough. 'I fear Sarah's life might also be in danger. So listen carefully, I'm going to get someone I can trust to come over here and look after you both while I tend to some urgent business. Under no circumstances must you allow Sarah to leave the house, understood?'

Visibly shaken Chrissie nodded vigorously and asked whether he was hoping to find their Maddie that day, bring her home, as tears brimmed and ran down a cheek.

'She's coming home,' he said firmly giving her a hug before dialling Vytas' number.

Fifty minutes later he was sitting in the small briefing room at Police HQ where DI Reed had the floor and was showing the gathering a grab taken from CCTV footage showing the face of the suspect killer of Hasan Abdul-Karim. The technical crew had overnight managed to trace his progress via the laundry to the SICU and back analysing the recorded data from several camera sites before selecting three images capturing his features most clearly.

Present in the room was the Assistant Commissioner, Commander Michaels, Casadio the Special Operations Group (SOG) leader together with his three team members, DI Reed and his newly assigned partner, a fresh faced Detective Sergeant Donna Jones.

And Riad who was wishing someone would open a window, the room hopelessly too small for the occasion but chosen because of security reasons. Standing where he was near the door he was squeezed in between Jones and a SOG member and one of them was wearing a particularly intriguing perfume and he hoped it was the woman.

'So far he does not come up on any wanted list, either local or international, but we are still checking', Reed said unaware of the frequent blowing motions into his palm that was eliciting shared looks of amusement from the SOG team. 'We have fingerprints from the syringe and these will be circulated but there is a chance he could be a cleanskin.'

'Way too professional a hit for that,' Casadio said, 'but how does this connect to the Maddie Green case?'

'We're not sure but as you know he is a person of interest in the disappearance of his stepdaughter and –'

He was interrupted by the Assistant Commissioner holding up a hand, 'Let Homicide handle that. So far the press is reporting it as a death resulting from a shooting so let's keep it that way for the moment. Now let's get on with the Bluenight briefing.'

'Yessir. *Shit!*'

'What?!'

'N – nothing, Sir,' Reed said hastily, furiously spitting in his hand while he paged through a sheaf of loose papers.

'Get on with it, man! We don't have all day!'

Riad listened with half an ear as a nervous Reed went over the details of the operation once more, his own thoughts far away. If no-one else had recognised Abdul-Karim's killer he certainly had. It was a face instantly familiar and he even had a name. On seeing that face a lot of things had suddenly dropped into place, all of them related to a series of killings in Kuwait City. Should he tell his Australian colleagues, especially now when they were at the pointy end of the search for Maddie? Somehow he did not think so, this had to do with another murder homicide altogether, in his own city, business he would attend to shortly. No, bringing this up now would simply confuse matters and take focus away from the plans of the day.

Likewise it was better not to bring into the open the role of Uncle Vytas in the matter. Vytas who was hopefully by now at the house in Drummond Street and keeping an eye on Sarah Green.

'Riad – Lieutenant Ajmi?' Snapping out of his reverie Riad saw Reed holding up what looked like a chunky black wristwatch and, in the other hand, a mobile phone. Satisfied that he had his attention Reed went on, 'This digital watch has been modified by our technos to contain the Life 360 app. This is a widely available tracking device working off Wi-fi and will enable us to track you to within a matter of meters. It also functions perfectly as a watch. The problem is range, indoors Wi-fi is good for about fifty metres, outdoors three times that. For extra range we have installed a hidden range booster in the trunk of the car you'll be driving but, of course, once you're away from the car we rapidly lose the connection. Here, try it on.'

The watch was passed along to Riad who took off his own to try it on. The sight of his old Rolex, a gift from his mother, led to some mumblings that detectives in Kuwait obviously were paid a lot better than in Victoria.

'Now for the mobile,' Reed continued, 'this one belongs to Nightcat 17 and has been uploaded with a similar tracking app as an extra backup. Riad, if you stay behind after the meeting I'll run you through its functions. We are using the mSpy program for this one.'

'What about a GPS tracker for the car?' someone asked.

'I was coming to that. The car is fitted with the standard fleet tracker device we use for our police vehicles which will enable the detectives in the pursuit car as well as the SOG team in their van to keep track of its whereabouts. The Wi-fi watch and phone is to pinpoint Lieutenant Ajmi once he's away from the car.'

'Is everyone clear on the schedule?' the Assistant Commissioner asked while consulting the messages on his phone.

'Yessir, we convene at the Frankston Police Station at five o'clock sharp and wait for Lieutenant Ajmi's call. Once he's been contacted by the target we follow.

'Thank you Commander Michaels and let me remind you that this is not a federal operation, it is still officially a missing person's case. DI Reed will be in charge.'

Riad had a question, 'Do I get a weapon?'

'I'm afraid not,' the AC said, rising and reaching for his cap, 'Far too risky and besides, as a foreign citizen you're not entitled.'

'Let's hope your karate skills are up to scratch,' the SOG leader offered to soft chuckles from his team.

CHAPTER 41

He was back at the house at ten and Vytas was there and enjoying a large plate of pancakes Chrissie had made. He smiled broadly as Riad entered the kitchen while unsuccessfully trying to tuck a large revolver into the back of his belt without Chrissie noticing.

'Riad! Good to see! You OK?'

Nodding wearily Riad sat down at the table and enquired about there being any more of those pancakes going around. And maybe some of that coffee he was smelling. While Chrissie busied herself at the stove he brought the big man into the picture while aware this was strictly confidential stuff and not giving a damn. If you couldn't trust family who could you trust?

Listening carefully a frowning Vytas asked whether he needed extra protection. Apparently Bubba had arrived back in the country only hours earlier and in spite of a minor injury – a flesh wound from a Syrian border guard's weapon – he was fit for duty and ready as always to help family.

Riad did not think it necessary to involve his other uncle at this stage pacifying Vytas' hurt feelings with a promise of maybe later. Then he asked whether Vytas had brought the item he had asked for.

'Of course,' came the answer, 'I get this from friend, iss clean, not used before.' Digging in a pocket he produced a slim spring action flick knife. Its handle inlaid with an emerald green motif. Weighing it in his palm Riad asked whether Vytas had tested it, checked the balance.

'Off course. She throw perfect.' Adding somewhat unnecessarily, 'And very sharp.'

'Hmm.' Folding back the blade Riad pocketed it, 'Let's hope I'm not the mug who brings a knife to a gunfight,' he said wryly. 'I have a feeling Mr Ruslan will not come quietly –'

Vytas looked worried. 'You want me take care of this Ruslan? No problem, I make it look like accident.'

Hastily assuring his uncle that would not be necessary, Riad proceeded to give him clear instructions regarding Sarah who was still asleep upstairs. 'She is not to leave this house at all until I return. Also no phone calls, I will take her mobile. And Chrissie, that goes for you too. Whoever killed her husband might be after her too, so you keep that front door locked and do not open it for anyone, clear?'

Both parties nodded leaving Riad with one last task he wasn't looking forward too. Asking Chrissie to stay in the kitchen he climbed the stairs to Sarah's bedroom. Standing for several seconds in the doorway he stared down at the sleeping form taking it all in, the tousled bedsheets, the sensuous curve of her hips as she lay facing the windows and the soft light streaming through the lace curtains casting shadows across the perfect contours of her face, the swan like perfection of her neck.

Where do you go to my lovely, when you're alone in your bed – She was so beautiful and so utterly vulnerable. What terrible things have you witnessed, Sarah Green? Does this life of fame and luxury ever make up for the past? Would anyone ever really see inside your mind?

Just what have you *done*, Sarah Green?!

Steeling himself he went over to the bed and sat on the edge. Staring down at the sleeping woman and being aware that he was burning that image of the most beautiful woman he had ever known into his mind and his memory forever, the words from an Oscar Wilde poem came to him, *Some love too little, some too long. Some sell and others buy; some do the deed with many tears and some without a sigh, but each man kills the thing he loves --*

Finally he leaned over and gently shook her awake. 'Sarah? Sarah, wake up. It's me, Riad.'

She rose from the depths of her dreams slowly, blue eyes fluttering before opening wide and finally focusing. 'Riad?'

'Yes, it's me. I have brought you some coffee.' He placed the mug on the bedside table as she slowly turned to face him while running a hand across her face. It was bandaged and blood stained and he wanted to caress it but couldn't.

'Wha – Why? What's going on?'

Giving her a few moments to become fully awake he told her that Abdul-Karim had died during the night. Offering no details he strove to make it sound like the result of his wounds. He watched in silence as the full impact of what she had just heard slowly struck home.

Riad did not know how he expected her to react but was still taken aback by the complete absence of any visible response. She sat upright and after a while nodded and sighed. So be it, was the message, or was it simply that she was too numb, too dead inside, to feel anything any more?

Wordlessly she took the coffee he held out and drank before mumbling a thanks and returning the mug. 'Hasan is dead,' she said slowly as she shakily brought cold white fingers up to her face to feel its familiar contours, a way of knowing she really was awake.

'Poor poor Hassan,' she whispered at length, 'always the one good man in an evil world –'

Turning her gaze on Riad she seemed puzzled then recognition flowed and she asked for Chrissie.

'She'll be here in a minute. Sarah, I want you to listen to me very carefully. Today is the day we, the police and myself, are going to try and get Maddie back. We have a good idea of where she is being kept. I want you to stay here, in the house, until I get back. I am leaving a bodyguard downstairs, someone I trust fully, as I believe your own life may be at risk. I don't want you to contact anyone at all, certainly not the press and not your agent. Fortunately all your appointments with the agency has been cancelled for the moment.'

He waited for a response but got nothing. 'I want to get up now,' she said at length. This was a signal for Riad to leave and send for Chrissie. Rising he went to the door and paused there, looking back at the woman in the bed. She met his gaze and was it his imagination or had the dazed look been replaced by something much more calculating, defiant even.

Shaking his head he went down the stairs. When, Riad, have you ever understood women, been able to fathom their alien thoughts?

After he had left Sarah lay back against the pillows and thought of the dream she had, the sudden clarity that had come to her after so many years. She remembered the house in Portsea now, recalled the bust of a guardian lion on each of the high gateposts. Even remembered how to get there, thoughts that had been repressed all these years.

She knew where her daughter was.

'It is disgusting that a police officer should know how to use that thing,' Zena said as she watched Riad tape the open flick knife to his left forearm with clear Sellotape and pull down the sleeve before declaring himself satisfied.

'So give me a gun and I won't have to carry this.'

She snorted but said nothing, turning up the volume of the car radio instead. It was a live broadcast of an Aussie Rules footie game and Riad suspected it meant as little to her as it did to him but let it go. They had been sitting in the parked car for the better part of an hour now and conversation had largely dried up to be replaced by a growing tension. For this was it, probably their last chance of finding Maddie Green.

Alive.

The call came at thirteen minutes past five. It was on the mobile belonging to Nightcat 17, the caller identifying himself as Ken after ascertaining he was speaking to a Mr White, the alias used by the paedophile. Leaning closer Zena was scribbling down the number while Riad listened to the instructions. In fear of inadvertent noises betraying the presence of a second person Riad had not gone onto speakerphone and as the call ended he put an impatient Zena into the picture.

'We are to proceed down the Mornington Peninsula Highway heading for Rosebud. There's a BP filling station opposite the entrance to the Bayview Motel and we pull in there and wait to be contacted. At this hour it should take us twenty minutes.' He waited while she relayed the instructions to Casadio and Reed on her two way radio, only to be informed by the SOG leader that he knew already, having a tap on the Nightcat 17 mobile. 'The signal is bouncing off Telstra's Droman tower so the perp is nearby.'

Uncertain as to how paranoid their quarry was and whether they had access to a scanner monitoring police channels, they were using special frequency hopping equipment but Riad still wished Casadio would be more cautious and not use terms like "Nightcat 17" on air.

And what about the corny "perp" that had him roll his eyes. Clearly the man was a fan of American crime series. Probably seen all one thousand episodes of NCIS.

'How will he know it's you,' Zena asked. 'I mean he doesn't have a description of either you or the car, does he?'

'I reckon he'll phone once he figures we're there, ask me to flash my lights or something. Anyway, it's time for you to get into the trunk and make sure the safety is on old Betsy,' he said nodding at the Glock showing under her jacket. 'Out you go sugar and try not to sprain something.'

'You sure know how to show a girl a good time,' she replied sourly, opening her door and flashing him a look somewhere between you bastard and my place or yours. 'And, you'd be surprised to know the positions I can get into –'

Smiling to himself Riad watched in the rear view mirror as she opened the trunk and got in, closing it with a solid clunk. It had been rigged so she could open it from the inside. At least, he mused, she didn't add the old cliché of if you play your cards right you could get lucky tonight.

But the message was clear, alright. It was the stress of the situation, he decided, with the adrenalin flow came increased sexual tension and why not?

As he eased into the late afternoon traffic a sudden thought had him hesitate, he hoped neither Reed or Casadio came up with the bright idea of racing to the rendezvous point to try and spot the contact before Riad arrived. Surely they would not be that stupid?!

Instinctively reaching for the radio tucked under his driver's seat he changed his mind. Too risky, Ken might just phone when he was on the radio and that would be that. The very reason he had left it switched off.

Storm clouds were moving in from the bayside and with it intermittent squalls, the low winter sun fast disappearing over a distant horizon. It gets late early here, he thought with a smile, thinking of the great Yogi Berra's famous saying while wondering if one of the celebrated Yankee coach's other sayings might surface when the next directions came up. "When you come to a fork in the road, take it!"

The thought made him chuckle out loud and for a moment he wondered whether Zena could hear him, wondered whether it was cold in the trunk, the car's heater now running full blast.

This is so you, Riad, he decided; whenever you're about to enter the valley of death you start clogging up your mind with trivial things. Funny things that somehow serve as a reminder of another, sane, world out there where things are familiar and safe and -- *Raindrops on roses*

And whiskers on kittens

Bright copper kettles and warm woollen mittens For the next few miles he tried to recall the rest of the lyrics and finally gave up, his thoughts returning to what lay ahead. Was Maddie still alive? Would she be there? What reception was waiting for him? And, most important, would people as ruthless as her captors let him take her away without things getting ugly? Zena thought they would, stating that in her wide experience in the field most paedophiles were pretty tame beasts, pathetic really and coming quietly once the game was up.

Riad was not so sure. If Ruslan was behind all this, like he thought he was, he would not go quietly. There would be blood.

After a while he followed the road signs for Rosebud taking him off the highway and onto Boneo Road, the traffic now thinning. There followed a series of roundabouts as he passed through a built up residential area and finally the T section with the BP filling station on his left and the entrance to the Rosebud Motel opposite. Directly across was a straggly line of trees and beyond that the long beach.

It was dark now, the forecourt of the place brightly lit with two cars at the pumps and three parked in bays near the entrance to the shop. Pulling into a vacant parking spot Riad switched off the engine and waited.

He waited for fifteen minutes while the temperature in the car slowly dropped and several vehicles came and went, half a dozen customers frequenting the shop, most to pay for fuel and some with small bags of purchases.

The phone rang. Even when expecting the call it still had him jump and he almost cut the call in his haste to pick it up. 'White.'

There was a pause as he listened to someone's breathing, then Ken said. 'OK. Here's what we'll do. I figure I've spotted you. Flash your lights twice if it's you in the white Commodore parked out front.'

Riad did as told and was ordered to get out of the car and enter the shop and head to the rear section where the large freezers were. Outside the car he hesitated, undecided whether he should lock the vehicle then decided no, Zena was there and he wasn't sure whether such an action might interfere with her escaping when the moment came.

Then he was inside the shop and heading for the brightly lit freezers, stacked with cold drinks and snacks, at back. There were few people in the place, two at the cash register where a girl young enough to still be at school was totalling up their purchases. Reaching the nearest freezer he paused to glance around finally spotting a tall gaunt man dressed in faded jeans and a chequered flannel shirt idly paging through the magazine rack. 'You White?' The stranger said, not looking up. A none too clean baseball cap with a John Deere logo topped off a straggly beard while lightly tinted yellow sunglasses hid his eyes.

'Yes.'

'Follow me,' the stranger said hefting a plastic bag containing his purchases, before heading for an as yet unseen exit at the back of the shop. A janitor was mopping the floor as they approached and stood aside for them to leave. Glancing over his shoulder Riad could see the girl at the cash register staring at them before returning her attention to a customer, the conclusion that the other man had already paid for his goods.

Then they were outside, a freshly sprung breeze from the sea bringing with it a sudden chill that had Riad shiver and thrust his hands into his jacket pockets. They were on the opposite side of the building and he knew without looking that they could not be seen from his parked car. This area was also not as well lit save for the headlights of the passing cars on the beach road.

Ken, Riad presumed this was him, set a brisk pace heading away from the forecourt and seconds later stopped at a parked Mercedes. 'Get in,' he said tossing his shopping bag on the back seat.

Then they were away and heading towards Sorrento, the evening traffic now considerably thinner with long stretches of wooded areas coming up as they left Rosebud behind. They travelled in silence while Riad thought whether he should put on a show of mounting excitement, after all, wouldn't that be how a paedophile on his way to a special treat would react?

Glancing at the man behind the wheel he decided it wouldn't make any difference so he turned his thoughts to Zena instead, had she by now clicked that there had been a change of cars?

He need not have worried. Parked a hundred yards away in the shade of a large tree Detective Inspector Reed had spotted the switch and radioed it in to the SOG team who as instructed were keeping way out of sight. This left him with the dilemma of how to get the federal agent out of the trunk without being seen. The car was parked under the bright lights of the forecourt and visible to those inside the shop including the cashier.

There was also a CCTV camera but that was the least of his worries. In the meantime Riad was being driven away and there was a limit to the range they could track him.

In the end there was no alternative to just pulling up next to the Commodore and help a disgruntled looking Zena out of the trunk and into the back of their car. There were no vehicles at the pumps and nobody inside the shop seemed to have noticed.

'Boy,' Reed said as they pulled away, 'I've heard of some guys being rough on their dates but to leave the sheila in the bloody trunk! That takes the cake.'

Commander Zena's reply was unintelligible but might have contained a lewd suggestion of what Reed could do with himself.

42

CHAPTER

After a while Ken pulled into a roadside rest area for truck drivers across from a caravan site and parked the car in a spot away from the sole streetlight. 'Get out,' he said and came around the car to where Riad was standing. 'I have to search you, we can never be too careful.'

Riad stood patiently while Ken patted him down, expertly checking the usual sites where a gun could be hidden then taking a close look at the mobile before handing it back to him. He was good but a real pro would have found the knife. Satisfied Ken pointed to the fat brown envelope he had retrieved from Riad's inside coat pocket, 'This the money?'

'Five thousand cash, just as agreed.'

Opening the envelope Ken ran the edge of a finger over the tightly stacked notes before handing it back. 'Looks OK. Let's go. But first, put this on,' It was a dark blue linen scarf rolled up to fashion a blindfold and smelled vaguely of a woman's perfume.

Obediently Riad, who had anticipated this, tied it around the back of his neck and allowed himself to be guided back to the car. The few seconds it took for Ken to walk around the back of the car was all Riad needed. Retrieving the small razor sharp disposable scalpel from its hiding place inside a bulky fountain pen he slid off the cap and in a few quick movements slashed a small square in the fabric of the blindfold before dropping the blade down the side of the seat. The opening was in line with his left eye and not visible to the driver now getting behind the wheel.

It was at the moment, thirty miles away on the other side of Melbourne, that Vytas Ayoub stirred and raised himself to an upright position on the couch. Instantly aware of a splitting headache and a mouth that felt like sawdust it took him a few seconds to regain his bearings. Then it hit him, the woman! She had given him a mug of coffee, a fancy strong one from a machine telling him it was a different taste but he should try it. Not long after he had suddenly felt sleepy and lay back against the cushions of the couch to have a quick snooze.

That was hours ago, when still daylight and what had happened in the meantime? Glancing around the kitchen alcove he could see Chrissie slumped over the kitchen table, asleep and snoring, her head resting on her folded arms.

Seven o'clock by his watch. *Merde!* He knew instantly they had both been drugged by the woman and where was she now? Hauling himself off the couch with some effort, his head spinning, he conducted a quick search of the house confirming Sarah Green was gone.

As was the Audi in the garage.

Bitch! And she was such a nice lady too.

Fumbling for his phone he remembered at the last minute Riad's instructions not to phone him under any circumstances but to contact Detective Inspector Reed if a dire emergency arose, a number being provided. How had his nephew put it,

don't hesitate to cope? Cursing under his breath he checked his messages to see that his contact at the harbourmaster's office had tried to get hold of him no less than three times, the earliest six hours ago, finally leaving a message. The Elena II had sailed at noon, her declared destination Darwin.

Double *merde!*

Locating Reed's number he sat for a moment then sighed and dialled, only to be immediately re-directed to voicemail. It seemed the detective had urgent business of his own and did not want to be disturbed. Did the caller wish to leave a message. He did not. Going over to the fridge to get a drink of water Vytas paused next to the slumped form of Chrissie. Her breathing shallow and rapid she was deathly pale and her skin was icy cool as he felt for a pulse which was thready and weak. The pool of vomit staining her top and hair clinched it. Christ! Whatever the bitch had doped them with, she had probably given this small woman the same dosage of what had nearly wrecked him. With a shaking hand he dialled 000 for an ambulance.

At that moment Sarah Green was driving into Rosebud and searching for a filling station, the empty warning light having been on for the past five miles. During the drive she had managed to compose herself and bring her raging emotions under some sort of control. No more crying, no more hysterics; she was going to Maddie and make things right.

If she thought at all about the dosage of the sedative she had dissolved into the coffee of Chrissie and the man, all of the twenty tablets the doctor had left her the night before, it aroused no concern. Maddie was all that mattered now.

Maddie was coming home.

Finally finding a filling station she pulled in at the pumps where a pimply faced youth in clean overalls was only to eager to help her refuel the Audi. Had she at that moment cared to glance out to sea through a gap in the trees she would have seen the bright lights of the Elena II as she slowly steamed towards Sorrento and beyond that the open sea.

In the spacious bridge Ruslan was sitting in the elevated captain's chair, a whisky in hand, watching his skipper slowly navigating their way through the treacherous shallows. They were in near darkness, most of the light coming from the battery of instruments glowing a soft green while the only sound was the rhythmic ping of the depth sounder and the occasional chatter interrupting the static on the radio.

In the reflections of the windows he could see the outlines of the skipper, the man's face a study in intense concentration as he made continuous small adjustments to the steering while finessing the throttle. Below their feet was the pleasant hum of the powerful diesels and Ruslan knew that standing on the lower rear deck one could just feel the subdued soothing vibration as the Elena II ploughed her way through the water.

It was pleasant up there and soon he would complete his final task and leave behind him Melbourne and Australia for good. He was about to go downstairs to the lounge, get himself another drink, when his mobile rang. It was Mikhail, 'It is as you suspected, boss. Ken's car is being followed, by three people, in a dark grey Camry. A man and two women. They have been careful to keep half a mile behind but I'm pretty sure they are following.'

'Police?' Ruslan asked as he felt the first stabbings of fear, the drink in his hand now forgotten.

'It's hard to tell but who else?' the standover man replied as Ruslan stepped out onto the open flybridge to find better reception. 'Another thing, boss, I think I spotted a special police unit in the area. Earlier, in Frankston. They were in an unmarked van but I spotted one getting out the back maybe to go to the toilet and he was in that full black gear they wear, you know the body armour and helmet.'

Ruslan thought this over for a moment then asked whether they were also following.

'I don't know. If they are they keep well back. But this is Mornington, boss, no crime here to bring out a special police team, no?'

Ruslan could only agree which made his plans all that more urgent. 'OK. This is what you do. You have the Sterling with you? Good. Head for the house and park somewhere close to the main gate from where you can watch but remain unseen. I'll be coming from the beach and rely on you to create a diversion if that police team attack, understood?'

'Yes, boss. The Sterling will be a nice surprise for any pig faced cop.'

Turning to the man at the helm Ruslan asked how long before they would be in position for him to take the service inflatable across to the beach where the house was. 'Fifteen minutes, it's low tide though so I'll have to anchor way out. Do you want Samantha to go along, secure the rubber duck while you're up at the house?'

'I'll be OK.' With that he went downstairs to change into a pair of dark slacks and a matching polo neck sweater, the outfit completed by soft soled boat shoes, a navy reefer jacket and a black beanie.

Checking the clip on a CZ automatic he tucked it into a jacket pocket as an afterthought adding a folded clasp knife.

He was ready to deal with Maddie Green and the would be clowns coming to take what was after all his possession.

Moving to the rear deck with its lowered transom he set about preparing the inflatable for launching. Even with the deck hand helping it was hard work which made the throbbing pain in his side all the more intense and as he sweated and cursed he wondered what his crew was thinking, decided he didn't care. They were well paid to run this boat, nothing more. Mikhail was different, the fellow Russian had been his bodyguard since the old days and he was in the full picture.

Ruslan knew he could rely on him with his life.

They were moving closer inshore now and through his night glasses Ruslan thought he could make out the house on the cliff, pick it out from its neighbours, most who were set on similar large acreage. The tide was turning and with it came small rollers and with the engines cut back the Elena II was starting to wallow. This would make it more difficult to get back on board on their return, all the more reason to get a move on. Reaching for his mobile he dialled a number and it was Martha who answered.

'Ruslan. I haven't heard from Ken, is he back with the customer?'

'No, sir. He's been gone for over an hour now so I expect him back any moment.'

'There's been a change of plan. I'll be joining you, so when they arrive I want you to stall. Don't let the man take Maddie to the room, understand? Not until I'm there.' A last thought had him add, 'The dog, is it tied up?'

'Yes, we always –'

'Good. I'll be coming up from the beach stairs. Don't say a word, I don't want the customer to know I'm coming.'

With that he ended the call and using the ship's intercom told the skipper to let him know once they were in position.

With the help of the young deckhand the launching of the inflatable went smoothly and the powerful outboard started immediately. If the deckhand, a South African on a working sabbatical, thought the whole operation strange if not downright suspicious, she had the good sense to keep it to herself having already decided to jump ship at their next port of call.

The crossing to the beach took twenty minutes as Ruslan steered by the lights of the houses on the cliff face as well as the smaller green beach level light glowing at the bottom of the wooden staircase leading up to his house. He had earlier instructed Ken to leave it on and also to unlock the gate at the top of the stairs. Had he been a romantic Ruslan might have reflected how that green light served as the same warning issued to Jay Gatsby from Daisy Buchanan's dock across the water but then he wasn't and the message was lost.

Approaching the beach he slowed until the craft struck sand then accelerated driving it skidding onto the firm wet surface. Killing the motor he moved to the prow and jumped off wincing as the sudden movement brought a sharp pain to his side. Gingerly bringing a hand up to the wad of dressings it came away wet with blood with did nothing to improve his fast souring mood. Securing the dingy with an anchor tossed well onto the beach he set off for the steps cursing softly as the soft sand made him stumble more than once.

A silvery moon was just showing through a window in the banked clouds and raised deep shadows that moved in the freshening breeze. Halfway up the steep steps he paused to catch his breath and stare back at the riding lights of the Elena II, reflecting how much more sensuous her sleek lines were than those of any woman he had ever known.

43
CHAPTER

The sea facing deck of the Portsea Hotel was ablaze with multicoloured lights from strung lanterns with pop music blending with shouting and laughter as formally dressed people danced between the tables. Riad figured it for a private party, perhaps a wedding and the irony of his own mission compared to the shared happiness inside that circle of light did not escape him.

'Not far now,' Ken said and this would be the first time he had spoken since their getting to know each other at the pat down session. They had left Sorrento behind, turning down Portsea Road from the centre of the small village where the streets were still crowded with holidaymakers and nary a parking spot in sight. They were now very much in a leafy neighbourhood reeking of old money, the houses set well back and hidden behind high walls and imposing gates. Riad knew from an earlier study of the Google map that they were close to the Nepean nature reserve with the ocean now on both sides and separated by less than a mile. He also knew there would still be Port Philip Bay's sandy beach stretching all the way from Frankston to the pier from which the ferry operated close by in Sorrento. He wondered about Ruslan and his boat and thought he should have insisted on a police boat being part of the mission but, no word from Vytas earlier so that angle was probably covered.

The music faded in their wake as they navigated numerous twists and undulations and now there were no people around and no cars and soon they would be running out of road. If Maddie was here she would be close.

And then they were there, Ken abruptly turning up a narrow lane that led over a ridge to several hundred yards further end in a cul-de-sac on a clifftop. There were large walled estates on each side, several with access to the lane. The one they stopped at had large adobe gateposts from which stared down two impressive bronze lions. The high wooden gates and eight foot walls precluded anyone from seeing inside. Ken pressed a pocket sized controller and the heavy gates swung open noiselessly providing a view to a long tree lined driveway and beyond that a Spanish hacienda style house with the ground floor windows brightly lit and streaming out onto the spacious lawns.

Ken paused, watching in his rear view mirror until the gates shut behind them, before slowly driving up to the house. Once there he switched off the engine and gave Riad permission to remove the blindfold.

Martha had opened the front door as they pulled up and welcomed Riad with an uncertain smile as she ushered him in. Ken could see at a glance that something was wrong given her questioning look but said nothing.

'Welcome, er –'

'Mr White,' Riad said with what he hoped was a suggestive wink, shaking the offered hand. They were in a spacious reception area, the ceiling supported by impressive wooden beams and the walls lined with heavy framed oil paintings, mainly landscapes but also portrait studies. Judging by the costumes it was extremely unlikely any of the subjects would ever have visited the house or were, in fact, still alive.

Had they visited they would no doubt have felt at home with the period furniture, the heavy wrought iron chandelier and the opulent oriental carpets. Mounted above an archway leading to the main area of the house was an impressive coat of arms flanked by crossed swords while a full suit of medieval armour stood to one side.

Decidedly a Spanish look, Riad decided, figuring an interior designer had been involved.

'Please, sir, if you would kindly come this way,' the woman said bowing him through to a sunken lounge with pretty much the same feel to it apart from heavy curtains lining a far wall and hiding what Riad guessed were glass doors leading to a veranda. Taking the offered seat and accepting the offer of a drink, whisky, Riad glanced around taking in his surroundings. A hallway led off to one side with a number of doors leading to presumably bedrooms and possibly a study. Directly facing him was a large dining room leading off to a kitchen and, on the opposite side he could make out the shape of a snooker table.

What made his pulse quicken however was the apparatus set up in the space between the dining room table and a sideboard. It was a slim metal pole stretching up from a broad metal baseplate to where it was attached to the ceiling.

It was the pole Maddie was seen dancing around on the porn video they had been shown. This was the moment he knew he had found Maddie Green. Should he activate the signal on the watch now? No, he decided, the others should be close by, better to wait until the moment he sees the girl.

In the kitchen where Ken was fixing Riad's drink Martha took him aside to whisper urgently that Ruslan would be here soon, coming from the beach access and that Maddie was not to go with the man until then.

'Did he say why?' a worried Ken asked as he added the ice.

'No, only that.'

Shrugging off a feeling of unease Ken went back to the lounge and handed Riad his drink. 'The girl will be here shortly,' he said, sinking into another chair and taking a sip from a beer in a stubbie holder. 'Martha is just getting her ready, you know.'

'That will be good,' Riad replied, 'it's been a while, you know. I've been thinking a lot about her.' This delivered with a leer which he hoped would go with his assumed paedophile image.

Ken laughed, 'I know what you mean, mate! You're in for a treat!' Suddenly serious he leaned forward, 'Let's have the money now.'

Returning the smile Riad shook his head, 'Uh uh, not until I see the cutie.'

Scowling Ken sat back and drank some more of his beer, he could wait and besides, Ruslan would be there soon, then they would take care of this bozo.

Standing in front of the mirror in her bedroom Maddie studied her image with a critical eye. Martha had dressed her in the French Maid outfit complete with the frilly white knickers as well as the lace cap and the feather duster she would use to tease the uncle with. Her hair had been tied up in a bun and Martha had carefully applied just enough makeup to accentuate the blue eyes and brushed pink blusher onto her cheeks.

Martha had watched critically as Maddie applied the pale pink lipstick herself, just as she had seen mummy do many times, finally nodding her approval. Then she had sat down beside her as they went over the evening's plans, Martha once again stressing that she would not allow this uncle to hurt her. She was just to be nice and maybe let him play a little with her but nothing nasty.

Long since unable to distinguish between "good" and "nasty" Maddie merely nodded. There was an unspoken agreement between the two of them that Martha would be close by, that the events of the other day would not happen again. Also, this time Minnie would not be taking part as she was having a night off.

And now she was alone and staring into the mirror and wondering what Mommy was doing to-night. As she studied the contours of her face she tried to recall what Mommy looked like but somehow the image in her mind remained distant, fuzzy. Mommy is beautiful she said softly to herself. Mommy is a supermodel and wants me to be one too. She says I'm beautiful and soon she will come and fetch me –

Unable to complete the seemingly impossible mental picture she went and sat on the bed and forced herself not to cry. Crying was for naughty girls Martha had said, it would ruin her makeup and Ken would be angry and we wouldn't want that, would we?

In the lounge Riad glanced at his watch and saw he had been waiting for twenty minutes. Something was wrong but what? There were no other cars about so no hint of another "customer" demanding the girl's attention. Had it been a simple plan to rob him and not deliver he reckoned that would have happened back at the truck stop already. No, something was wrong but Maddie was here, she simply had to be.

Without further hesitation he pressed the button to activate the go signal.

Parked five hundred yards away on Portsea Road and facing the turnoff earlier taken by the vehicle they were tracking, the alarm flashed on DI Reed's dashboard mounted receiver, at the same time it was received by Casadio's SOG squad where they were at that moment cruising slowly past the hotel. The car's occupants stiffened as they immediately became aware of the impending moment of danger, a young Detective Sergeant Brown flashing an apprehensive grimace at Zena as she fingered the butt of her service pistol. The comely brunette was newly seconded from Missing Persons and had never fired her weapon in the line of duty. Aware of her sweating palms she wiped them on the side of her pants hoping no-one would notice. This was it, hadn't she recently applied to transfer to homicide? The chase was on!

Not a word was uttered as Reed engaged the gears and prepared to head up the road at a pace. Car lights looming in his rear view mirror had him wait and then an Audi, travelling slowly, came up and, after a moment's hesitation, turned up the lane heading in the direction they were about to go.

Following a prudent hundred yards behind Reed instructed Brown to draw her pistol and have it ready. On the back seat Zena already had her own firearm unholstered and was intently peering at the scene ahead through slitted eyes. 'What the hell?' she said softly as the lead vehicle slowed down to pull up at a set of high gates which, according to the GPS Brown was holding was where their quarry was.

'It could be Riad —' Reed said between clenched teeth, immediately realising that was impossible, the signal was coming from beyond those gates. He slowed down before coming to a halt a safe distance away and switching off the headlights.

In the Audi Sarah was oblivious to the car following her as all her attention was now focused on those gates. Yes! This was it, the lions! This was the house. And her Maddie was on the other side of those gates and waiting for her...

She knew it would be futile to try and get through those gates, there wasn't even an intercom to call the house. But then she had been there before, had walked around the perimeter as she enjoyed the views down to the beach and the sea. She knew that if she followed the brick wall all the way down to the cliff edge it petered out and there was a rusty section of barbed wire disappearing into the scrub lining the rock face.

She also recalled there being a burrow of sorts under the wire, something perhaps created by a fox and maybe this was a way in. Getting back into the car she drove down to where the road came to an end and parked, leaving the lights on to outline the wire. Struggling over the uneven ground in her high heels (why hadn't she thought of wearing flat shoes?) she reached the wire and crouching quickly discovered that the burrow was no longer there, it had been filled in.

Indecisive while aware of a growing sensation of panic she stood gazing out at the blazing lights of the big house she could see so clearly through a gap in the bushes. Oh it was the house alright! The house where it had all begun, the whole ugly sickening business that had made her what she was and was now threatening to destroy the only true love she ever had. The one love she had betrayed so cruelly in an attempt to exorcise her own demons. And now the end was near... She *had* to get inside that house!

With a sob she rushed back to the car and got behind the wheel. Then gunning the engine to a crescendo she drove straight at the wire fence, the car leaping over the sudden drop to crash down onto the wires and hang there suspended as the wheels spun wildly on the wet grass and failing to find purchase. Moving as if in a trance now Sarah half climbed half fell out of the driver's side falling heavily onto the uneven ground before shakily coming to her feet. She had lost one of her shoes and angrily slipped off the other, tossing it aside before heaving herself up onto the car's sloping hood using the seat and open door for leverage.

Pausing for a moment to regain her balance she moved gingerly forward and leapt over the straddled fence to land on all fours on the other side. Behind her the twin headlights of the Audi were now tilted crazily skywards and seconds later the engine cut out.

way through the dense undergrowth towards where she knew the lawn and the house and Maddie was.

When Zena saw the other car drive crazily over what from But Sarah was now oblivious to all this as she slowly made her that distance appeared to be a fence around the property she hesitated no longer, jumping out and shouting at the others to stay there while she investigated. Not waiting for an answer she sprinted up the road towards the stranded car and in the half light of the moon was in time to see a shadowy figure launch itself from the hood across a fence and into dense brush. The light was poor but the figure was unmistakeably a woman and that meant only one thing.

With a curse dying on her lips she redoubled her effort while vaguely aware that to her rear another vehicle had appeared and was fast heading up the lane towards where Reed and Brown were waiting.

Crouching in the shadows of the property directly opposite the gates to the Ruslan house Mikhail studied the approaching fast moving van. He was right, this was the SOG team he had spotted earlier and they were coming this way! He had positioned himself twenty minutes earlier behind the closed gates of the millionaire's holiday home he knew to be deserted at that time of the year, having jemmied the gates and hidden the car in the driveway. Gazing through a barred aperture in the heavy wooden gates he now had an excellent view of what would be his line of fire as well as some protection from returning fire.

Parked less than fifty feet away and about to be joined by Lieutenant Casadio's team Reed and Brown were totally unaware of death now staring at them as they too waited for the anticipated reinforcements to pull up.

Come on, *tovarich!* Come to papa, the Russian said softly, teeth bared in a snarl as he cocked the Sterling and waited.

43
CHAPTER

It took Ruslan a matter of seconds to reach the house, his path across the lawn clear in the moonlight. Noticing Ken's car he decided to go around the back and enter through a side door to which he had the key. Noises coming from the direction of the service road had alerted him to the possibility of unwelcome visitors lending a definite element of urgency to his movements. Pausing to listen at the door he could hear voices coming from the lounge area and producing the CZ he held it concealed behind his back and pushed aside the heavy curtain to step inside the brightly lit room.

'Mr Ruslan!' Ken said jumping to his feet, 'Martha told me you might be visiting and –' He was silenced by an impatient gesture from the Russian who stared intently at Riad who had remained seated.

'Who is this?' he asked in the quiet voice Ken and Martha had come to know as a harbinger of trouble.

The two glanced uncertainly at one another and it was Ken who answered, 'Why, Mr White, of course –'

'No it isn't,' Ruslan said bringing the pistol into view. 'This man was on a press photograph taken in the company of Maddie's mother, Sarah Green.' He turned to Martha who had gone very pale, 'Go fetch Maddie, she's leaving with me. Now.'

There was a moment's silence as the woman scurried off down the corridor returning with an apprehensive looking Maddie by the hand. At that moment there was the cacophonic sound of shooting coming from the front of the garden and accompanied by shouting

———

and, seconds later, the boom of an explosion. Mikhail! Ruslan realised instantly, and he was firing at men trying to break into the property. And who else but the police?!

Seeing the gun Maddie suddenly broke free in terror and moving fast Ruslan lunged out to grasp her by the waist, the sudden movement springing instant tears of pain to his eyes. When he raised the pistol searching for Riad he found his target had reached up to grab a stunned Ken by the shirtfront dragging him forward and tumbling onto the couch where the two men were instantly grappling in a confusion of limbs as a desperate Riad landed punch after punch sending a spray of pink froth from the other man's shattered nose.

Locked in close combat the two had regained their feet and a cursing Ruslan could not get a clear shot at the policeman. In his grip the girl was wriggling madly and screaming and there was only one thing for it, he'd shoot both if necessary.

Seeing him raise the pistol at the moment Ken's arching back was the nearest Martha screamed and lunged at the gun taking the bullet to the chest and collapsing into Ruslan at the same moment as Maddie sank her teeth into his arm. The pain had him lose the gun and pushing the dying woman roughly away he forcibly picked up the girl with his good arm and made for the side door he had entered earlier.

Then he was outside and heading for the distant gate and stairs in a stumbling run and only partially aware of his kicking and screaming captive as his attention was drawn to the end of the driveway where an armoured car had now crashed through the heavy gates and was heading up to the house.

In the lounge Ken had momentarily broken free and was trying to reach Ruslan's dropped pistol that was lying mere feet away. Grimly hanging on to the man's wrist while desperately striving to clear his fuzzy vision from a blow Ken had landed seconds earlier Riad managed to trip the other man, sending him sprawling onto the carpet but nearer to the gun. It took Riad but a millisecond to realise he was losing this one which was when he ripped free the taped flick knife and threw it with all his force at Ken's broad back.

One of the few skills a young Riad had ever learnt from his Bedouin father was the dark art of throwing a knife and as the exquisitely sharp point sank deep into the other man's flesh Riad knew the blow would be fatal.

Gaining his feet with an effort for he was still groggy he picked up the pistol and set out to follow the fast escaping Ruslan.

Barely a minute earlier, when Lieutenant Casadio's SOG team had pulled up to the gates of the villa, the men spilling out of the back of the armoured car to be joined by Reed and Brown, Mikhail had opened fire with the submachine pistol, rapidly moving the weapon from side to side in a mowing action while battling to keep the wildly bucking barrel from kicking up and missing the target.

While two of his men went down only Casadio's lightning reflexes saved him as he dived behind the cover of the vehicle drawing his own weapon in one fluid movement. 'Get down!' he shouted at the momentarily frozen detectives but while Reed dived for cover Detective Sergeant Brown was too late, catching a burst of bullets that flung her six feet away as she still tried to raise her service pistol.

The Sterling has a firing rate of 550 nine mm rounds per second which means the 34 round magazine empties itself in a matter of seconds. Hence the experienced shooter would fire in controlled short bursts but Mikhail whose training had come from playing shooter video games where the ammunition never runs out, was no expert. Cursing he fumbled to change magazines and this was the chance Casadio, who had pinpointed the source of the lethal fire, needed. Pulling the pin on a fragmentation grenade he tossed it over the gate in a high arc to land behind the shooter where it exploded with ear splitting sound instantly killing the Russian whose smoking body landed sprawled over the blown down gate.

Pausing to check on his two fallen men, both who had miraculously survived with only lesser injuries due to their bullet proof flak jackets while the lady cop had not been so lucky, he ordered the armoured car's driver to crash through the gates and take them up to the house from where their urgently beeping homing signal was coming.

A lone figure was standing at the edge of the lawn and near the stairs leading to the beach below. From twenty yards away Ruslan could see it was a woman, knew instinctively who she was. Taking tighter hold of the struggling child and half carrying half dragging

Maddie to where the stairs beckoned he was confronted by a silent Sarah Green stepping in his way.

He was about to shout at her to get the hell out of his way when Maddie managed to wriggle free from his grasp while shouting Mommy! *You came!* at the top of her voice and running towards Sarah who stooped to pick her up. But the ground was uneven and in the poor light Maddie stumbled and fell and in two strides Ruslan had reached Sarah grabbing hold of her hair while a knife blade flashed dully as it was raised.

'Whoring bitch!' he shouted and then Maddie was upon them and a cursing Ruslan was kicking her away and then there was the loud crack of a single pistol shot close by.

The woman helpless in his grasp the Russian stood quite still, seemingly frozen in the moment, then slowly, almost in slow motion and still holding onto Sarah by her hair, he toppled backwards disappearing over the edge of the cliff and taking her with him. For a sprinting Riad, still yards away, it would be a scene forever etched in his memory, two figures side by side, almost but not quite in embrace and framed against the now silvery moonlight casting a wide beam of glittering light across the ocean and then, suddenly gone.

Nothing.

They fell without a protest, the only sound the crash of breaking branches far down and the cries of alarm from the disturbed seagulls scattering away to, for a moment, describe crazily looping black shadows against the night sky before disappearing down to where the safety of the beach beckoned.

He reached the cliff edge at the same time as an out of breath Zena who still had her pistol in the double handed shooter's grip.

Standing there on the edge of the abyss and peering into the darkness Riad could just make out the two bodies. The Russian was spreadeagled over a large rock while Sarah lay close by, sightless eyes staring up at him.

Even at that angle he could see the unnatural angle of her neck and knew she was dead.

They just stood there for a while, two people faced with an ending they never wanted, never saw coming. Then, gradually, they became aware of a third presence, coming between them and also staring at what lay below. 'Mommy?' Maddie whispered softly then before she could say anything more Zena had scooped her up holding her tightly in her arms, the little face buried in her hair, the dropped gun forgotten where it lay on the wet grass.

'Oh baby! My little baby –' she sobbed, as tears ran down her cheeks, 'It'll be OK. She'll be OK – '

And then she saw Riad shaking his head and they both knew it wasn't OK; it would never be OK again.

The others were fast coming up to where they were standing and still a few paces away they stopped as if sensing that something had happened here, something tragic and that they were imposters in the moment.

It was Casadio who finally broke the silence, 'Is this – is this *her*?' he asked to which Zena, too upset to speak, simply nodded.

'We found another small girl up at the house,' he replied as he glanced uncertainly from face to face, 'she was hiding in a bedroom and closet and I just thought –'

'There are two bodies down there,' Riad said as the lieutenant came up to see what they were staring at, 'The Russian and also Sarah Green.' He wanted to add, his daughter and the mother of his child but didn't. *It's just Chinatown* he said softly to himself as he followed Zena and an eerily silent Maddie towards where Jack Reed was waiting at the car.

Moving like an automaton as an ashen faced Zena led her away by the hand the girl never looked back over her shoulder. Following close behind Riad thought it was a matter of still being numb with shock at what she had just been through.

Later, he wasn't that sure.

44
CHAPTER

I f the desk attendant at the Holiday Inn thought it unbecoming for a guest to enter the foyer at three o' clock in the morning, looking somewhat shop soiled and in the company of an unidentified gentleman, she was enough of a woman of the world to limit her response to a reserved "welcome back, Miss Michaels."

An icy challenging stare from the federal policewoman probably played a role as the receptionist shrugged inwardly and turned her attention back to the movie she was watching on Netflix.

Bone weary and still numb from the aftershocks of the evening as well as the three hour debriefing that followed, Riad allowed himself to be led to the elevators by Zena who had driven them to the hotel from police headquarters. With the children in the care of the appropriate authorities at the Royal Children's Hospital and Chrissie under observation at a nearby hospital's Casualty for a drug overdose, there was little point in returning to the house in Drummond Street.

That, and he needed someone to help him through the night.

They rode the elevator to the sixth floor in silence and then Zena was digging for the room key before taking him by the hand and leading him inside the darkened room. As the door shut behind them and still in darkness Zena pressed him against the wall as she clumsily fumbled with the belt of his pants while unzipping her own slacks and quickly stepping out of her panties. He was instantly hard in her hand even while his whole body was shaking from he knew not what and as he tried to say something she hushed him with lips that crushed his as her tongue found his.

'Just fuck me!' she whispered urgently and then he was inside her as she hitched herself up wrapping both legs over his and forcing him to support her naked heaving buttocks as she moved in a frenzy of suppressed lust while he tasted the tears spilling down her cheeks. Stumbling towards where he thought the bed was he fell on top of her writhing sweat covered body as he ripped open her blouse to sink his searching lips over hard erect nipples while aware of sharp nails digging exquisitely painful furrows down his back.

And then she was coming and saying his name over and over while calling him a bastard and finally they lay exhausted in each other's arms as his night vision slowly returned and things in the room started taking on familiar shapes.

He thought they might be more comfortable if they took off their clothes and lay there patiently as she stripped him down while running warm hands over different parts of his body and remarking on the scars and wondering how he got them and deciding she'd rather not know.

'I needed that,' she whispered at length while drawing patterns on his chest as she snuggled up, her breath hot on his neck.

Riad said nothing as he felt the pent up tension of the night slowly be replaced by a deep seated weariness. It had been a long time for him too and as he stared through the semi-see-through curtains at the winking neon of the big city outside he knew that he liked this enigmatic woman, this outwardly hard human being who, like himself, had seen so much of the ugliness of the dark side of the street and yet still remained every bit a woman. Of all the women in his life, was this one not most like him? Did she not also dispel the widely held myth that old cops become hard and callous in response to the nastiness and often hopelessness of the endless battle?

Stroking her cheek that was still moist from the tears of minutes ago he thought of what George Orwell had said: *People sleep peaceably in their beds at night only because rough men stand ready to do violence on their behalf...*

He should have added women too.

She moaned softly as he ran a hand over the mound of her belly and down to where her sex was so very soft and wet and then they made love again, this time taking it slow before finally falling into a weary sleep while still deeply embraced.

His phone alarm woke him at six to find that Zena was already up and fresh from the shower, a towel wrapped around her hair while the rest of her was naked. 'Good morning, lover,' she said bending down to plant a lingering kiss on his lips. 'You'd better get a move on, we have a debriefing with the Assistant Commissioner at eight and I'd love to get some breakfast before then.'

Still woozy and with a slight headache Riad was thankful for the cup of steaming coffee she placed on his bedside table as he watched the Channel 7 news being read by an attractive blonde who took great care in her elocution at the expense of a fixed grimace that might once have been a smile.

In all fairness there was not much to smile about. The events of the night followed the latest update on the looming housing crisis and fresh scandals involving Australian rugby players. Six people dead in a police shooting in Mornington, including a police officer. This following a police raid on a suspected paedophile ring which led to the safe rescue of the missing Maddie Green as well as an as yet unidentified young girl. Both children having been admitted to the Royal Children's Hospital in Melbourne.

In a separate tragic incident the supermodel Sarah Green, who is the mother of Maddie, died in an accident involving a fall. No details have been released by the police who are investigating but it is not believed that this is related to the police shooting. The names of the deceased would be released as soon as police have managed to contact their nearest relatives.

The scene shifted to a warmly clad female reporter standing outside the wrecked gates of the Portsea house as she recited the earlier events in dramatic if not entirely factual fashion. How different the house looks in daylight he thought, almost tranquil with a bright winter sun in a cloudless sky and the excited chatter of birds in the background. As the camera panned to a wider sweeping view he caught a glimpse of the sea and thought he could make out the white hull of the Elena II where she lay at anchor. A sea patrol boat had boarded her in the early hours of the morning, arresting several crew members while the authorities had not yet got around to returning the vessel to the Melbourne marina.

None of this was known to the reporter but Riad had a feeling this tantalizing snippet would be leaked to the press before long.

The scene shifted to an interview with the shadow state Minister of Police who labelled the latest shooting as yet another example of how crime had gotten completely out of control under the weak Labour government while expressing his sympathy with the family of the police officer who had died in the line of duty.

With an effort he hauled himself off to the bathroom where he stood for a moment studying his face in the mirror. Was this stranger really him? This gaunt creature who could do with a shave and perhaps some sun and why not a good facial to get rid of those blue tinged bags under the eyes?

Sighing he got into the shower spending a full ten minutes as he let the piping hot water soothe away the grime and the bone weary tiredness of the previous twenty four hours. The hot water made the scratches down his back sting and that brought a wry smile to his lips for it was a good feeling, if somewhat painful. He'd have to watch out for those sharp nails next time he decided, while knowing that he very much wanted there to be a next time.

After a hearty buffet breakfast washed down with several cups of strong coffee Zena drove him to the house where she read the morning paper while he shaved and changed into fresh clothes. Then they drove down to the police station.

They were early, the others arriving with degrees of haste and with most carrying briefcases, one or two Riad did not recognise. Judging by the sober suits and worried expressions either lawyers or accountants.

Possibly spin doctors.

Fixing himself a coffee at a side table that also offered some sandwiches but no donuts, he spotted the Assistant Commissioner who, upon seeing him, strode across to unexpectedly shake his hand.

'Nasty business,' Addison said, then asked if Riad was alright.

'A bit shaken but I guess we all are.'

The Assistant Commissioner nodded sagely as he ran an appraising eye over the gathering group which was now sizeably larger prompting a move to a larger conference room. 'There will be quite a storm, I'm afraid. The minister is expecting a full report by lunchtime and then there's the press —'

Riad nodded, he knew all too well about the press.

'But life, and the work, goes on. I want to talk to you at the end of the meeting, in private. It's about a proposition I have been giving some thought to.' With that he moved to the front of the room to indicate to Detective Inspector Reed who held the floor, to start.

For a moment Riad feared the man would start by paying homage to the traditional owners of the land followed by the Lord's Prayer as he had noted formal Australian events start but there was thankfully no place for that here and Reed plunged straight in.

'*Shit!* Good morning everyone.' Visibly flustered he went into his fallback spitting in the palm of his hand routine before turning to a laptop open on a table and bringing up a PowerPoint display on the screen behind him. Going rapidly over the prepared slides outlining the previous night's events it culminated in an edited video taken from the helmet mounted cameras of the SOG team.

The firefight at the gates was especially graphic and Riad thought it an odds on bet it would find its way onto You Tube within days if not hours.

There followed twenty minutes of discussion time during which various parties brought up a myriad questions, most fielded by the Assistant Commissioner using a variety of assurances, vague promises to "look into that" and frankly a set of artful sidesteps. It reminded Riad of the state governor in *The Best Li'l Whorehouse in Texas* before deciding that was unfair. He liked the man.

Finally the matter of Sarah Green came up and here the attention shifted to Riad, introduced by Reed to those new to the investigation as the detective who perhaps knew her best. 'Lieutenant Ajmi, from Kuwait City homicide, was brought to Melbourne at the behest of the family to help with the search for Maddie and in the process gained some insight into the family dynamics which he believes played a pivotal role in the tragic events that unfolded.' This was delivered with a final suppressed *"cunt"* only partially masked by a cupped palm and spitting motion before the cop sat down to wipe his brow and thankfully accept a cup of coffee from a colleague.

There was a brief hubbub in the room as heads swivelled to assess the newcomer who now took up position at the table serving as a lectern. Seated near the back he spotted Zena who was in the company of two federal police officers who had flown down for the meeting. She was smiling at him and in a way this gave him the go-ahead to plunge right in.

'This is only the first of many such meetings and I'm sure it will take some time for this case to be fully laid bare. So I'm going to confine myself to the picture I have formed which I believe is probably as close to the truth as we're ever likely to get.'

'There are two criminal matters here but they are closely interlinked. Firstly, to understand what happed to Maddie we have to understand the mother. So, if you will indulge me, I will try and go over this as briefly as I can. The world knows Sarah Green as the beautiful supermodel whose four year old daughter was kidnapped from their home in Melbourne some months ago. Over the years her face has adorned many glossy magazine covers while her marriages to a millionaire Ross Green and later Hasan Abdul-Karrim, has been extensively reported in the press, as was the loss at sea of her first husband.'

As he paused to take a sip of his coffee Reed came forward to bring up a photo of Sarah the supermodel on the large screen followed by one of Maddie. Mother and child were smiling at the camera and the girl's face shone with the simple happiness of the very young and the very innocent. Looking at the picture of Maddie Riad felt a pang of deep seated pain and quickly returned to his narrative.

'But here's the real Sarah, the Sarah no-one really knew. Born to a London prostitute mother she was placed in foster care before being discovered at the age of sixteen by a modelling agent and that part is well know history. Only brought to light recently however was that Sarah mounted a DNA based search for her biological father who proved to be the international businessman, Dimitri Ruslan —'

At this a murmur rose from the room as several attendees scribbled notes. 'This was shortly before Sarah was married to Ross Green, a glittering affair that made the news around the world. At that stage she had met with Ruslan, at the Mornington Peninsula home where Maddie was held and last night's shootings took place, the only way she could have known the location of the house. What happened then we don't know but here's the shocking bit: Dimitri Ruslan is the father of Maddie Green —'

As expected this revelation led to gasps of shock around the room and if anyone had not been paying attention until then they were now. 'This we know from DNA tests commissioned by a suspicious Ross Green which proved he was not the father of his wife's child as well as Sarah's own investigation. At this stage Sarah, who had been a victim of self harm in her youth, began a round of what is known as doctor shopping with young Maddie. The child was seen by a number of top specialists who could never find the reason for Maddie's recurrent episodes of ill health as reported by the mother. Eventually child psychiatrists became involved and finally one, at a prestigious London children's hospital, raised the likelihood of the Munchausen by Proxy diagnosis.'

A show of questioning hands had Riad launch into a short explanation of the syndrome before picking up the narrative.

'Now we get to the next stage of the saga, the disappearance of Ross Green while on a private cruise in the Mediterranean on his yacht, the Fairy Knowe. On board was Sarah, Ruslan who was by now a family friend, Abdul-Karrim and a lady friend of Sarah's as well as several crew members. There is ample evidence that Ross Green started an argument accusing his wife of infidelity and that he was later that night murdered in their cabin by either Sarah, Ruslan or both and the body disposed of at sea. I doubt whether Abdul-Karrim was involved or knew about this.'

'So Sarah married Abdul-Karrim who soon became suspicious regarding firstly the frequent trips to the doctors with Maddie whom he suspects is not sick and secondly by the strange hold the Russian seems to have over his wife. So he hires a London based private detective who digs up vital information and who loses his life because of this. Probably at the hands of Ruslan.'

Pausing for a drink of water from a bottle provided on the table while allowing the furiously scribbling audience to catch up, Riad knew if they thought what they've heard that far was outrageous, wait for the next bit. 'Now we get to the bad part, the part where an increasingly unstable Sarah strikes a deal with Ruslan, the child's father, to stage a kidnapping allowing Maddie to spend time with her father; the father figure Sarah never had. We may well ask ourselves whether this was Munchausen by Proxy rearing its ugly head once more, projecting the mother's mental anguish onto the child?'

'What the deal was we shall probably never know but we do know that Ruslan – arguably one of the most evil men I have ever known, a true psychopath – starts using young Maddie in a variety of child abuse scenarios, some quite horrifying.'

'His own daughter!' a female in the front row gasped, burying her face in her hands while shaking her head. She was dressed in a dark business suit and the expensive shoes and crocodile skin briefcase had her down for a lawyer. Riad hoped she would be OK. Wanting to bring an end to the rising level of agitation in the room he pressed on, 'Suspecting his wife is meeting with Ruslan Abdul-Karrim hires a local private detective, Baker, to follow her. This ultimately leads to the shooting death of Baker recently at Camperdown and the wounding of Abdul-Karrim, presumably by Ruslan who was also injured in the altercation. We have good reason to believe Ruslan then orders the hit on Abdul-Karrim at the Alfred Hospital.'

'An increasingly desperate Sarah fails to get Maddie back from Ruslan and for obvious reasons cannot go to the police. Meeting me earlier at a psychologist's group session in Kuwait City where I had been sent to for routine counselling following a homicide incident, she sees in me someone who can perhaps be manipulated into getting the child back. An experienced detective who might just, with the right coaxing and hinting get the job done.'

'A stalking horse,' a voice interrupted, 'or was it just your body she was after?' This led to polite laughter quickly suppressed by a raised hand from the Assistant Commissioner who glared at Casadio, the SOG leader shrugging, his expression one of Whaat?

Riad wondered whether the tough talking commander's two injured men, one still in hospital, would appreciate the humour. Wondered if the man's PTSD matched his own, just finding another outlet. Shrugging off the thought he pressed on, 'So we go through this *dance macabre*, this charade where she sends countless clues my way including a bizarre session with a clairvoyant –'

'When do we get to the sex bit?' Casadio again, the response from the audience less pronounced this time.

'Lieutenant Casadio,' the Assistant Commissioner said softly without turning to look at the man, 'either offer something constructive – after Lieutenant Ajmi has finished his presentation – or shut the hell up, get it?'

A muted response from the rear indicated he did.

'Please go on, Riad,'

It was the first time the man had used his first name but they were all friends here now, were they not?

'I was slowly beginning to get the picture but too late for Sarah Green who began showing signs of unravelling, her behaviour becoming progressively more erratic as evidence came to light of what was happening to her daughter. I'm not sure whether she always knew where Maddie was being held or if it was simply an informed guess but in the end she did lead us there. We all know of the tragedy that unfolded next.'

Momentarily overcome with a sudden surge of emotion he paused, swallowing hard while aware others were staring at him quizzically, before pressing on in a halting manner, 'I...I just want to add one thought... about Sarah Green –'

Pausing again to gain control over a voice that had become thick with a choking sadness, he took a sip of water while seeking and finding Zena who smiled back at him with an expression that said "I know you loved her. It's OK—"

'—in the end it was love that brought back little Maddie. The simple all embracing self sacrificing love of a mother for a child ...'

Not trusting himself to say anything more he sat down abruptly and after a moment's awkward silence the Assistant Commissioner took the floor to wrap things up, announcing there would be a press briefing at twelve, the emphasis being on the safe recovery of Maddie Green as well as another young girl whose identity was still being ascertained. Also the tragic death of Sarah Green, the mother of Maddie, in an accident at the scene. During a shootout with the police several members of a suspected Melbourne based gang were killed with one police officer, Sergeant Janet Brown, sadly dying while two other officers were injured, both expected to make full recoveries.

There would at this stage be no need to bring up the role Lieutenant Ajmi played.

Question time was held to a strict limit and most were directed at Riad who had by now regained his composure and was able to field them without too much trouble. As to what happened next with the two girls, that was a matter for the appropriate authorities from Child Welfare and a statement from them would no doubt be forthcoming.

The meeting over they filed out but Riad was checked by the Assistant Commissioner who wanted a word. 'I shall of course read your report and fully expect there to be one or two, shall we say, *gaps* in the account. Facts that for reasons of your own you might want to hold back.' A sudden thought had him chuckle, his normally stern expression softening, 'I wasn't always a pencil pushing politician, you know. There was a time when I was a homicide cop, like you. Worked the east side from Brunswick in those days and sometimes, just sometimes I wish –' Shaking his head wistfully he took Riad by the arm to slowly walk towards the door, 'Let's just say, a homicide cop is lost without his contacts, informants and more, from the other side of the street. I can see you already have those contacts and that's fine by me. I don't expect you to bring them into the open, no need. But it has made me think.'

'We are planning to establish a Middle Eastern Crime Squad right here in Melbourne, similar to what operates in Sydney. I was thinking how a man with your skills, your background, would be invaluable in such a unit. I would like you to think about it, I know it's rather sudden and –'

'I'll do it,' Riad said.

'I fully realise it means uprooting and there would be some hurdles but I'm pretty confident we could arrange a speedy –'

'I'll do it,' Riad said, 'I'll be only too glad to join your department.'

Anticipating a hard sell the other man was momentarily taken aback, 'Eh? Oh! Splendid! Splendid, then let's get on with it!'

Later, over a coffee with Zena who was due to fly back to Canberra that afternoon, he thought back on his earlier discussion with Addison, his own instant decision to take up the offer. And why not? He had pretty much had it with Kuwait, not being a native his career was not going anywhere and now this business with Rania was another reason. A new start, for both of them. Who knows, he might even get used to the cold and the wet, it reminded him of an earlier life in Britain.

As if on cue his phone rang. 'Hello Chunky,' he answered with a sigh. It seemed there were aspects of his life he would never be able to leave behind.

45
CHAPTER

We will have an update on the events taking place yesterday in Melbourne on our nine o'clock newscast. Next, sport and here to provide a – Changing to a Fox Sports channel where Manchester United, his team, were strutting their supremacy, the Scorpion Master leaned back in his armchair while tentatively sipping his Coke and not really tasting the drink at all.

His thoughts were a thousand miles away. So, Ruslan was dead as was that bitch of a Sarah Green. So was Mikhail by the sounds of things and the Elena II being gone over by a forensics team even now. Frowning he tried to think whether he had left anything aboard the vessel that could identify him, decided not but there would be fingerprints, things he had touched. He had never been fingerprinted, never been in trouble with the law. So nothing to fear there.

But what if Ruslan had kept some documents pointing to him? Before the business with the boy assassins there had been other dealings along the line of internet porn, their core business. He had always been very careful but still...

The offices of Ruslan's companies, Hazelton Enterprises and Rosspolites Komersk, would be raided for sure. And who knows what the police would find that pointed to him? He had been careful always to use an alias in his dealings with the Russian but the man did know his real identity and could well have kept some or other record; perhaps for blackmail purposes?

Maddie? He only met the girl once, shortly after she had been taken to the house and he was meeting with Ruslan on some other matter. The offer was made to him but he declined, boys were more his thing but the Russian disapproved of that. Apparently it was decadent and disgusting. Would she recognise him if shown a photo? Maybe but unlikely and not worth worrying about.

Yet, back in Kuwait City, he would be safe, at least for the moment. Except for that interfering bastard of an Ajmi, he could pose a real threat and was likely back in the city any moment now. How did this nemesis ever get involved in the Maddie Green case in the first place anyway? That while looking into his own adventures here in Kuwait?

A coincidence? Perhaps but the risk this dangerous man could put two and two together was just too big to ignore. He would have to take out insurance, give himself time to plan a getaway to somewhere like Miami where he had had the foresight to stash away a sizeable fortune some years ago for just this kind of situation.

A plan, insurance. Was that not what his analyst always urged during their private sessions? How impulsiveness was his one big flaw, that so often led to the violent outbursts that they were working on controlling? That he wasn't really a psychopath but rather a highly intelligent individual often frustrated by the incredible stupidity of those surrounding him? Others who failed to see his genius and tended to get in his way when he was preparing to show the world a new way, the true power vested inside him. So she thought he might be narcissistic but what did that even mean, what did she know after all? Nonsense.

He decided he knew exactly what form that insurance should take.

Rising he went over to the elaborate control panels and brought up to the main screen one of the images from the other room. The boy, this one was not yet sixteen but was showing real promise, was standing legs spread on the mobility mat with both hands clasping the controls while his head and face were obscured by the virtual reality helmet. Several wires trailed across the floor and the first person shooter scene he was immersed in flickered across a big screen on a wall. The boy was not seeing the screen, that was simply there for the controller to assess and the wires were only in place during the training phase, such as now.

Later they would be replaced by WiFi but for now he was content to just let the student get comfortable with the controls. A glance at another monitor screen saw Romi, his manservant, seated at a small control panel at the back of the room. His function was to alter the level of the game depending on the boy's skill and as always it was important to judge this carefully. Too difficult it would lead to frustration and attendant recklessness and that meant losing control. Too easy and they ran the risk of the subject losing interest.

The boy was good, the animated way he moved and swayed his body indicating his immersion in the scene, the kill rate on the big screen very good indeed. There was no doubt regarding his suitability on a technical basis which meant the time was right to start working on the psycho manipulation aspect, the part the Master enjoyed the most. Signalling Romi to cut the session they would allow for a short break then move on to the next phase where he introduced the hallucinatory drops, nicely disguised in a soft drink and always being extremely careful and patient.

He had earlier decided this one was destined for the AK47, an earlier assessment using a handgun revealing the kid's marksmanship was not quite good enough to ensure a kill with just one or two shots before the target might shoot back. There would be no arguing with the staccato spray from the submachine gun. As anticipated the boy had hugely enjoyed the shooting session -- they all did -- and as always the Master had dressed it up as a demonstration to show how closely the virtual reality weapon and its controls mimicked the real thing.

That was immediately followed by a session using the fake AK47 handset and the transition had been seamless.

Normally he would work with a subject for a minimum of four weeks before they were ready, longer and there was the risk of being discovered and too short, well they wouldn't be ready. With this one (he thought his name was Ahmed) there had been an interruption of one week, the time he had been called away to Melbourne but nothing seemed to have been lost, the boy picking up straight from where they had left off.

He reckoned another two weeks would have been optimal. The problem was he did not have another two weeks, the homicide detective was expected back at any time and he needed a plan B to buy time. A realist he knew that regardless of that outcome, his time in Kuwait was finished. It would have been naïve to think this game (and it was a game, after all,) would not be found out sooner rather than later. It was time to relocate to where his talents and his product would be appreciated, even nurtured. But first he had to tie up a few loose ends.

Replenishing his drink he picked up his mobile and dialled a number from memory. She answered on the third ring, 'We have a problem,' he said.

On the way to the airport they stopped off at the Epworth private hospital to see Chrissie. She was sitting up in bed when they entered and the first thing Riad noticed was the huge bunch of flowers on the bedside table. The second thing he saw was the grinning hulk of Uncle Vytas overflowing the too small visitor's chair. 'Riad!' the pair exclaimed in unison, Chrissie's features lighting up in a warm smile that belied her wan complexion and the blue rings under her eyes.

'Come, come!' the big man said, jumping to his feet with surprising agility and drawing up two more chairs from the bedside of the patient in the next bay. If that patient's visitor, a gentleman of a certain age, who had been about to claim one of the chairs thought the action rude one look at the giant with the schoolboy smile had him decide prudence was a virtue after all. A passing nurse shared that thought and quickly found another chair.

Handshakes all around as Zena was introduced to the other two and sensing Riad's questioning look in his direction Vytas felt it necessary to explain his presence. 'Chrissie iss nice girl,' he began with an apologetic spread of shovel like hands. 'I worry. I feel bad I not able to protect her, you know —'

Feeling unexpectedly sorry for the big man Riad nodded in sympathy, 'You were not to know Sarah was planning to drug the pair of you, the way she did.'

'Chrissie, Miss May, she got very sick. Drug overdose the doctor say. First they treat in Alfred then send here.'

'Vytas has been so sweet,' Chrissie said as she patted his arm in a show of unexpected affection. 'First he saved my life by calling an ambulance and do you know, he never left my bedside, sat there with me in the Alfred's Casualty all night, the poor thing. Since then he has visited twice a day and brought me these lovely flowers!'

And here we are, Riad thought with an inward smile. First name terms and looking cosy together. Uncle Vytas turning on the charm again but there was something different going on here, the big man's taste usually gravitating towards the buxom brassy bottle blonde type. Who would have thought?

'Chrissie nice girl,' Vytas reiterated somewhat lamely as he looked at his nephew with puppy dog eyes.

They spent the next half an hour discussing Chrissie's future plans, she was due for discharge later that morning and Riad was relieved to learn that her finances were not an issue as the Abdul-Karrim's had been excellent employers. She was planning to return to London as soon as possible and promised to keep in touch.

Of no great surprise was that Vytas was planning to accompany his new friend, the stated reason being he needed a holiday. Apparently Bubba would be minding the shop and the thought of that loose cannon left unsupervised had Riad decide his own expedient departure from Melbourne would be a wise move.

The matter of funeral arrangements for both Sarah and her late husband came up and Riad thought that seeing it was still a matter for the coroner there was likely to be at least another week before the bodies would be released. Abdul-Karrim had relatives in Kuwait City and they were likely to claim the body. As for Sarah, she was a British citizen but seeing as other than Maddie she had no known relatives, she would most likely be buried or cremated right there in Melbourne, a city she had always loved. In neither case would money be a problem.

'She once mentioned a testament,' Chrissie said with a frown, 'likely lodged with a solicitor in London. I suspect she would want everything left to Maddie.'

Chrissie had earlier expressed the wish to see Maddie but Zena explained that at present the child was undergoing psychological assessment and therapy and none of them were allowed access just yet. There was the promise of a later meeting should Maddie so desire.

A few more matters were discussed and then it was time to leave if Zena wanted to make her flight. Leaning over to give Chrissie a peck on the cheek Riad was startled by the sudden presence of a television reporter and cameraman in his peripheral field of vision. 'Miss May?' the female reporter, a face Riad had seen on local TV, asked as she produced an oversized microphone while the cameraman proceeded to do a light check. 'I'm Chloe McMillan from Channel Nine, we spoke earlier and I believe you are ready to tell us your side of the Maddie and Sarah Green affair?'

'Oh yes,' a beaming Chrissie replied, 'my friends were just about to leave and I thought a good spot for the interview would be in a small chapel on the second floor. Normally it's deserted and I thought the stained glass windows would provide a nice backdrop. Knowing Sarah she would have liked that.'

'Excellent,' the reporter said as she passed Chrissie a hospital dressing gown from the foot of the bed. She hesitated as the young woman stepped into the light streaming from a window, highlighting her pale drawn features, 'Would you like a few moments to freshen up, perhaps a touch of lipstick, some blusher?'

'Oh no,' Chrissie said smoothly, 'don't you think the way I look now better highlights the pain and suffering I, Sarah and Maddie and I, have been put through?'

Riad decided Chrissie was going to be just fine. Perhaps not exactly a star is born but just fine.

'Keep it classy,' he said over his shoulder as he escorted a smiling Zena to the door.

They took the toll road to Tullamarine Airport, Zena expertly manoeuvring the rental through the afternoon traffic with a minimal amount of cursing at what she deemed incompetent elderly idiots that should not be allowed onto the roads in the first place. Personally Riad thought if she made even a token effort to keep to the speed limit and was less inclined to tailgate frightened fellow road users to a matter of mere feet, the trip would have been less stressful for all.

Privately he wondered if it was about last night and what had happened between them. Glancing at her profile he realised he cared for this enigmatic newcomer in his life, this strong woman in whose presence he felt so very comfortable. Was it because they were the same? The first woman he had known who shared his professional life, whom he could truly talk to about the world he moved in?

No, he decided, there was something more here. A real attraction and it wasn't just physical although that had been fantastic. He knew then that he wanted to spend time with Zena Michaels, quality time and who knows, something might come of it?

'Zena,' he said softly, 'I'm not very good at this but,' he paused, searching for the right words and this made her glance at him with an expression that said oh?'

'I think you're a very special lady, Zena. Someone I could really go for. I – I guess what I'm trying to say is I very much want to see you again. Soon and often –'

'I'd like that too,' she said as she squeezed his hand. This reckless move had them narrowly avoid a collision with a dump truck but had the effect of Zena slowing down slightly as they listened to Ronan Keating on the car radio. *If to-morrow never comes* sang the crooner and a part of Riad hoped the words would not prove prophetic.

Over drinks in the airport's Irish pub while waiting for her flight to be announced Riad told her about the Assistant Commissioner's offer and how he intended to take him up on it. Never one to wear her heart on her sleeve Zena's face remained expressionless but the touch on his arm said it all. 'It's fantastic news. When do you think you'll start?'

'As soon as possible; there's the matter of work permits, that kind of thing but he assured me it wouldn't take long. But I'll be back sooner, in a matter of weeks, for a little holiday and bringing along my daughter, Rania.'

'Perhaps I can arrange for us to see Maddie then, sooner or later Child Protection will be obliged to allow us access as she still has to be interviewed to hopefully give us leads on some of these paedophiles.'

'Yes,' Riad said simply, 'I really want to see Maddie again.' He didn't add that deep inside him there was a need to tell Maddie how sorry he was that he could not save her mother. How he would forever live with the regret that he could not see through the web of lies, the all enveloping charade, Sarah had woven around herself.

How once again, as it was with so many of the cases that had come his way over the years he was just that little bit too late to prevent a tragedy, like the time in the mountains of Al Hada when he couldn't save his own wife or Kuwait City where so many had to die before he could stop a killer who was staring him in the face all along? And was that not the story of his own fictional inspiration, the great Philip Marlowe? From *The Big Sleep* to *The Long Goodbye*, always a chronicler after the event.

And as he strove to shake off the sudden feeling of utter loneliness and with it a hopeless despair it was Zena's soft voice that brought him back to the real world. 'You did save Maddie,' she said simply caressing his cheek with a cool gentle palm while her eyes said *I know, I know ...*

<h1 style="text-align:center">45
CHAPTER</h1>

Riad's own Etihad flight to Abu Dhabi and on to Kuwait City was at eleven that evening and after seeing Zena off at the airport with a promise to phone soon, he took a shuttle bus to Southern Cross Station and at that hour found himself part of a river of suits as he walked from there down to DI Reed's office. The sidewalks were wet from an earlier shower but a wintry sun had broken through thinning clouds and there was a pleasant mix of exhaust fumes, food aromas wafting from small eateries and even the pungent smell of hot tar from where a crew in hard hats and Hi-Vis vests were fixing a section of the street leading down to the river.

Skirting a puddle while exchanging a smile with a pretty young woman whose face was half hidden by her umbrella he became aware of the sounds of the big city all around him. From the rumbling clack of the trams thundering past to the general hum of the traffic to the excited chatter of the young girls as they filed past in tight groups while never taking their eyes off their mobile phones. He could even hear the pigeons calling to one another on the eaves of buildings as well as the distant horns of the river traffic on the Yarra. How did the song go, a beautiful noise coming up from the street … it's got rhythm it's got beat …

Was it his imagination or did the rain really clear the air, drive away the smog, to the point where one's hearing became sharper? And what about things appearing somehow brighter, the colours more vivid, the girls prettier? A thought had him smile, the late French crooner Maurice Chevalier singing *thank heaven for little girls* ... Couldn't sing that one to-day, not politically correct even if you point out as he did that little girls grow up to be big girls one day.

The simple fact was he was happy, suddenly and for no reason at all, Riad Ajmi was happy. How did the old saying go, happiness is like a butterfly, if pursued it will always elude you. But if you turn your attention to other things it will gently settle on your shoulder.

Cute but he knew that was not quite the reason. For Riad Ajmi marched to an unquenchable hunger deep inside his soul that could only be stilled, temporarily, by that elusive butterfly known as the truth. A truth he now believed he had in his grasp after that phone call from Waleed less than an hour ago. His Kuwaiti sergeant coming up with that last bit of information that completed the puzzle of the identity of a serial killer that had been terrorizing a city for too long now.

Once again a mere hunch had paid off and now he was on his way back to tie up what was most likely to be his last case in what was fast becoming a foreign world to him.

On the way to the police station he hauled out his mobile and dialled Reed's number. A good thing he did for the detective was about to go outside in search of a bite to eat. So they met up in a pub diagonally across from Flinders Street Station and over a meat pie and a pint of bitter the conversation turned to Riad's plans to take the Assistant Commissioner up on his offer of a post in the new Middle East Crime Section.

'You'd be a natural, what with your knowledge of Arabic as well as the Lebanese lot,' Reed said between huge bites of pie. 'The Commissioner has asked me to forward some paperwork to you, a starter's pack of sorts now lying on my desk but I'll scan it and email it to you.'

'Not going back to the office to-day?' Riad asked, knowing the man's work schedule usually made for late hours and this being only mid afternoon.

'Nope. I shouldn't have even been there to-day it being a public holiday, Queen's birthday. But, work, you know.'

Riad said he knew then looked at the small object the other man had taken from a jacket pocket to place on the table between them. 'Sam asked me to give this to you, said you would know what to do with it. Fuck if I know what it is, some or other computer gadget. He said you asked for it.'

'Thanks,' Riad said as he pocketed the matchbox size gadget and took a fifty dollar note from his wallet, handing it to Reed. 'Please give him this and tell him I will keep my promise of giving him an update when I get back.'

'Yeah, right,' Reed said with a frown suggesting the whole business sounded a bit suspect to him but then did he really want to know? 'At least the kid's talking to me now,' he said, calling for a second beer and enticing Riad in joining him. 'I don't know what you said to him that time you came around but something seems to have changed in the little bastard now. Talks about becoming a detective, even asks me about cases and wants to come on a work experience, can you believe that?'

Animated hand movements morphed into a dry spitting motion and Riad braced himself for the random profundity to follow and was mildly disappointed when it didn't.

'Kids,' Reed said, dropping his hands by his sides in a gesture of defeat. 'Who needs them?'

'He's a good kid,' Riad said, 'It's all just a matter of capturing his imagination. With his kind of computer skills he'd be a real asset to any police force.'

Reed nodded and created space for the newly arrived beers while Riad fished out some cash. 'What about this case back in Kuwait? Any new developments?'

'I know who the killer is, I even know the reason for the killings. The challenge is to prove it.' He smiled over the foam of his beer but his eyes were cold. 'One way or another, I will stop him.'

Reed nodded knowingly, 'It's the old cop's dilemma, isn't it? Justice and the law. Occasionally the two coincide but every now and then it leaves us with that choice –' He looked at Riad calculatingly, 'Did you ever cross that line, take the law into your own hands?'

It was a serious question and Riad gave it some consideration. Well, there was the time of the Saudi rapist prince and then there was the Kuwaiti serial killer who couldn't swim... He nodded solemnly, 'Once or twice.'

Reed laughed, punched Riad on the sleeve sloshing some beer in the process, 'Dirty Harry! Man, I'm gonna love working with you!'

'What about you?'

'Nothing proactive, if you know what I mean.' Seeing Riad's puzzled expression he hastened to add, 'I've never planted evidence, never framed a perp. More a question of once or twice going cold on something that might have confused the jury, know what I mean?'

'Not what I've heard about Queensland cops.'

Reed shook his head, smiled, 'Australia's Wild Side. That was what the old timers call the good old days. No, it was never quite like that down here in Victoria, always a bit more subtle, if you know what I mean?'

This merited another beer as they swapped stories of cases past and Riad slowly built a picture of what his life was likely to be once part of Melbourne's police force. Different, yes but probably every bit as dangerous as it had been in Kuwait.

He would have to do something about those anger management issues though.

***

The girl looked up from the jigsaw puzzle she had been occupied with to meet the gaze of the smiling man in the white coat who was kneeling next to her and Sandy who had been helping her. Sandy was a young nurse who worked in the big sunny room and played with all the kids and she was always nice and even gave them sweets if they ate their meals and were nice to one another.

Sandy had on a pretty dress with lots of flowers and even a little bee amongst them. She wore a thin gold chain around her neck with a tiny golden heart hanging from it and it and when she came up and cuddled her it reminded the girl of her mother and that made her sad.

'How are we to-day little Maddie?' the man in the white coat asked. He spoke in a soft voice and put his face close to hers and it somehow bothered her and she turned her face towards Sandy who wrapped her arms around her saying, 'We're having a good day, aren't we Maddie? First we read some stories when the older children went off to school and now we're doing a puzzle!' Running a hand through the girl's hair she added, 'And dancing! You see that railing over there? Well she can do the most amazing things dancing around the upright beam. You love to dance, don't you Maddie?'

The girl said nothing as she snuggled further into the warm embrace of the nurse. The child psychologist, who went by the name of Dr Peters but was called Dr Peaches by the older children who laughed at his little party tricks, made eye contact with the nurse who made a dismissive motion. Nodding he straightened up saying, 'I'll tell you what, why don't we go for a nice walk in the garden outside? The rain has stopped with the sun smiling out there and I saw some pretty little blue wrens flying about. Would you like that?'

Her face still averted she nodded while saying she would like to visit the toilet. It was in the corridor and Sandy and the doctor watched as she went off. The doors at the end of the corridor could only be accessed by the use of a swipe card and Dr Peters asked whether Maddie had tried to escape again to which Sandy shook her head. 'It only happened that one time when old Professor McDonald came on the ward round. Something about him scared her and she withdrew sharply and ran down the corridor shouting for Martha.'

Peters nodded, 'I expressly wore this white coat to-day, as you know I don't normally but I thought it might distinguish myself from those paedophile she had been exposed to.' He shrugged wearily, 'I don't know if it makes any difference, she just doesn't seem to trust me.'

'It's only been a few days, the poor thing is still very traumatised; she keeps asking when her mommy will be visiting again and during the session with Dr Anne yesterday we tried to gently suggest that mommy was on a long journey and the best thing for Maddie was to be a good girl and that mommy was so proud of her and that in the end all would be alright.'

'You know I don't share this approach of my colleague, I think children, even small ones, handle the concept of death better than we think. But Maddie seems to have formed a tentative bond with Anne, Dr Nygaardt, so we'll go along with that.' A thought made him frown, 'Why do you think there was this strange reaction with the professor?'

'I don't know but he seemed a bit shaken himself.'

'Hmm... It's almost as if they had met before –'

'You don't think --?'

Peters glanced up sharply, 'What!? No! No, of course not. Just odd, that's all.'

Changing the subject he asked about the other girl, Minnie.

'She's currently in a session with Dr Nygaardt who feels she is holding back much more than Maddie. Almost as if she's built a shell surrounding her. You know we still have not managed to trace her parents? Aboriginal Affairs are involved of course but the impression is she's a runaway and might have been picked up interstate somewhere.'

'Are the two girls close?'

'Oh yes, they spend most of their time together and we have them sleep in adjacent beds.' They watched as Maddie returned, nodding when Sandy asked whether she had washed her hands. Minutes later they were outside and for once Maddie seemed happy as she spotted a tiny ladybird on a leaf and gently picked it up to hold the little bright insect in the palm of her hand. 'Mommy always says they bring good luck,' she chortled and this was so unexpected that the two adults glanced at each other in sheer surprise. And maybe, just maybe, Sandy ventured, they do...

It was the first sign of anything like a breakthrough they had experienced in the sad case of little Maddie Green.

It was later, over a cup to tea in the tearoom with Maddie having her afternoon nap in the ward , that Sandy took a seat next to Dr Peters who was idly paging through one of the stack of women's magazines that littered the place. 'Something strange that I forgot to mention earlier and that may or may not mean anything.'

'Yes?' the psychologist said in a disinterested tone as he ran an appraising eye over the latest glossy photos from Hollywood's glamour factory.

'You remember how I remarked on the reaction Maddie had upon meeting Prof McDonald? Well, I had been standing next to the other girl, Minnie, at the time and suddenly she grabbed my hand, really hard and as I looked down to see what was wrong there was this, this *look* in her eyes. Her whole little body had gone rigid. I didn't make much of it at the time but something had spooked her alright.'

'The old man probably reminds them of someone,' Peters said, turning the page, 'I'll think of a way to bring it up in our next combined session but I doubt whether it will lead anywhere.'

But it did mean something to someone. As he sat in his study glancing out over the spacious garden to where his man was washing the Rolls, the golden rays of the setting sun glimmering off the paintwork and chrome, his thoughts went back to what had happened the day before at the Children's Hospital. The girl had recognised him, no doubt about that. And then the other little vixen had been there and she too – What were the chances?! All it needed was for one to say something. And then there was the matter of the stab wound to his side, the visit to the Frankston Hospital. Not forgetting his own man who was now washing the car out there. He'd talk when the police came, place him at the house and that would be the final straw.

Tilting his chair to stare up at the portrait of his late father, the High Court Judge, he reflected with grim certainty how the old bastard would have taken the news. Probably have called for the black cap and pronounced the death sentence himself. And then there was his dear old mother, it would have destroyed her too. Now there was just his wife, long an alien to him and no doubt it would resonate around her bridge and tennis circle, the Bollinger and smashed avocado set as he liked to think of them. But they would quickly rally around the poor woman as those members of the lonely wives club normally do.

Luckily there had been no children and maybe that had been part of the reason he now found himself in this position.

The thought had him smile wryly, don't fool yourself old man, you're nothing but a dirty pathetic old paedophile.

As the revulsion washed over him he raised his glass in salute to the portrait of the judge before tossing back the cognac. Then, with a sigh, he pulled open a desk drawer to stare for a moment at the cold black object lying there before slowly raising it to his temple.

It made page four of the Melbourne Age the next morning: well known emeritus professor of paediatrics found dead in his study. No crime is suspected.

46
CHAPTER

Kuwait City

'Nice place you have here,' Riad said as he glanced around, 'Reminds me of mine. Calms me down.'

Ameera al Quarashi leaned back in her high backed tilting office chair and studied him from under hooded eyelids. Beautifully manicured nails hid her lips, long fingers steepled in prayer like fashion although he doubted she prayed that often. More a studied look he decided, wondering why he had insisted on seeing her that morning, alone, when there was available a perfectly adequate slot the next afternoon.

'You are feeling anxious?' she asked in a flat tone.

'It's more a feeling of excitement,' he said as he shifted to a more comfortable position on the chair.

'Oh?'

'Yeah. You know about the serial killer that has been terrorizing the city, the weird business of the link to computer games?'

No answer as she studied him, the hands now lowered, the carefully made up mask expressionless.

'I've solved it. Now it's just a matter of arresting the killers. That's the reason for this meeting.'

He let it hang there, finally forcing her to respond. 'Killers? You mean there's more than one?' She did not reach for her notepad, made no attempt to go through the motions of psychologist and patient. They both knew it was not that kind of meeting.

'Sure. You see the mastermind, the computer wizard using these boys has to find them somewhere, don't you think? I mean not just any teenager would do now, would they? No, it would have to be a kid who is suitable, someone with the personality or mental weak spot that would make them susceptible to whatever spell this Svengali is putting on them. So I figure he has to have some help. A talent scout of sorts. This is where it gets interesting, you see both boys we know of so far went to the same school. I think you know that school quite well, Ameera, it's one you do sessions at as visiting psychologist. We checked, both these boys were subjects of yours –'

'That doesn't mean anything,' she said, 'I consult at several schools. I don't know what you're getting at but this meeting is now over.' With that she leant forward to press a button on the intercom. 'Hala, Mr Ajmi is just leaving. Is my next patient here?'

A frown crossed her features as no acknowledging answer came and it was a man's voice that finally replied, 'She's been given the day off. There was a patient waiting but I've told them to go home, we'll be in touch.'

Riad watched as all colour drained from her face, the hand hovering over the intercom now visibly shaking. Good old Waleed he mused, he could have that effect on people.

'Of course, that's not all we have. There's the matter of the second killing, the slain computer boffin. You knew the murder weapon had been a samurai sword, information that was never released. Only someone party to the killing could have known that.'

There was a hint of sadness to his smile, 'Someone like you.   You were the talent scout that fed those vulnerable young boys to the monster that is Adel Rajab –'

There was a sharp intake of breath as any pretence the psychologist still harboured fell away leaving behind the naked face of one of the deadliest women Riad had ever encountered. 'Adel –' she said in a whisper, 'Ho – how do you know it's --?'

'One mistake, he made just one mistake.' Riad said as he watched her rise unsteadily to cross to where a crystal carafe with water sat on a side table. He watched as she poured water into a glass and swallowed two tablets from a small tin produced from a pocket of her jacket. She turned to look at him and sighed as he motioned her back to the chair with an inclination of his head. 'You see, killer that he is he could not resist killing one more time, in Melbourne. Someone he thought might be a risk to his mad enterprise. He banked on being unknown in that city, with no police record off the radar.

Faceless. The one thing he did not reckon on was me being there, being present when the police studied the CCTV footage. But I was there and I recognised him alright, from that group session we had right here in these rooms. That was the connection I needed to bring me here to-day. Then there's also the strange co-incidence that it was his Filipino driver, one Romi Fernandez, who happened to drive the car that ran over and killed the first shooter. Pretty suspicious don't you think?'

She was seated across from him once more and it could be his imagination or was there a strange light in those dark eyes?

'It's all circumstantial,' she said glancing out a window and seeing something in the shimmering blue of the distant bay that perhaps gave her comfort but meant nothing to the man now facing her across the desk.

Instead of answering Riad reached for the intercom and pressed the button connecting to the outer office. 'Got his address?' he asked Waleed who replied in the affirmative asking whether he wants the suspect's file as well.

'Everything. And Waleed, get the squad ready. We'll go there straight from here.'

If Ameera al Qarashi thought taking a patient's file without her permission was against all the rules she knew better than to protest for it would have been futile. This was Kuwait City, not New York.

'Now, where were we? Ah, yes, circumstantial you say? Maybe, but then of course we'll have the evidence of a certain Mr Adel Rajab, won't we? And I promise you, my lovely, he will sing like a canary when the time comes. And maybe there are other young boys currently in the preparation stage for his mad schemes? We are going through the school's records now to see who else you have been consulting.'

He studied her with interest and once again marvelled at how normal these cold blooded psychopaths often came across as. Deciding that was their secret, how well they blended with society, often in positions of trust and authority. In a way it filled him with a sense of helplessness; how many more were out there?

'Why did you do it?' He asked at length.

To his surprise she smiled, not a sad whimsical smile but a mocking one that suggested a mere policeman like him could never hope to understand her world. 'Why? Well, firstly because I could. Secondly because there is a PhD thesis in all this, my work. The old question, can under hypnosis a subject be made to carry out an act that is totally against that person's moral fibre, everything he has been taught? The convention says no but my work proves different –'

Riad shook his head, 'I don't think it does. These boys were doped and tricked into believing they were in a virtual reality game.' Checking his watch he decided it was time to go, 'One more question. Adel Rajab, this business of the women's shoes, is it real?'

This time she laughed out loud having Riad wonder what was in those pills she had taken. 'Nooo! That's just a story he made up. His real pathology is sado-masochism. More specifically, he likes to observe people in pain, especially mental anguish, that was the reason for his presence in the group session.'

'Sameera al Quarashi. I'm arresting you as an accomplice to murder. Anything you say may be taken down and used in evidence against you. You are entitled to a lawyer.' He didn't add the bit about if you can't afford one the court will appoint one, in the world of the rich there seemed little point.

She giggled as she rose unsteadily to her feet holding out her hands in mocking fashion. Whatever those pills were, they were potent stuff. 'What about the right to be silent?'

'No American Fifth Amendment in Kuwait City, here everybody talks, sooner or later,' he said simply as he led her to the door.

In another part of the city Adel Rajab stared at the images on his monitor screen as he once again picked the fruits of earlier video-bugging the psychologist's rooms. Of course it had been done for his own secret pleasures, all those juicy stories of pain and suffering but this time it could save his life. It had been purely by chance that he had checked that particular site this morning but then she had phoned him earlier, letting him know Ajmi was in town and wanted to see her.

Like himself she had been worried about how much the snooping detective knew or suspected, to the point of stating that she was putting an end to their enterprise. Upon learning about the incident involving Ruslan and the rescue of Maddie Green he had made some calls, setting up a safe house in Miami where he could reside incognito for as long as it took to assume a new identity while re-organising his business empire.

Glancing at his watch he calculated that Romi would have reached the apartment by now and hopefully have the girl. It was weekend so she should be at home, a safe bet as in their world young girls did not go out by themselves.

His man would bring the girl back here and with her as hostage he would have the time to plan his escape. Once out of Kuwait his money would buy his freedom. How to escape from Kuwait was the question though; at the best of times the city was a sealed unit. Across the land border to Saudi Arabia? He did not think so, the Saudi border forces were efficient and always on the lookout for illegals wanting to cross, especially after the Iraq War. And, truth be told, he would rather fall into the hands of the more gentle Kuwaitis if it came to a choice.

By air, on one of the many commercial flights every day? Once again there was the issue of passport control and with the girl as hostage it was a no go. He briefly considered an escape by boat, like many of his playboy acquaintances he kept a forty foot cruiser in the Sharq Marina but too slow, the authorities would be onto him long before he could reach Qatar or Bahrain.

No, it would have to be the relatively short road trip across the border to nearby Iraq. A long stretch was desert and poorly patrolled and in his Land Cruiser he could make it easily. Once in that wild place he could buy his way to anywhere in the world, no problem.

But he would need a head start, three or four hours at least before the alarm was sounded. And the way to buy that was to strike a simple deal with a certain snooping detective, an offer he could not refuse: the life of his daughter.

Riad was at the Salmiyah Police Station when his mobile buzzed. It was an unknown number and normally he would have canned it but something made him answer. The voice was that of a stranger, the opening words chilling, 'You know who I am. I have your daughter. Now listen carefully –'

Blindly reaching for the corner of the nearest desk to steady himself Riad tried to speak but his throat had gone dry. 'I – What!?'

'Shut up and listen. Rania is with me. Have a listen.' There was a brief pause followed by the shaky voice of his daughter, 'Daddy? I didn't do anything wrong, I promise. The man hit Yvette and there was blood everywhere -- I'm scared!'

The words cut through him with excruciating sharpness as Rania tried to say more but was cut short by an action that ended in a sharp yelp of pain.

'What do you want, Rajab?' Still shocked Riad had recovered enough to catch the eye of Waleed at the next desk in the detectives room, signalling him to come across as he switched to speaker phone. A finger across his lips cautioned the sergeant to be silent.

'Just you and I, Ajmi. In person, you bring in anyone else and Miss Pretty never makes it to prom night, get it?'

The shock of seconds earlier now replaced by a stone cold fury Riad said that he understood. His police colleagues would not be involved. How stupid were these self styled master criminals a distant part of his racing brain mulled, don't tell the police but meanwhile the person on the other side is on fucking speakerphone.

' Now listen carefully, you have my address?'

'Yes. Is that where Rania will be?'

Ignoring the question Rajab went on and this time there was an edge to his voice, 'Come over here straight away. Come alone. The front entrance to the building is on Marine Parade. Park directly across the road, I'll be watching and If I see any sign of others I'll –'

'No others,' Riad said quickly. Christ the man was beginning to sound panicky and that was never a good sign.

'OK. I'll buzz open the entrance door to let you in. Take the elevator to the top floor, I'm in the penthouse. And, Ajmi, no tricks.'

The line went dead leaving Riad and Waleed staring numbly at each other. 'Shit Riad!'

He nodded while glancing around to see if no-one else had overheard. They had only twenty minutes earlier booked Ameera al Quarashi who was by now on her way to the holding cells and he was about to phone the colonel who was at some or other meeting.

'Firstly, we keep this between us. If Omar finds out he'll follow some or other bloody protocol and take over and you know how that will end.'

Waleed nodded as he moved a shaking hand through his hair, 'A disaster.'

Sinking into his seat to allow himself a moment's clear thinking, Riad said, 'What could he want? I mean it's all over for him. There's no way he can escape being arrested so what is it?'

'He's mad,' Waleed offered, 'only a nutcase could have done the things he did. Maybe he wants revenge? This is not someone who thinks like we do.'

As he spoke he brought up Google Maps on his iPhone and was zooming in on the building in Sharq where the fugitive was holding Rania. In silence they studied the surrounds of the densely built up area noting that there appeared to be a ramp leading down to a parking basement on one side. No doubt with remote controlled access doors. Directly across was a low hedge of neatly trimmed bushes leading up to the sidewalk where several cars were parked.

'If you approached from that building there, keeping low behind cover of this fence, you could reach the cover of these cars and be directly across the street from the basement doors.'

'Yes,' Waleed agreed somewhat hesitatingly glancing down at his neatly laundered dress uniform while imagining what the kind of leopard crawling required over that stretch of ground would do to said uniform. 'But how do I get through those doors?'

It was with a warm feeling that Riad knew his partner would do anything to help him, no questions, no ifs. Just a matter of getting the practicals right. Blind loyalty and he knew instinctively they were going to win. Had to.

'We get another tenant to open the doors for us.' His mind racing now he held up a palm to forestall the detective's next question, 'The traffic department has the addresses of all Kuwaiti car owners on their computers. Remember that recent hit and run case where they gave us the driver's address within minutes? Well, let's give them the address and let them reverse locate the tenants.'

'How does that –'

'You get a tenant on the phone and ask them to open the doors and let you in.'

Seeing the look of incredulity on his friend's face he added, 'You're a cop, Waleed. Tell them it's police business, for God's sake! Scare the living daylights out of them if need be!'

A glance at his watch showed five minutes had already elapsed, he'd have to get going. 'I'll take my Cherokee, you come in the cruiser and make sure you're not seen. Get inside the building as soon as you can and send me a missed call then use the stairs, he might have the elevator covered on CCTV. Get in position in the stairwell and wait for my signal.'

'What signal?'

'I dunno! You'll know!' he answered, realising Rajab might well have taken away his gun by then.

Then he was racing down the stairs past startled staff who hastily made way as he pushed past the usual throng in the charge office to reach the doors and the parking lot.

He was halfway through the revolving doors when he remembered his mother. While running towards where he had parked the Cherokee he dialled emergency services and, identifying himself as a police lieutenant, asked for an ambulance to be urgently despatched to his apartment in Salwa.

CHAPTER 47

Mercifully the traffic at that hour was less hectic and it took him no more than fifteen minutes to cover the distance to the neighbourhood of Sharq. He decided not to speed, not to use the police lights for there was always the chance the all seeing all monitoring Rajab could have spying eyes out there and the sight might just freak him out. So he worked at calming down while feverishly trying to think how he was going to play it once inside the man's lair.

And it was futile, he knew. It always was in these situations. No two were ever the same and in the end it would come down to rapid situation assessment followed by unhesitating action. That, and blind luck.

And inside that place, at the mercy of a crazed mass killer, was his daughter. Oh dear God ...

As the familiar landmarks rolled past, people strolling and taking in the sea air; mothers with prams, delivery vans and female drivers in big sedans, some in black abeyas, he had to force himself to ignore these signs of normality. You're an existentialist Riad, remember? None of these things flashing by exist for you now, just the situation and time running out. Focus!

Then he was there and pulling up with screeching brakes. As promised there was a parking spot and wasn't that just like in the movies he thought. In the middle of downtown New York City Kojak would always slot right into that miraculously appearing parking slot. Maybe he *was* in a movie.

No! Concentrate, dammit!

Sitting behind the wheel for a moment he adjusted his service pistol, unclipping the holster from his belt and sliding the automatic down the back of his trousers where it rested against his back. Then, satisfied that his jacket would hide the weapon, at least from casual inspection, he got out the car and stood there for a moment, gazing up at the building across the street. The penthouse balcony stretched around one corner but fortunately not on the side of the parking garage entrance. Yet there would be windows on that side and he could only hope no-one was monitoring.

Another thought, what if Rajab had a camera monitoring the parking garage? It did not bear thinking and he shrugged it off, crossing the street to pause at the glass fronted doors of the building.

Almost immediately there was an audible click and the door yielded to his push letting him inside. Pausing for a moment to check his surrounds he noted the camera mounted in a corner and, next to the elevator, a large potted fern.

No mailboxes but then, even if Kuwait was big on mail deliveries which it wasn't, how would the mailman get inside?

Also no notice indicating the occupants of the different apartments. Apparently everyone in this exclusive abode knew where they were going. Luckily, so did he.

He rode the elevator to the top floor all the while aware that he had no plan for what to do once he arrived. Play it by ear? How did that ever work out for him and never before with the life of his daughter at stake. But a cold rage was building inside him and as he worked at containing it he knew he was going to end this, whatever it took.

As the elevator doors opened he found himself in a small alcove with a flight of stairs leading up to a steel door that at a guess gave access to the rooftop. Facing him was an impressive looking ornately carved door which yielded to his touch, swinging noiselessly open to a darkened room with the only light coming from curtained windows at the far end.

Aware he was offering a perfect target outlined against the brightly lit hallway he stepped quickly inside kicking the door shut behind him and moving to one side. Standing quite still for a moment while his eyes grew accustomed to the gloom he became aware of a faint pricking at the back of his neck. It felt sharp, much like a stiletto he'd say.

'Stand quite still, amigo,' a man's voice said as he was relieved of his pistol. A moment later the lights came on and he found himself in a spacious open plan lounge with an impressive well stocked bar to one side and a large kitchen dining area at back. Huge picture windows had their blinds drawn and at a guess they opened up onto the balcony he had observed from outside the building. A large open topped aquarium covered most of the opposite wall with several multicoloured exotic fish lazily swimming about. He couldn't be sure but thought one larger black one was in the process of tearing apart a smaller guppy.

'Thank you, Romi,' the man seated on the L shaped lounge suite said, 'you'd better check our guest for any other surprises. Mr Ajmi, please excuse my lack of courtesy but one can never be too careful, can one?'

'One can't,' Riad agreed wondering how long the politeness was planned to last. He stood patiently as the manservant patted him down, relieving him of his mobile and throwing it over to the man on the couch who looked at if briefly before casually tossing it into the fish tank.

'We won't be needing that,' Rajab said somewhat unnecessarily.

Dispassionately watching the phone drift down to the bottom in a series of gentle curves Riad said he guessed not. 'Enough of this bullshit, Rajab, where's my daughter?'

'Ah, the old proof of life, not so? She's fine, Ajmi, in the next room and you'll see her in a moment. I just had to check you were alone, you understand?'

Setting aside the open laptop he had been checking Rajab motioned him to a seat on the other arm of the couch which Riad, after a moment's hesitation took. It gave him the opportunity to look the manservant over. The Filipino was short, no more than five six but built like a brick wall. Dressed in a black tracksuit with white sneakers he stood legs apart while smiling at Riad as he cracked his knuckles. A brass knuckleduster on his left hand could be mistaken for a piece of ornamental jewellery in some polite quarters but not to Riad who had seen first hand the damage it could do.

Of the knife there was no sign, most likely a flick knife, he would have pocketed it.

'I sincerely hoped Odd Job here didn't lay a finger on my daughter when he abducted her,' Riad said in a low voice as he returned the Filipino's narrowed stare, 'I might have to hurt him.'

This merited a soft laugh from Rajab who, closing the laptop, had risen to his feet, 'I doubt it. The man's a black belt in karate amongst some other skills. Come, let's go next door.'

Leading the way through an archway and down a short corridor Rajab ushered Riad into a large windowless room where banked computer screens glowed on two sides. The room was oblong with an open area at the far end where there was a stage of sorts with the largest video screen Riad had ever seen covering the whole of the wall. A figure stood there facing the screen while slowly going through a series of languid poised movements suggestive of yoga or more likely a martial arts kata. The oversized helmet covering the head of the boy – he looked about fourteen – conjured up the memory of an earlier ET although Riad somehow doubted the innocent intentions of this individual.

Rania sat in a chair against the other wall. He noticed at a glance the duct tape securing her ankles and wrists to the sides of the chair while large frightened eyes glanced up at him. 'Dad –' was all she could manage in a small voice that had all the terror of the world in its fibre.

'It's going to be alright, Rania,' he said keeping his voice even as he scanned the row of flickering computer screens quickly locating the one showing the inside of the parking garage. The doors were closed, no sign of Waleed.

'How touching,' Rajab said as he went across to the banked screens, 'the father and daughter re-union. Wasn't there a song about that?'

Mother and child re-union, Riad thought, Paul Simon. He said nothing.

'Come over here,' Rajab said, 'let me show you my work.' He had taken a seat at the control panel and indicated Riad should take the adjacent one. Riad remained standing, 'Untie Rania first,' he said.

Muttering 'Oh please, alright then' and without glancing up from the screens Rajab waved at Romi to go ahead. 'Now, look at this!'

Reaching for a keyboard he tapped away, fingers moving at lightning speed while a free hand reached for a microphone. Across the room the boy stirred, picked up an automatic rifle from the floor, then stood and walked to the centre of the stage and faced the screen which remained blank. 'I've got him locked into the shooter game now, my own design. He's seeing it via the VR helmet but we can see it on this monitor. He's got the replica AK 47 now but,' he chuckled, 'when his time comes it will be the real thing, of course.'

'Interesting, how do you control him?' Riad said as, ignoring the chair, he perched on the long table supporting the screens positioning himself so his back obscured the monitor showing the parking garage. Rajab glanced up frowning but Riad's explanation that he could observe the boy better this way seemed to satisfy him.

'Let me show you,' the Scorpion Master said with more than a hint of pride in his voice as he clicked on the mike while the other hand clamped around a small joystick.

Come on Waleed! Riad urged as he motioned a questioning Rania to remain seated where she was.

At that moment the sergeant was cursing as he crawled over a wet patch of grass keeping his head below the cover of the low fence while risking the occasional peek to confirm he remained unseen. Discarding his earlier dress uniform he was in his goddamn new Levi's and AC/DC tee shirt which would be ruined after this not to mention the unmistakeable stench of sewage from the recycled water some dumb bastard had used to water the lawn. But he was almost there, the cover of the parked cars only a few feet away and then it was just a short sprint to those doors across the street.

He wondered how Riad was doing inside the scorpion's den, from his position he could see the Cherokee parked on the Gulf Road. Early afternoon now, Kuwait's dead hour when the shops and business had closed for siesta, so no-one about which, of course, might make him more obtrusive if spotted but no way around that now.

Riad's plan of finding out who else lives in the building then getting them to open the garage door! Please! Sometimes he wondered about the boss but after all the man was pretty stressed right now. Instead he had gone down to the technical boys who gave him the scanner he now had clutched in his hand. This, they guaranteed, would within seconds open any sonar activated garage door in the city, no problem and would he mind returning it asap. No-one mentioned the desirability of a search warrant, one look at the detective's scowling features having the backroom boys decide he probably knew what he was doing.

Grinning he pressed the button and sure enough, almost instantly the door started sliding up. He was across the street before it was fully open and then he was inside and closing it.

The garage was brightly lit and housed five vehicles with a sixth bay empty. A quick scan revealed two Corvettes, a Porsche, a black Suburban and a Land Cruiser.

All brand new, clearly a rich man's building.

Which one belonged to their man? More than one sported personalised number plates but none that said "Scorpion Master 01" or anything suggesting the identity of the owner. A thought struck him, what if several of these cars belonged to the man in the penthouse? Only one thing for it, disable them all.

But first things first; spotting the CCTV camera mounted next to the inside entrance he took a small can of black hair colour aerosol from a back pocket and quickly sprayed the lens of the camera, leaving an uneven dripping goo covering.

Less than optimal but the can of hair spray he kept in his desk at work to cover his bald spot before catching up with the ladies after work would have to do.

None of the cars were locked, what would the point be when secure in a garage? Starting with the Land Cruiser he opened the car hoods one after another before, without undue gentleness, ripping out whatever distributor cap or electric cables he could find. This took longer than he anticipated and halfway through he was sweating as he paused to check his mobile.

Still no word from Riad.

At that moment Riad was watching the boy in the VR headset going through a bizarre set of motions as a grinning Rajab moved the joystick while hissing instructions through the microphone. The electronically operated AK 47 shuddered as the boy swung it around, silently firing from the hip at rapidly moving targets with amazing accuracy.

'Is he seeing exactly what we're seeing on this screen?' Riad asked, feigning interest as his mind raced. For the moment there seemed nothing he could do to defuse the situation, the Filipino had his gun and besides that it was two against one not counting the boy.

The boy... The unknown factor, could an attack possibly come from that quarter? Come on Waleed!!

As if in answer to his query the man at the controls flicked a switch and whispering something in the mike had the boy discard the toy AK 47 to stride across to a corner table and pick up a samurai katana that looked awfully real from where Riad was sitting. 'Now,' Rajab said rubbing his hands together in gleeful anticipation, 'let me show you how good young Hamed has become with the sword!'

An unseen signal had a grinning Romi haul over a full sized mannequin, a clothes shop figurine by the looks of it, and place it centre stage facing the boy.

'Just this last little demonstration then I'm afraid I'm going to have to leave all this behind,' Rajab said wistfully as he glanced around taking in the playpen as Riad had come to think of it. A playpen for a very sick young man.

'Isn't it time you laid out your little escape plan?' he asked, 'always presuming your tiny little mind has managed to come up with one?' It was time to goad the man, stir up his anger in an attempt to provoke a rash action which might just make him vulnerable to a strike.

Putting aside for a moment the controls the other man sighed and swivelling his chair, fixed Riad with a narrowed look. 'Sarcasm doesn't work on me, Ajmi. I am beyond that.

You want to hear the plan? Simple; we leave here in my Land Cruiser heading for the Iraq border, let's say somewhere near Basra. I have hired a small plane to fly me from there to nearby Iran where I have, shall we say, good contacts. Once there I will release you. See, simple!'

'What about Rania?'

'The girl?' he glanced across at where a terrified Rania was glancing fearfully from him to her father. 'Such a pretty little thing, she could have had a great future but, alas, already past her best before date –'

'Unlike Maddie Green –' Riad heard himself say.

'Quite. No, I'll let her go. My own preferences lie elsewhere.'

'These boys?'

A look of anger flashed across Rajab's handsome features, 'I have never touched even one of these boys! Never!'

No, Riad reflected, just turned them into killers then eliminated them, like so much cannon fodder.

'Romi, give me the lieutenant's pistol, then go down to the garage and get the car ready. Then come back upstairs.'

Nodding the manservant left, pausing in the doorway to give Riad a long glaring look, the message *don't even think of it.*

'Oh, Odd Job, would you mind bringing me a cold beer while you're at it, there's a good chap?' Riad called after him thinking you touched my daughter, you big ape, I'll have you for that.

'Move over to that wall and go down on your haunches,' Rajab snapped, waving the gun at Riad who had his hands half raised in a placatory gesture. He wasn't even sure whether this nutcase was safe with an unfamiliar handgun.

As he reluctantly obeyed he glanced at the monitor screen to find the garage CCTV partially obscured by what looked like dripping black goo. Conclusion: his man was inside!

The other man had not noticed yet, his attention now taken up with the boy on the stage who had suddenly sprung into motion, the sword flashing as with lightning speed and impressive skill he took the mannequin apart, the incredibly sharp weapon sending head and limbs flying in all directions. Then, in slow motion, he regained his previous motionless position, the sword held in an almost ceremonial ready position.

'I can show you the game and his interaction but we're running out of time. There's a few items I have to collect so, I turn this camera onto you and,' nimble fingers flashed across a keyboard, 'with the wide lens camera on you, you are now part of the game! I'd be very careful if I was you.'

On cue, the boy turned to face Riad across the room. 'Just an extra security measure, *old chap*, at a signal from me I'm afraid you're toast. So do stand still, won't you?'

The sudden switch to faux English public school, complete down to the accent, had Riad wonder whether the man had multiple personalities. Now is not the time to unravel, Rajab! I can only handle one madman at a time. He watched as the Scorpion Master started gathering up several hard drives and disks from a drawer tossing them in a holdall while scanning the room for anything else that had to go.

In the garage Waleed was busy with the last of the cars, a Corvette, when he heard the inside door open. He ducked quickly under cover of the nearest car but was just a fraction too late as Romi spotted him, the big Filipino stopping in his tracks. 'You! What you do?!'

Not answering but stepping into the clear Waleed said nothing but studied the hulking form warily, searching for signs of a weapon, his own hand on his service automatic.

It took but a moment for Romi to take in the situation, the cars with their hoods open, then with a low growl he moved towards the policeman, a switchblade appearing in his hand as if by magic.

Without a moment's hesitation Waleed slid the Glock from its holster and fired twice, the first bullet catching Romi full in the chest while the second flung him back two paces where he slumped against the side of a car before slowly sliding to the cement and laying still. Stepping over to check the fallen man's pulse and finding nothing, Waleed eyed the open doorway and decided it was time to go upstairs, see what the boss was doing.

Staring down at the dead man at his feet he said softly, 'Just like a dago to bring a knife to a gunfight...' The thought had him grimace, it was the kind of thing Ajmi would have said; he was spending too much time around the boss, picking up on his bad jokes. Shaking his head he made for the door.

At that moment, in the games room, Rajab had moved close to where Riad was to slide open another drawer and scoop its contents into the holdall. As he did so he saw the monitor screen where enough of the gooey paint had dripped off the lens to clearly show the prone form of Romi sprawled across the floor.

'What the --?' Momentarily stunned the gun hand dropped by his side and this was the chance Riad had been waiting for. Using the wall at his back for leverage he leapt up and forwards crashing into the other man and sending them both flying, the gun spinning away across the floor to fetch up in a far corner.

'Kill, kill!' came the hysterical shout into the headset microphone as the two men grappled, Riad slamming painfully into the table's edge as he encountered unexpected strength and from a corner of his eye saw the camera swivel to remain focused on him while, somewhere in a distant universe, he heard Rania scream. With a superhuman effort that brought a searing pain to his old wound, he hurled Rajab hard against the console panel, the other man grunting in pain.

The boy was on the move now, the katana raised as he advanced steadily on Riad, the single eye of the headset camera never wavering. Realising he had no chance against that weapon, even in the hands of a boy, Riad reached inside his shirt, in the process ripping off a button, to grasp the object suspended from his neck by a light chain. It was the Node MCU, the jammer Sam Reed had given him, attached to a tiny power source. His fingers fumbling, the boy now but yards away and closing relentlessly, the katana flashing in the overhead light, he finally found the on switch and pressed as a silent prayer flashed through his mind.

What happened next was a sight never to be forgotten. The sword raised high, ready for its deadly strike, the boy froze. Time stood still as Riad, his mind dazed by the sudden sharp pain in his side, stared at the scene only half believing what he saw.

For the boy slowly lowered the sword finally letting it drop from his hand to fall on the floor with a dull thud. Then, still moving slowly he reached up and took off the VR helmet to stare at Riad blankly as if seeing him for the first time.

'What is happening?' he asked in the thin reedy voice of a juvenile. Unable to answer Riad just shook his head, finally managing to say, 'It's alright, boy. It will be alright—'

'Dad? Dad?!!' Rania's sharp voice had him glance over to see her standing there, the gun in her hand and pointing shakily at Rajab who was only feet away from her and steadily advancing as he held out a hand, indicating she should give it to him.

Riad knew he could never reach there in time, knew what would happen if Rajab got hold of that gun. Rania would have to do it! 'Shoot him, Baby! Just point and pull the – '

There was a sudden loud explosion and Riad watched in numbing shock as the Scorpion Master staggered back clutching his shattered arm as he stared uncomprehendingly at the very red blood now seeping through his fingers and staining the carpet.

Then Waleed was in the room, the smoking Glock in his hand as he quickly scanned the surroundings before putting it away. 'You OK, Boss?' he asked uncertainly as he noticed a smear of blood on Riad's shirt.

'Fine,' Riad gasped, 'My old wound has opened up but I'm OK.' He glanced across at his daughter who, still holding the gun while seemingly unaware of it, was shaking all over as tears steamed down her cheeks, 'Dad? I – I...'

'It's OK, Baby,' he whispered as he reached her to hold her tight, the tears warm in his neck. 'I'll always be there to protect you. Always.'

And, as always, the image of his Fareeda, the love of his life he could not in the end save, flashed before him and instinctively he held Rania tighter whispering over and over, 'I love you, I love you...'

Rising from where he had been checking on a loudly moaning Rajab and clearing away the dropped sword, Waleed glanced at the pair with a look of embarrassment before stating, 'He'll live.'

'What was my score?' the boy asked, his voice flat while dark eyes shone unusually bright.

Riad and Waleed exchanged glances and Riad made a dismissive motion to his partner, turning to the boy to say 'You scored well. We are finished for to-day, OK?'

'Yes. To-morrow again!'

There was no answer to that Riad could think of.

Motioning at the boy, who was glancing around uncertainly as if unsure where he was, to take a seat in a corner, Waleed dialled for police backup as well as an ambulance. 'And send a meat wagon,' he added as an afterthought, 'there's a stiff down in the garage.'

The corny toss aside had Riad shake his head, clearly the sergeant had been watching Kojak again. 'No double tap this time? Shooting for the man's arm when a miss could have been fatal?' he asked as he led a still shaking Rania to a seat.

Waleed shrugged, 'No problem. I am the best shot in the department, remember? And we need the punk as a witness to help us find the rest of these boys.'

Somewhere in the distance they could hear the sounds of approaching sirens. 'Sergeant Waleed,' Riad said with a sigh, 'As thankful as I am, my head now hurts almost as much as my wound. Please, no more of the Dirty Harry speak. I just can't take it any more.'

'Sure thing, Boss,' the detective said but his grin said it all; they had each other's back and always would.

48
CHAPTER

Melbourne, 3 weeks later.

It was eleven o'clock on a sunny Sunday morning when Dr Peters used his swipe card to allow Riad and Zena access to the children's ward. They had met over a coffee earlier in a small bistro across the street while Zena made some calls finally getting permission for them to see Maddie Green with the understanding that it would be in the presence of the attending psychologist. Apparently there had been some as yet unresolved therapeutic issues and things were at a sensitive stage.

A surprisingly patient Zena had explained that there were also some urgent police matters regarding the cracking of a widespread paedophile ring and that the girl might just provide the key. There was a twenty minute delay as various people were consulted, including the Victorian Health Minister who after a conversation with the Assistant Commissioner gave permission for the meeting to go ahead.

'Maddie was making real progress,' Peters said, 'Until something seemed to upset her a few weeks back. We're not sure what but the same incident had a similar effect on little Minnie. She's however doing better.'

'What incident?' Zena asked as they followed the psychologist past the nurses' station to where sunlight was streaming through large windows into an open space lounge.

———

341

Peters checked his stride and glanced around before dropping his voice, 'Well, it was during the grand round –' Seeing his guests' puzzled expressions he hastened to add, 'Every Monday morning we have this large combined ward round where all our patients are presented and discussed by the full team. That includes visiting private paediatricians who have sessions in our clinics. Well, it was upon coming face to face with the visitors that the girls reacted in this strange way.'

Scratching his head and shrugging he added, 'Of course it might just have been the large group that scared them but there was something odd about it. I did try and raise it with the children but to no avail, I have the feeling they, especially Maddie, are shutting it out.'

They had resumed walking now to find themselves in what was clearly a children's playroom of sorts with a central table and chairs surrounded by assorted cut down furniture, boxes of toys and children's books scattered about and colourful posters of cartoon characters adorning the walls. To one side was a large pasteboard covered with dozens of crayon drawings presumably done by the kids.

In a corner two small kids, both boys and with shaved heads were intently listening to what a nurse was reading from a picture book. The bigger of the two had a slim plastic tube trailing from his nose and taped to the side of his head. They did not look up.

The room was otherwise vacant.

'Who was present at that meeting that the girls had not seen before?' Riad asked as Peters indicated they should wait there, have a seat at the table, while he went off to find Maddie.

'Eh? Oh. Well, only the few visiting consultants, I guess.' He rolled off a short list while Zena took the names down. It was the last name that caught her attention. 'Professor McDonald? Isn't he that suicide from a while ago, the papers were full of it?'

Looking embarrassed Peters nodded, 'Yes. Very sad.'

Exchanging glances with Riad she asked whether the hospital could provide photographs of these visitors. It transpired all had photo IDs provided by the hospital and these photos would be on file. 'Good,' she said, 'Could you get someone to bring up a print out of these photos? I'd like to show them to the girls.'

'You mean right now?' a perplexed Peters asked while glancing at his wristwatch.

'Yes. Now.' Noting Riad's grimace she added grudgingly, 'Please. It's important.'

Excusing himself he went back to the nurses' desk and made a call. A nurse came up to them and said Maddie was at playschool in an adjacent ward and she would fetch her and be with them shortly. 'What about the other girl, Minnie?' Riad asked.

'She is also there but I thought –'

'It's better we separate them during sessions,' Peters said as he re-joined them, 'they've formed this bond, a protective measure, that have them close up to outsiders as they seek comfort, security rather, in one another.'

A few minutes later the nurse brought in an apprehensively smiling Maddie. She was dressed in a warm pink jumpsuit with an apron that had paint stains on it and warm Ugg boots that had little bells stitched to the sides. The bells jingled softly when she walked. He hair was tied back in a ponytail and the pink Alice band had flecks of glitter in it.

She came up to the table without hesitation and allowed Nurse Sandy to pull up a chair and help her onto it. 'Maddie,' she said smiling at the girl while smoothing away a stray lock of hair, 'this is Mr Ajmi and Commander Michaels. It was they who brought you here that day from the other place. They are our friends and wanted to visit you, is that OK?'

Biting her lip while rolling big blue eyes up at Sandy she nodded but did not speak. Riad noticed that her nails were painted a multitude of colours and there was a tiny woven wristband with a Frozen pendant.

'Maddie,' Dr Peters began, 'Did you enjoy Lizzie's birthday party yesterday? I believe there was lots of lollies and cake too.'

She nodded and from his vantage point Riad could see the little legs rhythmically swing to and fro. 'And how was school this morning?'

'It's not over yet,' the girl said as she glanced over to where Sandy had taken a chair.

'It's fine, Maddie, we'll go back to the others before long.'

Peters looked questioningly at Zena who produced a slim file from her briefcase and placed it on the table. Inside was a sheaf of A4 sized photographs lifted from the police files of known paedophiles. Turning to the girl she smiled while saying these were photographs of people they wanted to talk to and if she showed them to Maddie, would she recognise any of them? Was it Riad's imagination or was there the slightest recoil from the child and he decided his fellow officer might have come dressed a trifle less intimidatingly than the blue serge dress uniform and cap that now lay on the table between them. At least the chocolate cake in its box Zena had picked up earlier was a good idea.

Dr Peters nodded slightly to Zena's querying glance and then she placed the first of the photographs in front of Maddie. It was of an overweight middle aged man with a goatee and oversized glasses. He peered at the camera over flabby cheeks and the background with its height measuring yardstick suggested a police mugshot.

No reaction.

A series of photographs followed all meeting with no sign of interest. Finally she produced a photo of Ruslan, this gleaned from a society event in London, a year ago.

'It's my daddy,' Maddie said, drawing the picture closer and smiling. 'He's with Mommy now and looking after her.' Then, fixing them with a look of defiance, she said in a clear voice, 'He'll come and fetch me, he and Mommy. You'll see.'

The visitors exchanged glances while Peters looked strangely embarrassed. He cleared his throat and did not look at them as he spoke, 'the concept of the finality of the next world is not fully established in the very young. Especially after a traumatic event we tend to not emphasize it, rather work on a more –'

'You mean false hope?' Zena said offhandedly.

Dammit Zena!

'I—well, let's –'

The awkward situation was interrupted by a uniformed orderly arriving with a large brown multi-use envelope which he handed to Peters with the explanation it was from Admin.

They watched as he drew out five foolscaps of paper, each with a photograph in the top right hand corner. These appeared to be photocopies of the face pages of personnel. As he silently handed them to Zena Maddie slid off her chair while saying to an attendant Sandy that she was cold and wanted to go over to where Jasper was sleeping in the sunny spot by the window.

Jasper was a fluffy toy dog, Sandy explained as she rose to follow Maddie, adding over her shoulder that she was only little and it was time for the morning tea break.

'Just a few more minutes' Zena said as she followed the pair to the corner taking the photos with her. Rising Riad followed while Peters remained at the table as a call came through on his mobile.

Maddie was seated on one of the diminutive children's chairs while cuddling the toy dog and whispering inaudible somethings into a floppy ear. Pulling over a low chair to gingerly lower himself onto the awkward seat Riad took up position next to Zena who displayed unexpected flexibility by sitting cross legged next to the child. Yoga he decided, making a note to try it sometime but in all honesty, seeing Zena in that position brought other thoughts to his mind, thoughts that he quickly suppressed.

'We're going to have nice tea in a moment, Maddie and you know what? I've brought some cake. You'd like that, wouldn't you?'

More nodding but still whispering in the stuffed toy's ear. Placing the first of the photos on the tiny table Zena asked whether she had seen this man? No reaction. Shrugging she produced the second photo.

Maddie stared at the photo for what seemed like several seconds, the stuffed toy dropping to the floor. Then, without a word and moving like an automaton, she went over to the multicoloured play framework and paused there for a moment. Then, as the party watched in stunned silence, she slipped off the Ugg boots and without a backward glance grasped a supporting metal pole and, using it as a prop, started dancing.

Pole dancing to be precise, the kind they had seen her do on the porno videos. The fact that this time there was no music made it all the more surreal. And as she danced, the tiny body gyrating around the pole as she went through her routine, her eyes never left those of Riad and Zena.

They were dead eyes with no expression at all and as she came around again, her head arched back in mocking pose, she smiled and Riad thought it was the saddest thing he had ever seen. After a while Sandy went over and tenderly coaxed her down, leading her out of the room without a word.

Riad glanced down at the photo. 'Professor McDonald,' he said.

Zena nodded, 'I'll get a warrant.'

The both knew the dead man's computer might just hold some answers, lay open the secrets of a viper's nest. Forensics would always be able to unlock a computer no matter how hard someone has tried to wipe its memory. So far Ruslan's encrypted computer had proven hard to access but this might just be the break they needed.

As Dr Peters walked them to the door Riad asked about progress regarding Maddie's future.

'She's a British citizen,' he said, accepting the cardboard box containing the cake Zena had purchased earlier at the café. 'So far the Brits have been unable to trace any relatives. Well, apart from Ross Green's ex-wife and two grown up sons. They want nothing to do with the girl. As for the others, well, they're all dead, aren't they?' He shrugged glancing down at the box in his hands as if wondering how that got there. 'No, for the foreseeable future she stays with us. As you've seen, there's still a long road to go before she's back to normal.'

He expressed the word normal as if that was a sure thing given enough time but Riad wasn't so sure.

'What about the other girl, Minnie?' he asked.

'She's doing better, we've managed to trace some family in Wollongong, a grandmother, who's willing to take her. The mother, she's only eighteen, is in jail for drug related offences with the father unknown.' Holding open the ward door for them to pass he smiled sadly, 'Poor child, she's tested positive for gonorrhoea. Hopefully early and we can cure it. But imagine, a four year old ...'

With that final comment he stepped back the door closing softly behind him leaving Riad and Zena to walk silently back to where they had parked the cars.

There did not seem to be anything to say.

After arranging to meet that evening for a meal where she would get to meet Rania and Yvette, he watched Zena drive off. It was pleasantly warm in the rental Commodore and he sat there for a while letting his mind travel back over events of the last few weeks and the case of Maddie and Sarah Green which he knew would forever haunt his increasingly frequent nightmares.

Sarah and Maddie. Mother and daughter and, come to think of it, hadn't the tragedy already started with the mother of Sarah and that fateful relationship with Dimitri Ruslan? How did the Old Testament put it, the sins of the fathers will be visited upon the children to the third and fourth generation...?

But just who was the sinner and who was sinned against?

He thought back again of how Oscar Wilde had put it in The Ballad of Reading Goal: *Yet each man kills the thing he loves...*

...Some do it with a bitter look,
Some with a flattering word.
The coward does it with a kiss
The brave man with a sword ...

Could he have saved Sarah Green? Maybe just maybe if he had been able to find a way through those windmills of her mind that forever seemed to be throwing up more and more false leads amidst desperate cries for help. What if he had trusted his gut feeling, those battle hardened instincts that spoke of so many cases, so many tragedies, so many times all that in the end stood between too late and just in time was acting on that hunch?

What if he had not been blinded by his love for that beautiful haunted impossible woman?

With a sigh he started the car and, after a moment's hesitation, decided to drive out to Portsea, to where the memories now seemed to draw him.

He drove slowly, the radio tuned to some station playing a mix of old and new music tracks between the inane chatter of a talkback host and callers, the topic being things that have happened to you when you did not lock the toilet door. A giggling woman told of how her sixteen year old son walked in on her while she was self administering an enema.

Much laughter while Riad reflected on how banal things had become; the sublime giving way to the ridiculous. She considered therapy for her son, a sensitive soul but decided it was better to simply not mention it ever again.

It never happened.

Switching off the radio he drove the rest of the way in silence.

Rosebud came and went, the spot where Ken had pulled up to frisk him passing in a vaguely recorded blur, then Sorrento with the outgoing ferry blindingly white in the wintry sun and finally the turn off from the main street to take the winding road to Portsea. He was nursing a takeaway coffee now, picked up from a small bistro and bakery where a queue had formed to await a fresh batch of the best vanilla slice in all of Mornington. Waiting for the coffee he had sampled one and it was great and made him feel slightly better about the world, thinking of how often it was the little things in life that made it all worth carrying on in the end.

The Portsea Hotel came and went and then he found what he was looking for, the small service road that led up to the house. Driving slowly past the large gates that had blue and white chequered do not cross police tape crisscrossing them he noted that some repairs had been done and a large padlock was in place. A hundred yards further, at the end of the road, he parked and got out. The fence where Sarah's car had straddled it was back in place but the bushes on the other side were still broken with dead limbs visible. Come summer it would pose a fire hazard.

Standing at the top of the cliff and gazing out to sea he contemplated for a moment scaling the fence then saw what he was looking for, a narrow stone strewn path winding its way down to the beach below. It was half hidden by the undergrowth and only became visible when he was standing over it. It looked perilous but clearly others had used it so, treading carefully, he made his way down to the rocky beach where patches of kelp were glistening as the water washed about them.

A light sea breeze had sprung up and with it came a sudden chill and he turned the collar of his coat up and shoved his hands deep inside his trouser pockets as he slowly strolled towards where Nepean Point was obscured in the fast disappearing remnants of the morning's mist.

Save for the seagulls the beach was deserted as far as the eye could see. They were riding the breeze, just floating out there without the slightest sign of effort as they scanned the world below for any stray morsels while all the time keeping a beady eye on the stranger who might just be the key to a feed.

Others were floating on the shallow water with some preening their feathers with that fast jerking motion so typical of the avian world. He marvelled at how well fed they looked, and how clean. For weren't they after all carrion feeders, junk food slaves, arch opportunists? Shouldn't they show outward signs of the seedy squalor of their existence?

But then, they were kings of their own underworld and like the scions of his own human underworld they would always be immaculately, even flashily, dressed now wouldn't they?

But above all, they were free! For no reason the words of Robbie Burns came to him, the Scottish poet his all time favourite: *Ye flowery banks o' bonnie Doon,*

How can ye bloom sae fair;
How can ye chant, ye little birds,
And I sae fu' o' care!

Some unseen intrusion scared them off and as he watched them scatter and fly amidst loud cackles of protest a sudden deep sadness brought a lump to his throat. He had reached the wooden stairs leading up to where he could see the garden gate and, to one side and slightly lower the rocks where Sarah had died. For a moment he contemplated climbing the stairs to look down upon the spot but instead sat down on a sandy mound to stare out at the lapping waves slowly rolling in. It was low tide and it made him think of what someone had once said about how there was a tide in the affairs of men.

He had never felt quite as low as now. This, this was the ebb tide.

Picking up a few flat flintstone pebbles he sent them skimming across the water in a series of skips before disappearing under the surface. How many more skips can you do, Riad Ajmi, before you sink under that tide of human misery?

Rising he scanned around finally finding what he was looking for. A flat piece of hard blue stone, large enough to write a message on. Sitting down again and using a sharp pointed pebble it took several minutes to scratch some words on the surface. Then, hefting the stone which was heavier than he had realised at first, he climbed up to where the sandbank gave way to the creeping undergrowth.

Moving gingerly, slipping and sliding, careful not to tumble down the wet sand he reached the spot. It was directly beneath the large rocky outcrop where Sarah's body had lain and he placed the stone and wedged it into the sand. Then he stepped back and looked at what he had written: For Maddie. Remembrance of Innocence Lost.

Then, glancing up to where he had last laid eyes on Sarah Green he said softly, so here we are, my lovely, as promised; a stone for Maddie Green.

His words were lost in the breeze but it didn't matter, they would forever resonate in his mind.

Back on the beach he reclaimed his seat on the sandy mound and sat there staring out to sea. The wet was slowly seeping through the seat of his trousers but he didn't care for he was far away. Soon he would rise and go back to his life, back to Rania and the new challenges that awaited them in the promised land but for now he was just sitting there and watching the gulls and the sea.

His mobile rang and mechanically he reached for it. 'Yes?'

'Riad! It's me, Chunky! How you doin' bro?'

'We're not brothers, Chunky but I'm OK, thanks.'

'What do you mean, Gigolo? Details are being finalised and a wedding is in the air! Soon now we'll be brothers-in-law!'

For a brief moment Riad wondered if he had entered a parallel universe but the sting of the breeze on his cheek was real as was the sharp cries of the gulls, the familiar feel of the phone in his hand. Chunky al Thani, and for all he knew right now ensconced in some pleasure dome surrounded by scantily clad beauties while attended by servants. And why not?

'What's up, Chunky?' he asked, wearily accepting there was no escape, 'is it about Pudding Johnson's party? I'm sorry I couldn't make it; work you know.' Even as he said it he realised how incomprehensible the latter aspect would sound to someone like the sheikh.

'What? Oh that? Never happened, old boy! Turned out there was a problem about death duties or something, the boy's a bit short. Staying in his London flat at present. No, I'm planning a little cruise off the Greek Islands. Just a dozen or so old friends, and thought you would be an ideal guest. It would give us time to rekindle old friendships, you know? Oh *do* say you'll come!'

'Well, I –'

There was a moment's silence as he mulled this over. Maybe that was what he needed, a break from all this. Take Rania along? And what about Zena? How would she cope with the kind of people Chunky mixed with? Confidently he reckoned, she'd have them wary and disciplined come happy hour. What about himself? Would he want to be a member of a club that has members like himself? The old Woody Allen quip made him smile and it was with surprise that he realised it was the first time he had smiled in a while.

Sometimes banal is all we have.

'When?' he heard himself say while thinking there was a lot of things needed settling first.

'Any time you want to join, little bro. We'll be out there sailing for at least the next two months.'

'I'm in,' he said and cut the call.

He stood there for a while, drinking in the sea breeze that made his eyes water. Then he turned to take a last long look at Maddie's stone knowing he would never come back there again. Knowing that before long the wind blown sand would cover the stone, bury it forever. Some memories are better buried.

Far out on the horizon there was a haziness building. It looked like rain. But, as he headed for the car, he saw the rainbow.

THE END